the gift of love

W9-APR-860

the gift of love

LORI FOSTER

JULES BENNETT

HEIDI BETTS

ANN CHRISTOPHER

LISA COOKE

PAIGE CUCCARO

GIA DAWN

HELENKAY DIMON

BERKLEY SENSATION, NEW YORK

THE BERKLEY PUBLISHING GROUP
Published by the Penguin Group
Penguin Group (USA) Inc.
375 Hudson Street, New York, New York 10014, USA
Penguin Group (Canada), 90 Eglinton Avenue East, Suite 700, Toronto, Ontario M4P 2Y3, Canada
(a division of Pearson Penguin Canada Inc.)
Penguin Books Ltd., 80 Strand, London WC2R 0RL, England
Penguin Group Ireland, 25 St. Stephen's Green, Dublin 2, Ireland (a division of Penguin Books Ltd.)
Penguin Group (Australia), 250 Camberwell Road, Camberwell, Victoria 3124, Australia
(a division of Pearson Australia Group Pty. Ltd.)
Penguin Books India Pvt. Ltd., 11 Community Centre, Panchsheel Park, New Delhi—110 017, India
Penguin Group (NZ), 67 Apollo Drive, Rosedale, North Shore 0632, New Zealand
(a division of Pearson New Zealand Ltd.)
Penguin Books (South Africa) (Pty.) Ltd., 24 Sturdee Avenue, Rosebank, Johannesburg 2196,
South Africa

Penguin Books Ltd., Registered Offices: 80 Strand, London WC2R 0RL, England

This book is an original publication of The Berkley Publishing Group.

These stories are works of fiction. Names, characters, places, and incidents either are the product of the authors' imagination or are used fictitiously, and any resemblance to actual persons, living or dead, business establishments, events, or locales is entirely coincidental. The publisher does not have any control over and does not assume any responsibility for authors or third-party websites or their content.

Copyright © 2010 by Penguin Group (USA) Inc.
A continuation of this copyright page appears on page 361.
Cover photograph: "Feminine Presents with Paper Flowers" by Jeff Von Hoene / Photographers Choice / Getty.
Cover design by Rita Frangie.
Interior text design by Kristin del Rosario.

All rights reserved.
No part of this book may be reproduced, scanned, or distributed in any printed or electronic form without permission. Please do not participate in or encourage piracy of copyrighted materials in violation of the authors' rights. Purchase only authorized editions.
BERKLEY® SENSATION and the "B" design are trademarks of Penguin Group (USA) Inc.

PRINTING HISTORY
Berkley Sensation trade paperback edition / June 2010

Library of Congress Cataloging-in-Publication Data

The gift of love / Lori Foster . . . [et al.].—Berkley Sensation trade paperback ed.
    p.   cm.
ISBN 978-0-425-23428-0
1. Domestic fiction, American.   2. Families—Fiction.   3. Love—Fiction.   4. American literature—
    21st century.   I. Foster, Lori, 1958-
PS648.F27G54   2010
813'.0108355—dc22   2010004308

PRINTED IN THE UNITED STATES OF AMERICA

10   9   8   7   6   5   4   3   2   1

Contents

for the love of wendy

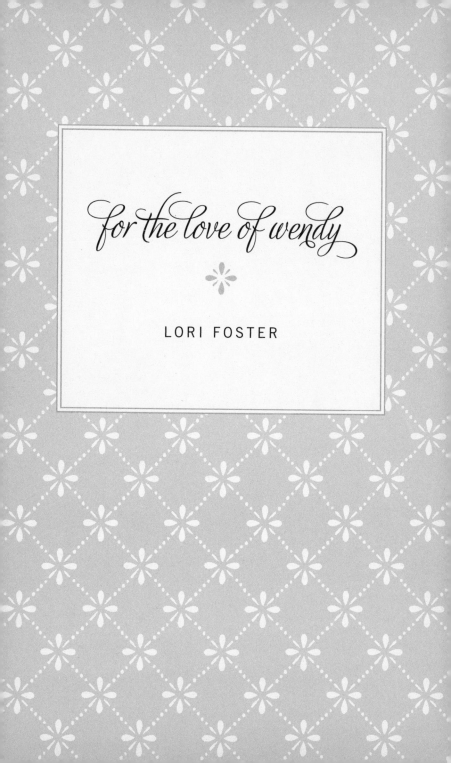

LORI FOSTER

one

❋

Standing at the dining room window, hands stuffed in the pockets of his dress pants, his tie hanging loose over a partially opened dress shirt, Jack Burke watched his five-year-old daughter in the backyard. Her movements were methodical and involved as she studied a yellow flower.

Sometimes his emotions overwhelmed him until he felt his eyes burn, until his throat tried to close with unending regrets, savage rage, and despair.

Though it had been five years, there were days that he felt the loss of his wife, Melanie, as the sharpest blow, as if it had just happened, as if the doctors were once again pushing him out of the way in a race to try to save her—and then later, presenting him with his premature child.

A daughter who looked like him.

A little girl Melanie would have loved with all her heart and soul—if she had lived. The emotional turmoil of losing a wife and gaining the responsibility of a precious, tiny child was enough to flatten him.

His baby girl had survived physically intact, but still not whole.

His heart didn't give a damn; he couldn't possibly love her more. To him, she was perfection in every way.

To the rest of the world, she was a child who had suffered trauma while still in the womb, and as a result, her intellectual maturity would never match that of her peers.

At birth, Wendy had weighed less than four pounds, and still she'd snuggled into Jack and seemed comforted by him. So little, so helpless—all he had left of Melanie.

He would raze the earth for her.

But what she really needed, what he knew would be best for Wendy, was a full-time mother. God knew he tried to give her everything, but he wasn't obtuse. Children needed the influence of both a man and a woman, the balance of nature, the gift of united love.

It was past time.

Hands fisting, Jack drew a slow, deep breath, and then another. He could not keep doing this, strolling down memory lane, reliving that heartrending day. It helped no one, least of all his daughter.

With an effort, he switched his gaze from Wendy to Briana. For two years now, he'd known Bri, and he'd watched her care for his daughter, grow to love her. Briana treated Wendy as her own, and that's what mattered.

At twenty-three, Briana was only nine years his junior, and she was so smart that carrying on a conversation was easy. But in many ways, *physical* ways, she still reminded him of a teenager. Rangy in build, doe-eyed, and too sweet, she gave the appearance of youth, yet she had the soul and compassion, the calm temperament and concrete sense of responsibility of a woman.

He saw Briana as a gifted academic, a cute brainiac who effortlessly juggled college with working part-time as Wendy's caregiver. She was rarely sick, and he'd never heard her really complain. She showed a contagious enthusiasm for life and an intellectual understanding of people that sometimes left him amazed.

Sweat from the overly warm June day left the pixie cut of Briana's short, dark hair a little glossy. Short, curled tendrils clung to her forehead, her temples, and her nape. As often happened, her glasses had slipped down the bridge of her nose, forcing her to tip her head back to see through them. Her gaze was serene and happy as she handed another flower to Wendy. Jack knew they were working on colors again, given all the yellow items laid out on the blanket.

Briana was so damn good with Wendy, so enduring and smart. And best of all, she made learning fun. She knew how to engage Wendy when so many others didn't. Her positive influence was invaluable.

He and Wendy were lucky to have her. But as his mom had just pointed out during his routine visit with her, it wasn't enough. Wendy would benefit from having Briana around more. And *he* needed to get on with his life by looking to the future, instead of the past.

As painful as it would be, it was time to create a new family.

Determined, Jack slid open the door, took a step out to the patio, and waited.

Wendy looked up when Briana prompted her, and then she scurried to her feet, and in that silent, stilted way of hers, she ran to him.

Scooping her up, Jack held her close to his heart as he so often did, and he thanked God that even though Melanie hadn't survived the awful collision, his baby had. Learning disabilities aside, she'd made it when the doctors had feared she might not.

He would always be eternally grateful.

Breathing in her sweet little girl scent, Jack kissed her sun-warmed cheek. "I love you," he told her.

"I love you more," she said back.

Even at five, there were few things Wendy said; sharing her love for him was one.

Calling out to Briana was another.

Jack felt Briana watching him, something she did a lot, as if curious about something, as if she looked at him in a more intimate manner than he viewed her.

Or at least, how he used to view her.

Now he looked at her, and he took in the charm of her big blue eyes behind wire-framed glasses, the wisdom in her demeanor, the lack of sophistication in her simple outfit of jeans and a college logo T-shirt. She'd kicked off her sneakers, and he saw that her feet were small, narrow.

Somehow appealing.

Jack felt a moment of guilt, then solid resolve.

"Briana."

She stood and brushed off her backside. "We were just finishing up. Why don't you two go in for a drink and cookies, and I'll be there as soon as I gather up everything?"

Without looking at him again, she stepped into her shoes and then began putting the items all on the blanket to make it easier to carry them inside.

Wendy touched the front of her bright tank top and said, "Yellow."

"Yes, yellow." Pleased with her, Jack nuzzled her cheek until she squirmed and giggled. "Very pretty yellow."

"Yellow," she repeated.

Jack smiled. "Let's go get a cookie, sweetheart. What do you say?"

Her green eyes, so much like his, lit up. She smiled and put her head on his shoulder. Seconds later she gave a huge, inelegant yawn.

Nap time was approaching fast, apparently.

Jack had just gotten Wendy settled in her seat with her snack on the table before her when Briana came in.

"What would you like to drink?"

She said, "You just got home. Sit down and I'll get it."

He leaned against the counter and crossed his arms. They went through this routine every time, with Briana determined to go the extra mile, even when it wasn't necessary. She was the most considerate person he'd ever known.

"My meeting didn't last that long, and then I visited my mother." That was something he did every Wednesday since his mother's stroke. "You went to school and then tended my daughter. I'd say we're even on being busy today."

Briana tilted her head, seemed to consider his words, and then shrugged. "I'll take milk."

Why her choice of drink amused him, Jack wasn't sure. Maybe because it only added to the idea of Briana being so young.

He poured her the milk and set the glass in front of her, and then prepared a cup of coffee for himself. "How were your classes?"

"Short day." Propping her chin on a fist, she bit into a peanut butter cookie. "I'm free the rest of the day now."

"Any work to do at home? Papers, studying?"

"Nope."

"Good." For some time now they'd coordinated their schedules around the time that Wendy needed them.

Just as parents would do.

Sometimes Briana worked too hard, carried too big of a load. He enjoyed seeing her with a little downtime.

Briana glanced over at Wendy and smiled. "It's only two o'clock, and she's already pooped out for the day. Look at her."

So much affection sounded in her tone that Jack couldn't help but be drawn to her. No, Briana didn't physically fit his fantasy woman, but she loved his daughter, and that meant she could have been a gnome and he would still deeply care for her.

"Was it the sunshine?"

Bri nodded. "After her kindergarten class, she ran around the yard like a little monkey for twenty minutes before I could corral her."

With cookie crumbs on her face and her milk only half gone, Wendy slumped in her seat. Her eyelids drooped until she looked more asleep than awake.

"I suppose you chased her?"

Grinning, Bri admitted, "I like a sunny day as well as the next person. And the physical exertion is good for her, too. First and foremost, I want her to be happy just being a kid, you know?"

His heart swelled with unfamiliar emotion. "I know that no matter what type of day it is, you make her happy." As a three-some, they'd built snowmen in the winter, raked leaves in the fall, and planted flowers in the spring.

Once during a thunderstorm when the electricity had failed, Jack had hurried home from a meeting, filled with worry—only to find Bri and Wendy tucked under a homemade tent in the living room, reading with a flashlight and having a blast. He'd gone to his knees and crawled under the quilt to join them, and they'd weathered out the storm with plenty of laughs.

As Wendy slipped off in slumber, Jack stood. "Come on, sleepyhead. Nap time."

Unlike other kids, Wendy didn't object to napping unless she was sick, which meant she'd be grumpy about everything. Jack lifted her into his arms, and she slumped boneless against him.

Smiling again, Briana set aside her napkin and stood. "See you tomorrow, Wendy." She came over, leaned closer to dust the crumbs from Wendy's rosebud mouth, and then kissed her cheek. "Love ya bunches."

Jack felt the touch of Bri's hair on his forearm, smelled the sun-warmed scent of her skin and hair, and felt the heat from her body.

It wasn't the first time she'd gotten so physically close to him, but it was the first time since he'd decided to stop thinking of her in a strictly platonic way.

"It's early still." *And she had claimed to have some free time.* As she made to withdraw, Jack cupped his hand around her neck. It felt right to touch her, comfortable and familiar and still . . . exciting. "Don't go anywhere, okay? I'll get her tucked in and be back in a few minutes."

She blinked and, because of the physical contact, held herself very still. "Oh, but . . ." Her eyes shifted to look at the dishes. "I was going to put these away and then—"

"Stay." Against his will, his thumb brushed along her jaw. So soft. "I want to talk to you." *And he needed privacy from his daughter to do this right.*

"Oh." Now she looked worried. "Okay, sure. No problem."

Jack let out a breath. "Bri, it's nothing bad. At least, I hope you don't think so."

"Nothing bad. Okay."

She didn't sound convinced, but Jack made a hasty exit anyway. He knew that if he didn't, he'd end up having the discussion with his sleeping daughter in his arms. Given how he hoped things would progress, that would never do.

two

Less than fifteen minutes later, with Wendy sound asleep in her room, Jack returned to find Briana standing at the sliding doors, looking out into the yard. After setting out fresh cups of coffee, she'd cleaned the kitchen—and tidied her hair.

Jack saw that as promising. Briana might be young, but like all women, she recognized male interest when it came knocking. He only hoped she reciprocated, because at this point in his life, he couldn't see himself with anyone else. Hell, he could barely see himself with her. He still loved his wife and he knew it.

But Melanie was gone and he wasn't, and he had to consider what was best for Wendy.

Lounging in the kitchen doorway, Jack took a moment to study Briana. At five-seven, she stood more than half a foot shorter than him. Any curves she had were understated: small breasts, narrow hips, long thighs—a pert ass.

Yeah, it shamed him to admit it, but now that he let himself think about it, he imagined . . . things. Sexual things. Like holding on to that taut little behind while he—

"Jack?"

Dragging in a sharp breath, he moved into the kitchen. "Thank you for waiting."

She nodded with uncertainty. "Everything with Wendy is okay?"

"Yes." He held out a chair for her at the kitchen table. "She'll be down for about an hour, I'm sure."

Bri sat. "Your mother?"

"Mom is fine, all things considered." Several months ago, his mother had suffered a stroke. Initially, Jack had hired a girl to help daily with the cooking and cleaning, but even ailing, his mother was too independent for that. She could tend to herself in most ways, so the girl now did chores only twice a month. Working from his home as an engineer, Jack was able to check in on his mother each week, and over the weekend he brought Wendy by to visit.

Briana lifted a cup of coffee for a sip. Unlike him, she used plenty of sugar and cream—the same way Melanie had preferred it.

And that's where the similarities between the two women ended.

"I like your mom a lot, Jack. She's always fun to be around. Even with her health struggles, she keeps her sense of humor."

Jack wondered if Briana would feel the same when she found out what his mother wanted of her.

"You know," she said, sounding cautious, "I worry about you, too."

That surprised him. "Me?"

Full of sincerity, she set her coffee down and crossed her arms over the tabletop. "You're not only a single dad, but you have the responsibility of caring for your mother now, too. Between working, raising Wendy alone, and worrying for your mother's health, it has to be a terrible strain."

Jack frowned. He wasn't a weak person; he was a grown man

who always met his obligations head-on. "I'm fine." Busy, definitely, but still . . . fine.

Bri just watched him.

He gulped down half the hot coffee, but it didn't help. "It's nothing I can't handle," he felt compelled to add.

She shrugged. "You're a very capable man, Jack, I know that. It's . . . one of the things I've always admired about you. And I know you don't see caring for your mother or Wendy as a chore."

"God, no." He cherished his time with each of them.

Briana's smile flickered. "Because you love them. I understand that. But it's still a lot for one person to deal with."

He'd lost his dad when he was young, so yeah, his mother had done the whole single parent thing, which made them exceptionally close. He adored her, so of course he worried about her.

She hadn't had a reoccurring stroke, thank God, and she'd managed a lot of recovery. But the doctors couldn't make promises for continued good health, and that factored into what he needed for the future—guaranteed stability for his daughter.

Bri fidgeted. "You wanted to talk?"

Jack sipped at his remaining coffee. "You're very good with Wendy."

Her brows lifted. "I adore her."

She said that so matter-of-factly that Jack knew he was making the right decision. "She adores you, too."

"I know." As if confiding in him, she leaned forward and said in a hushed voice, "Her teacher at the new private school is nice, and of course she's qualified, but Wendy doesn't respond to her as well as she does to me."

"You're special to her." Jack saw the spark in her eyes at that admission. "And actually, that's what I wanted to talk to you about."

As if awaiting something monumental, Bri folded her hands on the tabletop. "Okay."

Her attitude stymied him a little, but he forged on anyway. "I do the best that I can with Wendy—"

"You're an *excellent* father in every way."

Jack paused. She always flattered him, but sometimes her faith in him was humbling. "Thank you." Surely she recognized his flaws. He had them and he knew it. Plenty of them. "I do my best, but Wendy still needs a mother, too."

Too quickly, Briana said, "A mother's influence can never be discounted."

That rapid-fire agreement threw Jack but didn't take him completely off course. "Mom made a good point today during our chat. If something should happen to me—"

"Don't even say that!" She turned fierce and flustered. "You're a big, strong, healthy man and—"

"And accidents can happen to anyone." He knew that better than most. He and Melanie had thought they had their whole lives ahead of them. But she'd driven off one routine morning, and everything had changed.

Briana looked so alarmed that Jack reached for her hand and enfolded it in his own. "My mother loves Wendy unconditionally, but with her health issues, she's not capable of caring for a child, especially one with special needs."

Briana stared at their clasped hands, licked her lips, and nodded. "I'm capable."

Damn, but she was making this easier, and far more confusing, than he'd ever imagined. "I agree." He squeezed her fingers. "That's why I'd like to marry."

Her gaze shot up to his. "Marry?"

"It's important to me for Wendy to have a mother in every way, including legally. If you're my wife, you'll both be protected."

For once she was mute.

"Should the need arise, I want her looked after by someone who truly cares about her."

Briana swallowed, nodded again, and after biting her bottom lip, she said, "I've been waiting for you to ask."

That took him aback. "You have?"

She pulled her hand from his. "And I will marry you, of course."

Of course? What did that mean? Had Briana already thought about it? Jack shook his head. That didn't make any sense. Sure, he caught her looking at him sometimes, but never had she made a move . . .

"Jack?"

"Well . . . all right." Now he had no idea what to say.

She rolled in her lips and flushed. "That is what you were asking, wasn't it?"

"Yes." But he'd planned to do a lot more explaining and, if necessary, cajoling.

Briana pushed her glasses up the bridge of her nose and straightened her shoulders. "Good. I think this will be the perfect solution."

"You do, huh?" He should be celebrating her willingness, not looking for catches. But she was such an intelligent little . . . nerd, that he'd expected some reserve on her part, some practical arguments.

"Yes, I do. But I have some stipulations to go over first."

Jack put his head back. "Stipulations?" Briana was not the type to make stipulations. She gave of her heart and her time without ever asking for anything in return.

"I want more children, Jack."

Though he was sitting, he reeled. At least figuratively.

She rushed on after that bombshell to say, "You're a wonderful father, and I love Wendy completely. You know that, right?"

"Yes." If he didn't know it, if it wasn't a fact, he would never marry her.

"But she deserves siblings. I expect us both to have a long, healthy life, but we *will* age." Briana leaned closer to appeal to him. "It wouldn't be fair to leave Wendy left alone without people who love her. Without . . . *family*."

Jack tapped his fingers on the table and scrutinized her. What she said made sense to him, so he had no issue there. And if she wanted plain speaking, then he had no problem with that. "It's a mercenary way of looking at more children, don't you think?"

"It's a pragmatic way," she corrected, "but never doubt that I'll equally love any child I birth."

"Equally?"

Indignation brought her brows together. "You know I would never shortchange Wendy." With a fist to her heart, she said, "I love her like she is my own. Another child would just mean more love, and a better opportunity for Wendy to learn as she interacts."

"More children." Jack mulled that over, and finally said, "I would like that." He loved kids, and he liked Briana's rationale. Hell, between them, they could love a half-dozen kids with no problem.

Had she thought about the process of getting pregnant?

Beaming, Briana relaxed. "Wonderful. So *that's* settled then."

Meaning there was more? Curiosity gnawed at Jack. "What else?"

"I'm going to finish school. I would be fully committed to marriage, I swear, but I still need my independence, and you need to know that you're not responsible for me."

Jack started to speak, to correct her, but she held up a hand.

"No, Jack. I know you, and you feel responsible for everyone.

Me being younger, well, that just means that in many ways you still see me as a kid."

He didn't refute that. At twenty-three, she wasn't that far out of her teens, for God's sake. But in the long run, it just didn't seem to matter to him. "You are young."

She frowned again. "Although I assume you realize I'm a woman or you wouldn't ask to marry me."

He wasn't ready to go there yet. "I agree that you should finish your education. In fact, it's my hope that once we're together full-time, our schedule will offer up more opportunities for each of us. You could even take more classes if you wanted. And while I enjoy working from home, I've had to turn down big jobs that might've taken me away from Wendy too much. Between us, we might be able to make things more workable all the way around."

"Sounds perfect." She beamed at him. "Then we've got that settled, too."

But Jack could tell she had more on her mind. "Is that it, then?"

"Not completely, no." After a lot of nervous hesitation, she blurted out, "If we do this, if we get married, I want you to . . ." Her chin lifted. "To try to love me."

That profound demand froze Jack. He stared, blank-brained, as Briana flushed, adjusted her glasses, and maintained eye contact.

Damn. Usually Briana was so circumspect, so tactful, that he'd never quite imagined her saying something so . . . so *ballsy*. Or so emotional. She was an egghead. Smart, practical, matter-of-fact in all things.

Love? The idea of it hurt him, left him hollow and sick.

The silence built, but she didn't back down. She apparently knew what she wanted, and she was willing to state her case.

He admired her, and he didn't want to disappoint her, but he refused to lie. "Briana—"

"I know." She held up a hand to forestall him. "Your feelings for your deceased wife are still very real. I understand that. And I think it's admirable that your vows meant so much to you, that you gave her your heart in such a complete way."

He felt a very big "but" coming on.

"But I'm a woman, Jack, and I deserve everything. So if you want to marry me, regardless of the reasons, you can't set Melanie on a shrine so that I'm always relegated to second best."

Behind the lenses of her glasses, Briana's blue eyes looked huge and uncertain, but also determined. Jack knew she'd forced herself to have this conversation, and his heart softened.

"I see." She wasn't demanding love, but the opportunity for love. "I wouldn't want you to be disappointed."

Briana drew another deep breath. "If it turns out that your feelings for me never grow beyond fondness, then so be it. I'll deal with that."

How? Was she saying she was okay with a marriage in name only? He hoped he hadn't misled her with his intent.

"The thing is," she continued, "I don't want you to fight a growing connection between us or feel guilty about it if you *do* start to care for me."

Jack went straight to the heart of the matter. "Don't you think you're jumping the gun a little here? We only just discussed a new relationship, and you're talking about love."

For a single heartbeat, she looked sad before she turned pragmatic again. "For you, it might be new. For me, well, I've known how I feel—about you and Wendy both—for some time now. That's why it's important to me for you to give us a fighting chance."

Some strange emotion stirred inside him. "How do you feel?"

One side of her mouth quirked with chagrin. "I've been in love with you for a while."

Oh, hell. How could he have missed that?

"I didn't know."

"You made a point of not knowing. Because of that whole guilt thing, I think. But it's okay. You were putting Wendy first, as you should, and you didn't want to muddy the waters."

Astounding. He'd never known a woman like her. "I'm already fond of you, Briana. I wouldn't even consider marriage if I didn't like and respect you, and enjoy your company."

"And you think that should be enough?" Her mouth firmed. "I don't."

"Bri." What the hell could he say?

She stood to pace. "If you want to change your mind, I'll understand. But you won't find another woman who'll love you or Wendy more than I will."

Setting his coffee aside, Jack stood, too. He stared into Briana's eyes, and he saw so much—things he'd always missed before now.

"My motives are not all altruistic. Yes, I want what's best for Wendy." He moved closer and felt his muscles tightening. God, it had been so long. Far, far too long. "But I want for myself, too."

Her lips parted.

"Marriage has many conveniences. Coordinating schedules. Easy conversation with someone whose company you enjoy." As he advanced, she leaned back against the counter. "Shared interests, compatible personalities."

She nodded. "We can have all that."

His voice dropped. "But I want more." He stepped closer and braced his hands on the counter behind her, enclosing her with his nearness. "I want a warm, soft body sharing my bed."

Briana's jaw loosened. "Oh." A pulse went wild in her throat, and color flushed her face. "Me, too."

Her reaction turned him on.

"There are times," he whispered, "when I'm sick with the need for sex. Not lights out, rushed sex with a stranger."

She looked at his mouth, and then into his eyes. "No."

Jack removed her glasses and set them on the counter. Without them, she seemed somehow vulnerable.

And a little naked.

"I miss the intimacy, Bri. I miss the emotional and physical closeness. So if we do this, if you say yes, do so knowing that I want the kind of sex that lasts hours and makes two people sweat and burn." He cupped her face. "I want that with you."

Her hands lifted to his chest. She sucked in a hungry breath and, without saying a word, went on tiptoe to kiss him.

three

Briana couldn't believe this was happening, but she relished every second. He tasted wonderful, felt better than that, and her insides shimmered with need, with joy and fear and uncertainty.

Moments after meeting Jack, she'd fallen in lust. A few weeks after that, after watching him with his daughter and getting to know him as such a remarkable man, she'd fallen head over heels in love.

She'd seen signs, so many signs, that he felt more for her than gratitude toward the hired help. But always between them was the tragedy of his wife's death and the responsibility of always, *always*, putting Wendy first.

And that had only made her love him more.

How many men would deny themselves anything but duty? What man would fill his life with his daughter's needs and be joyous about it? How many men could juggle work with single parenthood and the care of an ailing parent?

Briana knew no other men like him. For her, Jack was the only man.

Now, finally, what she'd always wanted, what she'd dreamed of having, was being offered to her.

Except that Jack didn't admit to loving her. She had to believe that, on some level, he already did. She had to believe that eventually he'd love her every bit as much as he did Wendy and his deceased wife.

He was so tall, at least a half-foot taller than her. And where she bordered on thin, his physique was big bones, layered muscle, strength, and ability.

Next to him, she felt feminine, like a woman instead of an egghead. The traits that had made her unappealing to other men were things he'd often admired—like her intelligence, her dedication to her studies, her curiosity, and her ability to think through situations.

And given his heavy breathing, he liked other, more corporeal things about her, too.

Both of his hands now cradled her face, and he deepened the kiss until she felt his tongue. At the first touch, he groaned like a man in agony.

Her heartbeat sped up; desire twisted through her. To her disappointment, he pulled back, but he didn't leave her. He pressed her head to his chest and just held her tight.

With his heat surrounding her, Briana heard the pounding of his heart, inhaled his incredible scent. Against her belly, she felt the rise of his erection, and her knees almost gave out.

"Jack?"

He turned his face in to kiss her temple, and murmured, "Hmm?"

"I don't want a big wedding."

He went still, and then tilted back to see her. He continued to caress her, her back, her shoulders. Looking disappointed in himself, he admitted, "I hadn't thought about it."

She didn't care. "I don't want a big wedding, and I don't want to wait." As far as she was concerned, the sooner they could wed the better. "How long will it take to make the arrangements?"

His slow grin oozed sex appeal. It was the first time he'd ever grinned at her like that.

"In a hurry?"

"Yes." She crushed herself close to him. "You have no idea how long I've wanted you."

He threaded his fingers through her short hair. "That's nice to know, Bri."

Nice? God, what a vanilla word for how powerfully in love she felt.

He tugged gently on her hair so that she looked up at him. After another soft, deep kiss that curled her toes and raised her temperature a few degrees, he said, "I can get us in front of a judge within a few days. Will that work for you?"

"Yes."

"You're sure?" Considerate as always, he said, "I don't mind doing the whole fanfare if that's what you—"

"No." Self-conscious, she gestured down at herself. "You've known me awhile now, Jack. Can you picture me in a fancy dress? A *wedding* dress?"

His gaze went over her body. "You'd be beautiful."

Pleasure left her face warm and her breath shallow. "Well, I can't imagine it." She cleared her throat. "I don't want to imagine it. Dressing up is not my thing. Ditto on long formal ceremonies. I'll be much happier if we just get it done."

He gave a low laugh of indulgence. "We'll have the formalities behind us in no time, I promise."

"Good."

Then he sobered. "Until then . . ." He searched her face. "I care for you, Briana. I already told you that."

"I know." She more than cared for him. She loved him. Completely. And she knew he liked her, probably more than he

realized. She was far from dumb, and she had an astute understanding of human emotions. Right now, Jack felt grateful to her
because she loved and cared for Wendy. He also took pleasure in
their relaxed conversations, something he didn't indulge in with
many other people.

For a man like Jack, a man burdened with so much, she considered their easy camaraderie a great beginning.

"I don't want to rush you or make you feel awkward in
any way."

She was so busy with her own thoughts and with relishing his
nearness, she didn't understand. "Awkward how?"

He trailed his fingertips from her neck, down her collarbone,
and finally over a breast. Briana gasped—and an explosion of
sensation spread out through her body.

Jack's expression tightened as he cuddled her in his palm.

For her part, Briana wanted to melt all over him.

He sought her gaze, watching her intently, maybe gauging
her response as he continued to touch her, to find her nipple
with his thumb.

Oh, God, he couldn't know how that affected her, how she
felt it deep inside herself. "Jack . . ." she whispered.

With his other hand, he caught her hips and drew her in
closer to his body. "If you feel uncertain about spending the
night before we're married—"

"I don't." She wanted to be with him. *Right now.* For so long
she'd dreamed of this. Desire this strong was new to her, and she
wanted to explore it in every way.

To make herself clear, Briana looped her arms around his
neck and leaned into him. That felt good. Too good.

Voice trembling, she said, "Wendy will sleep for a while,
right? She always naps for an hour or more."

Jack said nothing, but his eyes darkened.

"I'm ready now. I've been ready." Whether he realized it yet or not, she'd waited her whole life for him. "Will you please make love to me, Jack?"

He went still for two heartbeats, and then he grabbed her hand and started walking her down the hall to his bedroom. Briana couldn't believe this was happening. He left her at his door long enough to peek in on Wendy again, and then he came back, rushed her inside, and closed and locked the door.

Before Briana could even take a breath, he started kissing her and undressing her at the same time.

She hadn't thought about it until just then, but she'd been outside all afternoon playing with Wendy. In the sunshine. In the heat.

"Jack?" He took her mouth and didn't give her an opportunity to speak again until he pulled her T-shirt off over her head.

Shocked at being bare-breasted in front of him, Briana said, "Shouldn't I . . . I don't know. Freshen up?"

His gaze devoured her. His nostrils flared and his eyes narrowed.

Rather than reply, Jack wrapped a strong arm around the small of her back, arched her upward, and drew her nipple into the heat of his mouth. All hesitation on her part disappeared. She sank her fingers into his thick brown hair and went lax in his embrace. The way he stroked her with his tongue, how he drew on her . . .

She whispered, "I had no idea," on a soft groan.

Just when she thought her knees wouldn't support her, he scooped his other arm beneath her bottom and lifted her to carry her to his bed.

He came down over her, kissed her long and hard, and then rose up to say urgently, "Briana, I'm sorry."

Without her glasses, she couldn't accurately read his expression, but he sounded worried. "For what?"

"It's been a long time for me . . ."

She knew that. Jack was a most discriminating man, and he rarely afforded personal time for himself.

"Me, too." Like forever. *Or never.* But he didn't need to know that yet.

He closed his eyes. "I need to slow down, but—"

"Please don't. What if Wendy wakes up? What if you change your mind?" Anything that kept him from her now would be unbearable. "Please don't slow down or apologize or anything." Biting back words of love, she kissed him and said, "I want this. Exactly as it is."

He put his forehead to hers, and then a second later he was standing again, his hands at the waistband to her jeans. He undressed her hurriedly. While staring at her body with absorbed fascination, he stripped off his own clothes.

Briana came up to her elbows. She'd seen him in nothing more than swim trunks, so she already knew how his body turned her on, how lean and hard and athletic he was built. But now, naked . . . wow.

He turned to the side a moment, and Briana realized he was donning a condom. When he came back to her, he stretched out beside her and kissed her again. This time, when they touched, it was skin to skin, and so exciting that she forgot to be reserved.

Provoked by love and curiosity, Briana reached down and clasped his erection.

He went rigid, suspended on a held breath, and then he cursed low and caught her wrist. "Not yet."

Awed, she said, "I love how you feel." It was pretty amazing.

He didn't understand, saying only, "I like how you feel, too." Pressing his hand between her thighs, he explored her, stroked over her—and then in her.

It was too much. Briana kissed him, clung to him, and when he moved atop her, she opened her thighs around him and locked her ankles at the small of his back.

For only a moment he looked at her with a wealth of senti-ment in his gaze. But it didn't last long before he was kissing her hard and deep, and then he thrust into her.

Briana stifled a gasp at his burning intrusion, clenched her whole body around him, and held herself still. She'd known what to expect physically, but she hadn't counted on the emotions swamping her, choking her, leaving her eyes damp.

She loved him so much, and finally they were together.

Jack froze. Against her breast, she felt the furious pounding of his heart; deep inside her, she felt the pulsing of his erection.

He put his face against her neck and, more gently now, withdrew.

Briana was about to protest when he slowly sank back in again. She caught her breath.

"That's better." While leisurely kissing her neck and stroking her hip, he started a rhythm that rocked her.

Everything felt amazing, every touch of his mouth or hands, the friction as he repeatedly filled her, and it all contributed to a near frantic need that kept growing stronger.

"Jack."

"Much better." He eased back enough to slip a hand between their bodies, and when his fingertips moved over her clitoris, she felt every sensation sharpen and burn until the climax rolled through her.

Only vaguely was she aware of Jack's response, how he fisted a hand in the sheet beside her head and began thrusting hard and fast, so powerfully, until he muffled a deep groan against her throat and went rigid over her.

Briana was still breathing too deeply when Jack rolled to his back and pulled her into his side. She glanced up at him and found him watching her.

"I was a virgin."

He choked on a sound of humor. "Yeah, I know that now. You could've told me beforehand."

"You might not have—"

"Oh, I would've all right." He inhaled and let his breath out slowly. "But I'd have made it easier on you."

"It was . . ." There were no words. "I loved it."

His grin went crooked. "You're a surprise, Briana. An amazing surprise." He yawned.

She said, "Can we stay like this for a few minutes?"

As an answer, he kissed the top of her head with clear affection. He closed his eyes, but he was smiling.

Satisfied, Briana allowed herself to doze off.

JACK awoke with a start. His first thought was of his daughter; panic wracked him—until her soft laughter reached him. It sounded like she was in the kitchen, and she wasn't alone.

As he assimilated her safety, his second thought was that Briana wasn't beside him anymore. He heard her say something indistinct to Wendy. So they were in the kitchen together—and he'd been napping like a child?

He never napped.

Sitting up, he found a sheet covering him and the bedroom door ajar. No doubt Briana had left the door that way on purpose, knowing he'd awaken with alarm.

He dropped back again against the rumpled bed. So many things ran through his mind: Briana's virginity, her sweet sexuality, her . . . love.

He scrubbed both hands over his face. The idea of her loving him was strangely satisfying. He didn't want to dwell on why that might be, on what his own feelings for her might encompass.

There were worries and a niggling of guilt, but damn, the

smile wouldn't stay away. For once the future—*his* future—looked bright.

All because of one innocent, uber-smart young lady. Without even trying, Briana had just rocked his world.

Anxious to see her, Jack threw off the sheet, left the bed, and dressed in a hurry. He wanted to talk to her, to be with her.

Because it was all new, he told himself. Not because he already half loved her. Not because, without him knowing it or accepting it, she'd crawled into his heart.

And yet, he knew when he'd thought of marriage again, his brain had gone to Briana, and only Briana.

Shaking off the disturbing possibility that he didn't know himself or what he wanted, Jack walked into the kitchen. Briana and Wendy were at the sink together. Standing on a stool, Wendy helped Briana with salad preparations. They kept bumping hips, laughing about it, and then doing it again.

Seeing them together like this sent insidious warmth curling through Jack.

It was . . . contentment.

Because he hadn't felt it for a very long time, Jack took a few moments to relish the sensation. It was a nice thing to know that, with Briana in the picture, he and Wendy would have everything they needed.

Though not more than an hour or so had passed since he'd taken her, he already looked forward to having Briana tonight. They'd be less rushed, and he'd be able to hold her all night long.

Wendy suddenly glanced over her shoulder, saw him, and hopped down off the stool. She ran into his arms and Jack swung her up for a hug.

Damn, but this just might work out.

four

By the end of the week, things were looking great. Jack was stunned by how quickly they all fell into an easy routine. It was almost as if Briana had been with them forever. And now, God willing, she would be.

Yesterday they had married. What should have been a momentous occasion proved only a hiccup in their lives. There was no fanfare, no crowds or formality, just their immediate families, a judge, and lots of smiles.

Briana had surprised him by wearing a blue print maxi dress that gave her the look of a flower child from the seventies. Thanks to Wendy's assistance, tiny flowers were haphazardly arranged in her hair. His daughter wore a matching sundress and flowers laced together as a necklace.

Both of his ladies had looked adorable, but then, they always did. He'd teased Briana, whispering in her ear, "A dress?"

She'd said back, "Not traditional white or lace or uncomfortable. In fact, I could get used to dresses like this." Then she'd confided, "Your mother suggested it, and I have to admit she was right."

Jack had already noticed that his mother beamed whenever Briana was near. Her approval couldn't have been more apparent. Luckily, Briana liked his mother just as much.

And to prove the point, she wore a dress now, at the zoo. Seeing her bare shoulders, the delicate nape of her neck, made him want to kiss her. But he didn't mind waiting, especially since Wendy was having so much fun.

They'd spent the week enjoying an odd, impromptu honeymoon by visiting local places such as the water park, the theater, the history museum—and today the zoo. It was Briana's idea, a way to commemorate their marriage without interrupting Wendy's schedule.

Like him, she put Wendy first.

Jack lifted Wendy off his shoulders, where she'd been perched to better see the bears. The second her feet hit the ground, she reached for Jack's hand—and Briana's. They stayed that way through the aviary, the aquarium, and the reptile house.

When they boarded the trolley, Wendy climbed into Briana's lap, and Briana put an automatic kiss to her crown. As the trolley rode along, Briana pointed out the sites and Wendy repeated each one.

For his part, Jack watched them, charmed, emotionally moved, and more than a little in love.

"I want ice cream," Wendy said.

Briana looked at Jack, caught him staring at her, and smiled. "I could use an ice cream, too. What do you think?"

"I think it'll be a sticky mess in this heat, but why not?"

She shrugged a bare shoulder. "If you can't be messy at the zoo, what's the point?"

Wendy repeated, "What's the point?"

Jack couldn't help but laugh. "True enough. We'll get off at the next stop."

Acting silly, Briana got Wendy to cheer with her.

She wasn't like Melanie, Jack admitted to himself. It wasn't that she was better or worse. She was just . . . different. Unique.

And how he felt about her was special.

He should probably tell her that he loved her. He knew he did. Again, not in the same way that he had loved Melanie. Five years changed a man. Being a father added dimension to his character in unexpected ways, forever changing him. He wasn't the same person that he'd been with Melanie.

He wasn't even the same person he'd been before marrying Briana.

As if she read his thoughts, Briana leaned against his shoulder. And damn, that felt right, so naturally comforting and secure.

He loved her.

In myriad, mysterious ways, Briana had taken his heart without him realizing it. Everything about her, her scent, the small sounds she made during sex, how she looked at him right before she came, filled some deep emotional well that had been empty for far too long.

He found himself looking forward to her company more than ever, but he now realized that he'd grown to rely on her in ways he hadn't before considered, ways that had nothing to do with his daughter.

Love.

He had to admit it to himself . . . but to her? His throat tightened, and a pang struck his chest, his heart. He'd loved once, and he'd been demolished. Wasn't it enough that they'd married? She was happy; she told him so every day.

For now, that would have to be enough.

IT had been so easy to move in with Jack. Before him, she'd never really seen herself as a wife. A student, yes. A teacher, eventually. Even a mother, given how she loved caring for Wendy.

But a wife was something different, and Briana found that it suited her.

Mysterious things became clear to her almost overnight. Like how Jack wallowed in her natural sexuality. Who knew that a previously virginal woman who was mostly uninterested in things of a carnal nature would love sex so much?

And she did love it. A lot.

She knew many women complained that the reality wasn't as magical as the storybook telling. But for her, it was.

She enjoyed surprising Jack; she could turn him inside out without even trying. A look from her, a whisper, and he was ready. And patient and tender and unselfish.

Thanks to him she now understood a woman's power over men. Before Jack, she hadn't associated power with her femininity. In fact, she'd never felt all that feminine.

Now, in so many different ways, he showed his appreciation of her female qualities. But he also appreciated her intelligence, when usually it intimidated people. He constantly smiled over little things she'd do, especially when it involved Wendy. She'd give the little girl a hug or show her patience when Wendy struggled with a new concept, and Jack would look at her with so much . . . emotion in his gaze.

She wanted to believe it was love that she saw, but he remained so protective of his heart that she just didn't know.

Still wearing her knee-length nightgown, Briana went to the counter to pour a cup of coffee. She wasn't exactly a morning person, but she wasn't someone who needed hours to wake up either, which was a good thing considering how active Wendy was in the morning and how cheerfully Jack faced each day.

She heard the shower shut off and knew that Jack was dressing. She sighed. Life couldn't be more perfect—unless he loved her.

But she knew going in that this was a marriage of convenience for him, so she wouldn't let it shadow *her* happiness. He would learn to love her; she had to believe that. Somehow, in some way, she would eventually win his heart.

A few minutes later, Jack walked in, shoes and a tie in one hand. He was still buttoning up his dress shirt, and to Briana, he looked gorgeous all freshly shaved with his hair still damp.

Wendy reached up for him, and as usual, he paused at the table to give her a hug. Always so much affection, Briana thought as she watched father and daughter.

"If you're all done eating," Jack told Wendy, "you can go brush your teeth."

She loved doing things on her own, so she raced off to the bathroom.

With love filling her heart, Briana smiled at Jack. "Coffee?"

Stepping into his shoes, he looked her over with proprietary admiration. "Thank you." He came close, took the coffee with one hand, and with the other he drew her closer, bending for a kiss. "I always knew you were a brilliant little nerd, but I swear, I never realized how sexy you are, too."

Her nightgown was cotton, striped, and practical—far from sexy. And right now, her hair stood on end, and behind her glasses her eyes were puffy.

Briana laughed at him. "If I'm sexy, it's because of you and what you do to me."

Setting the coffee aside, he put both arms around her. "Yeah, well, I'd love to do it to you again . . ." He gave her a soft kiss. "But I have to get to that meeting."

She sighed, accepting that the honeymoon was officially over. "I know."

"I can be home before you have to leave for your classes."

"There's no rush." It was rare that Jack got to take in an actual business meeting, and this would be to discuss a promising project, so she didn't want him hurrying on her account. "I'll drop Wendy off at school, so you just need to be done in time to pick her up."

"You're sure?"

They had a partnership, and she always wanted to do her part. Besides, she enjoyed her time with Wendy.

"Positive." And then, because she couldn't help herself, because the words were bursting inside her, Briana said, "I love you, Jack."

Wendy chose that inauspicious moment to come running back into the kitchen. She wrapped her arms around Jack's knees and repeated, "I love you."

He continued to look at Briana with a special heat in his gaze. She bit her lip and waited.

After the tension became nearly unbearable, he smiled and lifted Wendy up into his arms. "You're becoming a regular little parrot, aren't you?"

Wendy nodded. Jack scooped an arm around Briana, too, including her in the embrace. "Hearing that I'm so loved by my ladies is a very nice way to start my day."

He didn't say words of love in return, but Briana decided that he didn't have to. The look in his eyes, the way he touched her and spoke to her, said it all. Together they made a happy family, and that was what mattered most.

AFTER Jack left, Briana dressed and helped Wendy get ready. The exclusive private school was wonderful for Wendy, and Briana looked forward to the day when she would be qualified enough to teach at a similar place. She had plenty of education ahead of her, but she enjoyed the educational process, and now, by living with Jack, she had a much smoother schedule so she saw no reason not to continue.

The day was sunny and hot, not a cloud in sight, and she and Wendy sang on the ride to the school. Wendy held her hand as they left the car in the parking lot out front and went inside.

As usual, Wendy's instructor was friendly and accessible, but Briana didn't like to hover. It was important for Wendy to interact in a typical classroom atmosphere, and that didn't include a parent who wouldn't let go.

As she pulled out of the school parking lot to the main street, Briana was thinking about that, about how Wendy had kissed her good-bye with no clinginess at all. Every day it seemed that Wendy changed, growing more confident, more independent. It was a wonderful thing to see, to take part in.

Briana had gone only a quarter of a mile when she noticed a tractor trailer pull off a side street and crowd in too closely behind her. Glancing in her rearview mirror, Briana frowned and slowed, hoping to discourage the aggressive driver.

In an obvious hurry, he reacted by accelerating and switching lanes to pass her, but he did so without first checking that it was clear. When a horn blared, he swerved back to her lane—and hit the rear right end of her car.

The impact forced her car sideways, across both lanes. Briana tried to hit her brakes, to right the car, but an SUV plowed into her with jarring force.

Her head snapped back and then forward again, hitting the steering wheel hard enough to snap her glasses in half. The air bags opened, all but suffocating her.

It all happened so fast that Briana couldn't think straight. She'd hurt her knee on something, and sticky blood dripped down into her eyes.

She felt instantly nauseated, rattled, scared—and all she could think about was Jack.

Through the driver's door window, she saw that all around her, people had out their cell phones.

A man got her door opened, looked her over, and spoke to her in a calm, confident voice. "Try not to move, okay? I think all that blood is from a cut on your head. Head wounds bleed like that. But I'd rather you stay still until we know for sure."

The kind, take-charge voice reassured Briana. "Thank . . . thank you." Her head was swimming, and if she moved even a little, pain wracked her body.

"Shhh." He touched her shoulder. "Just breathe, okay? Para-medics are on their way."

She tried to say, "Thank you," but nothing came out past the crushing pain in her chest.

He reached beyond her to the floor where her purse had fallen and dumped. He pulled back out of the car with her cell phone. "I'm going to call someone for you, okay? You won't be alone."

"No . . ." The word emerged as a whisper, and Briana's vision blurred. Oh, God, Jack was the first number in her phone, but if he got that awful call . . .

He'd gone through this with his first wife, and he wouldn't know that this was different. He wouldn't know that Wendy was safe at the school.

Briana tried again, but her vision receded, faded into noth-ingness. She breathed Jack's name, and then oblivion took her.

WITH his heart in his throat, his knees quaking, his guts in knots, Jack ran into the hospital. Too familiar. All too fucking familiar.

He turned a circle in the entrance, unsure where to go, how to find her. A line waited at the reception desk, so he bypassed that and followed the signs to the ER.

The white walls, the antiseptic smell, the milling of depressed, worried, or despondent visitors—it all closed in on him until only a red-hot, desperate rage kept him moving.

He could not lose her.

Someone directed him toward the ER reception, and another rubber-shoed nurse took him to a curtained cubicle.

Pausing outside the curtain, Jack inhaled and tried to calm himself. The last thing anyone needed was hysteria. He was a man, *her husband*, and he had to hold it together.

God, please let her be okay.

He pushed the curtain aside and stepped into the small space—and then froze. Briana was on a bed, her head hastily wrapped with blood-soaked gauze, an oxygen mask on her face. Without her glasses, he saw the purpling bruises around her closed eyes.

"Briana."

Her eyes snapped open, and she turned her head toward him with a wince.

Emotion burned his eyes, tightened his throat. He couldn't seem to move.

Briana reached up and removed the oxygen. "Jack," she whispered in a voice so faint he barely could hear her. "Jack, it's okay."

He stared at her as he breathed hard, as he tried to collect himself adequately to sit with her, hold her, take care of her.

Tears mixed with the dried blood on her cheek. "Jack." She reached out to him in near desperation. "Wendy wasn't with me, Jack. She's at the school."

He swallowed hard, nodded. "I know that, sweetheart."

Her eyes looked heavy, maybe with pain medicine or just . . . pain. She licked dry lips. "You . . . you already knew?"

If he didn't sit down, his knees would give out. Cautiously, Jack lowered himself to the edge of her narrow bed. He touched the bandage on her forehead, felt the stiff blood still in her hair, and winced.

"The principal reached me just as my meeting had gotten

under way. The wreck was close enough to the school that they knew of it."

Her eyes sank shut. "Wendy? Where is . . . she?"

Jack cupped a hand to her face. She was hurt but alive. Warm and soft.

And his.

"She's fine. The school is caring for her."

"But . . ."

"She's playing, Bri. They'll give her lunch and keep her busy until I can get there." Such an amazing young lady, even now making others her main concern. "But you . . . you're a mess."

Eyes huge and bruised, she said, "I'm sorry. I know this isn't how we planned things. I never, ever wanted to add to your burdens."

She sounded so weak that Jack felt himself shaking. "Briana—"

A nurse parted the curtain. "Jack Burke?"

"Yes."

"Oh, good, I'm glad you're here." She pushed a rolling table with various items on it close to the head of Briana's bed. "She's been more worried about you than anything. But as you can see, with some TLC, she'll be all right. The doctor just left her. We think she might have some broken ribs, and we're getting ready to do some X-rays. On her leg, too."

Jack looked down, but the sheet covered her lower body. "Her leg?"

"She hit her knee pretty hard. It could just be a deep bruise, but we want to check it."

The nurse's easy attitude made him feel better. She displayed no sense of urgency, just competent care. "The cut on her head?"

"That's a doozy, isn't it? But don't worry, we'll get her stitched up, and once she heals, you'll never be able to see it. She was lucky that an off-duty EMT was on the road and called in the accident so quickly."

Briana said, "He was a very nice man." She reached out for Jack. Without her glasses, she missed the mark a little, so Jack caught her hand and lifted it to his mouth. "I think my breaking glasses are what caused the little cut on my head."

"Little," the nurse repeated with humor. She lifted the gauze and Jack got a look at the gash on her forehead. He grimaced for her.

The nurse asked, "You don't need the oxygen anymore?"

Briana shook her head. "I can . . . breathe . . . okay."

"Uh-huh." The nurse started to put the oxygen back on her.

"Please. I need a minute to talk to him."

Jack kissed her knuckles. "Dear God, Briana, I thought . . ." Tears welled in her eyes, ripping at him, leveling him. "Oh, sweetheart, don't. Please don't cry."

"I'm sorry." She hiccupped, sniffed, tried a deep breath, but couldn't manage it. "I knew you would think the worst and that was the hardest part for me! I wanted them to tell you that Wendy was okay, but I . . . I don't know. I passed out for just a second or something, and then I was in the ambulance and—"

He put a finger to her mouth. "Of course I'm relieved that Wendy wasn't in the car with you."

She drew in a shuddering breath. "I'm so sorry about this."

He'd been a coward and a jerk, and now she was suffering for it when there was no reason. "Briana, I love you."

Overflowing with tears, her eyes widened. She blinked fast, glanced at the nurse in disbelief, and then back to Jack. "What did you say?"

His voice broke. "You are so smart, Briana. How could you not know that I love you?" When she continued to watch him, he kissed her knuckles again and pressed her small hand to his heart. "I've loved you for a while, even if I didn't admit it to you—or to myself. But you know me, honey. Do you really think I'd marry a woman I didn't love just for convenience?"

"I . . ." Her hand fisted in his shirt, and then, since she was so smart, realization dawned in her expression. "You love me."

Jack smiled at her, reassuring her. "So much, you can't even imagine."

The nurse cleared her throat and stepped outside the curtain. Jack appreciated her patience and her tact.

"I'm going to be out of commission for just a little while."

Did she really think that mattered? Jack braced his arms on either side of her on the bed and, being very careful not to hurt her, leaned down to kiss her forehead, the bridge of her nose, her quivering mouth.

"I love what you do for Wendy, but what you do for me is pretty terrific, too."

"What do I do for you?"

"Everything. You do everything for me." He knew she didn't understand, so he explained. "When Melanie died, part of me died with her. I just didn't know it until you brought me back to life."

The nurse stuck her head in again. "Are we done romancing?" She smiled. "The doctor is waiting for us."

Jack stood. "We're going to have a long, wonderful life together. There will be ups and downs, and we'll deal with them. All that matters is that you're with me. With us. Forever."

Her smile trembled, and finally she nodded. "Okay then. Send the doctor on in." She put a hand to her aching ribs. "And you," she said to Jack. "Go and get our daughter."

ava's haven

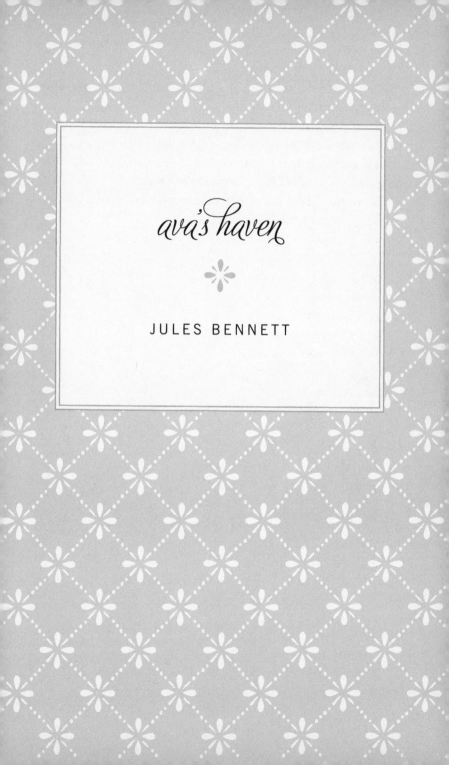

JULES BENNETT

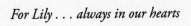

For Lily . . . always in our hearts

one

❋

"I'm here for Carly Myers."

The Stratton Police Department didn't seem too overly busy for a Friday evening, but at seven o'clock, the midsummer night was still young in the small town of Stratton, Alabama.

Olivia smiled at Officer Jenkins, the thirty-something man who usually greeted her with a slight nod and an apologetic smile on the rare occasions she had to come into the SPD. Easing the creaky chair back, he came to his feet.

"Have a seat, Miss Mathis." He motioned to the area with folding metal chairs.

Worried for Carly, Olivia didn't have time to care that the only vacant seat was smack-dab in between a prostitute who had, literally, the bare necessities covering her breasts and what appeared to be a homeless man slumped down in his chair. Olivia feared one wrong move and the frail man would be either on the floor or, worse yet, on her.

When her cell chirped from her purse, Olivia dug out her BlackBerry to check her texts. Ava's Haven could run just fine without her, but she always kept her phone on the highest volume so as not to miss an emergency. Emergencies happened when least expected and at the most inopportune moments. She should know.

"Livie."

Her hand froze around her cell, her heartbeat a bruising rhythm against her chest. The voice was just a little too close to her heart, a little too familiar in her mind.

No one ever called her Livie. No one at the shelter, none of her friends. No one.

Except Colin Parker.

At the risk of memories best left in the past rushing to the surface, Olivia lifted her head, and sure enough, there stood the man she'd intended to marry. The man she'd intended to have children with.

A stab of pain sliced through her as she settled a hand against her empty womb. So many memories flooded to the surface. They bypassed all the dreams she'd thought she'd buried, thought she'd never have to face again.

She was wrong.

"What are you doing here?" he asked, his brows drawn together.

Olivia came to her feet, well aware of the crackling tension settling in the air between them.

"I'm here to pick up a friend." She clutched her cell in one hand and her purse strap in the other, willing her knees to stay locked and keep her upright. "You work here?"

She took in his shoulder holster, dark jeans with distressed pockets, and dark gray button-up shirt. His shoulders and chest were much broader than when she'd last seen him. Of course, that had been twelve years ago, when they'd both been twenty and in love.

Or so the dream went.

"Detective." His eyes raked over her as if doing his own assessment. "Who are you here to pick up?"

Before she could answer, Carly came down a narrow hallway with Officer Jenkins escorting her. The normally petite, beautiful girl now had puffy, swollen eyes. Her hair hung in stringy ropes that looked as if it had once been in a low ponytail. Her young, baby face had red scratches.

"I'm so sorry, Olivia," Carly cried as she fell into Olivia's arms. "I—I . . ."

Olivia tightened her hold and smoothed the ratty blond hair down Carly's back. "We'll fix this. It's okay." Whatever "it" may be.

When Carly had called crying, the only audible words were "arrested" and "pick me up." Olivia hadn't hesitated. Fear had radiated through Carly's tone . . . a fear Olivia had once felt herself.

The police station began to bustle, but Colin kept his dark eyes locked on to this private moment. Olivia really didn't want to try to divide her attention between her past and her present. Her present, and Carly's future, won hands down.

As Olivia lifted her gaze, she caught the questioning look from Colin. He crossed his arms over his wide chest, leaving Olivia no choice but to look away. She couldn't focus on Carly's problems and helping her stay clean if she was thinking about how she'd made a mockery of her own life after Colin had left. Not that he was to blame. No, she'd brought all the evil, fatal damage upon herself.

The past couldn't be helped but the future could, and right now there were people who needed her. Starting with Carly.

Olivia eased back and pulled a tissue from her jeans. "Here. Dry your tears so we can talk."

"You're not mad?" The young girl sniffed.

She offered a smile. "Do I look mad?"

With mascara running all over her tinted, scratched cheeks, bright red nose, and quivering lips, Carly shook her head. "Thank you for coming. I promise I didn't start the fight, Olivia. I was just in the wrong place . . . again."

Olivia hugged the girl once more. She knew all about being in the wrong place in life. Not so long ago, she'd turned to the wrong crowd and got sucked in before she ever knew what happened. By then it was too late and the repercussions had been deadly.

But Olivia knew from experience, reprimanding Carly would get them nowhere. But maybe, by the grace of God, love, understanding, and patience would.

"Ready to go?" she asked.

Carly nodded and turned toward the door.

"Miss Mathis," Officer Jenkins called. "Here is her purse and I need you to sign here."

Olivia took the large pink tote and passed it over to Carly.

"Livie."

She dropped the pen on the desk and turned to face Colin, for what she hoped was the last time. "Yes?"

He glanced around the crowded station and stepped closer, lowering his voice. "Can we talk?"

"Now's not a good time." Thank God she had a valid excuse to get out of his powerful presence. "Carly needs me."

The muscle in his jaw ticked, and he nodded in understanding. "You still live here?"

Olivia glanced back toward the door to see if Carly was waiting for her. "Yes."

"I'll be in touch, then."

She whipped her head back around. "What?"

"To talk."

One corner of his mouth kicked up slightly as if he were trying to hold back a grin. A grin that would no doubt have even more emotional memories rushing back.

Great. Just great. She'd been in his presence for ten minutes, and she'd already experienced that intoxicating charm. Obviously he was just as potent now as he was then. But Olivia wasn't naïve, she wasn't a dreamer. Not anymore.

"Better go." He nodded toward the exit. "It's starting to rain and your friend is getting wet."

Thankful for an out but frustrated she'd been staring down the eyes of the past, Olivia rushed to the door and out into the now steady rain. With her arm protectively around Carly's shoulders, she hustled her through the parking lot and into her cherry red Jeep Wrangler.

Dealing with Colin was the dead-last thing Olivia had time for, not when Carly and countless other people needed support. And even if she did have the time, she wouldn't indulge in teenage fantasies.

Oh, who was she kidding? She didn't have the mental capabilities to rehash anything from her past with Colin. That portion of her life only led to destruction.

Talk with Colin? Was he serious? All that disastrous confrontation would accomplish would be opening old, deep wounds that Olivia couldn't dwell on. If she did, she'd be worth absolutely nothing.

People depended on her, so venturing down the path to the past was the worst possible thing she could do. Every bit of her time and energy had to remain on the future, not only for her own sanity, but for the welfare of everyone at Ava's Haven.

Luckily, Carly lived with a group of college girls who would watch out for her and who were extremely supportive. Once Olivia dropped her off and made sure she was okay, she promised to check back in tomorrow. But she made the girls promise to call if there was any sign of trouble.

Carly was just like Olivia at that age—always eager to please others at the expense of her own happiness and trying to find her place in life. Not to mention they both came from broken homes, but who didn't these days? Married couples who stayed together were becoming extinct . . . right along with Olivia's own dreams of being a wife, a mother.

Olivia sighed and prayed she could direct Carly down the right path. So far, though, Carly was already one step ahead. She hadn't fallen for a smooth-talking junkie, and she hadn't become hooked on anything. And Olivia would do everything in her power to make sure Carly stayed clean and headed in the right direction.

As Olivia guided her Jeep through the downtown streets, she knew she really needed to go back to the office and get some work done, but she simply couldn't. Seeing Colin again after twelve years had taken a major toll on every fiber of her being.

How could the man look even better than before? His once thick, wavy dark hair was now military short, completely taking away that boy-next-door look. Nearly everything with Colin's physical looks had changed. Now he appeared harder, tougher. His chest and shoulders were broader. His arms filled out his dress shirt, and his chiseled face looked more like a man than the boy who'd walked away.

But those eyes. Those navy blue eyes were just the same. Just as potent and capable of turning her insides to a quivering, jumbled mess.

What had he been up to all this time? Had he lived an entire lifetime in the last twelve years like she had?

Olivia turned into her drive, hit the button for her garage door, and pulled into her two-story cottage. She loved this house. Loved the lake she shared with only a few other scattered homes. But most of all, she loved the innocence this house represented.

This was her haven. The home she'd grown up in. The home she'd dreamed in.

The very same home she'd once run away from when she'd been lost.

And that was precisely why talking with Colin could and would be detrimental. She'd been in his presence for all of ten minutes, and already those feelings that were always right there at the surface threatened to explode with volcanic proportions. Why couldn't the past just stay buried? And why did every single detail come back with a vengeance? Each moment of that dark period stabbed at her, forcing her to choke back a sob.

Swallowing the lump and tears clogged in her throat, she closed the garage door, grabbed her messenger bag and purse, and went inside her empty home. She needed a dog. Or a cat. She was much more a dog person, but with all the crazy hours she worked, a cat would be more compatible. Maybe she would hit the local shelter next time she was going by just to see what they had.

Yeah, right. Like she could just go in and *not* pick out a pet. All her life, she'd wanted to save things, people. First her parents' failing marriage when she'd been only ten, then her relationship with Colin.

Too bad she hadn't put forth any effort to save her child.

Olivia set her bags and keys on the center island in her kitchen. The pain was always there, always waiting for the moment in her life when she least expected to be slapped in the face with reality. Some days the ache lessened, but some days it consumed every second of the day, every fiber of her being.

Actually, ache wasn't quite accurate. An ache would be a welcome feeling to the sharp jabs she often felt when dwelling on all the ways she'd ruined any chance of having a family of her own. But she had the shelter, and every person who came through that door was like a brother or sister. They were her family, and they were a close-knit unit.

No one, however, knew the details of her past. She tried not to dwell on it in public. Putting up a strong attitude and a let's-move-forward persona was the only way to assist others in making the proper decisions.

The knock at her front door jolted her from venturing too far into her morose past.

Olivia tried to peer out the sidelight as she walked through the narrow foyer. Even with her porch light on, she couldn't make out who stood on the other side of the door. She guessed the visitor to be a man from the size of the one bulky shoulder she saw.

But one quick glance through her peephole and Olivia froze.

Colin.

How on earth? She'd just run into him less than an hour ago, and he was on her doorstep already? He must've left not long after her.

As much as she wanted to ignore him and run upstairs and bury her head under the covers of her Queen Anne poster bed, she had to be mature about this. They were adults now, nothing could change what went on years ago. She was over the initial blow of seeing him, so another encounter shouldn't have her so flustered.

With a deep breath and a hand to her churning stomach, Olivia opened the door and pasted on a smile.

"Colin, how did you know I'd be living in my mom's house?" Realization dawned on her, and she held up a hand. "Never mind. You looked me up in the system. Right?"

That cocky, yet charming grin she'd always loved spread across his face, and it still made her knees weaken. "Guilty. Can I come in? Unless you have plans or are in the middle of something."

Her hand gripped the doorknob. "Uh . . . sure. Come on in."

She stepped back and gestured him through. Now what? Did

he really want to talk? Catch up on old times? Olivia knew they had absolutely nothing in common . . . not anymore.

"I just got home," she told him as she led him to her cozy living room. "Can I get you something to drink?"

"No. I'm fine."

Colin Parker was in her house, her living room. He seemed to dominate the entire space with his height, his muscular frame. His questioning gaze.

"How is your mom?"

Olivia swallowed. "Actually, she passed away when I was twenty-three."

Colin took a step forward, as if to comfort her, then stopped and shoved his hands in his pockets. "I hate to hear that, Livie. I'm so sorry."

"She had a brain tumor," she offered. "She didn't suffer, though. Once the doctors found it, she only lived another month. I'm sorry you didn't know. I know how much you loved her."

His sultry eyes leveled with hers. "I loved you, too, Livie. I would've been there for you if I'd known."

Okay. Awkward and most definitely *not* a topic she wanted to cover. No way could she just jump straight into how they did or didn't truly love each other.

"Have a seat."

Taking the lead, she eased down onto the butter yellow sofa and grabbed a bright red throw pillow to clutch on her lap. She needed a prop to hide her shaky hands.

He sat on the opposite end, rested his elbows on his knees, and sighed. "I'm sorry for just popping in unannounced like this, but seeing you . . . well, it was nice, and if I didn't stop by now, I never would've gotten the nerve to do so."

"Nerve?"

The Colin she remembered never feared a thing. Just one more way they'd grown in opposite directions. But she had to admit, he hadn't lost that sexy, slow Southern drawl. That smooth talk could still melt any coolness she felt toward him.

He glanced over. "I haven't seen you in twelve years, Livie. I wasn't sure you'd even want to talk. Not after how I left things."

Olivia swallowed, pulled her legs up beneath her, and toyed with the decorative beading on the edge of the pillow. "It was a long time ago, Colin. We've moved on."

"Still . . . I didn't know if you'd welcome me." He eased back onto the sofa and smiled. "I'm glad, though. When I accepted this transfer, I wondered if I'd run into you."

"Really?" He'd actually thought about her?

She tried to hold her eyes on his but found it too hard. Glancing away, she could only pray he hadn't heard what a mess she'd made of her life. But all he'd have to do was ask around, and he'd know every sordid detail.

Olivia gathered courage from deep down and brought her eyes back to his. "How long have you been back?"

"About six months. I bought a house out on Hutton Lane, and I've been renovating it in my spare time. It's a small bungalow built in the thirties, so it needs quite a few updates."

Six months? "I've been in the station in the last six months. I can't believe I haven't run into you."

"I work crazy hours. Perhaps I was there and just back in my office." His thick dark brows drew together. "Do you often have to come in and bail out your friends?"

Olivia tilted her chin in both defiance and pride. "Actually, I don't have to come in that often, and the people I come to bail out have no one else to call."

"Why is that?"

Surprised, and a bit relieved, she asked, "You mean no one told you?"

Colin crossed his ankle over his knee and shook his head. "I didn't ask anyone about you. I just went into my office, looked up your name on my computer, and found your address. I try not to share my personal life with my coworkers."

The fact that he'd just lumped her into his personal life concerned her, but she'd have to address that later. Or avoid it at all costs.

"I own a shelter," she told him. "Well, it's more than a shelter. I started it as a shelter for pregnant drug addicts."

His mouth dropped, and his brows rose. "No kidding? That's great, Livie. How long ago?"

"Almost nine years." She forced herself to trudge on and not think about the reasons behind her motivation. Colin didn't need to know what kept her moving forward every day. "We've actually grown, and I've been able to take on more staff. Now we work with runaways, pregnant teens, whether they're drug abusers or not. We also assist in finding jobs and housing for young adults looking to get off the street.

"Basically, we want to help anyone who took a wrong turn in life."

For a moment Colin just sat there, his dark eyes never wavering from her face. She wanted to know what he was thinking, but she didn't dare ask. She also didn't want to get lost in that mesmerizing gaze. Colin always had the ability to hypnotize her with those intense, sexy eyes.

After a moment of utter silence, which was only a wee bit awkward, Olivia could practically see the wheels in his head turning.

Please, God, don't let him ask what prompted my choice of careers.

"Livie, that's . . . wow." He shook his head as a smile spread across his handsome, chiseled face. "That's amazing. And this is your job, right? Not volunteer work?"

"I have volunteers, but this is my only job." My life.

He drew a knee up onto the couch and eased one long, tanned

arm across the back, as if reaching for her. "But how do you get paid? How do you keep things running?"

"By the grace of God and the generous donations that keep coming in."

Speechless again. Olivia was pleased to know that she'd impressed Colin to the point of silence, but if not for her careless actions after he'd left town so long ago, she wouldn't have the business and she certainly wouldn't be helping people.

And this was one of those times where she was thankful she could help others, but she'd much rather go back in time, redo the period in her life from the ages of eighteen to twenty-two. She wanted to go back to that innocent love she and Colin had, the dreams they'd shared.

She wanted to go back to the time before she got caught up in a world she didn't understand, a world nobody, especially a young adult, should have to encounter. A world full of lies, evil, and deceit. Maybe then she wouldn't have nightmares about burying a baby she barely remembered conceiving, barely remembered holding.

two

✳

Colin couldn't believe he was sitting in Olivia's family room. The same family room he'd sat in and told her he didn't think they were right for each other after three years of dating and talk of an engagement.

He didn't know what amazed him more, the fact that she was the owner of this remarkable shelter that gave so much or the fact that she was even more beautiful than he'd remembered. He wasn't surprised, though, that she was in the business of helping others. But this was quite a leap from what she'd always intended.

"What happened to your dreams of becoming a nurse?" he asked.

Her pale green gaze leveled his. "Dreams die."

Ouch. "Guess I deserved that," he murmured.

Livie closed her eyes and sighed. "No, you didn't. It's just seeing you, I'm forced to face all those memories."

Now that he understood. "Want me to go?"

Her lids lifted. "No. No. I'm just tired, and that's no excuse for being rude. I apologize." She smiled once again. "I see you did exactly what you said you'd do."

Colin nodded, thankful they were on a somewhat safer topic. "Yeah. After five years in the marines, I took a job with the Atlanta PD. I stayed there up until six months ago when I found out about the opening here. I'd always intended to come back home."

If she didn't quit toying with that beaded pillow, the thing would fall apart. Did he really make her that nervous? He was used to intimidating suspects, but this was the one person in the world he wanted to feel safe.

She glanced back to him, still worrying the colorful beading. "Not much has changed since you've been gone."

"You have."

Her deep brown eyes widened; her fingers stilled. "Me?"

"You've gotten prettier, something I didn't think possible."

Those wide eyes lowered to her unsteady hands. She looked so adorable tucked in the corner of her sofa, especially now that her cheeks were pink from his compliment. With her soft golden curls hanging around her face, she looked the picture of innocence. But he had a feeling there were secrets lurking behind this façade. Oh, everyone had a secret or two, but something about the worry and panic in her eyes when he'd brought up her career and her dreams had him wondering what she kept hidden.

Occupational hazard to always want to dig into people's minds and see the reasons behind their actions.

"Sorry," he told her. "I didn't mean to embarrass you."

She cleared her throat. "Did you ever marry?"

"No. I was so busy with work." Honesty, he had to be honest. "I also never found anyone I wanted to be with for the rest of my life. What about you?"

She shook her head, still looking down to the pillow. "No."

Okay, that was simple. He wanted to know more. He wanted to know everything. Mostly, he wanted to keep her talking so he had a reason to stay. He didn't want this moment to get any more awkward than it already was.

What did she do when her mother died? Did she have anyone to turn to during that rough time?

"So, what did you get your degree in? You were working on nursing when I—"

Left.

"I, um, didn't finish college," she told him. "I dropped out after you enlisted."

That shocked him. Dreams and reaching goals had been Olivia's number one priority. Besides, she'd been the class valedictorian and the one person Colin would've bet money on would not only get that BSN, but also go on to get her PhD.

"What happened?"

Livie tossed the pillow down, came to her feet, and crossed the room to the window overlooking the lake. He thought she was going to tell him, but when she wrapped her arms around her waist and dropped her head, he realized he'd asked the wrong question.

Obviously those secrets he'd feared hidden behind her sweet smile and girl-next-door persona were bubbling to the surface. Damn. He was so used to badgering witnesses and suspects, he hadn't meant to probe an innocent woman.

He, too, came to his feet and moved to stand behind her. "I'm sorry, Livie."

Something terrible had happened after he'd left. His gut told him she was both humiliated and fearful of this secret.

Before he could say anything else, her shoulders shook and she sniffed. Oh, God.

He placed a hand on her shoulder and turned her. "Liv."

She held up a hand and stopped him from pulling her into his arms. "No. Don't. I can't talk about the past. I . . . just . . . can't."

Taking a step back, he nodded. "Fair enough. I'm sorry I upset you."

He couldn't stand it, that lone tear track on her face. He took her face in his hands and swiped the dampness with his thumb. Those doe eyes staring up at him made him damn glad he'd found the courage to come to see her, but at the same time, she wouldn't be crying if he'd stayed away.

"Colin," she whispered.

Everything about her drew him in. Her sweet, floral scent, her soft, smooth skin beneath his palms, her vulnerability—a vulnerability he shouldn't take advantage of. He could no more stop his actions than he could stop her hurt. But maybe, just maybe, he could make her forget for a moment.

He eased forward, ever so slowly, giving her ample time to stop him. Just one taste, that's all he needed to see if the sparks were still there.

With his hands still framing her face, his lips touched hers. When she parted her lips, he nearly sighed with relief at her acceptance.

He was both right and wrong. Yes, the sparks were still there, but he'd need more than one taste. She was just as intoxicating as he'd remembered. Just as potent.

Her soft, gentle hands cautiously slid up his forearms, gripped his elbows. That small, simple gesture was the only thing keeping Colin from stepping back. She hadn't leaned into the kiss as most women did, nor had she offered more than he was taking.

But now she was. The kiss wasn't fast, wasn't aggressive, but he'd lost control just the same the second she'd touched him.

He knew she was in a difficult place in her mind, and wherever that lonely, depressing place was, Colin wanted to take her somewhere else. And selfishly, he wanted it more than his next breath.

Before he frightened her completely, Colin released her lips, but not her face. He didn't want to lose that connection, no matter how small. That silky skin beneath his rough palms should've proven to him just how different they were now. But he didn't care about the differences. He cared about Livie.

"I can't apologize, Livie. I'd be lying."

Her lids fluttered, and when she looked into his eyes, she immediately dropped her hands. "No, this isn't happening."

When she stepped back, he had no choice but to release her. Her whole body shook, the tip of her nose was red, her eyes still misty.

"Can you talk to me?" he whispered. "We used to talk about everything."

The corners of her delicate mouth tipped up in a sad smile. "That was a lifetime ago, Colin. And it's a place I cannot go back to. Especially with you."

Guilt slammed through him. Obviously, whatever held that haunted look in her eyes was caused by his actions. Had breaking up with her really been that life altering? Yes, they'd talked of marriage, but at the age of twenty, they had still been too young. At least, he'd thought so then.

What was she hiding that had her so scared to let him in?

"I'll go," he told her. "If you ever need to talk, I'm here. I won't be going anywhere."

When she closed her eyes and turned back toward the window, Colin knew that was his silent cue to leave her alone. She wanted to be alone, and he would oblige.

But that didn't mean he had to give up on figuring out just what the hell had happened to this vivacious woman after he'd left.

three

Working from home was something Olivia rarely did. Only when she'd had the flu, twice in nine years, did she stay holed up in her bedroom with her files, laptop, and tissues.

After Colin had left last night and she'd pulled herself together, she'd gone over to the shelter to retrieve some of her files and her flash drive. She'd left a voice mail for her assistant stating that she'd be working from home if they needed her.

Still in her gray lounge pants and matching cami, Olivia booted up her computer and tried to concentrate on her job. But her mind wasn't on work. How could she focus after the trauma, both mental and physical, she'd endured last night?

First Colin had wanted to play the "let's get reacquainted" game. Then, as if dredging up past memories wasn't enough of a blow, he'd gone and kissed her at the weakest moment she'd had in quite a while.

And, God help her, she'd enjoyed feeling his lips against hers. How long had it been since she'd allowed a man to touch her? To hold her? It had taken every bit of her willpower not to lean into him and allow the comfort he so eagerly offered.

But she doubted even his strong, muscular arms could bear the weight of her past.

Her eyes darted over to the small, framed set of footprints on her nightstand. Ava's footprints.

Even after a decade, the stab to Olivia's heart was just as sharp, just as fierce. There were only three things she had to keep her daughter's memory alive: the frame of footprints on pink card-stock, one photo of the fragile baby, and Ava's hospital bracelet.

The bracelet and photo had long since been put away. Seeing the shape her baby was in, seeing how small the bracelet was, only made the suffering that much worse . . . if there actually were levels of misery.

For so long, Olivia had kept the photo and bracelet beside her bed as well, but the collection reminded her of a shrine. As if she'd needed a reminder of the life she'd ruined and taken by just two short years of misguided judgment.

Moving the items had been hard, but there was no way she could start each day seeing her baby's face. She had to make some sort of peace with herself.

A bitter laugh escaped Olivia as she opened a document on her laptop. Peace? She would never feel peace again. Every bit of innocence and peacefulness she'd had died along with her baby. All she could do now was draw strength from the lives she'd influenced in a positive way.

This was no way to try to work, she scolded herself. Beating herself down wouldn't help others, and right now she needed to concentrate. She had to put the finishing touches on the arrangements for the shelter's annual fund-raiser, which was in three short days.

Not the most convenient time for her to stay home and have

a self-pity party, but she really needed to be alone right now. Being alone while miserable was always best. No need to go into the shelter and have her depressed mood rub off on people who were there to look for a positive atmosphere.

Right now, though, the pity party would have to be put on hold. This fund-raiser needed her full attention, and worrying about Colin and him finding out about her past had no place in her mind today.

The silent auction and Texas Hold 'em poker tournament was the biggest fund-raiser Ava's Haven had. She hoped they would top last year's donations of twenty-six thousand dollars. Yes, that was a lot of money, but to keep a business open twenty-four hours a day, seven days a week, all year long, was expensive. Thank God for volunteers and donors throughout the year.

Olivia looked over the spreadsheet of businesses and their donations, making sure they were all checked off for having delivered the merchandise to auction. Once she completed that task, she made sure all the poker players' funds had been received. The number of players was certainly up this year, and in a bad economy, she was even more grateful. Thankfully people were still in the spirit of giving.

By the time she'd checked off all the to-do lists she needed to, she glanced to the corner of her computer and saw it was nearly two o'clock. As usual, she'd worked through lunch. And as if on cue, her belly growled.

She set aside her computer and the folders, and padded downstairs to her galley kitchen to make some lunch—not that she was in an eating mood. Maybe just a cheese sandwich or some yogurt.

Just as she opened her fridge, the doorbell chimed.

She gave a once-over to her ratty, pajama-clad, braless appearance and shrugged. Her house, her day off, she could dress how she wanted. Even if it was late in the afternoon.

But when she opened her door and Colin stood on the other

side with a small bundle of bright, happy-looking daisies in his hand, Olivia really wished she'd considered showering and dressing this morning. At the very least she wished she had on a bra. She suddenly felt so . . . vulnerable and naked.

"A peace offering," he said, extending the flowers to her. "I'm not here to stay or to talk. I just wanted to say how sorry I am for last night."

He looked even sexier today, in his crisp long-sleeved white shirt with the sleeves rolled up on his tanned forearms, dark jeans, and shoulder holster. Everything about this man screamed authority and power, yet he stood at her door with a sheepish grin, guilt in his eyes, and delicate daisies in his hand.

Shocked at the gesture, and a bit flattered, Olivia took the bouquet, resisting the urge to bury her nose in the yellow and white petals. "Thank you."

"I was hoping to ask you something while I was here," he said, leaning an arm against the door frame.

"What's that?"

"I want to make dinner for you and show you my new place."

Olivia couldn't help but smile. "That wasn't a question."

Colin's low, rich chuckle washed through her, sending tingles throughout. "No, I guess not," he agreed. "But would you come? Just as friends."

Friends? God, she hadn't done something with friends in so long, she wouldn't know how to act. But in the light of day and after thinking about him all night, she had to admit the idea of having Colin back in her life, on any level, would be good for her never-ending healing process.

And as much as she hated to admit it, he was softening her hard edges. They'd only been reacquainted less than twenty-four hours, and already he'd broken through a layer she'd built around herself. Who knew what could happen if they actually spent more time together?

"I'd like that." There had to be stipulations, though. "But no more talk of the past. Deal?"

His sexy mouth split into a wide, adorable grin as he straightened to his full height. "Deal."

He gave her directions and left, leaving Olivia staring as his unmarked police car pulled from her brick drive. Once he was out of sight, she lifted the bundle of flowers to her nose and inhaled.

Calming, pleasant, irresistible. Much like the man himself.

This was exactly what she'd needed. Something good to remind her she was still alive, still working hard to keep her life on track for Ava's sake and for all the other people out there who'd taken a hard left in life when they should've stayed straight.

Olivia closed the door and went to find her short, square pink-tinted vase to put the flowers in. She didn't know the last time she'd received flowers.

Actually, never. She cut the stems down and spent a crazy amount of time fussing over the arrangement, breathing in the sweet aroma.

The fluttery schoolgirl feeling should've made her feel silly, but it didn't. She wanted to savor this moment. She deserved that much.

Olivia showered, dressed for dinner at Colin's, and left a bit early. She had several errands to run before the fund-raiser on Saturday. And, she had to admit, she was a bit too anxious to wait at home for the time to tick by.

Several hours later, Olivia pulled into Colin's drive and smiled. The deep brown bungalow looked cozy, yet masculine.

The small porch glowed in the light of the antique lanterns hanging from either side of the large oak door, and an American flag hung proudly from a tall pole in the yard with a simple light shining on the stars and stripes.

Olivia fisted a hand over her abdomen. Why had she agreed to do this? Yes, she still felt something for Colin, but that had to be old feelings creeping up. Well, that and the soul-searing kiss he'd given her last night. Okay, so the flowers really added another layer to the emotional foundation she was trying to stand on.

She cursed him for bringing those flowers. Sneaky guy.

Resisting the urge to throw up or stick her car in reverse, Olivia grabbed her purse and the bottle of Chardonnay she'd brought.

As she stepped from her car, Colin opened the front door and greeted her with a smile, and the tension and nerves evaporated. He'd always had that ability to calm her, to make her feel safe. Looked like some things hadn't changed after all.

But she was realistic. Olivia knew this wasn't *The Colin and Olivia Show: Take Two*. Even if he wasn't scarred by a haunting past, she was. Friendship was one thing; romance and falling in love were another.

She shoved the doubts and nerves aside, ready to have a nice evening with an incredibly handsome man. Colin met her half-way on the curved stone path leading to the porch.

"Did you find the place okay?" he asked, taking the wine off her hands.

"I did." She followed him into the house and caught a whiff of something amazing. "What are you making? My mouth is watering already."

"Lasagna. It's my mother's recipe."

Thoughts of happier times filled Olivia's mind, leaving room for nothing else. "You remembered?"

As he entered the spacious kitchen, he threw a glance over his shoulder and smiled. "That it was your favorite? Yeah, I remembered."

God, why did her heart have to get gooey all over again where this man was concerned? Just friends. That's all this could be. Her heart couldn't take another blow.

"Then I'm really glad I accepted your offer," she said, easing up onto a wrought-iron barstool at the center island.

Colin slid the pan from the oven and laughed. "You weren't glad before you smelled the lasagna?"

"I have to admit, I was nervous." She hung her purse on the back of the stool. "I haven't been on a date, friendly or otherwise, in years, much less in a man's kitchen."

He set the potholders on the charcoal granite countertop by the stove and came to rest his hands on the opposite side of the island. "You're kidding me?"

"I've been too busy."

He raised a questioning brow. "Too busy to eat with a man who's interested in you? I find that hard to believe."

Honesty. She'd always vowed to be honest with people. Another positive influence from Ava.

"All right, I haven't been in a comfortable place with my life to allow myself the luxury of dating."

He studied her in that examining, cop-like manner that more than likely came second nature to him. "Which begs the question, why did you agree to come here?"

She shrugged, hoping to keep the conversation light. "Because I know you and I know you'll respect my wishes of keeping the past in the past. With dating, I didn't want to have to go through that get-to-know-you stage."

Her answer seemed to pacify him, for which Olivia was grateful.

As they ate, he asked more questions about her shelter, and Olivia was all too eager to discuss the upcoming fund-raiser. Maybe it was the two glasses of wine, or maybe it was just Colin's undivided attention that had her so chatty. Either way, she was pleased when he nodded and smiled and told her how amazing he thought her work was.

"I asked a few of the guys about your shelter," he told her as he led her to his screened-in patio room overlooking a small pond. "They all sang praises to you and your employees. Seems you single-handedly built that shelter from nothing."

The airy room allowed the summer breeze to flutter through and the moonlight to spill in. The intimacy of the moment sent a trickle of panic up her spine, but she reminded herself she deserved this. She needed to relax, take time for herself. Why shouldn't she indulge in a few hours of calm? Her sanity would thank her later.

Olivia set her wineglass on the squatty brown wicker table and took a seat on the navy padded wicker sofa. "A good reputation is what keeps the donations coming in and the needy people eager to seek help."

He settled in beside her, closer than he'd sat with her last night at her house. "So where does the name 'Ava's Haven' come from?"

Olivia cleared her throat. She'd been prepared for this question. "'Ava' means 'like a bird' or 'flying.' I want everyone who steps through those doors to know they can go out and achieve anything."

Colin eased an arm along the back of the two-seater sofa. Even in the dim lighting, his piercing cobalt eyes seemed to study and probe her. She couldn't help but glance down to his lips, but she quickly looked back up.

"So the name 'Ava' was just a random name you chose for the meaning?"

Olivia swallowed and glanced down to her lap, then back up. That honesty thing niggled at her to tell him a portion of the truth, but not all. If he did indeed stick around, he would learn everything on his own anyway, so she might as well tell him pieces and ease him into that darkness of her life.

She leveled his intense gaze. "My daughter's name was Ava."

To Colin's credit, he didn't drop his mouth or act shocked. "Was?"

She nodded, pulling up strength she had stored in reserve for when this topic came up. "I delivered her at twenty-four weeks. She lived forty-six hours."

Colin didn't offer apologies or empty words. He simply took her hand from her lap and squeezed it. "How old were you when this happened?"

"Twenty-one."

"And the father?" he probed in a softer, caring tone.

Olivia cringed at just the thought of Josh. "He was with me at the hospital, for the funeral. But we parted ways soon after."

"Is this man the reason you quit nursing school?"

Olivia jerked her hand from his and came to her feet, keeping her back to him. She concentrated on the moonlight glistening on the ripples of the pond instead of the niggling urge to throw up.

"That's all I can tell you now, Colin. There are things that happened; I'm not proud of them, but I can't revisit that place."

He, too, came to his feet and wrapped his arms around her waist, pulling her back against his chest. "Okay, baby. Okay. I'm sorry for prying."

His chest vibrated with each soothing word, and Olivia allowed herself the luxury of leaning, if only for a minute, against his hard, strong body.

Maybe he could handle the whole truth, but she wasn't ready to see disappointment or, worse, pity in his eyes. He may have been ready to handle it, yes, but she wasn't.

"You're one tough lady, you know that?" he whispered in her ear.

Olivia laughed. "Not hardly. I just did, and continue to do, what I had to in order to get through each day."

His warm breath tickled the side of her neck. "You amaze me."

He turned her in his arms and kissed her.

four

Colin couldn't resist another minute. Livie's soft lips parted beneath his. She tasted of wine and sorrow. He wished he could make all her pain go away. Wished he could make her smile like she used to when her eyes would glisten and she'd throw her head back in silent laughter. But those days were gone, and Colin had only the here and now.

He'd take it.

When she turned fully in his arms, he didn't hesitate to envelop this perfect woman. Granted she saw herself as imperfect, but she was perfect . . . for him. Anything she was willing to give, he'd humbly welcome.

Her arms wound around his neck, toyed with his nape, sending shivers down his spine.

When was the last time a woman gave him shivers?

Holding, touching, none of it was enough. He was near begging, and he didn't care. He'd never begged for a thing—especially where a woman was concerned.

His hands roamed from the delicate dip of her waist up her

spine and found the clip in her hair. He slid it out and fisted all that thick, wavy hair in his hands.

What started out as a simple kiss quickly turned heated and overpowering. And like last night, he lost control the moment she responded to his touch.

She pressed her body deeper into his, and he fought to keep upright. Livie humbled him, made him want to take his time and show her the good in life . . . even though he didn't fully know the darkness he was fighting against.

"Colin," she murmured, pulling back. "I wasn't expecting this."

"Want me to stop?"

She bit her swollen bottom lip and brought her wide sparkling eyes up to his. "No. No, I don't. I need this. I need you."

Something about the way her eyes darted down and to the left gave him pause. "What is it?" he asked, tipping her chin up.

"I . . . have scars. Horrible ones from the delivery of the baby."

"Liv, I don't care about scars, inside or out." He tried to keep his tone soft, reassuring. "I only care about pleasing you."

"It's just that, I haven't been with someone since then." She closed her eyes. "I'm just . . . afraid. The scars—"

He kissed her lightly on the lips and lifted his head. "Every part of you is more beauty than I deserve. Don't belittle yourself because of your past or the reminders you still carry with you."

When she lifted her lids and looked at him with hope in her eyes, she said, "Make me forget."

Without hesitation, Colin captured her lips once again. He didn't rush, didn't take control. Livie had to remain in charge and comfortable with this decision. She may put up a strong front but beneath that steely exterior lay a vulnerable woman, and Colin thanked God she'd chosen him to open up to.

Nerves fluttered in his stomach. He and Livie had never made love when they'd dated before. She'd insisted on waiting until they were married. But that never happened.

No, he would not dwell on his past mistake of leaving the best thing that had ever happened to him. This was a second chance for both of them, and he was going to take hold with both hands and hang on.

Tonight. Right now, he would make love with the one woman who obviously still held his heart. He'd wondered when he'd come back to town how he'd feel if he ran into her again. He figured tension was inevitable, but beyond that, he really had had no clue.

Well, now he knew. They were combustible. The slow, easy pace was killing him, but he wouldn't rush. Not only did Livie need the gentle intimacy, but he wanted this to last as long as possible.

"Wait." Painful as it was, he pulled back. "The windows."

Her eyes widened. "Oh, God. I completely forgot where we were."

"I'll take that as a compliment." He took her hands and led her back inside. "You're still sure?"

She squeezed his hands. "For tonight, I don't want to think about anything else but this. Whatever else is wrong in my life, past or present, doesn't have a place here."

Even though he wanted to go slow, he couldn't make that long journey down the hall into his bedroom. He led her to the oversized leather sectional sofa in the living room and settled into the corner. His heart warmed at her words, and he lifted his arms in invitation.

With her delicate hands in his, he almost felt clumsy, but she eased down beside him, the soft leather groaning beneath their weight, and he knew this was right. Everything about this moment was meant to be. This beautiful, broken woman was giving a piece of herself to him, and he couldn't believe how lucky he was at this moment.

He'd never dreamed his vivacious Livie would ever question herself or find negativity in life. But something deeper, almost sinister, lurked during that gap when he'd been gone. Thankfully, though, she'd put it aside for now. Colin had slid through a crack in the barrier she kept resurrected around herself. Hopefully, he could knock the whole thing down.

With an easy manner, Colin removed her simple white sundress. After she assisted him in removing his clothing as well, she remained in control but increased the pace.

Hands explored, eyes roamed. So many years he'd wondered how this would be. So many times he'd cursed himself for leaving her behind. And he'd left her behind only because he'd thought they were too young, too serious, and he'd wanted to explore the world.

None of that now. If she was leaving the worries and questions of the world outside, then he would, too. He concentrated on each touch, each taste, each soft sigh from her lips.

When they came together as one, Colin knew in his heart there was no way he'd ever let this woman get away again. He wasn't a fool.

Their lovemaking was more than he'd ever hoped for, more than he'd dreamed. But he still hadn't had enough of her. Not even close.

As he lay there, half reclined into the corner of the sofa with Livie resting against his chest, he realized she may only be looking for a distraction, but he wanted to provide her with so much more. He wanted to be the one she turned to when she was sad, when those past memories came back in full force. He wanted to know what he could do to make her days better, to make her look only toward the future.

A future he wanted to share with her.

"Tell me this wasn't a one-time thing."

His own private thoughts penetrated the silence, but he wasn't sorry he'd spoken without thinking. He needed to provide her with total honesty.

Liv lifted her head and looked into his eyes. "It can't be more, Colin. I just don't have any more in me to give."

When she tried to ease off his lap, he held tight. "I don't believe that. You give so much to others, why not allow yourself the chance to see what you can have? I want to see where we can go with this."

She put a hand to his chest. "It can't go beyond this couch. I'm not the same person you left behind, Colin. I'm damaged. Yes, I've overcome my problems, but my heart is not capable of taking on any more pain."

He tamped down the jab of pain at her words.

"Who says I'll cause you pain? Maybe I want to help you overcome whatever nightmare you're still living every day."

"Nightmare?" She jerked out of his grasp and clambered off his lap. "You have no idea the nightmare I live each day. I killed my baby, Colin. I killed her, and at the time, I didn't care. All I wanted was my next high."

Guilt tightened in his chest. "I'm sorry, Livie. I didn't realize. I just wanted—"

"What?" she shouted. "What do you want? Do you want to know that I was so strung out on meth that I didn't even realize I'd been cut open and my child had been removed?"

"Liv, don't do this." Colin came to his feet, reached for his pants, and pulled them on. "Don't blame yourself."

Still naked, now sobbing and pointing to the X-like scar high on her abdomen, Livie continued like he hadn't even spoken.

"Do you see this? The baby was so far up, the doctor had to cut me open, go in, and pull her out. I didn't even feel pain afterward or the following day because of all the drugs in my system. I hemorrhaged so much, I cannot carry another child or I run the risk of not only killing the baby, I could die myself."

Colin stepped closer, gathered Olivia into his arms. She crumbled against his chest. Warm tears hit his bare skin, burning a hole straight through to his heart. Not only had she dealt with getting hooked on drugs, but she'd lost a baby and her own mother. No wonder she shied away from any kind of intimacy.

In his career as a cop and now as a detective, he'd dealt with many drug abusers and dealers. Never once had he felt sorry for them. In his eyes, they'd brought everything upon themselves.

But right now, Livie needed compassion and mercy. He wanted to give her both, but she had to get to a point where she was able to forgive herself before she could accept anything from anyone else.

"I d-don't remember her," she muffled against his chest after several long minutes of silence, save for her crying. "That's the w-worst part. I don't remember anything. All I remember is thinking how tiny the casket was."

Colin guided her back to the couch and eased her down onto his lap. Had anyone consoled her like this since the terrible tragedy? Was there anyone in her life now that realized all of this was still bottled up inside her?

And then it hit him.

"Livie," he whispered. "This happened how long after I left?"

"Two years."

"Was the baby's father on drugs, too? Is he the one who got you hooked?"

When she only nodded, Colin felt both sorrow and rage. How in the hell had this innocent, strong-willed young woman gotten turned on to such an evil, deadly way of life? It was a wonder she hadn't died herself. Of course, a piece of her had with the death of her daughter. Ava.

"Did you name your baby?" Colin asked. "It's so beautiful and meaningful."

Livie lifted her head, smiled through the tears. "I did. I had a baby name book and was actually excited. I loved the name, but I loved the meaning even more. I wanted my child to be able to fly away, to dream and soar and do anything she wanted to do when she got older."

Colin couldn't stand the pain reflecting in her eyes. He swiped each cheek with the pad of his thumbs. "There was still good in you for you to be anticipating the birth of your daughter, to pick out such a powerful name."

Her smile fell; her eyes closed. "No. There's no good in someone who refuses to give up an addiction for the sake of a child. It's selfish and irresponsible."

What could he say? Hadn't he always thought that of the overdosed, pregnant drug addicts who'd come into the station? He'd considered himself hardened after all his years as a cop, but he found himself softening second by second, teardrop by teardrop. Things weren't always black and white; Livie was a shade of gray.

At this point, all he could do was hold her and listen as she poured out years of bottled-up anger, resentment, guilt, and sorrow. She'd literally been through hell. No wonder she wanted to push him away. But giving up wasn't an option.

"What can I do?" he whispered.

She shook her head, sniffed. "Nothing can be done. I just wanted, no, needed, you to understand why we can't be anything more than this one-time thing."

"I disagree. Now, more than ever, you need to be with someone who cares for you." He forced himself to remain calm. Yelling at her wouldn't do one bit of good. "If you're not interested in taking this further, that's one thing. I happen to believe you're still punishing yourself and you won't allow any happiness in your life."

Livie eased back, searched his face. He could only hope his eyes revealed his true emotions. But he was also realistic. She hadn't fully healed, and she wouldn't do so tonight. But he would stick out this storm.

"I get happiness each time I help a pregnant teen go back to her parents. I get happiness when I find employment for a homeless father with two young kids. And I definitely get happiness when I get a drug abuser into a program and they are successful in getting and staying clean."

Colin brushed his knuckles across her tearstained cheek and slid her soft blond hair over her shoulder. "But who do you go home to at night? Who do you confide in when you're having a bad day? Who do you spend holidays with?"

Without a word, Livie came to her feet, gathered her dress off the floor, and jerked it over her head. Colin didn't dare move, even when she disappeared into the kitchen and came back with her purse, then slid into her tiny sandals.

She was pushing this moment, and him, away. This intimacy they shared that he knew was so much more than a one-night stand. Which just proved to him she wanted more. If she didn't care about the intimate moment that had just occurred, she wouldn't be so shaken up right now. Granted, she was upset because of dredging up her past, but she couldn't even look at him.

"I don't need anybody, Colin." She opened his front door then looked over her shoulder. "Don't try to save someone who doesn't want to be."

five

Olivia had to force herself to go to work. The fund-raiser had come and gone and, as usual, was a huge success. Ava's Haven ended up raising thirty-one thousand dollars between the poker tournament, private donations, and the items auctioned.

Now that the chaotic weekend was over, Olivia had time on her hands to reflect on her evening with Colin. She didn't believe he was simply acting on feelings from their past. She feared he was truly falling for her . . . if he hadn't already.

But how could he? They'd been reacquainted for less than a week.

Even so, she couldn't lie to herself. She'd felt something she'd experienced only one other time. Colin always made her feel safe, loved, and cherished—both then and now.

How fair would it be, though, for Colin to be stuck with her? She couldn't provide kids for him, she was practically married to her job, and the nightmares that still consumed her would only trickle over into his life.

So why was she even contemplating this? No. Absolutely

nothing could come from the evening they'd spent together. But she had those amazing memories to hold on to for the rest of her life.

His taste still lingered on her lips, and the way he looked at her, like she was the most precious person in his life, sent tingles racing down her spine. God, she could still feel his strong jawline and stubble beneath her touch.

She glanced down, found herself rubbing the tips of her fingers against her palms.

The tap on her door jerked Olivia from her all-consuming thoughts. "Come in."

Carly stood in her doorway. Her shirt hung off one shoulder, nasty red welts ran down her arm, and one eye was swollen and bruised.

Panic gripped Olivia. She jumped to her feet and came around her desk. "Carly, what happened?"

"I was on my way out of that doctor's office where you'd set me up an interview." Carly let Olivia lead her to a worn leather chair in the corner. "I was jumped by two girls who I used to hang with."

Olivia went to the water cooler in the opposite corner and filled a small white cup. "How did you get away?"

"Your friend happened to be driving by. He picked me up and brought me here."

She passed the cup. "My friend? Who?"

"Me."

Olivia turned to see Colin in her doorway. As usual, he had on dark jeans and his shoulder holster, but today he'd donned a navy blue button-down shirt that perfectly matched his eyes.

"Th-Thank you."

"Can I talk to you for a minute?" he asked.

She knew he meant alone. "Carly, will you be okay if I step out for a minute?"

The young girl nodded. "I'm fine now, just shaky. Go ahead."

Olivia offered a smile. "I'll be right back."

Leading him into a small break room next to her office, Olivia waited until he entered before she closed the door. "I can't thank you enough for bringing her in."

He shrugged. "I'm just glad I was running late for work this morning or I wouldn't have been able to help."

She studied him for a moment. The creases around the corners of his eyes, the intensity of his dark gaze. "You have a habit of saving people."

He smiled. "Occupational hazard."

"And what did you do with the other girls?"

"One took off when she realized who I was. I've got the other in custody for disturbing the peace. If Carly wants to press charges, I can add that to her list."

Curious, Olivia asked, "How did you know Carly didn't start the fight?"

He shrugged, rolled up his sleeves. "Because I saw how grateful she was when you came to get her the other day. I also saw how she was dressed and assumed she'd been in that office building for a good reason and wouldn't just come out onto the street and start pummeling people."

She couldn't help the smile that filled her from within. "You're a pretty good judge of character."

"Another occupational hazard."

Colin took a step closer. Having him so close, breathing in his fresh, masculine scent, was pure torture. His dominating presence filled the tiny break room, not to mention the fact he hadn't taken his eyes off her since they'd come in.

"Is that all?" she asked, praying he'd nod and leave.

A corner of his mouth kicked up. "You tell me."

Startled, Olivia stepped back. He stepped forward. The

advance-retreat dance went on until she bumped her back against the wall.

"What's all this?" he asked, looking over her head.

She knew what he'd spotted. "Those are pictures of all the people Ava's Haven has helped over the years. The ones who've stayed employed, stayed sober and clean . . . whatever their happily ever after may be. Everyone's is different."

Heavy-lidded eyes came back to hers. "What about your happily ever after?"

"Colin," she whispered, holding out a hand to stop him. "Don't."

He lifted her fingers, kissed them one at a time. "Don't what? Kiss you? Care about you? Love you? Too late."

Before her knees could give way, he hooked one big, strong arm around her waist. "I've got you."

Those piercing blue eyes captivated her. "For how long? How long will you put up with my past, and the day in and day out chaos of my job?"

"How long will you put up with mine?" he countered. "Our jobs aren't so different, Livie. We both want to help people. You just go about it in a much nicer, calmer way."

Why fight it? Why fight the fact she'd always loved this man, even though over a decade had passed? She'd thought of him every day, and here he was offering a second chance.

"What if we don't make it?" she asked, holding on to his shirtfront.

His lips captured hers for the briefest of moments, but enough for her to have hope. Something she hadn't had in a long, long time.

He smiled down at her, his eyes gleaming. "What if we do?"

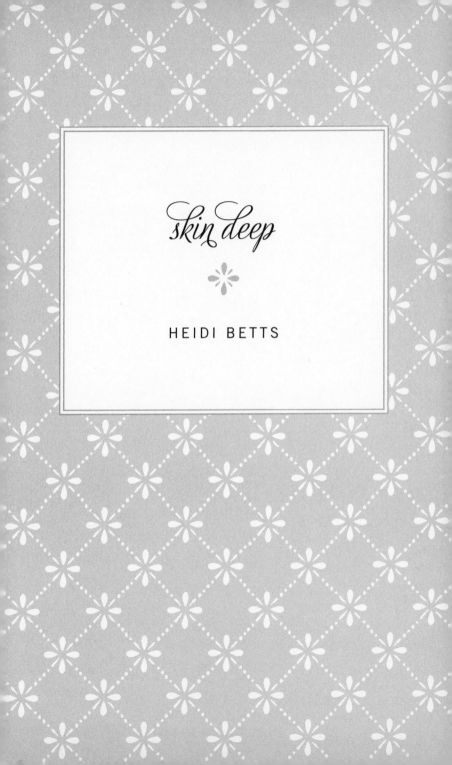

skin deep

HEIDI BETTS

*With thanks to Lori for being such a great friend and
a wonderful inspiration, and for taking me along on this great ride.
I hope we can do it again soon!*

one

✣

"Hello, Mac."

The soft words, spoken from behind his back, caught him off guard and made him pause in the act of rearranging his equipment.

He didn't go by the name "Mac" anymore, and no one in the small Pennsylvania town where he'd relocated a few years ago knew he'd been called that in his former life. Or his former career.

He straightened and turned slowly to find a tall, lithe blonde standing just inside the door of his downtown family photography studio. Babies and weddings and newly engaged couples—that was what he shot these days. It didn't exactly set his soul on fire, but at least it paid the bills and kept him out of trouble.

"Sorry," he said quickly, dismissively, "there's no one here by that name."

With any luck, the intruder would take him at his word and go back the same way she'd come.

One corner of the woman's mouth quirked and she took a step forward, decidedly *not* going back the way she'd come.

"Really? Because you look an awful lot like Rob MacGregor, former high-fashion photographer from Manhattan."

His gaze narrowed. "Who are you?" he asked, studying her more closely, but unable to place her. Of course, considering how drunk and high he'd been in those days, he wasn't entirely sure he'd recognize his own mother if she walked in the door.

The woman flashed a winsome smile and took yet another step forward. "Come on, Mac. I know it's been a few years, but I haven't changed that much, have I?"

She was within arm's reach now, so he studied her, really studied her. Long blond hair the color of rolling wheat fields. Bright green eyes and a heart-shaped mouth on a narrow face with great bone structure.

She was wearing a long, brightly flowered dress in some thin, flyaway material that covered her from chest to calf and shoulder to wrist. Attractive enough but not gorgeous, and she was a woman who could pull off gorgeous. If she put her mind to it, he suspected she could be downright hot with a capital *H*.

And that's when it hit him. He pictured her out of the dress and in a gold lamé string bikini instead. Four-inch heels; hair curled, teased, and shellacked; a pound of cosmetics making her features pop.

"Soph?" He jerked as though he'd been slapped, the shock of seeing her again—here, of all places—leaving him nearly speechless.

With a laugh, she closed the remaining distance between them, pressing a kiss to his stubbled cheek while she hugged him close.

"Sophia LaRue." He breathed the name that hadn't passed his lips since he'd left New York and his former life behind. "I can't believe it."

Pulling away mere inches, she rolled her eyes. "It's just plain

Sophie Lawrence these days, Mr. Rob MacGregor of Happy Endings Photography."

A ripple of embarrassment went through him at what he'd become, followed immediately by a wave of anger. What did he have to be ashamed of? He'd made some mistakes, done some things he wasn't proud of. But he'd gotten help, gotten his life back on track, and was doing just fine.

"Yep, that's me," he muttered. Disentangling himself from her hold, he backed away and returned to what he'd been doing— resetting his equipment and backdrop for a toddler shoot the next morning.

"Hey," she said, coming up behind him and once more laying a soft hand on his arm. "I didn't mean anything by it, Mac. I'm proud of you. You were a mess the last time I saw you, and I was terrified you were going to overdose or do something equally stupid to get yourself killed or thrown in jail. Every day I opened the paper and *didn't* see your name in either the obituaries or police log, I breathed a sigh of relief."

She didn't know how close she was to the truth on that. He'd had a few run-ins with the law because of his drug and alcohol abuse, and with the amount of junk he'd been shooting and snorting toward the end, he was *damn* lucky he hadn't wound up on a slab in the morgue. He knew it and reminded himself of the fact every single day.

Turning to face her again, he let out a long breath and met her moss green gaze with a dark, serious one of his own. "Why are you here, Sophie?"

One side of her lower lip disappeared as she worried it between two rows of perfect white teeth.

"The 'just dropping by for old times' sake' thing isn't working, hm?"

It was a rhetorical question and they both knew it, so he didn't bother answering.

She licked her lips and on a sigh admitted, "I need your help, Mac."

SOPHIE'S stomach clenched with nerves while she held her breath, waiting for Mac's reaction. He couldn't know what it cost her to come here, to track him down and lay herself bare—both figuratively and literally—in front of him.

He wasn't her last hope . . . he was her only hope. There was no one else to turn to, no one else she trusted as much as she trusted Mac, no one else who could help her get her life back the way he could.

Anxiety wasn't the only thing rippling through her belly and making her heart beat faster, though. She'd been attracted to Mac the first time she'd met him, several years before. With his shock of spiky blond hair, chocolate brown eyes, and lean, muscular build, there wasn't much *not* to be attracted to.

In those days, she'd been much more carefree, more live-for-the-moment and out to have a good time. Mac had been at the pinnacle of his career, partying hard on a regular basis to celebrate his success. Which was why it hadn't taken them long to fall into bed together.

There had been something between them . . . a friendship, a camaraderie, something more than simply a model sleeping with one of her photographers. Not that they'd ever had the chance to explore whether or not there could be more to their relationship than casual sex. She'd been too flighty, too self-absorbed, and he'd been too high.

But she was a different person now, and so was he.

"What kind of help?" he asked, drawing her thoughts back to the present. His low voice slid through her blood, heating her from head to toe.

"If you need a head shot or are looking for a family portrait, I'm your man. Otherwise, I'm afraid you're shit out of luck."

Rather than blurting out what she wanted of him, she sidestepped and changed the subject slightly. "You heard about my accident?"

She made it a question rather than a statement because she wasn't sure he *had* heard. It had been big news back in New York, and to a lesser degree across the country, but Mac had been fighting his own demons around that time and could easily have missed it.

His brows—a darker brown than his bleached hair—knit in concentration. "Yeah. I mean . . . I think I remember hearing . . ."

His voice trailed off and he ran the flat of his hand over the top of his head. "Sorry, no. I've been away from that world for a while now, and I wasn't exactly sober when I was in it."

She nodded, lifting a hand to the top button at the front of her dress. "Two years ago, I was sharing an apartment with three other girls."

Her fingers slipped the first button through its hole.

"One of them came home late from a party, drunk and probably a little high."

Button number two fell free.

"She left a lit cigarette on the nightstand in our room before passing out on the sofa."

Three.

"I'd taken a sleeping pill so I could get a good night's rest and so I *wouldn't* hear anything when my roommates came home and started banging around the apartment, but that meant I also didn't smell the smoke or hear the flames when the curtains and bedclothes caught fire."

She loosened buttons four, five, six, opening the full-length, brightly colored dress more than three-quarters down her body.

"I was lucky not to die of smoke inhalation before the fire

department got there, but I wasn't lucky enough to escape completely unscathed."

With that, she shrugged the dress off her shoulders, letting it fall to the crooks of her arms to reveal the flesh beneath.

Being in the modeling industry since she was eighteen had lowered her modesty levels significantly. She'd posed naked, walked runways in swimsuits that were little more than strands of dental floss, stripped down to nothing in front of umpteen people backstage at fashion shows while changing from one outfit into another.

So standing in front of Mac—a man she'd slept with once or twice in the past—in her matching bra and panties, dress still on, if not fastened and covering her, was nothing. She wasn't even particularly concerned about someone entering the studio behind her.

The only thing that made her moderately self-conscious about her appearance was the burn scars marking her body like a crude map of the continents. They weren't nearly as bad as they had been, but they were never going away either, no matter how many lotions or ointments she slathered on twice a day. The wide red splotches and puckered white lines were a part of her now. Forever.

"I was burned over more than twenty percent of my body," she told him softly. "I was in the hospital for months and rehabilitation for nearly a year after that."

Mac's gaze, she noticed, was riveted on her torso, on the worst of the scarring. But to his credit, he didn't look disgusted or horrified. His expression bordered on pity—a sentiment she'd seen too damn much of since the accident and had quickly learned to despise—but was saved by the hint of genuine concern she saw reflected in his coffee brown eyes.

"I'm happy to be alive, believe me. And well aware that it could have been worse. But looking like this doesn't exactly lend itself to a burgeoning modeling career."

two

Mac couldn't tear his eyes away from Sophie. Yeah, the burns were a distraction. His stomach tightened at the pain and trauma she must have suffered to get them, but they didn't make her any less beautiful.

Maybe it was because he hadn't been with a woman in . . . God, he couldn't even remember. Not since before his recovery, that was for sure.

Maybe it was because they'd been together before and he knew what she looked like completely naked, knew how soft her skin was, knew her breasts were firm, knew the cradle of her thighs was more than welcoming.

Or maybe it was simply Sophie herself who took his breath away. She always had. Even when he'd been under the influence and hadn't known his ass from a hole in the wall. Even with a hundred other gorgeous models strutting around, flashing their Ts and As in his face in an attempt to catch his attention.

Something about Sophia LaRue—a.k.a. Sophie Lawrence— had always called to him, drawn him in like a moth to a flame.

Their few brief sexual encounters had been blistering hot, no doubt about it, but they'd also stuck with him more than any of the others he'd had with the random models and actresses who'd trotted past his camera lens and into his bed.

Arousal thickened in his veins, sending long-dormant signals of longing and want to his groin. But then, there was a half-naked woman flaunting herself in front of him, so it wasn't like anyone could blame him for having such a reaction.

Even the scars didn't deter him from looking his fill and enjoying every minute of it. There was no rhyme or reason to the markings; there was simply a blotch here on her upper right arm, there just below the bra line of her right breast, then to a larger, more encompassing degree along her waist and down to her left thigh.

She was right that the burns would make a modeling career difficult. In an industry that revolved around perfection, that pushed its models to be stick thin and where "heroin chic" was considered healthy and attractive, the smallest flaw could keep a model from booking jobs and even securing agency representation.

Swallowing hard, Mac dragged his attention up from her white lace bra and panty set with the tiny pink flowers embroidered on each and away from all the pale, soft, mouthwatering flesh the garments didn't cover, and forced himself to once again meet her eyes. He was well aware that not all of his brain cells were firing properly, thanks to the massive amount of blood that had abandoned his gray matter and taken off for places much farther south.

"I'm sorry," he told her. "I hadn't heard."

And it really was a shame to have such a beautiful woman marred in such a way, especially when the injury would have had the added trauma of putting a screeching halt to her promising career.

"I'm not sure what that has to do with me, though," he added, hoping the statement didn't sound too harsh. It wasn't that he wasn't sympathetic to both what she'd been through and her current circumstances, but he had to be careful of who he got involved with and how much he let into his life.

With a delicate shrug, she pulled the dress back up over her smooth shoulders and began to rebutton it down the front. Mac did his best to roll his tongue back into his mouth but had to admit he was sorry to see her cover all that glorious female flesh.

"The scars make a modeling career difficult, but I'm hoping not impossible," she said.

Several beats passed while he waited for her to finish her thought and reveal what she needed—or perhaps simply *wanted*—from him.

With the dress once again wrapped neatly around her tall, shapely form, she dropped her arms to her sides. "I need a new portfolio, with photos of me *now*, so I can start looking for a new agent and hopefully start booking new jobs. And I want you to be the photographer."

THE silence was daunting, filling the oversize studio space like the inside of a deep, dark cavern with no discernable exit. Sophie held her breath, so hopeful that Mac would agree to shoot a new portfolio for her . . . and so afraid he wouldn't. Her heart pounded in her chest, her palms damp as she fought the urge to fidget.

Just about the time she thought her lungs would explode, he dropped his head, gave it a small shake, and replied, "Sorry, no. I don't do that anymore."

"Oh, come on, Mac." Rushing forward, she grabbed his arm and held on tight, doing her best to convey her desperation. "You're the best; you always have been. And there's no one I trust more to help me with this."

He shrugged her off, not roughly but enough to move away and return to toying with his equipment just as he'd been doing when she first walked in. "I can't, Soph, I'm sorry. You don't know what it took for me to leave that world . . . or what that world did to me while I was in it."

The words were soft and filled with regret, and suddenly Sophie understood. It wasn't that he didn't want to help her or that he'd lost his edge where his photography was concerned, but that he was afraid of falling back into old habits of excess and abuse.

Walking a few steps away, she took a seat on a small white platform draped with a dark blue fleece where she assumed children sat or were propped during their photo sessions.

"You told me once that all you'd ever wanted to be was a bigtime photographer. It was your dream to live in New York, capture beautiful images of models and celebrities on film, and have your photos appear on the covers of magazines, billboards, and in major ad campaigns."

He gave a derisive snort, pretending to be more focused on fiddling with the camera currently attached to a tripod between them than she suspected was truly necessary. "Yeah, and you see how well that turned out."

"Don't knock yourself," she told him, propping her arms behind her and leaning back slightly. Legs crossed, she negligently swung one sandaled foot back and forth. "You were amazing. And you were much more talented when you were sober than when you were hopped up on God knows what."

He glanced in her direction, flashing her a wry smirk. "Gee, thanks."

She chuckled at his obvious annoyance. "It's true. I never understood why you got messed up with that junk. Oh, I get the lure," she added.

Lord knew the stuff flowed freely in certain circles within the modeling industry. She'd been tempted herself a few times. But she'd seen too many friends get strung out and either destroy their careers, become all about the drugs, or worse yet, lose their lives.

"But you were better than that, and I always thought it was a shame you chose drugs over a brilliant career."

"I didn't exactly choose them," he murmured quietly. "I just couldn't stop once I got started."

She nodded again, because she knew exactly what he meant. "But you're doing better now, right? Got yourself back on track and under control?"

He sent her another sidelong glance. "Yeah. But you know what they say—one day at a time."

Sophie studied him for a second, wondering just how hard a struggle sobriety was for him. There was a time, not so long ago, when she wouldn't have cared. She would have considered an addict weak and probably stupid to boot.

Then she'd had her own accident, and while in recovery and rehab, she had met a number of different people working to overcome any number of different things. In the hospital, she'd made friends with other burn patients, but also those who were sick with both terminal and treatable diseases or who had been incapacitated in some way. In rehabilitation, she'd spent time with others who were trying to regain their mobility or to learn to live and function in a wheelchair.

It had humbled her and also made her realize how lucky she truly was. Sure, she might have been in a fire, might have burns covering her from chest to pelvis both back and front, but she was alive. She had all her limbs and was able to return to her old life—give or take—without constant, unbearable pain or a major change to her physical body.

She'd also come to understand that *everyone* was dealing with something. Whether it was an injury or an illness or an emotional stressor from some type of ongoing negative situation, no one ever *really* knew what another person might be going through in their personal lives. She tried to keep that in mind now when dealing with others and hoped it was one lesson she would never forget.

Which was why she hoped so much that Mac had been able to truly banish his demons and overcome his addictions.

She still needed his help, though, and hoped asking for it—pressuring him into it, if necessary—wouldn't jeopardize his sobriety.

three

Mac didn't know why, but he let Sophie stick around. Not just stick around, but talk him into going out for dinner.

No doubt so she could spend a few more hours trying to convince him to shoot her portfolio.

The problem was, he wanted to.

Having Sophie waltz into his studio had awakened more than his long-dormant libido . . . it reminded him of how he'd felt when he'd been behind the camera shooting magazine covers, swimsuit issues, and ad campaigns for everything from Calvin Klein underwear to Estée Lauder perfumes.

He'd felt like *somebody* back then. Powerful and confident and destined for greater things. Now, he wasn't destined for anything more than senior pictures at the end of the school year.

He could shoot some film for Sophie and send her back to New York with a full portfolio strong enough to get her a few call-backs, at least, if not actually book her some jobs. He didn't need to go there himself, didn't need to return to that life.

But when she started popping up again, making it clear she

wanted to revive her career, his name was bound to come up, if only in relation to who had photographed her post-scarring. Then the questions and curiosity would begin.

Mac MacGregor . . . whatever happened to him?

I heard he OD'd . . .

I heard he's living under a bridge . . .

I heard he moved to Idaho and joined a cult . . .

The worst speculation, though, would be if they remembered the truth—that his life had spun out of control due to drug and alcohol abuse. He'd dropped out of society to go into rehab and then hadn't been able to hack it sober.

Not that he'd ever tried. He'd gone straight from rehab to small-town Pennsylvania without bothering to return to New York or even *attempting* to reclaim his old life.

Why? he wondered now.

But he knew the answer: fear.

He was afraid that if he went back to New York and started doing what he used do, hanging out with who he used to hang out with, he'd fall right back into past destructive habits. Wasn't that what they'd drummed into him during his recovery? That if he wanted to stay clean and sober, he needed to stay away from all the places he used to use and all the people he used to use with.

The funny thing was, thinking about returning to the city either with or soon after Sophie didn't make him crave his old lifestyle. He didn't have a sudden urge to reach for the bottle or order a glass of wine with his dinner. He wasn't wondering how far from the restaurant he'd have to go to score.

But he *did* miss his old studio. The accolades that had come with his work. And he realized suddenly that he'd missed Sophie.

She was more than beautiful; that was the outside packaging and didn't even scratch the surface of what made her genuinely attractive. She was also funny and quick, always ready with a witty observation about their surroundings or the people seated near them in a restaurant.

From the time they'd been together before, he also remembered that she had a big heart and compassionate nature. She loved animals and children, and had always been volunteering her time or name to worthy causes.

She apparently wasn't letting her desire to get back into modeling affect her appetite either. As soon as they'd been shown to a small corner booth at Luigi's, the lone Italian restaurant Summervale had to offer, she'd grabbed the menu and practically recited it to their waiter. She started with a spaghetti appetizer, was currently plowing her way through a plate of eggplant parmesan with the help of several slices of garlic bread, and had been making noises about how delicious the tiramisu sounded.

"You must have the metabolism of a hummingbird on crack," he muttered, taking a conservative bite of his own three-cheese lasagna.

Her eyes widened at his mention of the word "crack," and she swallowed hard, making the tendons of her throat rise and fall erotically.

"It's all right," he said, allowing a ripple of real laughter—the first he'd experienced in months—work its way up from his diaphragm. "I'm allowed to say 'crack.' The rule is that you're allowed to talk about something as long as you used to be addicted to it."

He said this with a straight face, and for a minute she merely stared at him. Then she seemed to get the joke and chuckled right along with him.

"Very funny," she told him, taking a sip of her water with a lemon wedge squeezed in before digging back into the lightly breaded eggplant. "But I happen to know you had more expensive tastes when it came to the junk you put into your body."

"Yeah," he agreed with a wry twist to his lips, "I had a very discriminating palate."

"Oh, I don't know," she murmured softly, lifting her head to meet his eyes. "Your taste couldn't have been that bad. After all, you did choose me once or twice."

A jolt of desire raced down his spine and pooled in his belly like heat lightning. She was looking at him as though she were remembering every moment they'd spent together with their clothes off. Or most of them anyway. There had been a few times they hadn't gotten that far.

And damned if he wasn't remembering, too.

He shifted in his seat, trying to find a more comfortable position now that his jeans seemed to have shrunk a couple sizes in the area of his crotch.

"We were good together, weren't we?" he ventured, wondering if their few scattered encounters had impacted her as much as they had him.

His bedroom had practically had a revolving door back then, and he was sure he hadn't been her only lover either. But *she'd* stuck in his mind more than any of the others, and a deep, dark, sadistic part of him hoped he'd stuck in hers as well.

Sophie smiled across the table at him, a soft smile that teetered between angelic and wicked and went straight to his soul.

"Yes, we were."

She plopped the last piece of her entrée into her mouth and chewed thoughtfully. He watched the motion of her mouth, her lips, the sleek line of her throat, and felt himself grow even harder beneath the white cloth-draped table.

Washing down her meal with a sip of water, she set the glass carefully aside and then added, "I wonder if we still are."

Mac nearly swallowed his tongue. His heart pounded in his chest like a jackhammer, and if he'd thought his jeans were tight before, it now felt as though his fly was trying to strangle his penis like a boa constrictor out for blood.

"That's part of the reason I came to you," she continued when all he could do was sit across from her and gurgle like a brain-dead zombie. "I didn't want just any photographer to shoot my portfolio and help me get back on my feet. I want someone I have a connection with. Someone who can really understand what I'm trying to do and who'll care about the pictures he's taking because he knows how important they are to me."

He had to clear his throat a couple of times, but finally managed to say, "So we're not talking about retesting our compatibility with sex?" He knew he sounded petulant and more than a little disappointed, but . . . dammit, he *was* disappointed. And horny as all get-out.

Their waiter returned to the table just then, interrupting their conversation and keeping him from getting a much-sought-after answer to his question. The waiter took their empty plates and asked if they were interested in coffee and dessert.

Mac passed, knowing he was too tense to eat another bite and that caffeine probably wasn't the best thing for his already elevated blood pressure. Sophie, however, flashed a toothsome grin and requested a nice, large chunk of the tiramisu she'd been fantasizing about since they walked in the door.

As soon as the young man left them alone, she turned her attention back to Mac. Shrugging a slim shoulder, she murmured, "Who says the two have to be mutually exclusive?"

four

Mac's gut clenched even as he admired her ability to jump from one thing to another without missing a beat. And thank God. He'd much rather discuss the possibility of spending a few hours with her doing the horizontal mambo than mascarpone-layered and coffee-liquor-soaked Italian desserts.

"I'm going to try really hard not to launch myself across this table and attack you right here and now," he told her matter-of-factly, then sort of ruined the effect of that promise by leaning forward menacingly.

"That would be good," she told him, not the least intimidated if the smile playing at the corners of her lips was any indication. "This is supposed to be a family restaurant, after all."

He growled, using his elbows to drag himself toward her another inch.

"What I'm thinking about doing to you right now is *not* rated G for all audiences," he practically snarled.

"No," she said simply, "G definitely isn't high enough in the alphabet for what's going through my mind either."

His nostrils flared and lust pounded in a white-hot wave through every cell of his body. *"Soph,"* he grated in warning, as close to spinning out of control as he could ever remember.

And then the damn waiter showed up with her dessert, breaking into the riotous sexual tension swirling around them thick as a funnel cloud.

With a curse, Mac fell back in his chair. His arousal hadn't lessened, not one freaking iota, but he could tell by the way Sophie was poking her fork gently into the soft edges of her cake that they weren't getting out of here anytime soon. She was going to enjoy every bite to the fullest, playing with her food the same way she was playing with him.

Before the waiter could disappear again, Mac asked for the check. At least then, the minute Sophie finished scarfing down the last ladyfinger crumb from her plate, he could grab her hand and drag her out of the restaurant, out to his car. He didn't know what would come after that. He *hoped* it would be hot and sweaty and not require underwear, but he didn't *know* if that was actually where this was going.

While she took minuscule bites of cake, worked them around in her mouth for what seemed like an eternity, and then swallowed with small, stroke-inducing groans, he decided he should find out for sure what was going on between them. If she was teasing him, working him into a lather just to get him to help her with her portfolio, then he wanted to know up-front.

Oh, he might still fuck her, let her believe there was a chance he'd shoot some film for her before kicking her to the curb. And if not . . .

Wow. If not, he may very well be in big-ass trouble.

"So what if I say no to the photos?" he asked, tossing the question out there without warning, without preamble. "Just flat-out no. Does that mean sex is off the table?"

She studied him for a moment, continuing to chew as though

he was no more or less interesting than the sugary end to her meal. And then she opened her mouth and socked him in the stomach for maybe the dozenth time since waltzing back into his life.

"I wasn't planning to have sex on the table. At least not *this* table."

His cock jerked behind his fly and his balls started to throb. "Stop messing with me, Sophie," he bit out, not sure he could take much more before exploding . . . and he wasn't certain it would be in the good way.

Setting down her fork, she pushed her plate away and laid her hands lightly on the edge of the table. "I'm not messing with you. Teasing you, maybe, but not because I'm trying to be cruel. I like you, Mac, and even though I didn't come here with the intention of reviving our relationship, I have to admit that it's crossing my mind now."

"Do you want me, Sophie?" he blurted in a low, passion-laden voice.

She licked her lips and swallowed hard. "I'm not sure it's the smartest thing ever," she responded slowly, "but yes, I think I do. And before you ask again, my answer would be the same whether you agree to help me with my portfolio or not. Happy?"

Freakin' ecstatic.

He hadn't known until that moment what his decision was going to be concerning that, but suddenly he found his lips parting and the words spilling out. "I'll shoot your new portfolio," he said with a sharp nod of his head. "And it's not just because you're going to sleep with me."

A spark of humor lit her green eyes. "I am, huh?"

Another sharp nod. "Oh, yeah. If you ever finish putting away enough food to feed an army, that is." He dipped his gaze to her empty dessert plate, wondering if she intended to pick it up and lick it clean with her tongue.

With the corner of her lip twitching, she did him one better. Licking the tip of one finger, she ran it across the plate to pick up stray crumbs and sauce, then popped the digit into her mouth.

Mac's eyes were glued to those lips surrounding her index finger and sucking slightly, and he nearly came in his pants.

"That's it," he growled, the sound barely audible from between his tightly gritted teeth.

The chair almost toppled as he lurched to his feet, but he just didn't care. Rounding the table, he grabbed Sophie by the hand—the one *not* still in her mouth, doing erotic, mind-numbing things to his equilibrium—and pulled her up, dragging her with him straight out of the restaurant.

She gave a tiny yelp, followed by a low, throaty chuckle, practically running to keep up with his long, determined strides. Ten feet from his Jeep, which was parked at the curb, he hit the button on his key fob to unlock the doors. Two feet away, he reached out, yanked her door open, and all but shoved her inside. Stalking around the front of the vehicle, he climbed behind the wheel, cranked the engine, and pulled into traffic, cutting off a small red sedan and almost causing an accident he didn't have the time or patience to deal with.

"Well, that was certainly an entertaining exit. Imagine the whispers and speculation running rampant through that restaurant right now."

Mac heard the amusement threading through Sophie's voice, but damned if he could find it in him to join her. He was too tense, too wound up, too desperate. And he didn't give a shit what a bunch of strangers in a restaurant thought of him or her or their hasty departure.

"Either you're going to get a *lot* of curious new customers in the next couple of weeks, or everyone in town is going to start taking their own family portraits with those little disposable cameras," she added with a teasing note.

"Let them," he growled.

"So where are we going?" she asked. And then she reached across the console and laid her hand on his jean-clad thigh. The muscle there jumped, as did the one higher up, throbbing for escape from behind his zipper, and he nearly ran them off the road.

Muttering a colorful curse beneath his breath, he jerked the wheel and eased the Jeep back between the white lines.

"My place," he told her.

If they made it that far. Swear to God, if he saw a dead-end street or wooded turnoff where they weren't likely to be arrested for indecent exposure, he was going to take full advantage. The idea of leaning across the seats, shoving her skirt to her waist, and taking her up against the door was almost too tempting to resist.

But mental images were nothing compared to flesh-and-blood Sophie, who seemed determined to send him off the deep end.

She gave his leg a gentle squeeze. "And what will we do once we get there?" she asked so innocently, she might have been inquiring about his favorite flavor of ice cream.

A growl rattled in his chest, and his knuckles went white on the steering wheel. He could tell her. Oh, could he tell her. Explicitly and in no uncertain terms.

But he'd prefer to show her, and in just a few more miles, a few more minutes, he would.

At the sound of his self-control quickly nearing the breaking point, she leaned over and pressed a soft kiss to his stubbled cheek. The fingers on his thigh slid a few millimeters closer to ground zero, sending his temperature skyrocketing.

"Good things come to those who wait, you know," she murmured just below his ear.

Taking one hand from the wheel—which wasn't entirely safe at the speed they were traveling—he covered hers where it rested on his leg. It took all of his effort to move it away rather than toward his throbbing erection.

"I don't want good," he told her, tires squealing as he made a sharp left onto his street. "I want freaking fantastic."

"That's quite a bit of pressure to put on one sexual encounter."

They were at his building. The Jeep shot into the rear parking area like a bullet until he jammed on the brakes, sending them both lurching toward the dash, then slamming back in their seats.

Mac cut the engine, palmed the keys, and turned to pin Sophie with a smoldering glare. Hooking a hand around her neck, he yanked her close and whispered, "Not really, since I'm counting on a hell of a lot more than just one." Then he took her mouth in a long, voracious kiss that threatened to set the inside of the car on fire.

When he finally found the strength to pull away, they were both breathing hard, and all Mac wanted was to dive in for seconds. Instead, he let his arm drop from her nape and said, "Out. Now."

Without waiting to see if she would do as he'd commanded, he opened his door and crossed the gravel lot to the rear of his studio. A back staircase led to his apartment on the second level, but even though it was probably only ten or twenty steps away, it might as well have been miles.

Unlocking the back entrance to the studio, he turned to see if Sophie had, indeed, gotten out of the Jeep, and found her only a few inches away.

Good girl, he thought. Followed a split-second later by, *Thank God.*

He grabbed her by the wrist and tugged her forward, closing the gap between them, then snaked an arm around her waist, holding her flush to his chest. Their lips meshed as he walked her backward into the building, kicking the door closed behind them.

five

The inside of Mac's studio was dark, and he didn't bother turning on a light. Not that it mattered, since Sophie's eyes drifted closed more often than they were open.

It wasn't that she didn't want to look at Mac or see her surroundings, but simply that she was overwhelmed by the sensations roaring through her system. His kiss jellied her knees and melted her bones . . . and her brain wasn't far behind.

She'd always been attracted to Mac MacGregor, no doubt about it. He was a good-looking man, with his tall, lean, muscular build and the spiky blond hair at such contrast with the tan of his skin. The first time she'd met him, her stomach had done a little flip-flop, and his handshake had caused a zap of electricity to skitter down her spine.

And though they'd traveled this road before, the sparks were still there, stronger and sharper than ever.

Thank goodness, she thought as the door slammed shut behind them and he turned her again, backing her up against the hard, flat surface.

She hadn't come here for this, had meant only to ask Mac for a favor that might help her resurrect her career. But getting the chance to be with him again, like this . . . well, it was an unexpected, but very welcome, perk.

Her head cracked into the door as his mouth slid down her throat to her chest. Buttons popped as he ripped her dress open, and she moaned at the hot, wet kisses he trailed down to her breast. Her already puckered nipples tightened even more when he nuzzled the scalloped edge of her bra and then suckled her through the lacy material.

She ran her fingers through his hair and arched into his touch. Mac continued to tear open her dress, washing her body in cool air until he pressed against her, blocking out everything but his heat, his scent, the delicious friction of cotton and leather and denim on bare skin. He pressed the hard bulge of his erection into the notch between her legs, and suddenly she wanted him—needed him—as naked as she.

Shoving at his jacket, she wrangled it down his arms until he was forced to lower his hands from her waist to shrug it off. His shirt followed, her nails raking the firm planes of his abdomen and chest as she pushed the fabric up and over his head.

He growled in her ear, leaving biting, sucking little marks all along her skin while he allowed her to undress him. His own hands were busy stroking up and down. Her midriff, her thighs, the undersides of her breasts. Everywhere he could reach, his rough palms grazed her, set her on fire.

She fumbled with his belt buckle and then the snap of his jeans. He tugged and yanked at her panties. As soon as he had them down and off one leg, he pushed her hands aside and finished unzipping his pants.

He didn't bother taking them all the way off but shoved them down just enough to free himself. Then he was lifting her, wrapping her legs around his waist, and driving into her.

A single long, hard thrust buried him deep and forced a gasp from her lungs. She hadn't been with a man in years, not since before the accident—and a while before, at that. Partly because of the burns, she supposed. They'd made her self-conscious about her body, insecure about the one thing she'd always had the utmost confidence in.

More so in the beginning than now, which was why she was so determined to get back into modeling. To prove to herself—and the world—that she was still beautiful, still worthy of admiration. And to show other women and young girls that just because you weren't perfect, just because you had a few physical flaws, didn't mean you covered yourself up or hid yourself away. You picked yourself up, held your head high, and made the world meet you on your terms.

The other reason she hadn't taken a lover was frankly because no one had appealed to her in the months since she'd been released from physical therapy and returned to her (almost) normal life. But Mac appealed. Oh, did he ever.

And the length of time since her last sexual encounter didn't seem to matter to her body or her mind. She was so aroused, so hot and wet for this man that he slid right in, filling her in a way that made her feel whole, complete.

Hooking her arms around his neck, she tugged him in for a soul-stealing kiss. He groaned as his tongue tangled with hers, sweeping inside her mouth to tease, to taunt, to drive her crazy.

His fingers flexed on the soft curve of her hip, and she tightened her grip on him. She couldn't pull him any closer, but she also wasn't letting him get away.

"You feel so good," he murmured against her lips.

"Mmm." It was the best she could do to voice her agreement.

"You never should have come here," he told her, pulling out a few scant inches before sliding back into place. "I was doing fine before you came." Out again. "And now . . ." In again. "I don't think I'll ever get enough."

Each time he pulled back, the sensations caused her to take a deep, shuddering breath. Then when he slid in again, she had to bite her lip to keep from crying out.

She hoped he was right about never getting enough, because she wasn't sure she ever would either. She could easily imagine dying a happy woman if she could make love like this with Mac every day of her life.

His mouth sucked tiny love bites on the side of her throat and she purred, actually purred, while she rubbed her breasts along his chest and dug her nails into his shoulders like a cat kneading for cream.

"Mac," she whimpered, "stop teasing me."

"Not teasing," he responded, nostrils flaring. "Just trying to make it last."

"Don't need it to last. Need it now. Hard, fast, *now*, Mac."

Before the words were even out of her mouth, he'd hitched her up another inch around his waist, his fingers digging into her hips, her thighs. Her back and head cracked against the flat panel of the door, rattling it on its hinges, but she barely felt the impact. Wouldn't have cared if she had.

All she felt was Mac. All she cared about was having him inside her, hot and hard and pounding to oblivion.

And he gave her exactly what she wished for. No more words, no more soft touches or unnecessary foreplay.

His mouth captured hers. One hand came up to clutch her breast and tease the nipple. Then he was thrusting, driving into her again and again, harder and faster, just as she'd begged. Demanded.

She didn't have a lot of room to move, but neither could she resist canting her hips, lifting and falling to meet him as he pounded her like a drum.

Thank God.

Mouths parting, they both gasped for air. Sophie's blood felt as though it was about to boil out of her body. Her skin tingled as if she'd touched a live wire, and the sensations building between her legs and low in her belly made her want to moan and whimper and scream all at once.

"Sophie," he grit out, nipping at a muscle in her throat and following its taut line to her bare shoulder. "Sophie, Sophie, Sophie."

His rough grating of her name punctuated each of his hard thrusts, knocking her into the door over and over, and all she could think was *yes, yes, yes*.

Her lips parted and the words slipped out. "Yes, yes, yes. Mac!"

She cried out as the orgasm ripped through her. Powerful, intense, shooting through her body like a falling star, ricocheting off every bone and internal organ until she was nothing but an oozing mass of liquid goo.

While her head was still spinning and small aftershocks were still rippling up and down her spine, Mac continued to drive into her. Once, twice more. And then he, too, gave a shout of completion, stiffening as he spilled inside her.

six

✳

Sophie tried not to laugh as Mac moved around in front of her. First on the right, then the left. One minute standing, the next hunkered down on the balls of his feet.

She hadn't seen him this animated, this energized, in years. At least not without the assistance of drugs or alcohol.

And though she was used to being naked in front of photographers, she *wasn't* used to her *photographers* being naked in front of her. Which is why she was having a hard time keeping a straight face.

"Watch your expression," he chastised, not for the first time. "We're going for sexy and ethereal here, not happy and ready for anything."

"That would be easier if you'd put some pants on," she told him.

He looked down, as though he'd forgotten he was flapping in the breeze. Then he shrugged, uncaring, and went back to work.

After collapsing to the floor in a heap, boneless from their bout of lovemaking up against the back studio door, they'd crawled their way unceremoniously to the small, brown velvet sofa on the opposite side of the room. Mac had taken the bottom while she'd sprawled on top of him, and they'd lain there for what seemed like forever, giving the depleted cells of their bodies a chance to recover. Then they'd gone at it again—not quite as hot and heavy as the first time, but still steamy enough to leave Sophie once again drained and gasping for breath.

When Mac had begun to recover the second time, he'd decided they should start shooting photos for her portfolio. She'd laughed at his announcement, certain he was joking.

He wasn't.

He'd climbed to his feet, naked as a jaybird, and started setting up his equipment. Thank goodness the front of his studio was dark, the blinds drawn—otherwise anyone passing by on the sidewalk might have seen Mac dragging her off the couch and positioning her in front of his camera Lady Godiva-style, right where he wanted her.

She'd argued with him, protesting that she wasn't ready to be photographed, especially not for something so important. And that she needed a better wardrobe than her now-torn dress for a fully rounded shoot. She needed a bikini, a little black dress, a long, flowing gown. Because though the idea behind the new portfolio was to get modeling agencies and fashion designers to accept her *with* her scars, it wasn't about flaunting them or leading people to believe that she couldn't model unless she was showing them off.

And last but not least, she needed to do her hair and makeup, sure that both were a disaster after having Mac's hands and mouth all over her. Her portfolio should convey a number of different looks, a number of different hair styles and makeup jobs, not simply "rumpled" and "thoroughly ravished."

But he hadn't listened. He'd been determined to snap some pictures and wasn't taking no for an answer. And since it had been so long since she'd seen him this way, seen him so enthusiastic and passionate about his work, she hadn't had the heart to refuse.

He had her sit on the floor, legs crossed at peculiar angles, head tilted, her floral dress draped strategically to look like simply an extraneous bolt of fabric. Then he pulled her up and had her stand completely nude, hands crossed and covering her breasts. Every other inch of skin, including the full extent of the burn scars, was completely visible and captured forever on film.

Then, surprising her, Mac set up his tripod and connected his camera to a timer. He pulled his jeans on, leaving the top button loose before joining her and snapping shots of the two of them together.

His hands on her body, his bare chest against her back, sent heat spiraling through her. And imagining how the photos would turn out—sexy, sensual, hinting that they were more than just old friends or impulsive lovers—made her stomach dip nervously.

Was there more to their relationship than casual sex or a favor between friends?

Did she want there to be?

She didn't have an answer, and before she was forced to think about it too long, Mac's hands began to wander, intent on more than producing a seductive pose for a photograph no one else would ever see. Leaning into him, she let him distract her, let him ease her to the floor, impromptu photo shoot forgotten.

Which was fine with her. As strong as her feelings were for Mac, she didn't know where this was going or how he felt about her. She would rather keep things light, enjoying the moment and whatever time she had with him.

The rest, as the saying went, would take care of itself.

❋

TWO weeks later, Sophie's portfolio was complete and she was ready to return to New York. She'd spent much longer in Summervale than she'd planned . . . longer with Mac, both in bed and out . . . with only a couple of short trips back to the city for wardrobe changes and other items needed for the shoots.

But the moment of truth had arrived. Her portfolio was strong. The pictures Mac had taken were incredible, if she did say so herself. It wasn't even that she was blindingly beautiful or exceptional in any way, but that he was amazing behind the camera. She suspected he could shoot a can of pork and beans and have it come out looking like a movie star.

And even though her scars were readily visible in nearly every photo, Mac had made them look good. A part of her, he'd made them look almost like a work of art splayed haphazardly across her body.

That didn't mean agents or designers would be accepting of the injury and shower her with contract offers, but it was the very best she ever could have hoped for.

They stood on the sidewalk now, in front of his studio, hands clasped, faces long with regret.

"You could come with me, you know," she suggested, reluctant to let go, walk to her rental car, and leave him and this small town that had grown on her over the past weeks. "See old friends, keep me company while I make the rounds. Hold my hand and distract me while I wait for the phone to ring." She wiggled her brows, letting him know exactly what she was envisioning as a distraction.

One corner of his mouth twitched even as he gave his head a small shake. "My answer is the same as the last fifteen times you mentioned it—no. I can't risk it, Soph. I had to leave that place and that life behind along with the drugs and alcohol."

She leaned forward, pressing herself close to the long, hard planes of his tall, lanky frame. "You're better than that," she told him. "Stronger than you think. Nobody in that world made you do anything, you just got wrapped up in the fast and crazy lifestyle. And I firmly believe that if you don't want to go back to it, you won't, and no one you meet along the way can make you."

He lowered his head, resting his brow against hers. "You're good for me, you know that?" he murmured in a low, heartfelt tone. "You have more faith in me than I have in myself, but I'm glad you came. I needed this."

So had she, more than she'd realized when she'd first driven into town.

"Guess this means I'll be making a lot of trips to this little 'burb. When I'm not jetting off to Jamaica or Paris for million-dollar photo shoots, that is," she added with a hopeful half grin. Hopeful that she really would be flying off to places exotic or otherwise as a working model. But more that he wouldn't shoot down her hint that she'd like to continue their relationship, long-distance, if necessary.

Holding her breath, she waited, wondering how he would respond.

Lifting a hand, he brushed his fingers through her hair, tucking a strand behind one ear. "You know where to find me," he said simply.

As commitments went, it wasn't exactly a marriage proposal, but she would take it. Mac was too special, and she found herself too wrapped up in him to walk away without a backward glance.

"You'd better get going," Mac offered gently. Lowering his head, he pressed a long, soft kiss to her lips before leading her to her car and seeing her safely inside.

He stood on the curb while she drove away, and she watched him in the rearview mirror every minute until he disappeared from sight.

seven

❋

A month had passed since she'd driven away from Summervale. Away from Mac. And though things were going well for her, she'd missed him every second of every minute of every day.

So much so that she was rethinking her decision to pursue getting back into the modeling business. It was what she knew, what she'd always done before the accident, and what she'd thought she wanted more than anything, fighting her way back from her injuries just so she could return to work doing what she did best.

But now . . . If Mac wouldn't come to New York and she was busy with shoots and fashion shows all over the country, as well as internationally, when would they see each other? How often could they truly expect to be together?

Not very often, she admitted with a sad sigh.

Maybe it was better to give up the idea of modeling. After the fire, everyone had assumed her career was over anyway.

And what would be so wrong with moving to a small town in Pennsylvania and finding a job she enjoyed? Dating a man who made her elbows sweat and who she was pretty sure might be The One. Maybe one day marrying that man and starting a family.

When she thought of it in those terms, she wasn't sure getting back into modeling held a candle to the rest.

The only problem was, she currently had her toes dipped firmly back into the modeling world, which made the decision a much finer wire to have to cross.

Stepping through the lobby doors of the tall office building in the middle of Manhattan, she stopped at the edge of the sidewalk and wondered what she should do.

Instinct drove her to dig her cell phone out of her bag and dial Mac. For better or worse, she was brimming with excitement and happiness, and couldn't think of anyone else she was as eager to share her news with.

Moving down the street in the direction of her loft apartment building, she listened to the rings and waited for him to pick up. When he did, with a simple hello, the very sound of his voice sent skitters of awareness and longing dancing down her spine.

"Hey," she said, her tone low even as she had to raise her voice to be heard over the loud background city noises around her.

"Hey," he said back, and she couldn't tell if he was happy to hear from her or not.

Because she couldn't think of anything else to say, she blurted out, "I've got some news."

"Yeah?"

"Pulse Model Management just offered me a contract. They loved your photos and said my burns may actually be an asset to some designers and in some arenas. But even if they're not, they're easy enough to cover."

"Way to go. Congratulations, Soph, you deserve it."

He sounded genuinely pleased for her, and warmth burst in her chest, spreading outward. She smiled, adding a little bounce to her steps.

"So what are you up to?" she asked, wishing she had the nerve to ask if he missed her . . . if he would reconsider his decision never to visit the city again . . . if there was any way for her to slip away this weekend to visit him . . .

"Oh, nothing much. Hangin' out with a few friends." A horn honked and the blast seemed to echo through the phone line. "Thinking about you," he added softly.

The earlier warmth of contentment that had filled her chest heated by several degrees and moved lower, into her belly and between her legs.

"Really?" Geez, could she sound any more like a pathetic high schooler?

"Sure. Your silky blond hair, your ruby lips, the way you fill out that sexy red raincoat."

She chuckled, imagining his spiky, even blonder hair . . . the way he filled out a pair of faded blue jeans . . . the mouthwatering sight of his smooth bare chest . . .

"Hey, wait a minute." Her footsteps faltered as she frowned into the mouthpiece of her phone and glanced down at herself. "How do you know I'm wearing a red raincoat?"

How did he even know she owned one? She hadn't had it with her while she'd stayed with him last month.

"Because I'm standing in front of your building, watching you walk this way looking confused. Hurry up, babe, you've kept me waiting out here long enough."

Her head shot up, her gaze rushing past the few strangers littering the tree-lined street until it landed on his towering form. She didn't know if it was Mac himself or her desperate need to be near him that drew her attention so unerringly, but she locked on his short, near-white hair, the leather jacket over a plain black T-shirt, his usual worn jeans and work boots . . . and her heart lurched. Her lungs stopped working and tears pricked behind her eyes.

And then she was moving again, walking, then jogging, then running the last few feet to reach him. She threw her arms around his neck, and he caught her, lifting her in his embrace for a tight hug, her legs swinging off the ground.

"What are you doing here?" she asked when she pulled back to look at his face.

He opened his mouth to answer, but she covered it with two fingers. "And don't say you're standing here waiting for me to get home. I mean what are you doing *here* in Manhattan after your insistence that"—she lowered her voice and wrinkled her brow, mimicking his low, masculine tone—"'I can't go back there, I can never go back'?"

He grinned at her lousy impression and smacked a quick kiss on her lips. "A funny thing happened after you left. I started getting phone calls from old friends and contacts. Folks asking where I'd been, why my photos were suddenly showing up in your new portfolio, and when I was planning to pick up again where I'd left off."

Her eyes widened, surprised at the response his work had gotten from just the few places she'd circulated her portfolio. Granted, his photos were fabulous and deserved all that attention and more. But usually when a model went looking for work, *she* was the one to hold center stage, not the photographer who had shot the images.

"I ignored them at first, but the calls kept coming," he continued, his cheeks coloring slightly in embarrassment. "Phil Jackson . . . you remember him, right? . . . invited me to stay with him for a few days if I wanted to come into the city and feel things out."

"You've been here for a few days? Without letting me know?" she demanded, a scowl turning her mouth down at the corners.

He at least had the grace to look chagrined about that, too. "Yeah, but I have a good reason. I wanted to be sure."

"Sure about what?"

"That I could do this. That I could be back in New York without wanting to hit all my old haunts or having the urge to go back to all my old habits."

Her fingers, which were wrapped around his firm upper arms, squeezed gently and moved up and down in a comforting, supporting motion. "And?"

"I hung out with old friends, talked about the business, even went to a couple parties just like I used to."

Sophie's stomach tumbled. He sounded so serious, she feared things hadn't gone well. That the demons from his past had caught up with him and gotten him to do something he didn't want to do.

"And . . ." He drew the word out, building the tension, making her every muscle and tendon draw tight with worry. "Nothing. I enjoyed myself, and started to recall why I loved the business so much and got into it in the first place. But even though the booze was flowing freely—along with several less legal substances, I'm sure—I didn't need it. Didn't have so much as a twinge as trays of champagne floated past or when someone offered me a drink directly."

Letting loose a tiny squeal, she jumped up and wrapped her arms around his neck once again, hugging him close. "I'm so proud of you," she told him. "I always knew you were stronger than that garbage."

"Yeah, well . . ." He cleared his throat, which had gone thick with emotion. Nuzzling his nose against the curve of her neck, he said, "I realized something else these past few days, too."

"What's that?" she asked without moving away from his snug embrace.

"I'm thinking that if I had someone here to keep me on the straight and narrow, to go along with me to those parties and give me something to think about other than drugs or booze . . ."

He shrugged a shoulder, hugging her even closer. "Well, that could be a pretty strong incentive for me to move back and start shooting the good stuff again."

Heart beating double-time behind her rib cage, Sophie pulled back until she could see his face and meet his dark brown gaze. She licked her lips nervously. "Got anyone particular in mind?" she asked with much more bravado than she felt.

"Oh, I don't know. Phil would probably be an okay choice. Or maybe Bruce Trevoti."

Pulling her arm back, she punched him none too gently in the stomach. "You big jerk!" she charged. "You'd better be talking about me or you can haul your butt right back to that dump you call a studio and take pictures of drooling babies for the rest of your life."

He threw back his head and laughed, a deep, rich sound that rolled through her veins like honey.

"Yeah, I'm talking about you. Thought maybe you'd let me crash with you for a while till I can find my own place and get back on my feet."

Her heart continued to race, but for a whole different reason this time. "That would probably be all right," she replied carefully, not sure how excited she should get when everything was still so uncertain.

"If things work out," he went on, "we can talk about finding another, bigger place together. Maybe do the whole Manhattan version of the white picket fence, two-point-five kids, a dog in the yard."

His fingers were in her hair now, stroking it away from her face while he cupped her jaw and kept his eyes locked with hers. "I love you, Sophie. And I want the next drooling baby I capture with my camera lens to be ours."

Everything past *I love you* flew at her in a rush and made her feel as though she'd slipped into an alternate reality. But she was game. She was very, very game.

"I love you, too," she told him, running her fingers over his rough cheeks and pressing a soft kiss to his lips as she struggled to hold back tears of joy. "But let's take things slow, okay? Give me a couple years to enjoy being back on the runway and in swimsuit editions before you knock me up and turn me from a model into a mom."

One corner of Mac's sexy mouth lifted and a wicked glint sparkled in his eyes. "Fast or slow, baby. You know I like it both ways."

She chuckled, ready to explode from the complete and utter happiness pinballing its way through every cell of her being. Reaching into her handbag, she came up with a set of keys, dangling them in front of him.

"I'm in 4B. Care to go upstairs and prove it?"

The glint in his eyes grew even brighter, edged now with the short fuse of unleashed desire. He pulled open the glass front door of her building, bracing it with his body before scooping her into his arms.

"Quicker than you can say 'cheese,'" he told her, carrying her upstairs, where he proceeded to demonstrate the very best of everything.

atticus gets a mommy

*

ANN CHRISTOPHER

To Richard

Special thanks to Lester S. Duplechan, MD,
who answered my endless questions with patience and enthusiasm.
Any mistakes are, of course, mine.

one

✣

"Who's the guy?"

Whoa. Was that his voice? Growling like that?

Yeah. Unfortunately.

He, Keenan Evans, a successful architect and generally cool guy despite being a wheelchair-bound quad with limited use of his arms and hands and zero use of his legs, was about to lose his freaking mind.

Right here, at the elegant reception following his sister Lisa's wedding to his best friend, Cruz Shaw. Right now.

Why?

Because Diana Barker, another architect at his office and the most beautiful woman in the world, had shown up tonight with . . . Keenan had to swallow back the rising bile even to think the horrible four-letter word . . . a date.

A *date*.

Wasn't that just a kick in the teeth?

Apparently he wasn't the only one who thought so. Atticus, the capuchin therapy monkey that handled all his fine-motor tasks and was his constant sidekick, cocked his fuzzy little head as though he knew things were about to get bad. Settling into Keenan's lap, blue leash jangling, he looked into Keenan's face with concerned brown eyes. "Oooooh," he murmured.

Meanwhile, Diana, the object of Keenan's increasingly tortured obsession, looked around, delicate brows raised and a crystal champagne flute poised near her perfect lips.

"Excuse me?" she said.

She looked pissed, which was just fine with him, because God knew he was pissed.

Pissed because, in a roomful of two hundred or more people, he was the one stuck, undancing, in a wheelchair, even though the music's beat pulsed through his blood just like it did everyone else's. Pissed because he would never dance again, never walk, and never be free of this godforsaken wheelchair. Even after years of getting used to it, he was still pissed.

Most of all, he was pissed because Diana was here with some other guy who had four working limbs. She'd found the kind of guy she deserved, damn her.

The gnawing jealousy had already hollowed out his insides with its sharp little teeth. At this rate, he'd be certifiably insane before the newlyweds left for their Caribbean honeymoon in a couple of hours.

Diana. Even her name was an ache in his heart, and had been since the day she showed up in his office and his life, and looked into his eyes. *Diana*.

After dancing to the Black-Eyed Peas' "Let's Get It Started," "Electric Slide," and several other fast songs, during which she'd tempted him like Salome with her scarves, all swaying hips and lush curves in a filmy black dress that was classy and yet left plenty to his overactive imagination, she'd slow-danced. With him. Her—Keenan repressed a shudder—*date*.

The punk who'd had his clingy arms all around her like poison ivy strangling an oak.

Stuck in this lousy chair, Keenan had watched from the sidelines and seethed.

Now both he and Diana were spoiling for a fight. It was the perfect time because her date had hightailed it off to the cake line or some such, and they were as alone as it was possible to be in a packed ballroom.

"Your *date*," Keenan reminded her, with just as much aggression in his voice as before. So much for not snarling this time. At best, he'd managed to sound as though he merely wanted to maim the punk rather than kill him outright. "The guy who was all over you a minute ago. Remember him? Where'd he come from?"

"Evan?"

He'd preferred to think of him as *Punk*, *SOB*, or *Loser*, but whatever. Evan. If he had to have a name.

She shrugged and sipped her champagne. "We met at the gym—"

Of course. Because the gym was where you hung out when you had a whole body.

True, Keenan hung out at a gym, too, but it was a special one for people like him, where he could work on keeping his upper body strong even if his lower body was a useless combination of loose skin, atrophied muscles, and the sharp right angles of his bent legs.

"And he asked me out a few times. I finally said yes." She paused to stare him right in the face, the challenge bright in her eyes. "Why do you ask?"

They were gliding into treacherous waters here, but then everything about Diana felt dangerous to him and always had. Dangerous and endlessly fascinating.

Time to back off a little lest she realize exactly how much she meant to him.

Trying to match her nonchalance, he shrugged and navigated the wheelchair until it was next to her chair at the table and they were shoulder to shoulder.

Too close and yet way too far away.

Atticus, who was always on the lookout for a forbidden treat, took advantage of Keenan's momentary distraction and sniffed at the remnants of Diana's wedding cake. With sugar in the offering, he chittered with rapture and dug in with his tiny fingers, shoveling icing into his mouth. The dumb thing would make himself sick in a minute, but Keenan could deal with only one crisis at a time, and Diana was it.

"He doesn't seem like your type," Keenan told her.

"How's that?"

"You have an IQ. From what I've seen tonight, he doesn't."

There was something dark in her half smile, amusement that wasn't amusement at all, but something harder, almost bitter. "Just because he hadn't heard about the tornadoes in Topeka yesterday?"

Keenan snorted. "Honey, I'm thinking that unless they show it on Sports Center, there's going to be a lot he doesn't know. Have you checked to make sure he knows who the current president is?"

To his consternation, she laughed. *Laughed.* And then she did something far worse: looked off across the room to where Evan was now shaking hands with some guy over by the bar, and sighed, giving him a look of such frank sexual appreciation that it was practically a leer.

Keenan almost choked on his jealousy.

"Well," she said in a husky-sexy voice that was exactly what he'd imagined in all his overheated dreams of her, "Evan's got other things going for him. A lot of other things. So it's all good."

Following her gaze, he forced himself to look at Evan and take inventory. Again.

Evan was tall. Keenan used to be tall. Evan was the kind of dark and handsome guy that women universally went nuts for, the kind of guy Keenan was once. Hell. Keenan supposed he still was good-looking, from the waist up anyway, not that women ever bothered to look down at him these days. Being ignored by the fairer sex, when they'd once fallen all over him, wasn't good for his morale. To say the least. Evan, on the other hand, had all the confidence in the world, and why shouldn't he? He could have any woman he wanted, make love to any woman he wanted, and Keenan—

"What's wrong?" Diana asked softly, and the challenge in her expression had grown and intensified into open defiance. If he didn't know her better, his sweet Diana, he'd almost think she wanted to stick it to him and rub his face in Evan's perfection. "I thought you'd be happy for me."

The growing sickness inside him had a choke hold on his struggling lungs, and it took him forever to speak. When he did, it was in a weak voice that would have unmanned him if the car accident hadn't already done that so effectively.

"Happy for you?" he echoed.

Diana hitched up her chin, and Jesus, it felt like she was cocking her fist, getting ready for the right hook that would knock him out of the wheelchair and leave him flattened, facedown, on the ballroom's parquet floor.

"Didn't you tell me to find someone who could give me everything I need?" She smiled then, his Diana, a smile that was all flushed cheeks and sensual knowledge, as though she'd already enjoyed all the pleasures a man like Evan could give her and intended to enjoy them again as soon as possible.

That smile killed him.

"Now I have everything I need," she said. "Evan's giving it to me."

They stared at each other for several silent seconds, each more painful than the last, and he wondered how he could hurt so bad without a fresh physical injury.

Just when he'd come to the conclusion that they'd hit bottom and this night had gotten as bad as it could possibly get, a new thought blindsided him, one that made the thought of Diana having sex with some other guy—a whole, healthy guy—seem like a mere walk in the park on a sunny Sunday afternoon.

Oh, shit. Oh, Jesus. Oh, no.

And he shouldn't ask. They'd covered this ground already, and he'd made his position on any sort of a relationship with Diana perfectly clear: wouldn't happen. It was better for her, obviously, because she didn't need to be saddled with a cripple, and better for him because why get his hopes up that life might hold some happiness for him after all?

So, yeah, what she did with her personal life was no concern of his, and there was a speeding lightning bolt with his name on it, and then, once it struck him dead, a special place waiting for him in the hottest fires of hell for being a big enough bastard to even wonder, but . . .

God. He hadn't known it would feel like *this* to see her with someone else.

"Are you in love with him?"

That was it for Diana; he knew it even before her lips twisted with derision and her entire body stiffened to granite. Clunking her champagne flute on the table, she stood and stared down at him with icy brown eyes that glittered with the unforgiving hardness of diamonds. Working hard not to blink, he met her gaze and considered it a modern miracle that his testicles didn't wither and fall off before her quiet fury.

"That's none of your business, is it?"

No. It was none of his business at all, and they both knew it. And that didn't lessen the pain one damn iota.

Lobbing a final glare at him, she spun on her sky-high heels and walked off toward her date, the man who deserved her.

"Shit." Keenan was left alone feeling doubly paralyzed—physically, as always, and emotionally, because he just didn't know what the hell he should do now. *"Shit."*

Atticus, who'd devoured all the cake remnants and had the telltale white icing ring around his mouth to prove it, now had a moment to commiserate. Facing Keenan, he stretched up on his hind legs and stared into his face, his expression grave. Keenan stared back, not bothering to hide his desolation.

And Atticus, bless his little furry heart, patted his cheeks with both messy hands, offering what comfort he could.

two

Pull it together, girl, Diana told herself, and managed something like a smile just as Evan, her date, held out a hand to reel her in. Sidestepping the last couple of people at the crowded edge of the dance floor, she slipped into his welcoming arms, which were strong and muscular, and she felt . . . nothing.

Well, not quite *nothing*. She felt all the heightened awareness a woman automatically feels when she's near a handsome man, and there was no question about it—Evan was handsome. It was all going on right here, no doubt. He had the height and the shoulders, the sparkling eyes and the dimples. He smelled good, too, with a hint of cologne that was sophisticated and musky and should have been devastating rather than just pleasant.

The problem was, he wasn't Keenan.

"Hey." Putting his arm around her waist, he kissed her forehead with soft lips and then gazed down at her with open appreciation, as though the fun could begin now that he had such a fine woman back by his side. "You want to dance again?"

She hesitated, cursing her own ambivalence.

Okay. So here was a sexy man who had his hands on her and thought she was special. Special enough to want to have sex with anyway. She waited for her belly to quiver, but it remained stubbornly unmoved by this masculine perfection.

No surprise, really.

It was hard to get turned on by Evan when she was stupid enough to be in love with Keenan. Keenan, the man who'd rejected her on more than one memorable occasion. Keenan, who couldn't make it plainer that he wanted nothing to do with her, not unless he could back over her a couple of times with his specially modified car. Keenan, the man she'd never have even if she couldn't stop wanting him.

Man, she was an idiot. So much so that hot tears burned the backs of her eyes, putting her in danger of making a fool of herself in public.

And then she caught herself.

Not today, sister. No man was worth public tears. Not even Keenan.

This was her good friend Lisa's wedding reception, and Diana was here with an attractive man who wanted her. No way was she going to feel sorry for herself and let her doomed love for a moody quadriplegic ruin that. Tonight she was going to pull it together and have fun. Dammit.

She widened her fake smile, blinked back her emotion, and slipped away from Evan. "I'm just going to run to the ladies' room first."

Evan, good-natured as always, didn't mind. "I'll meet you back here."

"Sounds like a plan."

She dove into the crowd and headed for the bathroom, anxious to be alone long enough to get her game face firmly back in place. She'd just touch up her makeup and—

Oh, no. She froze just inside the swinging door. The place was full of primping women with lipsticks, powder puffs, and God knew what—all standing in front of the mirrors. Even the little seating area was occupied.

So much for that brilliant idea.

Backing out of the bathroom, desperate now for any sort of sanctuary, just for a minute, she hurried down the hall away from the ballroom and tried the first door she came to. Hah! Unlocked! It let into a dimly lit great room of sorts, with bookshelves, more sofas and chairs, a roaring fire in the gas fireplace and—oh, no—the bride and groom locked in a vertical embrace over in the corner, looking like they were seconds away from consummating the marriage.

Leave, girl. Just leave. Back out of the room and—

Too late; they'd heard her. Breaking apart, Cruz and Lisa looked around with unfocused eyes and tried to catch their breath.

The powers of speech failed them all, and they stared at each other for an excruciating beat or two. Awkward. This was what you might call an awkward moment.

"Umm," Diana began, fidgeting and stammering, her cheeks hot with embarrassment. "Sorry. I was just—"

"It's okay." Cruz gave her a don't-worry-about-it smile, wiping smeared lipstick off his mouth with his handkerchief in one hand and keeping the other slung low and possessive across his new wife's hips. "We should be getting back anyway. They'll be looking for us."

He tugged Lisa's hand and they started toward the door, but Lisa, beautiful in her sleek white satin gown and veil draped over the crook of her arm, gave Diana a sharp look.

"What's wrong, Diana?"

Oh, great. That dose of loving concern was sooo what she didn't need right now. Just like that, all the tears she thought she'd conquered, or at least temporarily blinked into submission, welled anew.

"Nothing," she tried, her bottom lip trembling.

Lisa didn't look convinced, what with her crinkled brow and all. Apparently it took more than her own wedding reception to throw her off the trail of romantic trouble. Maybe she was part bloodhound. "It's Keenan, isn't it?"

"Uh-oh." Amusement and interest sparked to life in Cruz's brown eyes. There was nothing he loved better than a fresh opportunity to tease Keenan about something. "What's up?"

Lord. Could this night get any worse? That's all Diana needed: to worry the bride on her big night while simultaneously giving Cruz a reason to needle Keenan.

Straightening her spine, she tried again. "Keenan and I had a little, ah, discussion a few minutes ago, but everything's fine now, and—"

Lisa's shrewd eyes narrowed. "He's jealous about your date, isn't he? I *knew* it."

Before Diana could work up any sort of denial, the door swung open again, and the night did indeed get worse.

Apparently all this talk about him had made his ears burn, because Keenan, looking grim and determined, his jaw tight, rolled into the room and studied their guilty faces.

"Can I talk to Diana for a minute?" he asked after an excruciating pause.

"No," Diana said, but no one was listening to her.

"Absolutely." Lisa smiled, looking so delighted it was a wonder she didn't twirl and skip her way out of the room. Tugging Cruz behind her—the groom was looking downright smug now, the light of mischief bright in his eyes—she paused only long enough to squeeze Diana's arm and whisper in her ear.

"Don't give up on Keenan, okay? He's crazy about you, even if he's too stubborn to admit it. Just hang in there and—"

"I can hear you," Keenan said sourly.

"*Good.*" Lisa was so full of gleeful triumph she all but levitated with it. "Because I'll have a word or two for you in a minute, brother."

This pronouncement sucked a good fifty percent of the smugness from Cruz's face, and his gaze flickered between Keenan and his new wife. "A *quick* word," he told Lisa. "You'll have a *quick* word with him. We've got some consummating to do, and we don't have time—"

The look Lisa shot her husband was pure desire in its most primitive form, so much so that Diana had to turn her head and Keenan cleared his throat.

Cruz stilled, utterly fixated on his bride.

"Oh, don't worry." Lisa gave him a thorough once-over filled with the promise of intense sensual delights that were still illegal in some states. "You'll get what's coming to you."

It took Cruz a couple seconds to get his husky voice working again. "I'm going to hold you to that."

The newlyweds left, taking all their sexual heat with them and leaving only a ringing silence that seemed to get worse with each creeping second.

Diana recovered first. "Where's Atticus?"

"Playing with some of his fans in the ballroom. I gave him a few minutes off, so he'll probably try to get his hands on more cake."

"Oh." She took a step toward the door. "Well, you and I've already talked, so—"

"Diana. *Please*."

She froze where she was, with one hand reaching for the door, because she just couldn't walk out on him when he spoke to her with such intense urgency. But looking at him was another matter, so she didn't do it. There was no way she could stare into those midnight eyes and feel nothing. She couldn't see him sitting, so proud and handsome in his double-breasted tuxedo, so emotionally wounded, and not want him. It wasn't in her.

So she spoke to the closed door, wishing she could just leave right now.

"You have two minutes," she told him.

"Sit down with me. Please."

He'd once mentioned that he hated always having to stare up at people from his chair, and she couldn't blame him. His long legs were wasted now, thin beneath the fine wool of his trousers, but he'd been tall once. She hadn't known him before his accident, but it must be hard to go from being one of the tallest people in the room to having even kids tower over him.

So she sat, grudgingly, and folded her hands in her lap. "What is it?"

He wheeled over until they were knee-to-knee. His words didn't seem to want to come, and she kept quiet, refusing to make anything easy for him.

God knew he'd never made anything easy for her.

"You deserve the best out of life," he said finally.

The best. Huh. Yeah. She'd heard this before, many times. Maybe she could look at him after all.

Staring him straight in the face, she mimed a yawn and checked her watch.

Red blotches appeared on his cheeks, but he kept calm and repeated the same old stupid script. "I want you to be happy, Diana. You'd never be happy with me—"

Wow. So now he was God, dictating her wants and needs to her from his almighty perch in that wheelchair. Wasn't she lucky to have him to run her life for her?

She had nothing to say to this. Why respond, anyway, when it was so fascinating to watch him throw everything and the kitchen sink at her—everything but the truth?

"And I want you to find the right guy—"

Okay. Enough was enough; she'd reached her bullshit quota for the night. "Have you got anything new for me—"

Keenan floundered.

"Or can you speed this up so I can get back to the reception while I'm still young and cute? I've heard it all before, and it's pretty boring, frankly."

His brows lowered until they were nothing but heavy slashes over his eyes, as unmistakable a warning sign as any she'd ever seen. To his credit, though, he took the high road and kept waving that olive branch of peace.

Too bad she wanted war.

"Why are you making this so hard, Diana?" There was a touch of rising frustration in his voice. "I just want you to understand—"

Oh, for God's sake. She didn't have time for this nonsense. "Understand what? That you're a coward?"

The C-word shut him up in a hurry. It hung in the air, reverberating between them, as ugly and devastating as she'd meant it to be. His fingers, already curled, tightened into fists in his lap, and that same tension ran up his arms until his shoulders squared off.

"Don't you call me a coward," he said in a low voice.

Oh, but she was just getting warmed up.

"Don't get me wrong." She shrugged, so nonchalant they may have been talking about this morning's rain. It was easy to remain calm while she twisted the knife, because he'd had this strong dose of tough love coming for months. And his blotchy color, a vivid red now, bordering on purple, told her she was hitting home.

She was only sorry they hadn't had this conversation sooner.

"You have some courage. I know that."

"Some . . . courage?" His voice was strangled.

"Well, you battled back after the car accident, right? You went through all that terrible physical therapy, and you rebuilt your life. Now you live on your own again. That's not bad."

Keenan looked apoplectic now, his upper body and facial muscles so hard and tight with rage that a single touch might be enough to make him crumble to dust.

She ticked off his accomplishments on her fingers, keeping her voice at a dismissive singsong that made him sound as though he'd done nothing more complex than learn the first half of the alphabet. "You can drive your own car, and you can play basketball with your wheelchair league, right, and you can enter your wheelchair marathons and earn all kinds of medals."

From out of nowhere, a white-hot rage swept over her, washing away the grim satisfaction she'd felt to finally say these things to him. For a minute, she was too upset to continue. He held her life in his hands, damn him, and he didn't have the faintest idea what his rejection was doing to her.

Her voice rose, pitching higher with her frustration and desperation, and she taunted him, going for his emotional jugular.

"You're a real marvel, aren't you, Keenan? There's nothing you won't do with that chair, is there? I'll even bet that if they set up a quadriplegics' expedition to the top of Mount Everest, where you strap your wheelchair to your back and claw your way to the top of the mountain without oxygen, you'd be the first one to sign up for it, wouldn't you? So, yeah, you have *some*"—she held up her thumb and forefinger, half an inch apart—"courage. I'll give you that. Actually, I'll give you more than that. You're the bravest man I've ever met." She paused. "Except when it comes to me."

He made a choked sound—of rage or anger, she couldn't tell which.

"Deep down where it counts, right *here*"—she reached out and, pointing her forefinger, jabbed him hard in the chest—"you're a cow—"

"*Don't you call me a coward*," he shouted, batting her arm away.

She yelled, too, getting to her feet and into his face, beyond caring if they made a scene at this beautiful reception and had to be thrown out by security. "You *are* a coward! When it comes to me, you're the biggest coward there is!"

"Screw you." Wheeling around her, he headed for the door. "I'm leav—"

"Leaving?" She let out a single bark of laughter, as derisive as she could make it. "Go ahead, Keenan. That's what cowards do in tricky situations, right? They run away, don't they? Isn't that what they teach in Coward 101?"

A roar of rage rose up out of him, so powerful that she wondered if it could lift him out of that chair and propel him to his feet. Two slashing downward strokes of his arms had the chair spinning back toward her and she had to fight the urge to run and hide.

"What do you want, Diana? What the hell do you *want?*"

That was easy. "Tell me what you're so afraid of. Please—"

"I'm not afraid." The way he snarled it, as though she'd insulted him, his manhood, his mother, and generations of his family going back to slave times, told her she'd hit a raw nerve. "I don't know where you're getting that."

Okay. Time to try another approach. "Fine. I want you to be honest for once. How would that be?"

"I'm always—"

"Don't." God. His audacity made her want to pull her hair out in frustration. Apparently no lie was too far-fetched and ridiculous to tell. "Don't even try it. You've never been honest with me a day in your life."

"That's not true," he said, but his voice didn't sound any too steady, and his gaze, so defiant a second ago, wavered.

"Oh, yeah?"

He stilled. They stared at each other, both knowing where

this was going and what was next. They'd been headed for this conversation—this single moment—for months, if not years.

"If you're so honest all the time, tell me how you feel about me."

She waited and watched while all that bright color drained from his face. And the same Keenan she loved, the one who was so fiercely strong and who had resurrected his life, battling his way back from a devastating injury that would have killed a lesser man, hesitated. Then he lied.

"You're a wonderful friend," he began, "but it's nothing more than—"

Diana wasn't sure which was more insulting: the lie itself or the fact that he thought she was dumb enough to believe it. Either way, she'd had enough and didn't plan to listen to another dishonest syllable.

"Yeah, see—there's that coward thing again. That's what I'm talking about."

"I told you not to call me—"

"Do you think I don't see the way you look at me?" she cried, her desperation making her so shrill and agitated she felt like a wasp trapped in a jar. "Do you think I don't notice? Do you think I'm too stupid to know when a man wants me? Is that it?"

Keenan cursed and turned his head away, but it was too late. She'd seen the wheels turning in his mind and the subtle schooling of his features, as though he could get that horse back in the barn if only he kept his face blank enough.

His plan apparently formulated, he met her gaze again. "You're beautiful, Diana. You know that—"

This wasn't about her looks, and they both knew it. Her pride whispered a warning, but her heart wouldn't let her stop now. "I love you, Keenan—"

"Don't," he said sharply.

"*Love you.*" Ignoring her skirts and heels, she dropped to her knees in front of him and grabbed hold of the arms of his chair. Now he was trapped with nowhere else to run and nowhere else to look. "What do you think you're protecting me from?"

Some of the fight seemed to go out of him while his eyes were heating up with that emotion he could never completely hide. Seeing the intensity there—the riveting focus on her and her alone in the world—gave her the last boost of courage she needed.

And she reached out and touched him.

The smooth skin of his jaw first, velvet over marble, warm and vital and more thrilling than anything she could begin to imagine. "Love you, Keenan."

He gasped, and she took that as encouragement.

Leaning closer, she stroked her hands over his heavy arms and shoulders, ignoring the tuxedo's fine fabric and searching for Keenan's strength. When it wasn't enough to feel the vigor in his biceps and forearms, she rubbed her cheek against his torso, which was hard and lean and thundering with his heartbeat. And here was the smell she craved, the one Evan didn't have: clean soap, sporty deodorant, fresh linen, and warm skin.

Wild now with the primitive thrill of doing *this*, something she'd wanted to do for so long—so long, God, *so long*—she eased lower, until she nuzzled his crotch, loving as much of him as she could, for now. His gasp deepened into a groan, and she looked up into his face so he could see her expression when she said this next part.

And then, when he was staring down at her with hot eyes, glittering eyes, and she was staring up at him, letting all her need show on her face, she hugged his useless legs close to her heart.

"I love everything about you," she told him. "*Everything.*"

Something broke free in his expression then, something joyous, bright, and uncontrollable even though he tried to blink it back and tamp it down. Breathing hard, he raised his clumsy fingers and stroked her face—the left side first, and then the right.

His touch was gentle . . . so gentle . . . and she closed her eyes with the pleasure.

Then his hands touched her hair, and he tilted her head back, anchoring her the way he wanted her.

Staring into his eyes, she held on to this moment.

"Tell me," she said.

A hint of a smile curled his lips. "I love you."

"I know," she said, because she did. But it was so much better to hear him say it.

He hesitated, and in that one moment, she saw every emotion under the sun pass over his features, all battling for supremacy: joy and sorrow, excitement and trepidation, desire most of all.

The desire won.

With a rough groan, he pulled her up, just enough, and kissed her.

three

There was no gentle meeting of lips, no gradual buildup of intensity from one to ten.

The kiss exploded the second their mouths connected, and there was no turning back after that. He held tight to her head, and she surged upward, starving for the taste and feel of him and needing to do this if she wanted to survive another minute.

His mouth was hot and slick, sweet from cake, his lips softer and yet more demanding than she'd imagined. He claimed her with his sweeping tongue, thrusting deep before backing off just enough to run his lips all over her forehead and cheeks, kissing every part of her he could reach.

She was just as desperate, clinging to his head and neck, and holding him close because she couldn't stand to ever let him get away, not after this.

Without warning, he broke free and jerked her away by the shoulders. Maybe he needed a break, a second to catch his breath, or maybe he couldn't believe that something this glorious could happen between them.

They stared at each other, both panting, and in his eyes she read astonishment, awe, and a dark, driving need every bit as strong as hers. The arrested moment pulsed and grew, heightening the tension until she felt it in every atom of every nerve ending in her oversensitized body.

Then, with a low groan, he kissed her again.

He was delicious, God . . . so strong and amazing, so unbelievably thrilling. He tasted like home and everything she'd ever longed for in her life, everything she'd ever needed. Parts of his body were damaged, yeah, but it didn't matter because the passion pouring from him now was more potent than she'd ever felt from any other man, and that was enough.

She wanted all of him and wanted him to have all of her. So when his lips slid down to her bare neck, she arched for him and pulled the bodice of her dress down, baring herself and offering everything she had.

So what if they were in the middle of a wedding reception? It was dim and secluded here, and the door was shut, and nothing short of a bomb scare and ballroom evacuation would force her to cut short this stolen moment with him.

He stiffened and stared, his eyes wide and fixated on her swollen breasts and dark nipples. There was no shyness or shame in her. She was ten—no, fifteen—pounds overweight, easy, and she'd felt like a stuffed sausage squeezed into the dress, but he seemed to have no problems with any of that.

"God," he said, cupping and caressing her. "You're perfect."

The words were right there, so she didn't hold them back. "So are you."

Tipping her chin up, she tried to reclaim his mouth and kiss him again, forever, but he jerked her away again, harder this time, and she knew it was over even if her bewildered body wasn't up to speed.

It took her a minute to shake off her sensual haze. "What—"

"Fix your dress." Turning away—she had the feeling he never wanted to lay eyes on her again—he swiped his mouth with the back of his hand, removing all traces of her lipstick and her.

Still kneeling, she fixed her bodice but then clung to the arms of his chair, unwilling to move away from him, even a little. "Did I do something wrong?"

His lips twisted in a disconcerting bastardization of a smile. Taking one of her hands, he pressed it against his crotch and held it there. "What do you think?"

Oh, God.

If he was trying to slow this train down, he'd just made the wrong move.

Her mouth dried out. She tried to remember that he was upset about something and didn't want this to go any further, but it was hard when his erection strained for her. Acting on instinct, she murmured appreciatively and—

Cursing, he shoved her hand away. "Don't."

Diana stood, and the weariness washed over her. She was so tired of being held at arm's length, so tired of putting everything she was on the line only to be rejected again and again.

But, she reminded herself after a minute, this was Keenan. *Keenan.* And he was worth the effort, even if his eyes were now flashing murder at her.

"Why?" Brushing her now-messy hair out of her face, she stared down at him. "Tell me why I can't touch you. If I love you, and you love me, and we want each other, then tell me—"

He snorted, the ugliest sound she'd ever heard. "Because it doesn't always work, that's why."

She let this settle for a minute, trying to come up to speed and reconcile what she'd read and seen about spinal cord injuries with what she'd just experienced. "But . . . you've had other girl-friends since the accident, and I thought—"

His eyes were hard and flat. "Well, that's the tricky thing

about incomplete spinal cord injuries, Diana. Sometimes it works and sometimes it doesn't. Sometimes I need extra stimulation and sometimes I don't. Sometimes—and this is where it gets really fun for the woman—it works for a while and then quits. Doesn't that sound like a blast?"

Was that it? She ran through these various scenarios in her mind, made peace with them, and then moved ahead. "Okay. I understand."

Another snort. "You understand?"

"Yes." She spoke slowly, determined to make sure *he* understood. "I understand."

"No, you don't." He flapped a hand in the direction of the ballroom. "This is why you need Cro-Magnon man out there. You won't have these kinds of problems with him. You'll never have to worry about pressure ulcers or infections—"

"I'm sorry." It was impossible to keep the sarcasm out of her voice, because, really—where was this going? Did he think if he framed a logical enough argument, he could talk her out of loving him? "I don't mean to be slow here, but you seemed to be doing a great job with a couple of other parts of your body just now. Your mouth, for one, and your hands—"

"There's no substitution for making love, and you know it."

"Actually, there are lots of substitutions, most of which you can buy online at some very tasteful and discreet stores—"

"You want to have sex with some battery-operated device?"

"If it's your hand holding the device and your lips kissing me, then yeah—you bet I do."

Shaking his head as though he just couldn't understand her willful refusal to listen to him talk sense, he pressed his hands to his temples and made a low, rumbling sound, like a growl. "You'd be better off taking your chances with whatshisname out there—"

Okay. He was really starting to piss her off again.

"Yeah," she said. "I'm sure Evan could screw me real good, if I let him."

Keenan shut up midsyllable, stunned and all but gagging on the tail end of his sentence.

Good. Maybe she could get a word in edgewise, for once. "But here's the problem with your dictating my life choices to me: I don't love Evan. I don't even want him. I want you."

"That'll change after the novelty wears off," he said flatly. "So why don't we call it quits here and save ourselves the trouble?"

Was she actually hearing this nonsense? "Are you really that idiotic, Keenan?"

He swore under his breath and looked away.

"Can I just point out that I have a few physical issues, too?" she asked.

"What the hell are you talking about?"

"Well, I'm fifteen—hell, who am I kidding?—no, twenty pounds overweight, for one."

His jaw dropped. "Not from where I'm sitting, you're not. From where I'm sitting, you're freaking perfect. And are you actually comparing being a quadriplegic to being allegedly over-weight?"

"No. I'm saying that everyone has issues. If I don't have one now, what if I develop one later? What if I turn up with cancer and lose a breast? Or heart disease? What if I'm in a car accident tomorrow? Would you stop loving me just because—"

He growled with frustration, cutting her off. "You don't understand. You *can't* understand."

"Try me."

"I dream about you," he said helplessly. "Almost every night."

Wow. And here she'd thought he'd already claimed her entire heart. How was it that he managed to keep stealing more pieces of it? "I dream about you, too."

His eyes narrowed into disbelieving slits. "Sexually?"

Remembering the last dream, just the other night, after which she'd woken, sweaty, aroused, and grossly unsatisfied, she shuddered. "God, yes."

This confession only seemed to agitate him. "Well, here's what I dream: that I have two good legs. That I can pick you up and throw you around the bed in all kinds of positions—"

She shuddered again, unable to control her responses to him, his longing, and his voice.

"Or against the wall. That we can do it all night—"

She held up her hand. "Let me stop you right there. I'm way too heavy for you to pick up anyway. Not that I don't appreciate the sentiment."

"Jesus," he muttered. "Will you listen to anything I'm saying?"

"No. Because you're not saying anything that matters to me. Do you want to know how it is when I dream about us?"

"No," he said quickly.

That was just too damn bad. "I dream that you're all over me. Your arms and your hands and your mouth. And I can't get enough of you. And when I wake up, and you're not there, I—"

She broke off. There was no way she could convey how lonely she was for something she'd never had anyway, or how much she missed him when she reached for him and he wasn't there.

He stared at her for a long time, his expression closed and unreadable.

"I can't give you what you need, Diana," he said finally.

"And you get to decide what I need?"

"In this case, yes."

"So what if I lost a breast to cancer? Or a kidney or a leg to diabetes? Would you not want me then? Are you that shallow, or is it just that you think *I* am?"

"Of course I'd still want you, but that's not the point."

She laughed then, bitterly, looking to the ceiling, because if divine intervention was coming, now would be a really good time for it to show up. "Then what is the point? Please enlighten me, because I'm not getting you at all, Keenan."

"The point is that you need to stop with the bullshit hypotheticals. I can come up with a bullshit hypothetical, too. Want to hear it? Here it is: Maybe Martians will invade earth tomorrow and blow us all up, and all of these issues will be moot. But until then, you have to face the fact that I'm not even sure I can produce kids—"

What? *What?*

"*Kids?* Is that what we're talking about here? Well, ease your mind, Keenan. I'm thirty-seven and I've never been pregnant, so as far as we know, my plumbing doesn't work either."

"Stop minimizing this," he shouted. "I'm trying to protect you."

Protect her. Right. And wasn't that the biggest bit of cowardly hypocrisy of all?

So now they were right back where they'd started.

"No," she said, too exhausted to keep her voice above a husky rasp. God, he wore her out. "You're trying to protect yourself. Because you're scared, and you think I feel sorry for you. Either that or you think I'll feel sorry for you one day in the future. And you're a coward hiding behind that chair."

Her little speech was exactly the wrong thing to say. And exactly the right thing.

Gripping the arms of his wheelchair, he pushed himself up as though he wanted to escape, his neck and upper body straining against the circumstances that had trapped him there, and against her, and against himself.

"*Don't you call me a coward!*"

"Why not?" she wondered. "It's the truth."

four

✻

Coward.

The word was still reverberating, a whizzing Ping-Pong ball trapped inside Keenan's skull, when the door opened again, emitting a burst of the thundering bass line from the reception, which was clearly in full swing.

He braced himself, hoping round three with Diana wouldn't lead to a KO with him spread-eagle on the floor in front of the roaring fire, but it was only his sister.

He relaxed a little, coming down off heightened alert.

He also felt the sharp pang of disappointment deep in his chest.

"Hey." Lisa crept into the room, peering around as though she needed to make sure the furniture was all still in one piece. Hell, she'd probably been listening at the door this whole time. "Someone's been looking for you."

She'd had Atticus's leash in her hand, but now she let it go. The monkey raced across the room, scrambled into his usual perch on Keenan's lap, and then turned his back on him, trying to hide something in his hands. It was . . . Keenan peered over his little shoulder for a better look . . . a bag of those pastel candied almonds, wrapped in that fancy netting stuff, tied with a bow that Atticus would have undone in two seconds.

Candy-covered almonds. Because that was what the monkey needed to wash down all the cake he'd eaten earlier. Nice.

But Keenan was happy to see the little guy. The sight of him, with his little black bow tie today, in honor of the occasion, was always comforting. God knew Keenan needed some comfort right about now. Raising his clumsy fingers, he scratched the thick mat of hair on the tiny little head. And Atticus grabbed the first almond and went to work gnawing on it in a two-handed grip, like a squirrel on amphetamines.

"How's it going?" Lisa asked.

"Peachy."

"Right. That must be why you look so happy."

The concern in her eyes was hard to face. Here she was, on her wedding day, looking like an angel in her white dress and veil, a beautiful goddess come to earth, and she was wasting time worrying about him.

He focused on the back of Atticus's head. "I'll be okay."

She looked dubious but said nothing.

He thought about today's significance. Man. Lisa, his big sister. A married woman. Amazing.

He remembered how far she'd come in the last few months, and how Cruz had helped her past her guilt. She'd been the driver the night Keenan was paralyzed. Not that it was her fault a drunk had plowed into them, but she'd still felt responsible.

Now, though, she'd let all that go. All the darkness, all the pain.

And here he still was, waist-deep in it.

Taking her hand, he tugged her to the sofa Diana had just vacated, and she sat.

He stared at the shiny band on her fourth finger and grinned. "I can't believe it."

She giggled, reminding him of that Christmas morning so long ago when she'd discovered a purple bike with a basket and handlebar streamers under the tree. "Neither can I."

"You're happy."

"I'm sooo happy."

He scowled. "You should be. I told you Cruz was a good guy."

"Yeah," she said, rolling her eyes. "Right after you threatened to knock his teeth down his throat for hitting on me."

Keenan scrunched up his face. "I don't remember that part."

"Riiiight."

Laughing, she squeezed his hand, and it hit him: Lisa didn't belong to him anymore—she belonged to Cruz. And that was the way it should be. Still, he wondered how many more private moments like this they'd have, just the two of them. She seemed to be thinking the same thing, because some of the joy dimmed from her face.

It was a poignant moment, but not sad.

"I love you, Lis."

"I know you do." Being Lisa, she got right to the heart of the matter. "And you love Diana, too, don't you?"

That choked him up. Way to go, sister. Rendering him speechless inside two minutes. That was a real record, even for her. He looked away, blinking back hot tears, and brushed some of Atticus's almond debris from his lap.

"Eeeee," Atticus said by way of thanks, and kept munching.

Lisa scooted closer and squeezed his arms, reassuring him just by being there. "She loves you, too, Keenan. I know she does. I can see it when she looks at you."

Through God's grace, he pulled it together. "That's not the point."

"Well, what *is* the point?"

Oh, come on. Did they really need to have this discussion? For real? "The point is: I'm stuck in this wheelchair."

She gave him a blank stare. "So? You made peace with that a long time ago. Before I did, in fact."

Was she serious? Was she really going to force him to explain? "It's one thing to make peace with it for myself. It's another thing to talk about having a relationship with a sexy woman who—"

"Oh." Lisa's expression cleared. "This is about sex, then. But you can have sex, right—"

Whoa. He wasn't quite up to discussing his sex life with his sister.

"I can't use my legs, Lisa."

There she went with the bewildered eyes again. "Yeah? So?"

Frustration crept into his voice. "So, I can't dance at weddings. I can't climb up on ladders and change lightbulbs—"

"*Diana* can change the lightbulbs."

"What if I can't have children?" he barked.

Atticus jumped and muttered with disapproval, but Lisa didn't miss a beat.

"What if you can?"

What the hell?

What was with these women tonight? Why couldn't they face facts and see what was right in front of them? Was there something funny in the wedding cake they'd been eating? "Diana deserves a man who—"

"Oh, bullshit."

Keenan was so stunned to see Lisa cursing and fierce while looking like an angel in her wedding dress that he snapped his jaws shut. Even Atticus froze and blinked at her.

"What's really going on here, Keenan?"

"I'm telling you—"

"*Keenan.* Please." To his absolute horror, she gently took his hand, kissed it, then pressed it to her heart and held it there. As though she held *him* there. As though she'd do anything, under-stand anything, protect him from anything. As though she needed him to need her. "There's nothing you can't tell me."

Just like that, she stripped him of all his defenses.

"I'm scared," he said simply.

This didn't seem to surprise her because the warm glow in her eyes never wavered. "Of what?"

"Of letting her see who I really am."

"She knows who you really are. She never even knew you before the accident."

"She's never seen my legs. She's never seen the ulcers I get sometimes, or seen me struggle to get dressed in the morning. She's never had to take care of me when I get sick, or—"

"Keenan," she said, bringing him up short.

God. Those repressed tears burned him again, trapped in his throat this time. There was so much kindness in Lisa's expression, so much love. It just tore him up.

"We'll all get sick if we live long enough. I just vowed to stay with Cruz in sickness and in health. I meant it. So did he."

This was so frustrating. What could he do to get her to fully understand? Would he have to bare his single darkest secret? Would that do it? Fine.

"I don't want to see pity in her face. Not ever. Not *Diana*. Do you get that? I want her to see me as a *man*."

Atticus, in his unerring way, cooed softly up at him in a monkey *don't worry, man, it'll be okay*, and patted his arm for emphasis.

"You are a man, Keenan," Lisa said. "And everyone knows that but you."

five

This was such a bad idea, Diana thought.

It was nearly one in the morning. She'd already had one piece of wedding cake—well, one and a half, to be honest—at the reception. But . . . she had brought home this one teeny-tiny piece, which was a souvenir for all the guests. And it was spice cake with gooey cream cheese icing, her favorite. And she had just endured yet another of Keenan's rejections and what was, all in all, the most crap-tastic night of her life.

She deserved this cake. She'd earned this cake. She needed this cake.

Dammit.

Tomorrow, she could worry about that twenty pounds she needed to lose, go to the gym to atone for all her sins, and that sort of nonsense. For tonight, however, a little self-medication was definitely in order. She was only sorry she didn't also have a fifth of tangerine vodka on hand. She could make cosmo-politans or something, and drown her sorrows by pickling her brain.

Ah, well. The cake would do nicely.

Unwrapping the plastic and setting aside the pretty little flower garnish, she took a giant bite from the icing-covered end. Oh, man. Talk about *heaven*. She closed her eyes and tipped her head back, the better to let the sugar high speed directly to her brain.

Yeah. That was better. Much better.

A movement in the corner of her eye caught her attention, and she turned in time to see Scout, already crated and bedded down for the night on her fake shearling pillow, give her a doleful look. Of course, all of Scout's looks were doleful, seeing as how she was a basset hound, but tonight even her droopy ears seemed especially disapproving.

"Don't you judge me," she told the dog. "I've had a rough night."

Scout merely stared, apparently too disapproving of Diana's gluttony to do more than yawn and rest her head on her paws.

Diana took another bite, smudging the icing on the corner of her mouth and not even caring. It wasn't like anyone was here to see her. Anyway, she needed to wallow in her despair, just for a minute, and now was not the time for napkins.

After the bride and groom left the reception, she all but took Evan's arm and frog-marched him from the dance floor, forcing him to take her home. Not that she'd been a fun date anyway, what with disappearing with Keenan and then spending the rest of the night trying not to cry. Finally, she'd bade Evan a fond and celibate farewell and climbed out of his car, ignoring the bewildered hurt in his eyes. Poor guy. It wasn't his fault she was in love with someone else.

Then she'd come up to her small but cozy apartment, taken her shower, and thrown on her T-shirt, Hello Kitty boxers, and matching fluffy slippers, all of which were childish but comfortable as a cloud lined in satin. When a girl was nursing a broken heart, it was important that she do so in complete comfort.

Thus outfitted and despite the late hour, she'd come straight to the kitchen and eyeballed the cake in a losing battle to have some discipline.

Now here she was, Miss Piggy herself. Not that she cared.

She took another bite of cake.

It was time to face facts with Keenan: they had no chance. Not for lack of trying on her part, God knew, but there was nothing else she could do with a man so determined to be a martyr.

Well, screw him, right? Since he was deep into his Greta Garbo act, wanting to be alone and all, let him cuddle up to Atticus on those cold winter nights. They could keep each other company. That would serve Keenan right, although it hardly seemed fair to the monkey.

Keenan. *Jerk*.

She took another bite of cake.

What she needed to do was quit her job at the firm and find another one somewhere else, where she didn't have to see Keenan. That wasn't healthy, working with the object of her obsession on a daily basis. A change would be good for her. In fact, maybe she needed a whole new city. Boston was great, but she'd also enjoyed the time she spent in Atlanta, and—

She paused, listening.

What the hell?

Was that someone knocking at her door? At this hour?

Putting the cake on the counter, she padded through the foyer and peered out the peephole.

And saw the top of Keenan's head, with Atticus perched on his shoulder.

Oh, God.

Her pulse went haywire. After swiping her hand over the back of her mouth and then running her fingers through her messy hair, she gave up on any remedial measures to improve her appearance. That train had already left the station the second she'd put on the Hello Kitty jammies.

She swung the door open. "Hi."

"Hi," Keenan said.

Atticus, now relieved of his bow tie, waved and chirped a hello.

"Hi, Atticus," she said, scratching his head.

The pleasantries dispensed with, she focused on Keenan, who seemed somehow sharper than he'd been earlier, almost as though he hummed with a quiet energy he hadn't had before. He'd changed, too, and now wore a T-shirt and dark track pants.

"What are you doing here? Why didn't my doorman tell me you were coming?"

He shrugged. "I think he went to the bathroom or something. I waited until someone else came out and I slipped in."

"Diabolical," she muttered. "I'm going to have him fired first thing in the morning."

Keenan gave her that new look again, the one that was so darkly indiscernible it was like staring into the heart of a black hole. "Take it easy on the poor guy. I really wanted to talk to you. Can I come in?"

"Umm . . ."

Having just decided that Keenan was out of her life and she'd be better off moving to San Francisco or some such, it wasn't a good idea to let him in so he could give her any more mixed signals. Unfortunately, he didn't seem too interested in her answer. Without waiting for her to move aside, he rolled forward with a couple of quick swipes at his wheels, and before she knew what'd happened, he was settled in her softly lit living room, right next to the sofa.

O-kay.

Shutting the door, she followed him.

Atticus, meanwhile, was going nuts. He'd spotted Scout in the crate and was chattering wildly, pulling on his blue leash and wanting to greet this new furry creature. Scout raised her head off the pillow and showed her excitement by making the most wildly enthusiastic gesture she was capable of: she raised her eyebrows and sniffed the air.

"Do you mind . . . ?" Keenan asked.

"Ah . . . no," Diana said, with no real idea what they were talking about.

But Keenan unhooked the leash, and Atticus, needing no further encouragement, jumped down and scampered across the floor to the wire crate. Which he opened. Before Diana could think to splutter a protest, he'd clanged the door shut again and headed straight for the food dish, helping himself to some kibble.

Scout, looking beleaguered, watched and tried to sniff Atticus's diapered butt.

Keenan grinned. "Looks like they're going to be friends."

Diana had no interest in pets at the moment. "What're you doing here?"

He gestured to the sofa. "Can you sit down with me? Please?"

A husky new note in his voice did delicious things to the pit of her belly, or maybe it was the way his appreciative gaze traveled over her body in a lingering sweep.

Whatever. She sat.

He eased closer, bringing all that masculine intensity with him, along with the fresh scent of soap and deodorant, as though he'd just showered. Diana tried to be brisk and unaffected, to look him straight in the eye with a cool gaze that couldn't be ruffled, but that was about as successful as pretending not to notice while a solar eclipse occurred overhead.

Keenan dove in without preamble. "I screwed up earlier."

"You did?"

"Yeah. I kept thinking how I'd've handled our situation if I wasn't in the wheelchair, but that's stupid."

"It is?"

"Yeah. Because inside, where it counts, I'm the same guy. That's what was throwing me off."

Diana hated to be dense, but she felt like she should ask. God forbid she hear something in this conversation that wasn't really there. Her hopes had already been smashed and pulverized enough for one night, thanks. "What are you saying?"

"I'm saying—can we try this again?"

No. No, they could not try this again. They'd been over this ground several times before, each time leaving her bruised and battered, and there was nothing more to say. She had half a slice of cake to finish eating, and then, when she was done with that, she was going to Google "Seattle" and "Phoenix" and see which city was hiring more architects. Then she was going to type up her letter of resignation.

No. The answer was no.

"Sure," she said.

He grinned, subjecting her to a potent combination of devastating man and boyish dimples, and she realized, for the first time, how tense he'd been. She was marveling over the thrill of having such power over a man like this, when his smile faded, leaving only naked heat.

Taking her hand, he held it in his warm grip.

"Hi," he said again.

Breathless, she opened her dry mouth. And tried to speak. And tried again.

Finally, on the third attempt, she managed it.

"Hi."

He lowered her hand to his lap and turned it over, palm up. And then he used his damaged fingers to trace a path from palm to wrist and back again, over and over again, that had her skin shivering and a deep ache developing high up, between her thighs. When she'd begun to squirm in her seat, he looked up at her, his eyes a glittering flash of brown crystal.

"I'm in love with you," he told her, his voice a seduction in itself. "Did you know that?"

At the moment, she didn't know anything, not even her name. "No," she breathed.

"Hmm." Looking down again, he took her hand and raised it to his mouth. With a gasp, she traced the bow of his top lip and the plump curve of his bottom lip, enjoying all of his tender textures, until . . .

He sucked her first two fingers into his mouth, hard.

"Oh, God," she said, and the ache between her thighs became a clenching need.

In no particular hurry, he pulled her fingers out, scraping them gently against his teeth and working them with his tongue, the suction hot, wet, and so arousing she nearly came from it.

"I want you," he said when his mouth was free again.

That gaze flickered up to her again. Hot. Primitive. Undeniable.

"I want you, too."

"I'm not seeing anyone else."

Her lips curved with pleasure, but managing a full smile just now was beyond her. "Good."

"I don't want you seeing Cro-Magnon man or anyone else. Okay?"

"Okay."

One of these days, when he'd satisfied the raging need in her body and cooled her hot blood, and she was able to regain her senses—in, say, ten years or so—she really meant to tell him not to speak to her this way, with his pronouncements and directives. Grown women like her didn't need a man bossing them around, and she needed to nip this bad habit in the bud. Someone was acting like a caveman, true, but it wasn't Evan.

But . . .

Until then, she'd let him claim her all he wanted.

And she'd claim him.

"Let's go," he said. "Which way to your bedroom?"

She got to her feet. "This way, but—what about them?"

They both looked around at Atticus and Scout, neither of whom seemed to need supervision at the moment. Atticus was lifting the dog's ears, presumably inspecting for fleas, and Scout had her snout back on her paws, submitting but staring at the monkey with her mournful brown eyes. Every time Atticus's frenetic movements brought him close enough, Scout would swipe at him with her great tongue, trying to get him clean.

The mutual grooming could go on for a while, which was good.

Diana fully planned to take a while with Keenan. "Let's go."

She led him down the hall. The lamp next to her big sleigh bed was lit and, knowing how Keenan felt about his body, she turned it off. The last thing she wanted to do was make him self-conscious, and—

"Hey. Turn that back on. I want to see you."

"But . . ." Diana hesitated, her hand still hovering near the lamp. "I thought—"

"And I want you to see me."

Well. She turned the light back on.

Now wasn't the time to get shy, but she did have a flaw or two and she couldn't stop herself from flushing furiously. Plus, he meant so much to her, and she didn't want to make some blundering mistake that would spoil the moment. And she fully intended this to be the last first time she ever made love with anyone in her life.

Staring into his brown eyes, watching as he heaved himself out of his chair and onto the bed, where he propped himself against the many pillows, she let instinct take over. All they needed to do was touch each other. The rest would take care of itself.

"Come here," he said.

She went, climbing up and straddling his legs, settling on her knees. Moving together, they lifted the bottom of his T-shirt and pulled it off over his head, and there he was. A sculptor's dream, heavily muscled with the kinds of chiseled ridges and curves that those health magazines purported to help men achieve. Over that was a layer of the smoothest brown skin that she could ever hope to see.

"Oh," she said, because she couldn't look at him and be eloquent at the same time.

Cupping her face, he pulled her down, closer, and then they were kissing with all the heat and hunger they'd had earlier, nipping and sucking, as though there'd been no interruption at all. The most wonderful rumbling noises vibrated in his chest, humming through both of them, and it was like the animal in him was gathering strength, preparing to break free.

The animal in her had already gone wild. It wasn't enough to kiss his mouth. She had to run her tongue down the strong column of his neck, tasting the faint saltiness of his skin, nuzzling his collarbones, suckling first one flat nipple, and then the other. The whole time, he ran his hands over her back and shoulders, touching everything he could reach.

"Where is your spot?" she whispered.

Keenan went utterly still and watched her with narrowed eyes, as though he didn't trust his ears. *"What?"*

"Your spot. I've done a lot of research, and I know that a lot of people with spinal cord injuries have one hypersensitive spot that's really—"

"*Here*." He indicated the back of his neck, at his nape. "Right here."

Easing him forward a little, so eager she shook with it, she ran her tongue around the smooth column, until she got to that spot. Then she latched on and sucked.

Keenan cried out and jerked away. She was afraid she'd hurt him—until she saw the awe in his expression, the naked heat.

A pregnant moment passed, with only their panting to break the silence. He recovered first. Running his stiff hands down the sides of her breasts, he squeezed them together. She moaned and dropped her head back, ready to do anything and everything for him.

"Take this off," he said, fumbling with her T-shirt.

She couldn't sweep it off fast enough, tossing it to the floor in a flash of pink and trying to make a joke because this moment was strained to the breaking point with meaning and she wasn't sure she could handle the climbing tension.

"Don't you like Hello Kitty?"

"I like it just fine. On the floor."

She started to laugh, but the noise died in her throat when he scooted lower, just a little, and caught one of her nipples in his mouth.

Ah . . . his mouth. The things he did—*God, what was he doing?*

Stroking and sucking with his tongue, scraping the nipple with his teeth—just *there*, with just enough pressure to make her writhe and cry. And then he shifted and she was tumbling to the bed beneath him. He loomed over her, bracing on his arms and blocking out the light . . . the bedroom . . . everything that wasn't him.

His mouth didn't miss a single inch of her torso. He savored it all, licking and nuzzling lower, dipping into her belly button and making her hips jackknife off the bed, until—

"Take these off for me," he said.

Her mind spun because this was the real Keenan, the one she'd always known was there, commanding and confident, and he stole her breath. Somehow she'd known he'd be like this, if she could only get past his armor.

Hooking her thumbs under her waistband, she shimmied out of her shorts and panties while he watched, riveted. When she was naked, she propped herself up on her elbows, waiting to see what he wanted from her now, but all he wanted was to look.

"God," he said. "You're beautiful."

"So are—ahhh—"

"And your smell. What're you trying to do to me?"

He wedged those wide shoulders between her knees, spreading her wide, and then his mouth was on her, right where she needed it most, and everything else went dark and silent.

The pleasure grew, notching higher and settling into a delicious pulsing knot, until finally the waves broke over her, so piercing and delicious she couldn't have stifled her cries if she'd tried.

Keenan. God, *Keenan*.

The ripples were beginning to fade and her head to clear, when Keenan shifted again, so that she was on top. It took a minute to refocus her vision and take in the breathtaking sight of him beneath her, hers for the taking. Now it was her turn to give pleasure, and his to receive.

Flicking her gaze up to his, she curled her lips in a wicked smile and felt his heart thunder when she put her hands on his chest.

Oh, yeah.

"Let's take these off." She slid her hands low on his taut belly, underneath the elastic of his track pants, and felt his upper body stiffen. But they'd come too far to let doubts overwhelm them, no matter what happened from here, and she wasn't about to turn back now.

So she tugged the pants and black briefs down, past his erection and thin hips, all the way to his atrophied thighs and wasted legs. Sudden tears burned her eyes, even though she'd thought she was braced and ready for this moment. She wasn't. To see the ruined parts of this vital man's body hit her hard, right in the gut, and she needed a minute to catch her breath.

But . . .

Keenan was watching, waiting for her reaction; she could feel his new stillness.

Anyway, she loved all of him. Had waited years to physically love him.

So she raised her head and smiled to reassure him, stroking the outsides of his long legs even though he couldn't feel her touch. "I love you."

Levering himself up on his elbows, he blinked furiously, trying to speak. "Diana."

"Shhh," she said.

She didn't need to hear it, whatever it was. Everything he felt was written all over his face.

Exhaling a huge breath that made his lungs heave, he smiled back, just a little, and that was all she needed. Lowering her head, she took him into her mouth.

He groaned, clamping his hands in her hair, anchoring her, and she worked over him, her head bobbing, until her mouth and tongue were tired and his breath raspy.

"Now," he said. *"Now."*

Pausing only to grab and open the condom he'd laid on the nightstand, she rolled it on him, working quickly. And then she slid up and over him as he eased onto his back, and angling her hips and taking him in her hand, she sank down until he was buried deep inside her.

Ahhh . . . God.

Leaning back and thrusting her breasts into his palms, she let the pleasure wash over her again. Nothing had ever felt this good, or ever would again; she had been born to accomplish this single thing on earth: making love with Keenan.

After a moment's adjustment for both of them, his breath hissed and he gripped her hips, encouraging her to move. She did. Faster when she wanted fast, slower when her hips and thighs got tired. Judging from his earthy sounds of encouragement, it was all good to him.

He couldn't move with her, and it didn't matter. Not even a little.

Only that point where he joined her body mattered, and the excruciating friction.

The contractions began again in her belly and crested over her, so rhythmic and powerful the breath died in her throat and her cries were silenced. She collapsed over him, gasping, and he caught one of her dangling nipples in his mouth, pulling hard. She pumped her hips again—once . . . twice . . . and then he said, *"Diana,"* and his neck arched back, into the pillow, and he shuddered beneath her.

Exhausted, sated, she buried her face in the sinewy hollow between his neck and shoulder, and sank into absolute, joyous oblivion.

Maybe she slept; there was no way to know for sure. When she raised her head again, it was to see that the shadows had shifted across the walls and the night had deepened. Turning slowly, trying to be careful not to wake him if he was asleep, she looked to Keenan.

He lay on his back, staring at the ceiling, lost in thoughts she couldn't begin to imagine. As she watched, a single bright tear trickled from the outer corner of his eye, down his temple, and onto the white pillowcase.

Oh, no.

Had she hurt him or done something wrong? Was he disappointed?

She tensed, just a little, a half-formed apology on her lips. He looked around at her, and their gazes connected.

He smiled then, a glorious smile of such hope and happiness that he was almost a stranger to her—it altered his features that much.

She waited, frozen, not wanting to speak or do anything to ruin *this*.

"Hi." He smoothed her hair out of her face, his touch unbearably gentle.

"Hi."

"You're a miracle," he told her. "You know that?"

"One of us is a miracle, yeah."

His smile widened, then dimmed, and she could feel the warnings coming, and the buildup of disclaimers and *whereases*.

"It may not always go that smoothly. You know that, right? We may have problems—"

Reaching up, she tapped two fingers on his lips, silencing him because she didn't want to hear it. As far as she was concerned, there was only one issue that needed to be addressed.

"Will it always be you here in this bed with me?"

He didn't hesitate, not even for a millisecond. "Yes."

"Good." Easing closer, she moved her fingers aside so she could kiss him again. "Then we haven't got any problems at all."

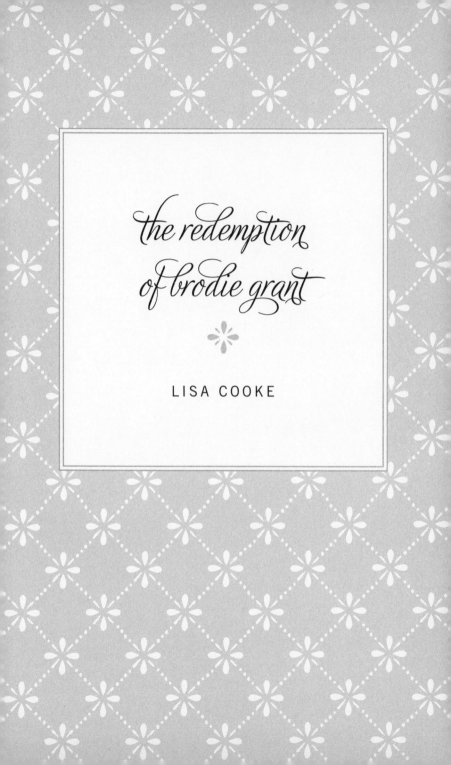

the redemption
of brodie grant

*

LISA COOKE

For Mom and Dad, thanks for always believing I could do it.

one

East Texas, 1886

Whoever said love was blind must have overlooked a few other senses, starting with the sense God gave a goose and ending with the sense to come in out of the rain.

Brodie Grant tapped his fingers against his leg as he watched his kid sister marry a first-rate bastard. Sara claimed she loved Leo Stover, but Brodie had thought their momma had raised her better than that.

"Does anyone have just reason why these two can't be joined together?" the preacher asked, and Brodie held his tongue. He knew at least a thousand reasons, including the fact Leo was a lying son of a bitch. But he stayed quiet. Quiet and fidgety. Quiet and fidgety and pissed and . . .

"I now pronounce you man and wife."

Hell.

His mother squeezed his arm, bringing him back from his general state of pissiness.

"She's so happy," Momma said.

Brodie looked toward the front of the church, where Leo was kissing his sister, and regretted for the thousandth time that he hadn't returned home sooner. Maybe if he had, he could have kept her from marrying a man that clearly wasn't good enough for her.

"You could act happier for her sake," Momma said, and Brodie didn't doubt that for a minute.

"You know how I feel about Leo," he said.

Momma patted his arm. "That was a long time ago, Brodie. Things change."

No doubt about that either. Things had changed in an instant ten years ago when all hell had broken loose, and Brodie had been blamed for it. Now, everyone looked down their noses at him like he was scum. Anger boiled up in his gut again, but his sister's blinding smile calmed it. Damn, if she didn't look happy, hurrying down the aisle on Leo's arm.

"You're staying for the reception, aren't you?" Momma's statement sounded more like instructions than a question.

He sighed. "Yeah, I'll go for Sara's sake, but Leo had better stay the hell away from me."

"Brodie, you're in the house of God," Momma said, tugging him into the aisle. "Watch your language."

Hell, he *had* watched his language.

MAGGIE Stover Walls waited patiently as the guests in the little white church filed into the aisle to leave. Everyone in town had attended her brother's wedding. A marriage between a Stover and a Grant was something to see. There had been bad blood between the families ever since Brodie had burned down the Stover's barn, killing a bull that was worth a fortune. Leo had said he thought it was an accident, but that didn't help things any.

The expensive incident almost cost her family everything they had. It had taken years for her father to save enough to buy the bull, and losing him before he'd sired a single calf had been devastating. Her pa had counted on that bull to produce the best breeding stock in Texas.

Because of Brodie's malicious act, Maggie's family struggled for years to regain their losses. Thank goodness he'd left the area the day after the fire and hadn't returned. Being civil to him after what he did would have taxed every bit of Christian charity she had in her possession.

Standing, she brushed her hands down her bodice and turned to step into the aisle. From her position near the front of the sanctuary, she could see most of the people leaving for the reception, including the back of Sara's mother and the large man escorting her. Maggie paused. A strange sense of familiarity washed through her. Could it be?

Nah, Brodie wasn't nearly that tall and broad when he'd left ten years before. Besides, what were the chances he'd return after what he'd done? She leaned in an attempt to get a better view of the dark-haired man, but all she managed to do was step on Lenore Mills's toes.

"I'm sorry, Mrs. Mills," Maggie said, still straining to see the stranger.

"That's all right, honey. I can't blame you for trying to get a look at Brodie. He's changed quite a bit, hasn't he?"

Maggie hoped her face didn't show the shock she felt. "Are you sure it's Brodie?"

"Yep," Lenore said. "He came home yesterday, just in time for the wedding." Lenore then tipped her gray head toward Maggie and grinned. "He sure grew into a handsome man, didn't he?"

Looks had never been Brodie's problem. Even at nineteen, he'd been fine to look at, and Lord knew, Maggie had done her share of looking. To a twelve-year-old girl, Brodie Grant was just

about perfect . . . until he ruined their lives. She slowed her step
so she wouldn't have to speak to him just yet. Seeing him unex-
pectedly had churned up feelings she'd tried to forget, and she
needed a few moments to regain her composure.

Unfortunately, a few moments were all she had. The reception had been set up in the yard outside the church. Tables with
food and drinks lined one side of the yard, and several chairs and
benches lined the other; the center area had been left clear for
dancing. Maggie glanced around the crowd until her gaze landed
on Brodie. He stood, somber and quiet, leaning against a tree,
watching the crowd as though daring someone to speak to him.

He didn't smile. He didn't interact or attempt to mingle with
the others. He just stood, glaring from beneath the brim of his
Stetson. He hadn't looked at her, not yet, and she was prepared
to look away the second he did, but for now, she couldn't drag
her attention away from him. Shifting his hand to hook on to
the front of his belt, his jacket pulled back enough to expose the
gun strapped low on his hip. What kind of man wore a gun to
his sister's wedding?

Brodie had changed. And not in a good way.

"Maggie?"

Maggie flinched and whipped her head toward her brother.
"Leo," she said, laying her hand against her heart, "you startled me."

Leo frowned and nodded in Brodie's direction. "Have you
talked to him yet?"

Heat crept up Maggie's neck. Her first thought was to ask
who Leo was referring to, but obviously, he'd seen her staring at
Brodie. "No." She patted a tendril of hair back into her chignon.
"I have nothing to say to him."

"Our families are connected now. Holding a grudge against
him doesn't seem to make sense."

Her jaw dropped. "I can't believe you said that. He ruined our lives, Leo."

"Did he?" Leo shrugged. "It was a long time ago, and I think we've done fine. Besides, it was an accident."

"You don't know that for sure. Pa has always said he did it on purpose." She lowered her voice when she realized others could hear. "If it was an accident, why did he leave so quickly?"

"Can you blame him? Pa was looking to kill him." Leo glanced to where his father stood, talking to some of the men before he added softly, "I would have run, too."

Maggie started to argue that their pa wouldn't have killed Brodie, but she wasn't sure that was true. Their father's temper was legendary. He'd never raised a hand to her or her mother, but she'd seen him whip Leo until he couldn't stand just for leaving a gate open. In his furious state the night of the fire, he very well might have killed Brodie.

"But that's all behind us now," Leo said, taking her hand. "It's time to move on."

It took Maggie a second before she realized Leo's intention. She didn't feel like dancing, but Jeff Powell's fiddle was humming, and Leo didn't give her a chance to refuse. Forcing a smile, she allowed him to drag her into a lively square dance—unaware until it was too late that Sara had done the same thing with Brodie.

A barking of calls and the dancers changed partners rapidly, stopping, as luck would have it, when Maggie was in the arms of Brodie Grant. He led her through the moves with little effort and even less enthusiasm until the dance ended. Then he turned toward her, truly looking at her for the first time. The corner of his mouth lifted softly as he raked his gaze across her face, his eyes landing on her lips, which were parted slightly from the exertion of the dance. He watched her mouth far longer than he should have before he turned his attention to her eyes. Deep and dark, hooded by the brim of his hat and something primal, his eyes held her frozen to the spot.

She'd never felt a gaze before, but she felt that one. It fluttered her pulse, warming her more than the dancing had, and for a brief instant, she forgot the last ten years. She forgot the fire, the anger, the hardship. She forgot her husband's death, her mother's illness . . . all of it. For just an instant, she was a twelve-year-old girl with a wild crush on her brother's best friend, longing for a kiss she'd never gotten.

Then he ruined it.

"I'm Brodie Grant," he said.

The turd didn't even remember her.

BRODIE hobbled back to the tree, trying to figure out why the pretty little brunette had kicked him in the shin. He hadn't stepped on her toes or insulted her. Hell, he hadn't even looked at her until the dance ended. Maybe that was why she was mad. Maybe she didn't like being ignored. Under normal circumstances, he wouldn't have ignored her, but he'd been dragged into the dance by his sister, and it had taken a few minutes before he'd loosened up enough to look at his dance partner.

Cheeks pink, curls brushing her face, her lips parted and looking like they needed kissing . . . it had taken all his willpower not to taste her mouth. But he hadn't because he didn't know her *and* they were in the middle of a crowd; otherwise, not knowing her probably wouldn't have made a difference. Luckily, he'd refrained from stealing a kiss. If she kicked men just for introducing themselves, she probably would have gutted him for kissing her.

He fought the urge to rub the knot on his shin as his mother walked over to talk to him. "Why did Maggie kick you?" she asked, handing him a cup of cider.

So, the woman's name was Maggie. "Haven't a clue." He took

a long drink of cider, all the while eyeing Maggie as she talked to a group of friends near one of the tables.

"I thought maybe you said something about Leo."

"Why would she care—" He stopped. Couldn't be. "Maggie *Stover*?"

"Who'd you think I meant?"

Slowly, Brodie returned his attention to the curvy, shin-kicking woman standing by the cookies. That couldn't be Maggie Stover. The Maggie Stover he knew was a skinny, freckle-faced tomboy, who wore boy's britches, rode bareback . . . and would have kicked him in the shin in a heartbeat.

"Holy hell," he muttered.

"You didn't recognize her?"

"She didn't look like that the last time I saw her." A quick calculation put Maggie at about twenty-two years of age. "Is she married? I don't see a husband hanging around."

"She was for a short time, but her husband was killed a couple of years ago by a rattlesnake. She's Maggie Walls now." Momma looked up at him, a little twinkle in her eye. "She grew up to be right pretty, didn't she?"

He had to agree, not that it mattered. Maggie could've been the prettiest woman in East Texas, and she still would've been off-limits. Leo's kid sister would hate him like the rest of the Stovers did, and if there was one thing Brodie had learned through the years, it was that it was a waste of time to try to convince people of something they didn't want to hear.

"Oh, there's Louise Thompson," his mom said. "I need to ask her something." She hurried toward Louise, leaving him alone under the tree, but he barely noticed. His attention was riveted on Leo's father, John. The big man was headed Brodie's way, and based on his expression, it wasn't to welcome him home.

"You got a lot of nerve to show up here after what you done." John Stover never was one to mince words.

Brodie forced his jaw to unclench before he turned his head slowly to look Leo's father in the eye. At one time, John Stover struck the fear of God in Brodie, but that time was long gone. Ten years as a scout had Brodie's hide tough enough to take anything the man wanted to dish out. "My ma needs me to help at the ranch."

"Then, you're staying?" Stover said as though he couldn't believe Brodie's audacity.

"Yeah," Brodie answered. "I'm staying."

A red stain crept up Stover's throat as he stepped closer to Brodie and lowered his voice. "Stay the hell away from me and mine. You and I both know what you did that night." He pointed his finger at Brodie's face. "You killed my bull so my stock wouldn't compete with your father's, and someday you're going to pay for that."

Stover spun away and stormed off before Brodie had a chance to answer—not that it would have made any difference. Brodie's pa had raised breeding stock for years, mostly so he wouldn't have to work a large herd of beef cattle. But Stover didn't understand enough about breeding to be successful at that game, and a man like him found it easier to blame others for his failures than to accept the blame for himself.

He regretted again that he hadn't stayed to defend himself that night, but as a nineteen-year-old kid, it never dawned on him to defy his parents. They'd insisted he leave the area so he did, no questions asked.

Shifting his stance, he darted a glimpse across the crowd and caught Maggie glimpsing back. She froze, and he couldn't help but wink at her, despite the warning from her pa. The pink blush to her cheeks pleased him more than it should.

John Stover be damned.

two

✳

Nothing cleared Maggie's head more than climbing onto her horse's back and heading across the open range. And in the two weeks since Brodie had returned, her head had needed a lot of clearing. She'd been widowed for nearly two years, and even though she couldn't say she'd loved Dave, she'd respected him, and for most women, that would have been enough. A good, levelheaded man was all she'd wanted, or at least, all she'd thought she wanted. So why did Brodie's sudden return have her twisted in knots? Why did her heart pitter pat every time he came near, and moreover, why did he keep winking at her?

She'd seen him only a handful of times since the wedding and there'd been enough people around that they didn't actually speak to one another, but whenever she'd caught his eye, he'd given her a wink that spoke volumes. Steamy, suggestive volumes that were improper at best and downright scandalous at worst.

And she couldn't stop thinking about them.

Maybe she should have kicked him a little higher.

"Drat," she muttered.

She'd come all this way so she wouldn't think about Brodie, and all she was thinking about was Brodie, which was not safe considering her location. As a child, she'd gotten into trouble more than once for riding alone to this part of her father's ranch. Located hours from the main house, the deep canyon had the ability to turn into a death trap in an instant when storms hit and flash flood waters rushed. But it was beautiful with its large boulders and bubbling stream, and once she'd noticed how close she'd ridden, she couldn't help but enter the canyon before returning home.

She glanced toward the heavens, frowning slightly as she realized how late it had gotten. If she left now, she should be able to make it back to the house before nightfall.

"Come on, Clyde," she said, turning the horse to guide him out of the ravine.

A blast from his nostrils and an immediate twitch of his ears heightened her awareness, but not quickly enough for her to stay on his back when the hiss of a snake's rattle sent her to the ground and the horse bolted from the canyon without her.

WIPING his brow with the back of his hand, Brodie took a moment to watch the clouds forming in the east as he leaned against a fencepost for a quick rest. The morning was already muggier than usual, even for August, and the air felt thick and ominous. He'd been repairing fence since dawn, and in the three hours since then, he'd made a lot of headway, but there were still miles more to go.

He pulled his pliers from his hip pocket and returned his attention to the broken barbed wire, wondering if the clouds would bring rain to help ease the drought. If they didn't, he feared the herd would pay the price.

"Brodie!"

He lifted his head to see his sister riding toward him, her horse stirring up swirls of dust as it loped in his direction.

"Something wrong?" he shouted, but his gut already told him something was definitely wrong.

She pulled her horse to a stop, talking without dismounting. "We need your help. Maggie is missing."

"Missing?"

"She rode out yesterday morning and didn't come back. John and Leo left to look for her yesterday evening, and they haven't returned."

"I'm sure they'll find her. Maggie knows how to take care of herself."

"We found her horse standing in the barn this morning. He came back without her."

That didn't sound good. "Was he hurt?"

Sara shook her head. "He was fine, but there was no sign of Maggie."

Damn, that didn't sound good at all. He removed his gloves and tucked them into his hip pocket. "John and Leo wouldn't want my help."

"Do you care what John and Leo would want? Maggie is out there and is probably hurt. You've been a tracker for the last ten years, right? If anyone can find her, you can."

He couldn't argue that, not that he wanted to. The thought of Maggie being lost and possibly hurt made his stomach drop. He headed for his horse.

"Do you need to go back to the house for provisions?" she asked.

"Nope." He swung into the saddle. "I'd planned to be riding fence for a few days when I left this morning. I've got provisions. Do you have any idea which direction she might have headed?"

"No," Sara said, pulling her horse beside his as they left the fence row.

"I'm going to have to start at the barn and follow her horse's tracks back to her."

They rode in silence for a few moments before Sara said, "Brodie? Do you think you can find her?"

"Yeah, I'll find her." he said, eyeing the darkening sky one more time. Rain played havoc with tracks, but after all these weeks of drought, what were the chances of it raining now?

MAGGIE gripped the side of the rock canyon to pull herself to her feet once more, but the rock was slick from the rain and her swollen ankle still too tender to allow her to do anything other than hop to another boulder to sit. Her belly grumbled. She'd been gone for more than twenty-four hours. By now, there was no doubt a search party would be looking for her, but she needed to get out of the canyon so they could find her.

Panting, she took a moment to study her surroundings. The rain had been increasing in intensity for the past hour, and based on the darkening clouds, it was nowhere near letting up. On the other side of the stream, a large rock overhang jutted from the canyon wall, providing a cave-like area protected from the strengthening storm. But more importantly, it was well above the rapidly rising stream.

The tops of a few boulders still poked out from the frothy water, allowing some slippery stepping stones to the other side. She weighed her options. If she attempted to cross to the cave, chances were high that she'd fall into the water. But if she stayed where she was, the flood waters would overtake her within the hour. At least she'd worn trousers when she'd headed out for her ride. Crossing the stream in wet skirts would have been impossible.

Taking a deep breath to help calm her stomach, she stepped to the first rock then paused to adjust her weight. The second boulder was a few feet farther away and would require that she jump, a task she normally could do with her eyes shut, but slick rocks and a swollen ankle complicated the situation. She took another deep breath. Focusing on the rock and praying with the zeal of a Methodist, she swung her arms to give her momentum and leaped.

Pain shot through her ankle as she landed, but a quick adjustment shifted her weight to her other foot. She teetered for a moment, concentrating on two rocks ahead of her. The closest had a rounded top, not nearly large enough for her to use, but the flattest one was farther away and partially submerged.

Her ankle throbbed. Her hair stuck to her face in soggy tendrils and the rain had soaked through to her skin, but the roar of the rising water kept her from focusing on her discomfort. If she didn't make it to the other side, she would likely die in this canyon.

She shook her head to clear away those thoughts. Death was not an option. Bending her knees, she swung her arms and lunged toward the boulder. She landed with a jolt. The pain searing from her ankle caused her leg to collapse.

"No!" she yelled in frustration, grabbing wildly for a handhold as she plunged into the rushing waters, the currents quickly sucking her under. She fought for the surface, gasping for air when her flailing arms managed to grab a tree limb caught among the rocks. Pulling her body into the limb, she wove her arms through the branches as the cold water surged against her.

She didn't want to die, not here, not like this. But the storm was nowhere near over, and soon the stream would overtake her. Squeezing her eyes shut, she prayed for a miracle.

"Maggie!"

Her eyes flew open. She turned her head toward the voice. Brodie was on the bank, sitting on his horse and swinging a lasso over his head. "Hang on!" he shouted, as though she had any other options.

She started to respond but gasped instead as her branch shifted in the water. "Hurry!" she yelled.

He threw the rope, but it landed in the water too far away for her to grab. Quickly, he pulled the lasso back to him for another attempt. Heavy now from the water, the next throw missed her as well, though luckily, it managed to grab on to one of the branches. Brodie tied the rope to his saddle horn.

"Step back," he said to his horse. The mare stepped back, tightening the tension in the rope like she'd been trained to do for roping calves. "Whoa." He stopped her then dismounted and hurried to the edge of the stream.

He cupped his hands to yell above the howl of the water. "Can you reach the rope?"

Maggie shook her head. "The water is too strong!"

Brodie ripped off his jacket, hat, and gun belt, tossing them over the saddle while Maggie attempted to move closer to him, but the current penned her to the spot. Brodie held on to the rope, maneuvering his way across boulders and rocks until he had no choice but to jump into the water. He grabbed the branch and pulled up to her, wrapping his arm around her waist to help her as they inched back toward the rope.

Suddenly, the branch snapped. Brodie grabbed for the line, barely snagging the end of a twig still tangled with the rope as the larger limb rocked in the water. Brodie twisted the rope around his arm and tightened his hold on Maggie's waist.

"Step back," he yelled. A boom of thunder startled the horse, causing her to sidestep and throw her head.

"Whoa," Brodie said, his voice calming the animal before he repeated his command. "Step back."

With a snort of agitation, the horse backed away from the stream, pulling Brodie and Maggie close enough to gain their footing and crawl from the waters. They collapsed on the bank, panting for breath.

"Thank you," she finally managed to mutter.

Brodie pulled himself to his knees then sat back on his haunches. "Don't thank me yet." He wiped the water from his face. "We still have to get out of here. Are you hurt?"

"I twisted my ankle when I fell from my horse." She pointed to the cave above them. "I was trying to get to that cave for shelter when I fell into the stream."

Brodie looked up at the cave and nodded. "Probably not a bad idea to wait the storm out there—" He stopped abruptly, frowning as he turned his head to listen to a distant noise. "Do you hear that?"

Maggie sat up and listened. The roar upstream was unmistakable. "Flash flood."

"Come on!" Brodie pulled her to her feet, wrapping his arm around her waist to scurry up the bank.

He lifted her to his horse's back, pitching Maggie the reins. With a quick swat to the horse's rump, Brodie sent Maggie and the mare scrambling up the hillside. Maggie allowed the mare to choose her path across the slippery stones and muddy ruts, knowing she'd do a better job at finding her way than Maggie could.

"Brodie," Maggie yelled, unable to turn around. "Are you behind me?"

"Yeah!" he yelled back.

She shifted her weight forward, leaning over the mare's shoulders to make her ascent easier. They'd barely made it inside the mouth of the cave when a wall of water crashed through the canyon below.

"Holy hell," Brodie said, stepping up beside her to watch the waters surge past.

Maggie didn't say anything, but her stomach dropped as she watched the limb she'd clung to wash free of the boulders and tumble out of sight. Had Brodie not come when he had, she would be dead right now. A chill ran down her spine.

She pulled her attention away from her would-be watery grave to the cave that was now her refuge. The opening of the overhang was at least twenty feet wide and fifteen feet tall. It reached into the side of the hill another twenty feet or so, providing a dry place to wait out the storm for them and the horse. The cave was dry, though she couldn't say the same thing for herself. Now that the excitement was over, her wet clothes felt like ice against her skin.

"Are you hungry?" Brodie asked as he helped her from the saddle and over to sit on a rock.

Rubbing her arms in an attempt to warm them, she forced a smile and said, "Starving."

"I thought you might be." He pulled the saddle from his horse and dug through his saddlebag. "I've got some beans, but we'll have to eat them cold. I don't think I'm going to be able to find any dry firewood around here."

"Right now, I think I could eat them can and all."

He smiled, handing her a now opened can with a spoon stuck in the beans. "You won't have to do that, but you are going to have to eat them from the can. I don't have any plates."

She reached for the can, but instead of releasing it, he paused for a moment as her fingers lay against his on the side of the can. His gaze locked on to hers, making it impossible to look away. His whiskey-colored eyes had always fascinated her, but now there was a depth to them that had been missing in his youth, a smoky intensity that made her temporarily forget about beans as he searched her face.

"Are you sure you're all right?" he asked, brushing a strand of wet hair away from her cheek.

She swallowed and nodded. Neither said anything for a moment longer, until he finally glanced away from her and mumbled, "That's good." Then he quickly returned to the other side of the cave to dig through his saddlebags for more beans.

The sight of him down on one knee as he opened another can thwarted her attempt to focus on the beans. Wet clothing clung to him, outlining his muscles as he moved. Broad shoulders, narrow hips, thighs bulging against the fabric of his trousers . . .

She jerked her attention back to the beans. She had no business thinking about Brodie's thighs or hips or any other part of him that looked as hard as the canyon walls. Hard and slick and . . .

Beans.

She shoveled in another spoonful, proud of her ability to divert such lustful thoughts with something as simple as beans. They weren't exactly what she would call tasty, but they were filling her belly and getting her mind away from scandalous thoughts that served no purpose. At the moment, beans were the center of her universe, the goal of her existence, and the purpose of her being.

"Are you finished?" he asked.

"Yes," she said, pleased that the last bite of the infernal beans squelched her errant thoughts once and for all.

"Good," he said, unbuttoning his shirt, "because you need to take off your clothes."

three

✳

"I—I beg your pardon?" Not a brilliant response, but it was
the best Maggie could do under the circumstances.

Brodie removed his shirt. "I only have two blankets. If we
wrap those around our wet clothes, they'll be soaked in no time
and then we'll have nothing dry to wear," he said . . . or at least
that's what she thought he said. It was difficult to focus on his
words when his hands were unbuckling his belt and the muscles
that had teased her from beneath the wet shirt were now on flagrant display.

"Maggie?"

Merciful heavens, he'd caught her staring at his flagrant display. "I . . . um . . . I'm not cold." Her declaration probably
would have been more believable if she hadn't shivered from her
nose to her toes at the end of it.

Shaking his head, he returned to his saddle to untie the bedroll. With a quick flip of his hands, the blankets unrolled. He
returned to Maggie, handing her one of the blankets, and said,

"I'll turn my back," which he did, returning to his blanket and the task of removing his wet clothing.

Her cold and trembling fingers attempted to work the wet fabric of her blouse over the buttons while her eyes glued themselves to his every move, as a precaution, of course. She had to be at the ready in case he turned around to catch a glimpse of her. But true to his word, he kept his back to her as he pulled off his boots, setting them to the side . . . and then he dropped his britches.

Thankfully, Maggie's gasp was quiet enough that he didn't hear it. Long, sleek, powerful . . . her husband had not looked like that. She squeezed her eyes shut, but it was too late. The image of him standing as naked as a babe was burned into her mind, probably forever.

"Are you done?"

She opened her eyes. Brodie stood with his back to her, the blanket wrapped around his waist and his hands resting on his hips.

She swallowed. "No. I'm having trouble with the buttons. I guess my fingers are colder than I realized."

"Want some help?"

She didn't want his help, but she needed it. Her boots were going to have to come off before she removed her trousers, and with numb fingers and a swollen ankle, she could not manage that alone. "I'm afraid so. I don't think I can get my boots off."

He turned toward her, running his hand back through his wet hair, which returned to its original place as though he hadn't touched it. As a young woman, she had dreamed of threading her fingers through his hair, cradling his head as he kissed her.

Whoa! Those thoughts had to stop. This was the man who had maliciously set fire to their barn, destroying a priceless bull and their future all in one night. How could she have forgotten that? It didn't matter that as a child she'd imagined herself in love with him. It didn't matter that he'd grown into the most handsome man she'd ever seen. It didn't matter that he was now kneeling in front of her with his well-muscled thigh jutting from the gap in his blanket.

He lifted her foot to place it on his muscled thigh. "This is the sore one, right?"

She nodded, unable to speak. Evidently, muscled thighs had that effect on her.

"Stop me if this hurts." He loosened the soggy lacings and gently pulled the boot from her foot. She winced when he rolled the drenched sock down her ankle and laid her bare foot against his thigh.

"Do you think it's broken?" she asked in an attempt to get her mind away from the feel of his warm skin against her foot.

"I don't know, but you'd better keep your weight off of it either way." He removed the other boot more quickly then looked up at her. "You really need to get those clothes off. Your skin is like ice."

She knew that was true, but when she attempted to unbutton her blouse, her stiff fingers couldn't force the button through the wet fabric no matter how hard she tried.

"Let me help." Brodie reached for the button, but she stopped him by clutching the button in her palm.

"I don't think that would be appropriate, do you?"

He pulled his hand back and sighed. "Maggie, I'm not going to hurt you. You were like a kid sister to me. Now, let me help you, or you're going to get sick."

Maggie hesitated for a moment, weighing his words, before she dropped her hand to allow him to help. He should have been relieved that she'd finally given in, but at the moment, relief was the last thing he felt. A dry, fully clothed Maggie was tempting enough. This wet, partially naked one was killing him.

She'd watched him undress. He had felt her gaze and heard the tiny gasp when he'd dropped his pants. A gentleman would have wrapped the blanket around his waist before he'd done that, but gentlemen led boring lives. A gentleman also would have warmed her hands in his until she could finish undressing without assistance.

He unbuttoned her blouse.

Would a gentleman close his eyes? If so, he would miss the white chemise peeking from beneath the blue chambray and the rounded tops of her breasts just below his fingers.

Thank God he wasn't a gentleman.

"I can manage from here," she said.

Damn.

"How about your belt buckle?"

"Oh." She looked down at her waist. "I might need help with that."

He lifted her to her feet, steadying her until she could balance herself without putting weight on her swollen ankle. Then he turned his attention to pulling the wet leather of her belt through the buckle.

She watched his hands tug on the belt.

He watched her breasts rise and fall with each breath she took.

By his estimation, he had a much better view.

"Thanks," she muttered, and he realized that sometime during the rising and falling of those breasts, he had finished unbuckling her belt.

"Do you want me to help get your pants unfastened?"

"No. I think I can manage."

He paused for a moment, not wanting to step away from her but knowing he had to. It would be easier if she wasn't looking up at him with doe-eyed wonder, her lips parted slightly and a drop of water trickling down her jaw. He brushed the droplet away just as a gust of wind and a loud clap of thunder brought his mind back from the thoughts of ravishing the wet woman in front of him.

"It seems to be getting worse," she said, and he wasn't sure if she was referring to the storm outside or the one brewing in him.

Step away, Brodie. She no doubt blames you for ruining their lives. You don't need that or her.

He brushed his hair back from his face then gestured toward the opposite side of the cave. "I'll be over here if you need me." As if there was anyplace else he could be.

Damn, he was turning into an idiot. He returned to his side of the cave, keeping his back to her while she removed the rest of her clothing, but the sounds of rustling fabric painted erotic pictures in his mind. Firm white breasts, nipples puckered from the cold, long lean legs leading to rounded hips and . . . hell. This wasn't helping anything.

"Are you finished?" His tone sounded a little harsh, even to *his* ears.

"Yes."

A deep breath and a personal reminder of who she was helped calm his body. Then, he turned around. She'd removed her clothes, laying them across the boulder to dry. Blouse, pants, chemise, socks . . . chemise . . . chemise. Hell. She'd removed everything. He'd told her to, but she'd never listened to him a single time when she was a kid. Why did she have to start now?

He returned to her and asked, "Are you warm?" Another stupid question. Women with blue lips were rarely warm.

Maggie swallowed, suddenly uncomfortable with his proximity. She wasn't sure if her shivers were because of the cold or because of Brodie. He stood just in front of her, and the only things separating them were a couple of wool blankets.

"I'm warmer," she said, but she could tell by his expression he didn't believe her. She pulled her blanket tighter around her shoulders, painfully aware that it stopped just below her knees, leaving her calves and feet bare.

"We would be warmer if we sat beside each other," he said.

He was right, of course. It was highly improper and would be dangerous if it were any other man, but Brodie had said she was like a sister to him. Luckily, he had no idea her thoughts were far from sisterly. She nodded and allowed him to help her to a dry spot where the boulder lay against the wall of the overhang. The huge rock blocked the wind that occasionally whipped into the cave.

She settled against the rock and adjusted her blanket while Brodie dropped down beside her and did the same. The cave to her left, Brodie to her right, she truly was between a rock and a hard place.

"Why are you smiling?" he asked.

She couldn't very well tell him she was thinking about how hard his body was, so she said, "I'm just glad you found me."

Folding his arms across his chest, he leaned his head against the bolder and said, "Me, too. I'd lost your horse's tracks about a mile away from the canyon, but once I made it that far, I knew you'd be here. You always loved this place as a kid."

He remembered. She hadn't even been aware that he knew she loved the canyon. Not only had he known, but he remembered. That thought pleased her for some ridiculous reason. "It's a big canyon. How did you find me in the stream?"

"I didn't at first. I was just about to leave when I heard you yell."

"I yelled?"

He chuckled and turned to face her. "Yeah, you yelled 'no.'"

She vaguely remembered yelling. Too many other memories were vying for her attention. Like the fact his lower lip was slightly fuller than his upper, and that when he grinned, his mouth turned up a little more on the left side than the right. She remembered his scent, the rumble of his voice, and the flecks of gold in his eyes. She remembered the barbed wire fence that had given him the small scar on his chin.

Still grinning, he said, "Do you remember the time I found you when you'd run off after getting mad at Leo? You'd shimmied up a tree like a little squirrel."

Yep, she remembered that, too.

"I thought the wolves were going to eat me."

His smile grew wider. "Wouldn't have been enough there for a full meal."

"Are you saying I'm too skinny to feed a wolf?" She bumped her shoulder against his in a playful manner that just slipped out. She shouldn't be so casual with him, despite their history—or maybe because of their history. Either way, it bordered on flirting, and a naked woman shouldn't flirt with a naked man unless she meant business.

He laughed, thankfully. But his smile softened quickly when he said, "You used to be too skinny to feed a wolf, but you've filled in nicely over the years."

How should she respond to that? Thanking him was out of the question. A lady doesn't thank a gentleman for making an intimate comment about her body.

Should she chastise him for looking at her when in truth it flattered her to no end? Scolding him would also be hypocritical, considering she'd been looking at his body every chance she'd gotten. Luckily, he shivered, allowing her a chance to change the subject.

"You'd be warmer if you'd wrap your blanket around your shoulders."

He lifted his brow. "Somehow, I doubt it."

She glanced at the blanket wrapped around his legs. Most of it was dark with wet spots from the rain. How had she not realized that sooner? He had given her the blanket from the inside of his bedroll, leaving the outer one for himself.

"You gave me the dry blanket," she said.

He shrugged. "You were cold."

And now she sat warm and dry while he shivered. And night was falling and the wind was howling and it was getting colder . . .

"You can share my blanket."

Lord, have mercy. Had those words just come from her mouth? Did she actually offer to let Brodie slip inside her blanket? Her face suddenly heated as she thought through the ramifications.

Brodie cleared his throat. "I, uh, don't think that would be wise."

He kept his gaze riveted across the cave as he spoke, like he was too embarrassed by her offer to face her. She should be relieved by his refusal, but the darkening cave was getting colder by the minute, and she could see the gooseflesh rising on his arms, despite the fact he had them folded tightly across his chest. He was refusing her offer of shared warmth because of some misplaced sense of decency. They were adults, for goodness' sake.

"You're being ridiculous," she said.

Slowly, he turned his head to face her, his brows rose. "You think I'm being ridiculous?"

"Yes." She lifted her chin, bracing for an argument. "It's getting colder in here, and you're going to catch your death if you don't share my blanket. These are unusual circumstances. It's not like we're children, Brodie."

His eyes narrowed as he looked into hers and said, "You aren't the least bit concerned about allowing a naked man to share your blanket? Because we can't do that without being next to each other." He paused for a second before he added, "Skin against skin," in case the image wasn't clear enough for her.

"You're cold." She repeated the point, though she wasn't sure if it was for his benefit or hers. But his expression didn't change. The man was still as ram headed as ever. So she cheated. "I'm cold, too."

And that changed everything, as she knew it would.

"You are?" he asked with genuine concern.

She nodded, then shivered a little—not too much, Brodie wasn't stupid. "Besides, I trust you to be a gentleman."

Damn. Of all the things the woman could have said, *that* tore apart Brodie's excuses quicker than anything else could have. She left him with no options except to crawl under her blanket to warm her or admit that trusting him to be a gentleman was the worst decision she could've made.

"Why don't you put your blanket under us," she said, "and we'll use mine to wrap up in?"

That was a logical and sound plan. It would give a layer of blanket between them and the ground, but, "There would be nothing between us," he reminded her.

She rolled her eyes as though he truly was being ridiculous. "I've been married. It's not like I haven't been next to a man before. I'm sure I can fight the temptation."

Ouch. She said it as though he held no appeal to her at all, as though being against him would cause no desire or lust in the least.

"I'm sure I can, too," he lied, standing to remove his blanket.

Her eyes opened wide. "What are you doing?"

He shrugged nonchalantly. "Putting my blanket down to sit on, as you suggested. What did you think I was doing?"

"Nothing. You just caught me by surprise, is all."

Brodie might have believed her act of indifference had Maggie not squeezed her eyes shut when he stripped his blanket off to lay it on the ground. "Well, are you going to share your blanket or are you going to leave me hanging, so to speak?"

Her cheeks turned red enough to see even in the dim light of the cave. Eyes still shut, she felt the ground for his blanket, then scooted over to sit on it. In a move that could only be described as amazing, she managed to hold one edge of her blanket across her body while she opened the rest for him to snuggle in.

This was his last chance to do the right thing. He looked at her—her lashes lying against her cheek, a long sleek leg peeking from beneath the blanket, her arm extended to welcome him . . .

"Hell," he muttered, wasting no more time in joining her. He pulled the blanket around him, nestling into her cocoon, and he had to admit the heat felt good. Too good.

"See? That wasn't so difficult," Maggie said, once some adjusting had taken place. "We can keep each other warm without anything indecent happening." Her posture contradicted her words. She sat stiff as a board, careful not to touch him under the blanket. Apparently she wasn't as indifferent to his nearness as she'd claimed.

And apparently Brodie was much less of a gentleman than even he had realized. "We would be much warmer if we wrapped our arms around each other."

"I'm warm. Aren't you?" she said, a little too quickly.

He didn't chuckle, but he rather enjoyed the hint of panic in her voice. Even as a kid, it had been fun to tease her, though he never dreamed he'd be teasing quite like this. "I'm still cold. I guess jumping into that icy river then giving you the dry blanket chilled me more than I realized."

Using guilt was cheap but effective.

A timid "Oh" slipped from her lips, causing him to notice they were no longer blue, but a nice kissable pink.

"Of course, if you don't think you can fight the temptation . . ." He shrugged.

She cocked her chin and said, "Of course I can," which was exactly what he knew she'd say. Then she wiggled closer to him to prove her point, but if anyone was going to do any point proving, it was going to be him.

He wrapped one arm around her shoulder and slipped the other around her waist to pull her against him. She gasped and suddenly the game wasn't funny anymore. Silky, soft, and smooth, her body melted into his like it had been there many times before.

Her breasts pressed against his chest and one leg curled across his instinctively. Only a few inches separated their mouths and the inches were disappearing fast. Neither spoke as they stared into each other's eyes.

A kiss. Just one kiss, then he'd pull away and quit teasing her before things got carried away. He leaned toward her, giving her a chance to pull back if she wanted to, but she didn't. Instead, she moved her mouth toward his.

Their breaths mingled then their lips touched, and all his intentions of pulling away vanished. Tipping his head slightly, Brodie deepened the kiss, slipping his tongue into her mouth to taste her. Maggie met him stroke for stroke, and her acceptance heated his blood even more. Cautiously, he brushed the side of her breast, growing bolder when his caress was met with a moan instead of a slap. He cupped her breast, lifting it as his thumb teased her nipple to a hard tip.

He broke free from her mouth to trail kisses down the column of her throat and across her collarbone. Lingering kisses. Nibbling kisses that didn't stop until they found her breast.

Maggie couldn't contain the gasp that slipped from her throat when he licked her nipple, then pulled it into his mouth. Fiery tingles shot through her body, landing with intensity in the juncture of her thighs. His mouth tugged and suckled her breast, stealing her thoughts and sending her body reeling with sensations. He caressed her thigh, moving slowly upward until his hand was a hair's breadth from her folds, and knowing he was so close yet not touching her intimately, made her hurt for want of him.

She shouldn't be allowing any of this, but despite how hard she fought to think of a reason to stop him, she couldn't find one. She couldn't find a reason to stop him from doing anything he wanted to do, because she wanted it, too. She had for years. Even when her husband had made love to her, it was Brodie's hands she had imagined on her body. But her wildest imaginings couldn't compare with the reality and now she knew why. She loved Brodie Grant.

Always had, probably always would.

With a masterful move, he twisted until she was on his lap, giving his hand more freedom to explore her curves. She cradled his head like she'd always dreamed of doing while he ravished her mouth, and his hand glided between her legs to tease a fire that was already to the point of explosion. He stroked her, and the moisture he encountered had nothing to do with the stream. His hand was calloused but gentle, his movements both languid and intense. With the skill of a master, he coaxed her body to a blinding need for him.

Then, he slipped a finger inside her . . . then another.

"Maggie," he whispered, his fingers still inside, "if you want me to stop, I will, but this is your last chance."

Stop? Unable to speak, she shook her head then kissed him while she ran her hand down his body to his arousal. She wrapped her fingers around him and stroked his length, marveling at the heat and hardness of him. He groaned into her mouth, his body tensing with need until he could take no more. Laying her quickly on the blanket, he nestled between her legs and in one quick thrust entered her.

Wrapping her legs around his waist, she rode him with more passion and fire than she'd ever felt with her husband. More than she ever knew existed. Each rocking thrust drove her toward a pinnacle of excitement until finally her body exploded with racking shudders, causing her to yell Brodie's name as he poured into her, and his groans joined hers in the darkness of the cave.

Then it was quiet. No sound except for their breathing and the drumming of the rain. He lifted his head from the curve of her neck where he had nestled it during their lovemaking and looked into her eyes. "Are you all right?"

Good question. She was naked in a cave with the only man she had ever loved still buried deeply inside her. It was wanton, shameful, and well-past sinful, and to make matters worse, he didn't feel the same. She had dreamed of him for years, yet at Leo's wedding, Brodie didn't even know who she was. He had no idea how long she'd loved him, and it wouldn't matter to him if he did know. What had she done? She'd made a fool of herself. That's what she'd done.

"I'm fine," she said, forcing a smile, but a tear spilled down her cheek despite her efforts.

Brodie frowned and immediately pulled out of her. "Did I hurt you?"

"No," she said, suddenly feeling cold. "I'm just tired. I need to get some sleep."

He nodded, but she didn't think he believed her lie. He quickly adjusted their blankets before wrapping his arm around her waist and pulling her back against his chest to keep her warm.

He kissed the shell of her ear. "Good night," he whispered.

Within moments, his even breathing told Maggie that he was asleep. His body curved behind hers like a husband would spoon his wife, with her hips cradled in his lap and his arm wrapped protectively around her. She had imagined this moment a thousand times before, but now it felt empty.

She'd made love.

He'd had sex.

And even though both acts occurred in the same embrace, they were millions of miles apart.

four

"Get your hands off my daughter, you son of a bitch!"

Maggie's eyes flew open in the morning light of the cave. It took a few seconds for her to remember where she was, but her father's voice she recognized instantly. Clutching the blanket to her chest, she sat up and searched the cave for Brodie. She spotted him jerking on his pants on the other side of the overhang.

Her father pointed at him and said, "I'm going to kill you for raping my daughter."

"Pa!" Maggie yelled. "Brodie didn't rape me. He saved my life." She wrapped the blanket around her and scrambled to her feet, but her sore ankle stopped her from running to Brodie's side.

"Where are your clothes, Maggie?" Her father's voice dripped with anger and disgust.

"I fell into the river and Brodie pulled me out." She clutched the blanket closer, suddenly feeling tawdry. "Our clothes were wet and we had to take them off to get warm."

"So you repaid him by lying with him like a whore?"

Brodie took a step toward her father, pointing at his face. "If you ever call Maggie a whore again, I swear, I'll kill you."

"Stop it!" She hobbled over to them, determined to end this before it got any uglier. Lowering her voice, she repeated, "Brodie saved my life, Pa."

Her father glared at Brodie then looked at Maggie with a shake of his head. "Get your clothes on, Maggie," he said as he left the cave.

She limped back to her clothing.

"Don't go with him," Brodie said.

"Why wouldn't I?" She waited, silently begging him to ask her to stay with him. But he didn't, of course. He had no reason to. She wasn't a virgin. She'd lain with him of her own free will, and he owed her nothing in return.

Brodie dropped his head and muttered, "No reason that I can think of."

She pulled on her cold, wet clothing and left Brodie, the cave, and a good part of her dignity behind.

ENOUGH was enough. Brodie spurred his horse, hurrying her to close the distance between him and Maggie. In the three days since they'd made love in the cave, he'd been unable to think of anything else. When she'd asked him why she shouldn't go with her father, the only reason he could think of was because he didn't want her to. But he knew that wouldn't be enough. Maggie's family hated him, and if he truly was guilty of what they thought he'd done, he would hate himself, too. What kind of man would maliciously set fire to his neighbor's property? Unfortunately, he was so drunk that night, he couldn't remember for sure what had happened—only that if he did burn the barn, it was an accident.

At first, he didn't care what they thought. He knew he

wouldn't do something like that intentionally, and their opinions didn't matter. But things changed. They changed when his ma needed him to come home. They changed more when his sister married Leo, and the change became complete when he made love to Maggie.

It was time to set things straight once and for all, then maybe, just maybe, he could convince Maggie that they belonged to-gether. He pulled his horse up to stop in front of John Stover's ranch house, but he didn't have his feet on the ground before John stepped onto his porch, with a rifle pointed at Brodie's chest.

"What the hell do you think you're doing here?" John said, his jaw clenched in anger.

Brodie raised his hands away from his gun belt to show he meant peace. "I've come for Maggie."

"You've wasted your time. My daughter's too good for the likes of you."

Brodie deliberately calmed his voice. "I did not set fire to your barn."

"Leo said he saw you leave, and the barn was in flames behind you. Why would he lie?"

Brodie shook his head. "I don't know. Maybe he saw someone who looked like me or maybe he was still drunk. I don't know, but I *do* know that when I left the barn that night, there was no fire."

John raised his rifle to look down the sight, focusing his aim on Brodie. "You're a lying bastard."

"No, he isn't." Leo stepped onto the porch with Maggie and Sara close behind. "He's telling the truth."

John frowned and lowered his rifle. "What are you saying?"

Leo stepped forward, leaving the porch to stand in front of Brodie. "I took Brodie to see the bull that night. We'd been drinking, and we had a bet on who had the best bull in the area. I set a lantern down in the barn and forgot it when I left." Leo dropped his head for a moment, then took a deep breath before continuing. He glanced at Brodie. "When I remembered, I ran back to the barn, but by then it was in flames, and Pa was scream- ing and cussing and saying he thought your pa had done it to kill the bull."

It took all Brodie had not to smash his fist into Leo's face. "So you told him you'd seen me down there."

Leo nodded. "I would have told him the truth after he calmed down, but you left town the next day, and I couldn't see any reason to tell him since you were gone anyway."

"You son of a bitch. For the last ten years, you let everyone think I'd done something like that."

Leo raised his chin. "If you want to whip me right now, you got every right, and I won't stop you."

"If he don't, I will." John Stover laid his rifle to the side and stormed off the porch toward Leo. He cocked back his fist and took a swing, but Leo caught his hand in midair.

"No, sir. You won't," Leo said.

Brodie stepped up beside Leo and folded his arms across his chest. If anyone was going to whip Leo's ass, it was going to be Brodie. However, it took a lot of guts for Leo to come clean like that, and if old man Stover wanted a fight, he was going to have to take on the two of them.

Leo glanced toward Brodie and nodded once in thanks. "I'm done taking your whippin's," Leo said, releasing his father's fist. "It was ten years ago, Pa. I done something stupid and I'm sorry. But it's over."

Stover looked at Leo then back at Brodie before he threw his hands up and headed back to his porch. "You're both idiots," he said, going into his house.

Maggie and Sara stood silently on the porch. Each staring at the men as though they didn't know what to say. Sara was the first to move, stepping slowly off the porch to Leo's side.

He dropped his head and said, "I'm sorry, Sara. Will you forgive me?"

She took his hand. "I always knew Brodie wouldn't have done that on purpose. I suspected you'd lied for some reason. I just didn't know what it was." She looked at Brodie. "Do you forgive him, Brodie?"

Brodie glanced at Leo then shrugged. "I'll work on it, but I might still whip your ass if it suits me."

Leo grinned. "I'd like to see you try."

It was at that moment Brodie realized why the lies had hurt so deeply. Leo had been the best friend he'd ever had, and as hard as it was to admit, he'd missed the son of a bitch. The bitterness would need a little more time to go away, but Brodie suspected it probably would eventually.

Sara led Leo back into the house as Brodie stood in the yard, still facing Maggie. "I came here for you, Maggie."

Maggie's heart pounded wildly in her chest. "Why?"

"I came here to do right by you and marry you."

She swallowed and asked again, "Why?"

He lifted his brows in surprise. "Because of what happened in the cave."

His words hit her like a slap in the face. "You want to marry me because we slept together?"

He nodded. "It's the proper thing to do."

"You can go to the devil, Brodie Grant." She spun away from him and darted into the house.

"Maggie, wait!" he yelled, but she had no intentions of waiting. No man was going to marry her because it was the "proper thing to do." She'd already had one loveless marriage, and she'd die old and shriveled before she had another.

She stormed through the house to her room and slammed the door, but not before she heard Brodie explaining to her father that he'd rip his head off if he tried to stop him from following her.

Evidently, her father believed him. In a matter of seconds, Brodie jerked open her door and entered her room. He didn't slam it behind him, but he closed it with certainty, then wedged a chair under the knob.

"Why did you do that?" she asked, watching him cross the room to her.

"Because no one gets out or comes in until we sort this out."

She turned away from him to stare out the window. "We have nothing to sort out."

His hands gripped her shoulders. "Maggie," he said, turning her to face him, "I don't know what I did or said that made you so mad, but I'm sorry."

"Why do you want to marry me?"

"Because a gentleman would do no less." He smiled, obviously pleased with his ridiculous answer.

She wasn't pleased in the least. She kicked him in the shin as hard as she could. Maybe that would knock some sense into him.

"Damn it to hell, Maggie!" He grabbed his leg and hopped over to sit on the bed. "Would you stop doing that?" Rubbing his shin, he said, "That's the same leg you kicked last time."

She would feel bad about hurting him, if she was sorry. But she wasn't. "Get out before I kick the other one."

"No."

Did he say *"No"*?

"Not until you tell me why you won't marry me. You owe me that much."

She crossed the room to remove the chair from under the doorknob. She needed to get away from him before she kicked more than his shins. "I don't owe you anything."

"I saved your life."

Well, shoot. He had her there. She paused for a moment to calm her anger, then turned slowly to face him. He wanted the truth. She'd give him the truth. "I won't marry a man who doesn't love me."

Brodie stood and walked over to her. "Is that all?"

"Is that all?"

The corner of his mouth turned up in the lopsided grin that always made her insides melt as he laid his hand against her cheek. "I think I've always loved you, Maggie. I just had to wait until you grew up."

Her eyes clouded with tears. "Really?"

He chuckled. "Really."

"You're not just saying that because you think I want to hear it?"

"No." He shook his head. "When you were a kid and you got into trouble, who always came to your rescue?"

She chewed on her lower lip for a moment as she thought. "You."

"And when you were upset and needed someone to talk to, who did you come to?"

She frowned. "You."

"There was always something special between us, Maggie. You've got to admit that."

Admit it? She'd lived on it for years, but he didn't need to know that just yet. "Well," she said, in an attempt to act nonchalant, "I suppose you could be on to something there. But do you think it's enough for marriage?"

"I love you, Maggie. If you don't agree to marry me, I'm going to pester the hell out of you until you do."

Her excitement bubbled to the surface in a giggle, despite her best efforts to control it. "In that case, I guess I'd better marry you."

"Good, 'cause I'd hate to have to drag you back to that cave until you gave in."

She thought of the delicious ways Brodie could make her give in while he wrapped her into his arms for a lingering kiss. Then he pulled back and said, "There is one condition. Promise you won't kick me in the shins again. That last one hurt like hell."

She raised her brow and wound her arms around his neck. "No promises."

"How did I know you were going to say that?" His eyes twinkled as he leaned in for another kiss, and Maggie decided she probably wouldn't kick him again.

At least, not unless he really needed it.

the wolf watcher's diet

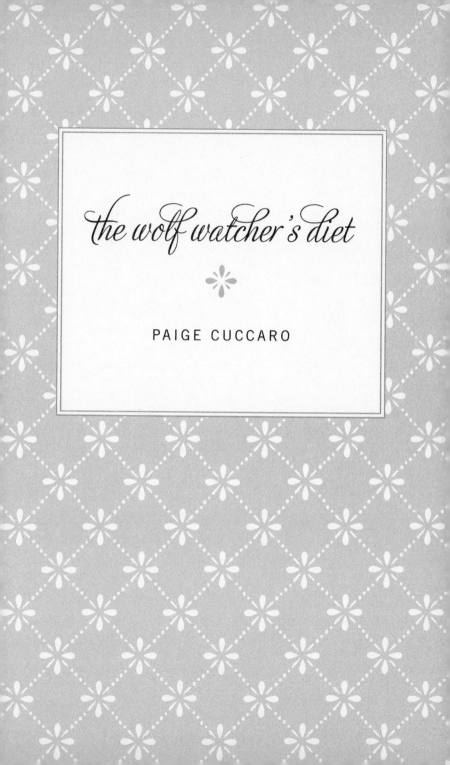

PAIGE CUCCARO

one

❋

You'd think after having a head-on collision with a tree in the middle of nowhere at half past one in the morning, my night couldn't get any worse.

Right? You'd be wrong.

Hot fudge topping and rainbow jimmies were everywhere. It was like an ice cream massacre. Soft-serve swirl had smeared all over the driver's side airbag, the dashboard, the cracked windshield, and pretty much every square inch of my face.

Gross, I had ice cream in my hair, too, which was worse than you think considering my hair is curly and coppery red. With the chocolate and vanilla swirl lacing through the kinky strands combined with the colored jimmies dangling off the ends, my head felt like a homemade Christmas ornament. I stopped thinking about it.

The door was stuck, and I had to jam my shoulder against it twice before it creaked open, letting loose a rain of chocolate-covered raisins from the floorboard. "Perfect."

I swung my feet from under the dashboard and rocked out of the seat into the high weeds. Ice cream drizzled down the side of my face, and I wiped at it with the back of my hand. I looked. It wasn't just ice cream. My hand and the sleeve of my white blouse were smeared with blood. I felt for the wound under my hair, and a jolt of pain pierced through my skull when my fingers touched the gash. Yeah, I know. What'd I think would happen?

"Just . . . perfect." The dark woods around me started to spin, but I took a few deep breaths and managed to clear my head, focus. I glanced around for the dog I'd swerved to avoid. No sign of him. Of course not. The fleabag was probably off somewhere licking parts of his body he had no business licking. "Stupid dog."

Next time, the mutt was toast.

Okay, it wasn't all the dog's fault. I may have been a little distracted. I'd dropped my plastic spoon and was trying to feel for it under my feet without dropping the sundae cup in my other hand. I'd almost had it.

Yeah, that sounds bad in retrospect. Anyhoo, I had to get help. My phone was in my purse, but glancing around at the bits of stuff that had once been inside my car and were now spread all over the woods, there was no way I'd find it.

"Okay, plan B." Get my butt up the embankment to the road and flag someone down. I started climbing. By the time I reached the top, blisters stung the palms of my hands from clawing at roots and weeds, and my lungs burned like I'd inhaled acid. Dirty, achy, and exhausted, I just wanted to go to sleep . . . or maybe I was starting to pass out. *Focus.*

The wooded road was just as desolate as it'd been when I wrecked. Cutting alongside a mountain, the other side of the road was an uphill grade into the night, covered with dense woods.

The moon was little more than a slit hiding behind rolling clouds. And if that wasn't enough, the hairs on the back of my neck kept tingling with the sensation someone was watching me. Paranoia is not my friend.

But then a low rumble crept up my spine from behind me and I turned. I didn't want to, but I'm a sucker for my curiosity. The forest was like a wall of black with only the closest trees visible to add contrast. Whatever made the creepy sound was down the hill past the blinking lights of my car.

I could hear something moving down there, dried leaves shuffling under its feet, the snap of a twig, the rustle of underbrush. And then I realized there was more than one. My heart shot into overdrive, and my body went still as stone. I thought about screaming, making noise to scare it off, but I couldn't get past the scared rabbit reflex to stand so still I'd become invisible. Yeah, doesn't work well for rabbits either.

Out of nowhere, headlights washed over me. I looked but had to close my eyes against the brightness. I'd been so scared I hadn't even heard the truck coming. I didn't care who was behind the wheel, I just ran to the driver's side door. He looked normal— *thank God*—forty something, short sandy hair, polo style shirt, and jeans.

I grabbed the side mirror and practically crawled through the window. "You gotta help me."

"Where'd you come from, little lady? Is that blood?" He turned off the engine.

"Yeah. I . . . I had an accident." I couldn't get a good breath. I'd been holding it too long without even realizing it. I swallowed. "My car's stuck down there against a tree and I think . . . I think there's something in the woods."

He opened his door, and I had to shuffle back so he could get out. My brain was starting to haze again. I couldn't figure out why the guy was getting out of the truck instead of letting me get in. *Whatever*.

"Where's your car, honey?"

Wasn't he listening? I pointed. "Down there, but—"

"Show me. C'mon," he said, shooing me ahead of him. Warning alarms blared in my head, but then they'd been blaring since I'd slammed into that tree. I ignored good sense and led the way to the edge of the embankment.

Staring down at my crunched car below, I said, "See?"

"Yeah." His arm snapped around my chest, trapping my arms against my sides. His other hand clamped a smelly cloth over my mouth and nose.

Surprise sucked a deep breath into my lungs and with it whatever he'd doused on the cloth. My thoughts went fuzzy quick, but I was sharp enough not to take another breath. I squirmed, trying to get my elbows up to jam into his gut, or stomp my foot in the right spot to crush his toes. I missed. He held me too tight, and I needed to take another breath before I passed out.

And then I heard it again, that weird low rumbling sound. Only this time it was closer. A lot closer.

"Oh, shit." The guy spun around, putting me between him and whatever it was. His hand slipped from my mouth, and I took a fast breath before my brain identified what I saw.

A dog, probably the same mutt that'd caused this mess, stood in the middle of the road, growling at us. He was a big dog, but this close the sound of his growl rumbled through my chest like it was part of the air around us and made the hairs all over my body vibrate. Goose bumps raced down my back. "Uh-oh."

"Get outta here," my savior—turned kidnapper—said to it. "Go on, get." He faked toward the dog, like he'd attack him. Problem with that was he still held me between him and it.

"Hey. Knock it off. Le'go of me." I pushed back each time the idiot lunged forward. Even I could see the dog wasn't buying it.

He was just making the thing mad, and it was a freaky big dog. Seriously.

Idiot's third fake-out triggered the reaction I'd worried over. The giant dog lunged, and my captor twisted, shoving me right into the biggest set of teeth I'd ever seen. Reflex brought my arm up, and its sharp fangs drove through my skin like it was tissue paper. I could've sworn I heard the snap when his teeth met.

I screamed, the pain blinding me for a second, and stumbled back. The dog let go, but I fell into the arms of the jerk who'd pushed me. With his hands on my upper arms, he used me like a human shield, yanking me this way then the other to keep me between him and the crazy beast he'd pissed off. Not that it worked very well.

You see, I have a small weight issue. In a society where thin is in, and there are more programs to help people lose weight than there are to help feed the poor or teach the illiterate to read, it's easy to get caught up in body image. Mine—ain't so great.

I've always struggled with my weight, but after graduating college two years ago without even a meaningless one-night stand, let alone the love of my life, to show for it, I gave up. There are plenty of more important things in life to worry about, like paying bills, keeping a job, inflation, war, frequent-flyer miles . . . I refused to waste another minute thinking about what I ate or worrying about how much I weighed. At least that's what I'd been telling myself.

So at my size I'm not that easy to swing around.

Within seconds, blood covered my forearm and hand. The front of my blouse and slacks were soaked, sticking to my body. My head was like an overfilled balloon with the prickly poke of the bite wound stabbing at me, threatening to explode my brains over everything. I couldn't get my footing, couldn't get away, and every other second I had the loud snap of teeth in my face followed by that chest-rumbling snarl.

I couldn't breathe around the pain, and my sluggish brain kept me a half beat behind, jerking back from the snap of teeth in the nick of time again and again. My feet scrambled over the gravel at the edge of the road, but I couldn't break the guy's hold on me.

"Stop it." I didn't know if he heard me. I didn't have the breath to raise my voice above a raw whisper. "Please. Let me go."

The guy brought me up hard against his chest, cowering behind me. "There's another one. God help us, it's a whole pack."

Opening my eyes made me realize I'd closed them. I was starting to pass out, but seeing the guy was right helped zero my attention. Three more giant dogs had come out of nowhere to surround us. Their muzzles trembled, baring their teeth, growling and snapping at us. The guy spun us around, guarding against one dog and then the next.

They held their heads low, the scruff between their sharp shoulder blades standing on end. Step by step they crept closer, the sound of their growls vibrating down to my bones. I freaked—a flash of wild panic. The guy hadn't been ready for it. The quick spasm tangled my feet. His grip slipped, and I dropped. I didn't even have the reflexes left to catch myself, and the side of my face smacked the hard rough gravel.

I groaned, wincing against the slam of pain, but otherwise couldn't move. It was a good thing.

Wind rustled my hair as one of the big dogs leapt over me, driving into the guy with a sickening thud. He screamed, but it couldn't mask the wet sound of his flesh ripping under those powerful jaws. He hit the ground somewhere near me, his boots scraping and kicking against the gravel. I didn't look.

His screams turned to gargled spurting sounds as his mouth filled with blood. A sharp clawed foot knocked against my thigh when one of the other wolves passed by me to join the frenzy. My heart jumped into my throat. I squeezed my eyes shut, terror petrifying my body.

A furry leg brushed against my back, warm breath snorted through my hair. I held my breath, and then a long, rough tongue licked the side of my face.

Just like that, the world went away.

two

"I'm sorry. Should've been more careful . . ."

Someone was whispering in my ear. And licking my arm. *Eww.*

I jerked my hand away and opened my eyes. One of the dogs that had attacked me lay inches away, staring at me.

"I'm not a dog," the male voice said next to my ear.

Wait. The voice wasn't coming from next to my ear. It was coming from inside my head. I looked at my hand, but all I saw was the hairy leg of another dog. I must've been lying on it. All the wild panic from before came rushing back, my heart pounding in my head. I had to get away. They'd killed that guy; I just knew it. I was next. I had to get away.

I jerked backward, but the stupid dog underneath me followed. I pushed up and watched the hairy paws move, too. They braced under me where my arms and hands should've been. How was that possible?

"Ohmygod, what's wrong with me? Is it my eyes, am I hallucinating?" I'd hit my head in the accident. Maybe that was it. *"Or maybe I died . . . and came back . . . as a dog."*

"*Ella, calm down. Let me explain,*" the voice said again. I ignored it. I mean, that's the first sign of crazy when you start talking back to the voices in your head, right? Of course, hearing voices in your head to begin with doesn't exactly scream sane. But I was pretty sure the train had already left the station on that count.

I pushed to my feet, all *four* of them. It wasn't easy. My dog legs were thinner than my human legs had been, and I wasn't much lighter. Apparently when the powers-that-be sent me back as a dog, they decided to send *all* of me back. So not only was I a dog, I was a plus-sized dog. "*Perfect.*"

At least I wasn't lying half chewed along the road. I was in a bedroom—a nice bedroom, big, tall ceilings, long windows. There was a four-poster bed and a separate bathroom from what I could see . . . from the floor. I looked at where I'd been lying. Muddy towels stained with blood were in a pile on the floor. "*Nice way to treat the dog.*"

"*You're not a dog,*" the voice said.

"*Really? Then I just have some sort of severe brain damage or something?*" Scary how hopeful I sounded.

"*No. You're . . .*" The voice trailed off, and I heard his sigh.

"*Great, I'm frustrating my own crazy voice. That can't be good.*"

The dog that'd been watching me sat up, shook his head with a hard snort. "*Let's take this one step at a time. First. Stop calling me a dog. I'm not. I'm a wolf.*"

"*Who?*"

"*Me.*"

"*The voice in my head is a wolf? What, dog's not good enough?*" My crazy voice had attitude. "*Perfect.*"

"*No. I'm a wolf.*" The dog in front of me stood, wagged its long bushy tail, its tongue lolling out the side of its mouth. "*I'm not just a voice in your head. I'm a wolf, a werewolf, a shape-shifter . . . like you. That's why we hear each other's thoughts in our heads.*"

"Shape-shifter? That's different." My crazy voice had a better imagination than I did. And what was with this dog, lookin' all perky and happy all of a sudden? Maybe he had to go out. *"Sorry, boy. No hands."*

Pretty dog, though. Looked like a husky, only bigger.

"No." The voice sighed again. It wasn't easy being my crazy voice. *"Listen. Please. The dog in front of you wagging its fool tail? That's me. I'm not your crazy voice. I'm a werewolf. I accidentally bit you last night and now you're a werewolf, too.* Not. A. Dog.*"*

"Seriously?"

He sighed, this time sounding more relieved than frustrated. *"Yes."*

"That's crazy."

"Ella . . ."

"Okay, okay, I guess it's the lesser of the insane possibilities and the evidence does seem to support it," I said.

"Finally." The dog—I mean, wolf—sat.

"So, uh, what should I call you?" I asked. *"Spot? King? Lucky—?"*

"Luke. My name's Luke." He was sounding a little frustrated again.

"Oh. Okay. I know a guy named Luke." I felt a nervous ramble coming on but was absolutely helpless to stop it. *"He's a teacher. So am I, by the way. That's how I know him. I teach seventh grade English. He's science. Am I going to get fleas? 'Cause I'm really not okay with that. You killed that guy from the pickup truck, didn't you? No. Never mind. Not my business. Anyway, I should be getting home. Got a ton of things to do, call a tow truck, let the school know I'm okay, grade some papers, and then there's the whole circling around twenty times before I lie down. That'll eat up some time. Am I ever going to stand on two feet again?"*

"Ella . . ."

"Hey. How do you know my name?"

Luke's pale wolf eyes looked away with a blink then back

again. They were pretty eyes, light blue rimmed with an ink black ring. Luke from school had eyes like that.

A preverbal light flicked on in my brain. My stomach dropped like I'd gone airborne for a second. I stopped thinking about it.

"After you passed out last night, we brought you here to the pack house. It's been twelve hours," he said. *"You were hurt . . . I mean, besides the bite wound. I hoped you wouldn't shift, but . . . you did."*

"Obviously."

"Sometimes the virus that alters human DNA doesn't spread. There was a chance, but . . ." He looked away again, like there was something he didn't want to tell me, or was ashamed to. *"I didn't want to infect you, Ella. I just . . ."*

"Hey, you didn't eat me, so I figure I'm ahead of the game," I said, trying to make him feel better. Not sure why, but whatever. *"Still haven't told me how you know my name. And shouldn't shifting shapes be, I dunno, part of being a shape-shifter? How do I get back on two feet?"*

"You should've shifted back already," he said.

"Huh?" Not a good sign.

"The initial shift normally alters your human DNA so you can go back and forth between forms, but it also heals the bite wound and whatever other health issues you have at the time."

I thought about that. My head didn't hurt anymore, and the bite wounds on my arm were gone. Well, as far as I could tell, seeing as how my arm was now a leg and covered in fur. *"So what's the holdup? What do I do?"*

"Nothing. It should just . . . happen." He stood, maybe sensing my growing terror. Maybe sensing he should get out of striking distance. *"The fact that you haven't shifted back makes me think there might be internal injuries from the accident that are taking longer to heal. It might be something you can't feel until it's too late."*

"Too late? Too late for what? No. Don't answer that. I'll be okay,

though, right?" The hairs down my spine shivered with the ice that whooshed through my veins. *"The shape-shifter DNA will heal whatever's wrong, right? Right?"*

Luke didn't answer. He moved closer, nudging his nose against my neck. I kinda liked it. Weird, 'cause, well, he was a dog—I mean wolf. Either way, I'm more of a cat person. Go figure.

"The virus should heal you, but we want to take you to our doctor just to be sure."

"Yes. Good idea." Anything that keeps me breathing is a brilliant plan in my book. *"Let's go."*

He stepped back, just far enough to stare at me with those pretty—uncomfortably familiar—eyes. *"I thought you might want to get cleaned up first."*

"Oh. Right." I'd forgotten about the ice cream swirl and rainbow jimmy hair treatment I'd given myself last night. Not to mention the blood from the gash on my head and the fang holes in my arm. I must've looked like crap. But then again, I was a dog—wolf. *"Where's the shower?"*

If a wolf face can look embarrassed, Luke had it down. He turned, not looking at me. *"That's the, uh . . . other thing I have to tell you."*

"Oh, crap." There was more? *"What? Am I going to have an uncontrollable urge to drink out of the toilet?"*

"Showering is going to be hard at first without, y'know, arms and hands."

"Oh. I hadn't thought of that."

"Don't worry. I'll help."

"You?"

"I'll have to shift. But I want you to remember . . . I didn't mean for any of this to happen."

I knew, but I didn't, at least I didn't want to. In the next few minutes there was no denying it. Luke the wolf sat, lowered his head, and took a deep breath that expanded his chest and sides, and kept on expanding. The skin on his back stretched, his fur separating, thinning. Within seconds he'd gotten larger, there was more skin than hair, and I could see his bones moving underneath. I could hear them snapping and scraping against each other as they changed shape and grew.

When those same pretty, pale eyes swung up to me peering out of a human face, I knew why they looked so familiar. *"Oh-mygod, it's you."*

The seventh grade science teacher, my colleague, Luke Danhurst, raised his hands, crawling toward me on his knees. *"Ella, wait. Listen . . ."*

I learned way more about Luke in that second than I really cared to know. For instance, he was circumcised. I felt my brows rise and I looked away. *"Whoa. Don't remember buying a ticket for that show."*

"Oh. Sorry, I . . . just a minute."

I peeked to see his high, tight bottom racing to the chest of drawers. I looked away again before he caught me looking. Luke was hot. Seriously. Hot. Jet-black hair that would hang in loose waves to his shirt collar, a lean-muscled body, square chiseled jaw, and eyes that almost glowed, framed by lush black lashes. In other words, the kind of guy who would never see a pleasingly shapely woman like me as anything more than a friend.

He was a sweetheart, a nice guy, always inviting me to sit with him at lunch. It didn't mean anything. How could it? His table was almost always filled with beautiful young student teachers eager for his attention. You'd have to tie three of those girls together to get one real-sized woman. If that was the kind of girl he wanted, I couldn't compete.

Still, he made sure to invite me to tag along when they made plans to go to the club on weekends. I never went, of course. If I'd wanted to see Luke Danhurst shake his goodie bag, I'd watch it in my dreams where I could choose his dance partners. We were friends, though. Of course, that was before he turned me into a werewolf. The relationship was lookin' kinda iffy now.

After a minute he was back, kneeling beside me. "Ella, you have to believe me. I was just trying to protect you. I was running with the pack, just messing around. I thought I'd make it across the road before you rounded the bend."

"That was you? You were the dog I almost hit?"

"Wolf. And yes." He'd put on a pair of underwear. Dark blue. Briefs, not boxers. Who knew? "You drive way too fast, by the way. If you'd been driving with your hands instead of your chin . . . Never mind."

He was right. If I'd been paying more attention, and yeah, slowed down a little, I might not have wrecked, that wacko wouldn't have stopped to help, the wolves wouldn't have attacked, and I wouldn't be standing on all fours.

This was my fault.

I sighed, though in my wolf body it was more of a wet snort. *Gross. "How, exactly, do you plan on helping me shower?"*

His eyes turned hopeful, but the expression flickered then faded. "We, uh, have a metal tub in the backyard. I'd use hot water . . . and shampoo."

Right. 'Cause how else would you wash a dog? *"Perfect."*

three

Luke drove a Jeep Wrangler with huge windows. I tried to resist hanging my head out with my tongue lolling from the side of my mouth, but . . .

Ohmygod, it was like crack! Seriously. I didn't even try to suck in the string of drool that stretched longer and longer from my bottom lip to flap in the wind. I *loved* it!

And then a bug smacked into the back of my throat and the thrill was gone just like that.

"You know, uh, there's a leash law in town." He wasn't so much asking as telling.

"Bondage. Yeah, that's what was missing from this experience. Nice."

"Really? I had no idea." He bobbed his brows. His smile softened the sharp masculine lines of his face. Made him look more approachable and less like someone you drool over from afar. I liked it. Too much. "You a BDSM girl?"

"Oh, yeah. The thought of the doctor sticking a thermometer up

my butt . . . Ooo, can't wait." I looked back out my window. *"This doctor going to be cool with you bringing a wolf into his office?"*

"Sure. Why wouldn't he?" Luke said, eyes on the road. "He's a vet."

My head snapped around to him. *"No, he isn't."*

Luke glanced at me, smiling. "Yeah, he is." The smile melted at the edges, then turned to confusion. "What?"

"I am not an animal." Great now I was quoting the Elephant Man. *"I was joking about the thermometer up the butt, you know."*

"Relax. Richard, Doctor Carter, is one of us. He's a werewolf. He went to school for general medicine then went back to get his doctorate in veterinary science to help the pack. Turns out he liked being a vet more."

"What a heartwarming story." I looked back out my window, trying not to think about all the indignities animals endure during doctor visits. *"If he asks me to pee in a cup, I'm screwed."*

Luke's soft laugh tickled through my belly. Crap. Of all the people who had to see me like this, why him? And here I thought having him wash the mud off my hairy stomach would top my embarrassment chart. How the hell was I going to get up on one of those high metal tables? And what would happen when I really did have to pee? Ugh. I didn't want to think about it.

"So, how many of us are there?" I asked, cleverly changing the subject.

He glanced at me then back to the road and shrugged. "In the world? Hard to say. But locally, there's just our pack. About one-fifty, although there are a few couples expecting."

"One hundred and fifty werewolves in Washington, Pennsylvania? That's not possible."

On the other hand, Washington was a small town surrounded by really small towns, surrounded by acres and acres of forest that blanketed the foothills of the Appalachian Mountains. I guess if there was going to be a spot on the planet where werewolves would multiply like rabbits, it'd be Washington, PA. We also have a large population of rabbits, coincidentally. Or maybe it wasn't a coincidence.

"We're not just in Washington. The pack house is here, but most are spread out and live in nearby counties." He looked at me for a second, glancing at the road and back. "We're normal people, Ella. Just like you. We have families, jobs, join bowling leagues . . ."

"Those people aren't normal."

"The point is that being a werewolf changes your life, but it doesn't have to change the way you live."

My gaze drifted back to the greenery whizzing past my window. *"Could say the same thing about incontinence."*

"You'll get used to it."

"I don't know. This is pretty much the weirdest thing that's ever happened to me. Was it like this for you?"

"No," he said, and his voice was softer, more private. "I've always been a werewolf. Born this way. Both my parents were pack members."

"Didn't know that was possible, both born and made werewolves. Not that I really thought about it." Up until about four hours ago I didn't even know there was anything real to think about. Live and learn . . . the hard way. *"Are most born werewolves?"*

"Yeah. At least in our pack. We're a pretty tight community. It's hard to find people outside the group who'd fit in. Only about an eighth of our members were bitten, and most of them were bitten for love."

Aw, sweet. I'm not jealous. *"How many were accidents?"*

"Uhm . . . counting you?" He suddenly seemed very focused on the road. Either that or he just didn't want to look at me. "Three."

"Three?"

"Yeah. Two of them were teething accidents. Cute werewolf

baby, a couple of admiring checkout girls who got their fingers too close. Y'know."

"I'm the only werewolf that was accidentally bitten by an adult?" It seemed too much like karmic payback, though I had no idea what I'd done to piss off karma.

I couldn't keep thinking about it. I sighed and stuck my nose out the window, catching the breeze. It wasn't a dog thing. People do that, too. *"So if only an eighth of the pack are turned for love, the rest of you must only date furry?"*

He flashed me a sideways glance, his sharp chiseled cheeks going red. "Mostly. Like I said, it's hard to find someone outside the group who shares our unique . . . interests."

"Like what, playing catch? Chasing tails? A deep fascination with fire hydrants?"

"You joke, but wait 'til you see one of those stout red beauties now." He whistled, and I hoped to God he was joking.

"Perfect." I stood and thought about lying down on the Jeep's little bucket seat. Wasn't going to happen so I sat again. My skinny little wolf legs were tired. *"So is there a sexy she wolf in your life?"*

I'd made it as casual a question as I could. Many a teacher, female and male, had thrown themselves at Luke and gotten nowhere. He'd nipped any further attempts in the bud with the old "I don't date colleagues" excuse. I guess I could be wrong, but from what I'd seen, Luke didn't date anyone. Not that I'd been stalking him or anything. He had plenty of friends. Everyone liked him. He'd even invited me along with the group to go dancing plenty of times. But group dates don't count. Besides, I'd never noticed him *noticing* anyone.

"Yes and no," he said. "The last few people I've dated were werewolves, but no one who's ever triggered my instincts."

"Is that a euphemism?"

He glanced at me, brows drawn in confusion. "Oh. No." He

laughed. "Wolves mate for life. When we meet our true mate, our instincts take over and we'll do . . . almost anything to be with them."

"Ah . . . good to know. So what if you don't meet the one? You stay single?"

"No." Luke shrugged. "Most of us marry, have kids, grow old, and die perfectly happy without ever feeling that overpowering animalistic draw to someone. Just like humans."

"Wow, depressing."

"No, it's not." He laughed again. I liked that I could make him laugh. Unless he was laughing *at* me and not *with* me. Wait. I wasn't laughing.

"We still fall in love, just like anyone," he said. "But you know how rare it is to find that special once-in-a-lifetime love."

"Yeah." Even harder to find that special someone who feels it back. *"So, uh . . . no special wolfy for you yet, then?"*

"No."

My heart did a little happy dance in my chest.

He rolled his shoulder. "Well, yeah. I mean, there's someone." Stupid heart. "She's . . . she's not my soul mate, but I've known her all my life. Our parents were pushing us together in our playpens. But . . ."

"You don't love her?" I'd cross my fingers if I had any.

"No, I love her. She's one of my best friends. It's just . . ." His gaze swung to me, and if I hadn't looked like a dog, literally, I might think there was something meaningful behind that glance. He looked away, hands white knuckling around the steering wheel. "It's complicated. Besides, there's a lot of politics involved. Makes a person's motives suspect no matter who they are."

Werewolf politics. That was a new one. *"You don't trust her?"*

"Of course I trust her. Well, no. I mean, I don't really trust anyone." He sighed, pulling to a stop at the first traffic light we'd come to in twenty minutes. We were getting closer to downtown

Washington. "My father's our pack's alpha. As his son, I'm in line to take over. My wife, whoever she is, will be the alpha female. That's a powerful position, with a lot of perks. It's similar to the wolf hierarchy, but more . . . civilized. Sort of."

"Sheesh, Luke, that's a horrible way to go through life," I said.

"I'm used to it."

"But if you never really trust anyone, how can you ever find love? Love without trust is like . . . like cotton candy without sugar, like lemonade without lemons, like ketchup without tomatoes, like—"

"I get the idea." He flashed me one of his heart-stopping smiles, and my belly felt like it sat up and begged. "My parents managed to find each other. I don't know. Maybe I've already met my true mate, and I just need her to realize it, too, for the instincts to trigger in both of us."

"Right." That would be my luck.

About ten minutes later we pulled in front of the Paws & Claws pet clinic. The stand-alone vet's office was on the outer edge of town in an old Victorian-style house.

Luke came around to open my door. He slipped the looped end of a nylon leash around my neck, so loose I hardly felt it through my fur. I crawled from the seat to the floor and peered at the sidewalk.

The distance to the ground seems a lot farther when you're traveling it head first.

Seriously.

"You need help?" Luke asked.

I glared up at him, though I think it lost something coming from a furry face. *"I got it."*

The sidewalk was as hard as it looked, and I landed on my skinny wolf front legs with a huff, followed by two quick shuffled steps while my back end dropped behind me. Ugh. So undignified.

"Wow, dude, your dog's huge." A young female voice stated the obvious. Both Luke and I looked at the college-age couple walking toward us. They looked like Barbie and Ken dolls, both tall, blond, and exceedingly tanned.

Was she seriously calling me fat? Like being furry wasn't bad enough. *Sheesh.*

"You're a werewolf. She meant your overall size, not your weight," Luke said through our nifty mental connection. *"Why would you think that?"*

I didn't answer.

"Aw, but he's a good-lookin' pup." College boy squatted in front of me, scratched the fur behind both my ears. I wanted to be offended by the gender screwup, but . . .

Ohmygod, the ear thing was *awe*-and then-*some*! It felt better than . . . than sex. Okay, not that good, but close.

"Eww, David." College girl looked like she might hurl. She flicked her long poker-straight hair over her shoulder and held her barf back with manicured nails at her pursed mouth. "Don't touch that thing. It's going to the vet. Who knows what diseases it has."

"Get over it, Shelly," he said, still scratching—*thank you.* "There's a ton of reasons you take a dog to the vet."

I was starting to like this guy. Never mind that in human form I'd be invisible to a hard-bodied hotty like him. Yeah. This werewolf thing wasn't all bad.

It was like being a whole different person. I was attractive in this form. People, men, noticed me. I liked it. Really liked it.

"Ella, all this time . . . Is this really what you think of yourself?"

I didn't answer. I couldn't. In that same instant an urge so strong, so foreign to me I didn't know to suppress it, overcame me. I raised my chin . . . and licked David, the college hotty, right on the nose.

He laughed and, to my surprise, kissed my nose back. Okay, yeah, even from my end there was an ick factor, but I could get used to it.

I thought Shelly might faint. She groaned and staggered back a step. "Oh, God . . ."

For the first time I felt a pull on my leash, and my brain tripped over the sensation. I heard Luke's smooth voice in my mind. *"That's enough, Ella."* Out loud he said to the couple, "I'm sorry. We're going to be late."

I pulled my head from David's scratching hold and looked up at Luke. His scowl was fixed on David, teeth clenched so tight I could see the muscles flex along his jaw. What was that about?

David pushed to his feet, wiping his nose with the back of his hand. Laughing, he leaned in to give Shelly a kiss, but she shoved him away. "You are *not* going to touch me until you wash the dog spit off your face and hands."

I stepped closer to Shelly, sniffed her leather flip-flop, her ankle, her knee. She stiffened under my curiosity, clutching at David's hand.

"He's just sniffing you," David assured her.

She smelled like wax and artificial flowers and too-strong perfume. The smells stuck in my nose, made me sneeze. Shelly jumped, squealing. "Eww, it spit snot on me."

Oops. Yeah, wasn't all bad.

four

I had never had my butt sniffed, but after I'd walked into the vet's office, the likelihood I would have my first up-close-and-personal dog-style handshake became a very real possibility. Doctor Carter may cater to werewolves, but they weren't his only clientele.

The place was packed. There were three cats in travel cages and one on a leash, which was just, y'know, wrong. I counted four dogs, a boy with a turtle in a box, another with a rabbit and—I kid you not—a hefty-sized man holding a tiny fishbowl. The bowl was empty except for the dingy water. My curiosity soared. But I couldn't ask. *Crap.*

I followed Luke to the receptionist's desk. The woman behind the counter peered up at him through thick glasses way too big for her face. Her brown hair, the color of a paper bag, was split down the middle, and pulled into two ponytails behind her ears on each side. Someone seriously had to tell her the look wasn't flattering. Not me, of course. I couldn't talk.

Her smile blossomed, coaxed to life by Luke's *GQ* looks. "Can I help you?"

"Yes. The name's Danhurst. He's expecting us," Luke said.

Like he'd used some secret code name, she sobered. "Yes, Mr. Danhurst. I'll let him know you're here. It'll only be a minute or two."

"Thank you," he said, but she was already on her way, disappearing through the half door and down a hallway.

Luke took the only seat left on a two-person bench. The scary-thin woman next to him held a cat carrier on her lap. The cat inside hissed at me. Every bone in my body wanted her to open that little door. *"C'mon, cat. You wanna piece of me?"*

Weird. I like cats.

As much as my brain balked at sitting on the floor, my body seemed to move on reflex, finding a spot next to Luke's leg. *"Do the employees know what you—I mean, we—are?"*

"Only Doctor Carter and his vet assistant, Linda, know. She's probably in the back with him. The others have just been told that the Danhursts are priority customers," he said to my mind without any outward sign that he'd spoken. This telepathy thing was pretty handy. Almost as fun as speaking a foreign language in front of people.

"Is Linda a werewolf?"

He draped his arm across the back of my neck and shoulders, his fingers digging into my thick fur, scratching. God, that felt good and not just in a dog kind of way. The feel of his hand on me, even through my fur, set my heart to a faster beat. My skin tingled under the dense hair, the sensation heating deep inside me, and my mouth went dry—and hot as an oven.

"No. She just wants to be," he said. *"She's been trying to get one of us to turn her for years. Not sure why."*

She probably just wanted to be closer to the pack, be a part of them. I know being a werewolf made me feel strangely connected to Luke in a way I'd never felt with anyone else before despite the short time that'd passed. It occurred to me that Luke had never touched me before he'd turned me into a wolf. Not that the opportunity had come up much. And granted, part of that was my fault. I'm not a touchy-feely kind of person. But still, I couldn't help wondering if all these casual kindnesses were because it was easy to forget the real me in this form.

I leaned into his leg, enjoying the closeness while I could. His scent surrounded me, more potent than I'd ever noticed before. Or maybe it was my wolf-enhanced olfactory sense that made the difference. Either way, I liked the sweet, masculine smell of his cologne, the clean soap scent, flavored by the unique phero-mone tang of his skin. I closed my eyes and breathed him in, letting the warm aroma seep into my bloodstream.

Here, in this office, surrounded by strangers, I was man's best friend, Luke's best friend, closer to him than anyone in the world. I was going to soak it up while I had the chance. Once I was back to my old body, the rules would change all over again.

"You're a frustrating bundle of contradictions, you know that?" he said.

"Uh . . . what's that?" I hadn't been talking to him, just think-ing to myself. He couldn't hear every thought that passed through my head. Could he?

Luke shifted in his seat, though he didn't move his hand from my neck. *"What rules? And who set them? Why do things always have to be so complicated with you humans? It's no wonder we're encouraged to steer clear of them."*

I glanced up at the tight, drawn lines of his face, the narrow slant of his husky-dog blue eyes. A sickening dread weighted my stomach. *"Hello? Testing. One. Two. Three. Can you hear me?"*

"I hear you, Ella. Not that it makes a difference. I thought the one good thing that would come out of my screwup was that I'd fi-nally hear your thoughts—understand you better." He laughed in his head, bitter. *"Hell, hearing your thoughts only make things more confusing . . . and maddening."*

"So you've been listening to everything I've been thinking? Everything?"

He looked down at me, blushing, emotion flickering through his eyes. At least he had the decency to look embarrassed. *"Yes."*

"Wow. Thanks for the heads-up. Am I hearing all of your thoughts?"

Luke looked away. *"No. Be grateful."*

What was that supposed to mean? *"Not fair."*

"You'll learn to shield your private thoughts. Takes time. Trust me, I realize now I want you to learn."

Sheesh, testy much? *"Who stepped on your tail? Why are you so grouchy with me all of a sudden?"*

He took his hand away and tucked it under the fold of his arms across his chest. *"Did you have to enjoy that guy putting his hands all over you so much? And I have never avoided touching you, Ella. I tried a million times to get closer to you. But no matter how many times I invited you to go out, you turned me down flat."*

"Whoa. Why does it bother you that I liked him . . . petting me?" The word felt wrong despite its accuracy in this instance.

Luke wouldn't look at me. *"It . . . it doesn't. Just forget it."* He tipped his chin toward the client door. *"Here comes Linda."*

Forget it. Yeah, like that would happen.

The tall brunette held the door open, her wide smile brightening at the sight of Luke. "It's so nice to see you again. Who've you got there?"

Veterinarian assistant Linda was pretty enough, if not a little tall in my opinion. She had a model's body, thin, long-limbed, and the kind of face that only really looked good in pictures. Too large eyes, too wide a mouth, the bones in her cheeks and jawline were too sharp, which made her face pretty but . . . intense.

She wore her oak brown hair in a neat bun at the crown of her head. When Luke led me toward her, I heard her heartbeat skip, smelled the light sheen of sweat, her eyes darkening as she stared at Luke. So it wasn't that she wanted to be turned so much as she wanted to be turned by Luke. I suddenly felt like the dumb dog in the room.

"This is Ella," Luke said, handing Linda my leash when she reached for it as we passed. She closed the door to the waiting room behind us, and it was just the three of us in the hall. "She's new. But there seems to be a problem. It's been more than twelve hours, and she hasn't shifted back yet."

Linda's face pulled with concern. She reached down and stroked my neck. "Well, she's absolutely beautiful. I love your coat color. Not many natural redheads in the pack. Who was she turned for?"

"No one." Luke led the way down the hall to the open exam room at the end. "It was an accident."

"Accident?" Linda laughed. "Right. There's no such thing when it comes to turning someone. Who's in denial?"

Luke stepped to the side once we were all in the small exam room. The muscles along his jaw flexed with his clenched teeth, face dark with reined anger.

After a few seconds, Linda glanced at him, seemed to study his face. She had her answer. "You?"

"It. Was. An. Accident." The more he said it, the more I started to wonder.

Linda's gaze shifted back to me, and the look in her eyes was decidedly cooler. "Well . . . I guess anything's possible." She tapped the metal table with her open hand. "C'mon, Ella. Hop up."

She jerked my leash, not enough I'd gag but enough to bug me. I think that was the point. A quiet growl rumbled out of me on reflex and drew Luke's attention.

"Is that necessary?" he said.

Linda's gaze swung to his, eyes wide and innocent. "Maybe you're right. She's a little . . . plump. Maybe it was her wonderful feminine curves that made you *accidentally* bite her."

I got the feeling she wasn't buying Luke's claim.

"That'll be all, Linda," a male voice said. I turned to see a lean man with peppery black hair, thin matching beard, and golden brown eyes wearing a white doctor's smock turn to hold the exam room open for his assistant.

She shoved my leash at Luke. On her way out she said, "If I'd known big breasts were your kink, I wouldn't have wasted my time waiting for you to ask me out."

"I think she likes me," I said.

A smile flickered across Luke's lips at my sarcasm, and then he shut it down and focused on Doctor Carter. Luke offered his hand. "Richard, sorry for the unplanned visit, but it's an emergency."

The doctor shook Luke's hand, but his golden eyes were on me. "So I see. Who's this?"

Luke didn't answer, and after the silence had turned awkward, I glanced at him.

"Richard's a werewolf, Ella," Luke said. "Remember? He can hear your thoughts."

"Oh. I'm Ella Blackwood. I don't normally look like this . . ." I felt I had to mention it. He probably already knew. But still.

"She was turned more than twelve hours ago after a car accident. She hasn't shifted back." Luke reached down and slipped the leash from my neck.

The doctor crossed an arm over his belly and propped his elbow on it to toy with the small graying tuft of hair beneath his bottom lip. He looked pensive. "Are you in any pain, Ms. Blackwood?"

I meant to shake my head, but it didn't feel the same with my wolf body. *"No. I feel fine. I mean, I hit my head in the accident, and my side was a little sore, but I'm feeling pretty good considering."*

Doctor Carter leaned over me, his fingers palpating up both of my back legs, rotating joints, feeling along my spine, down around my belly and chest, then over both front legs. I flinched at the occasional pinch of pain.

After feeling my neck, and under my jaw, the doctor stood, brow creased with thought. "Any broken bones have healed. Still some bruising. Could be a concussion, but the virus should've healed that. Might be internal injuries, still mending."

"Is that enough to stop her from shifting back?" Luke said.

Doctor Carter's brows drifted to his hairline. He looked from me to Luke and back again. "Possibly. However, Linda had a point. You're a beautiful wolf, Ella, and I'm sure you're just as lovely a woman, but there is a weight issue. Wolves are lean-bodied animals. As a human, your curves are a feminine asset. But your wolf half feels no need for the, uh, voluptuous padding."

"My wolf is trying to heal my big boobs and round butt?"

"I don't believe it," Luke said.

The doc shrugged. "I'll run some tests, get a few X-rays, a sonogram, but I'm fairly confident her wolf won't allow her to shift back until she's completely healthy."

"She is healthy," Luke argued. "She's a woman, and she looks like one."

"That doesn't mean her body fat index isn't higher than it should be and that it puts undue strain on her heart or other organs."

"Wait." I sat. Had to. I was feeling kind of woozy all of a sudden. *"You're saying that I'm stuck as a wolf until I lose some weight?"*

"Until your body becomes leaner, yes, I'm afraid so," the doc said.

I'd been trying to lose weight since I was fourteen. In nine years, my bra and jeans size had never changed. I was going to be an overweight wolf for the rest of my life. *"Perfect."*

five

Dieting was surprisingly easy when a large part of the menu consisted of food I had to catch first.

"You still have to eat." Luke wagged his tail, ears up and forward. He was such a cute wolf.

"I don't eat Thumper. Bring me a cheeseburger. I'll eat that," I said. *"I'm willing to wait forty-five minutes to get a seat at a good restaurant, but I draw the line at having to chase down my food. If it's got a pulse, forget it."*

"Trust me, you'll feel differently once you get started. Your wolf half will love it."

"But my human half prefers her meals medium well . . . with a side of fries." I plopped my butt to the ground, like the period on the end of my statement.

"Okay, never mind eating." He closed the distance between us, nuzzling his great-smelling head against my neck. I would never get tired of that. *"The hunt is great exercise and it's fun. You'll see."*

I laughed. *"Yeah. I bet."* I may not be the sharpest claw on a wolf's foot, but even I know when a person uses the words "exercise" and "fun" in the same sentence, their idea of one or the other is usually vastly different than mine.

"You're right. I don't want to push. If you're happy living the rest of your life in your wolf form, it's none of my business. I'll let the school know that your temporary leave of absence has become permanent." He looked away, oh, so coy. *"I'm gonna miss that great smile of yours, though. And I can't believe we'll never get the chance to dance."*

Not fair. *"Oh, so now you'd ask me out?"*

He looked back at me. *"I've asked you out a hundred times. You always turn me down."*

"You asked if I'd join the group and watch all of you dance. Not the same thing."

He sighed. *"You're right. I'm used to doing things in a group setting. I'll be more specific next time . . . the second you have a hand to hold again."*

Had he just promised to take me on a date? My chest squeezed, pulse racing. Not that it mattered. The only way we could go dancing was if I traded in two of my legs for arms, and the only way I could do that was to lose weight—body fat. Unless there was some new Weight Watchers plan for wolves, the odds weren't in my favor.

"Besides," he said, *"you're half wolf now. It's time you learn how to act like one. We do things as a pack, and that includes the hunt. Everyone is looking forward to you joining the group. But like anything, being a good hunter takes practice. I was hoping to give you a few tips before the rest of the pack tags along."*

I pushed to my feet. *"Fine. But can we start with something a little slower, like hunting a cow?"* At least it'd give me an outside chance at that cheeseburger.

six

Turns out hunting was . . . well, okay, it was fun. A blast, actually. Orgasmic. Right. Not really orgasmic, but close. It was freeing in a way I'd never known. And not really the hunting part, but the running.

Yeah, I dug the running.

I still hadn't gotten my cheeseburger, but Luke cooked a mean skinless chicken breast, and he had a way of making fish and vegetables that melted in my mouth.

We'd been "practicing" every day for two weeks, and I still wasn't tired of it. I'd gotten good at picking up the prey's scent, whatever it was that day—rabbit, pheasant, deer. We'd chase the game for an hour or more before cornering it. Luke encouraged me to take that last step and pounce. I just couldn't.

"Dude, it's Thumper, Bambi, and their buds." Luke didn't hold it against me.

I was getting faster. I knew Luke was holding back at first, shortening his stride, finding the path of least resistance through the forest for me to follow. Each run he gave a little more, ran a little faster, until I wasn't running to keep up, but matching him stride for stride.

Then last night everything changed. Last night was amazing. I led the hunt, zigzagging through the trees, the wind breezing through my fur, the scents of the forest seeping into my veins. I wasn't just running through the forest, I was a part of it.

The buck's heartbeat had echoed through my head, my own heart matching its rhythm. I could smell its fear, knowing death shadowed its every stride. Propelled by a powerful will to survive, the deer had raced through the woods, smooth, graceful, like a boat through water. But it couldn't escape me.

Luke and I split, him swinging wide to the right, me to the left, corralling the panicked stag, driving it where we wanted.

The smell of mud and moss and wet stone reached my nose twenty strides out. Without a spoken decision, Luke and I drove the buck straight for the stream. It would have to make a choice, stop and face death head on or leap into the unknown. As each long, hard stride ticked off the seconds, the deer had to know, like we did, what was coming.

It reached the high bank of the stream . . . and leapt.

I skidded to a stop at the edge, dirt raining down into the fast-moving water under my feet. Luke was beside me a second later, and together we watched the deer struggle, fighting the current until it reached the other side. Amazing.

I could still feel the pulse of the stag thrumming through my veins. I could still feel the soft give of the forest floor beneath my pads.

"Ella."

I could still taste the moist wooded air on my tongue, the sound of my howl on the wind.

"Ella, you're dreaming. Ella."

I opened my eyes to find Luke where I'd found him every morning, lying next to me with his arm draped over my chest. *"Did I just howl?"*

"Yeah, and your feet were twitching. Chase dream, right?"

"Yeah."

He shrugged. "Happens."

I stretched on the warm sheets and soft bed, my furry head snuggling deeper into the feather pillow. I may be of the canine species, but I'm no animal. After that first morning, I'd refused to sleep on the hard, cold floor when there was a perfectly good bed in the room. Luke hadn't argued.

He hadn't left my side since the first day, worried and waiting to see when I'd shift back. Every morning I found him nestled next to me, his hand on me to wake him if the change started. I'd grown used to finding him there, inhaling the scents that were so uniquely him, feeling his muscled body against my . . . fur. Still. It was nice. I'd miss it if—when—I turned human again.

Luke leaned into my back, his body molding against mine. He hugged me, digging his fingers into my fur. He whispered into my ear. "Tonight's the night. The whole pack is coming over for the hunt and to meet you."

"Oh . . . uh, goodie?" I'd met Luke's parents, Tomas and Sophia, a few nights earlier when they'd returned ahead of schedule from their European vacation.

Turned out, Luke looked more like his mom than his dad. Tomas was stocky with light caramel hair. Luke's mom's jet-black hair would reach the small of her back if she took it down from the soft pile on her head. She was only as tall as me, five-five, but she was lean and strong, like her son.

I liked them both instantly.

Sophia assured me their unexpected arrival was strictly a coincidence, but the goofy grin she kept flashing at me and the way she hugged Luke every time he passed by made me start to wonder. Mama wolf seemed to have high romantic hopes for her little pup. No matter how hard I tried to explain, I don't think she really believed we were just friends. I didn't worry about it. She'd believe me once I shifted back to my *real* body.

Luke laughed, hugging me tighter. "Don't sound so worried. Everyone's going to love you."

Not everyone.

"MADISON, this is Ella," Luke said, and I looked into wolf eyes the color of green pine needles. I'd seen her arrive about twenty minutes before I came out to the back deck at Luke's urging. She'd been human then, petite with a gymnast's body, powerful muscles, creamy peach skin, sunny blond hair, and a button nose.

"It's nice to meet you, Ella." She circled me as she spoke, sizing me up and, I think . . . sniffing me. Weird. *"I've heard so much about you. I must admit, I couldn't wait to meet our dear Luke's one enormous accident."*

I knew my infection, Luke's bite, had been an accident. And despite the way everyone continued to say the word with suspension, I didn't like the way Madison said it. The judgment and veiled disapproval in her tone touched the inner bitch in me. Maybe that'd been the point. Oh, well.

"I've been here for a few weeks. Didn't think you needed an invitation to visit the pack house."

"Normally, no. But you've created a curiously unique circumstance. New rules, new . . . complications," she said, brushing her body along mine.

For a human, it was an odd gesture, but for a wolf, it was borderline insulting. She was putting her scent on me, automatically placing me beneath her in pack hierarchy. Yeah, I know. I was the new girl, but like I said, I didn't like her tone.

I felt, more than saw, Luke shift forms off to my left. *"Madison, it's not Ella's fault I asked the pack to stay away from the house for a few weeks. She needed time to adjust."*

Madison finished her circle to stand in front of me. *"Really? None of the other turned members were given such focused attention. Especially from our future alpha."*

Luke positioned himself between us. *"The others knew what to expect. They'd been given time to prepare for their new lives."*

"Mmm . . . That's true . . . Isn't it?" She moved closer to Luke, nuzzling her nose into the midnight fur of his neck. *"But after two weeks alone together, you still expect us to believe your bite was an accident?"*

"It wasn't just the bite." He stepped away from her. *"She still hasn't shifted back."*

Madison's green eyes swung to me, a fraction wider. *"Still? I'd heard about her . . . problem."*

"Bite me." Admittedly, not really something you should say to a wolf. I hadn't thought that retort all the way through.

"She was gorgeous," Luke said before things got out of hand. *"Still is. Doc just said she needed to get her body mass index down. Heal some wear and tear on her heart."*

Gorgeous? Did he mean that?

Luke turned to me. *"Of course I meant it. You're the only one who didn't like your curves, Ella. I've always been a fan. So are a lot of men. If you'd stop wanting to be something you're not and accept the beauty you have, you'd have noticed."*

Madison snorted. *"Well, it doesn't matter if you just look like you fit in. That pretty coat and shiny eyes will only get you so far. You want to be part of this pack, you're going to have to prove you've got what it takes on the inside."*

"She's got it," Luke said, still meeting my eyes. *"She just needs to believe in herself."*

"Hi, Ella! Ooo, pretty coat." Two voices echoed through my

head in unison. I turned to see the identical wolves behind me, fidgeting, bobbing their heads, sniffing, and bumping into each other. They had to be teenagers.

Luke turned, too. *"Ella, these are my nieces, Chloe and Zoey. They're fourteen."*

"Twins?" I asked.

I heard giggles, but it was Luke who said, *"Yeah."*

"Wow."

"C'mon, Auntie Ella," one of them said, circling around behind me. The other flanked my opposite side. *"We'll introduce you to everybody and give you some tips on who're the best trackers and hunters."*

Auntie? What was that about? I didn't ask. I followed their lead as they introduced me to both humans and wolves.

The large gathering was an even mix of Homo sapiens and Canis lupus. The wolves were big and muscled with shiny coats and bright eyes. The humans were exceptionally attractive, all with toned, healthy bodies. Did I really look like I fit in here?

"You're beautiful, Auntie Ella," Zoey said on my left. *"Not that it matters. What counts is if you can be the alpha female Uncle Luke needs you to be. And that's all about what's in your heart, not what surrounds it."*

"Yeah, if being good-looking was all it took, Uncle Luke would've married Madison years ago," Chloe said. *"Being leaner will make you healthier, but it won't help you fit in."*

Did everyone know about my shifting problem? *Perfect.*

I'd heard it a hundred times. Who hasn't? What counts is the heart and soul of a person, not the outer shell. But I don't think I'd ever really believed it. Now there was no getting around it. For a wolf, it was all about self-confidence, skill, and determination. Luke was right. I had those qualities . . . when it came to teaching.

But now I had to learn to accept that my body type didn't

dictate whether or not I was attractive, or if I fit in. It was the way I saw myself that made the difference. And thanks to my wolf, I knew now, I had always had the soul of a kickass huntress.

Yeah. That's right. So bring it on.

By the time dusk set the forest sky ablaze with rich dark colors, I felt like one of the family. The crowd of wolves at the forest's edge had grown to sixty or more, all of them pacing, excitement rumbling through the air on hushed growls and anxious yips. Standing among them, I felt more complete than I'd known possible. God, I'd miss this.

Luke's father, Tomas, made his way to the front of the undulating mass of fur-covered bodies. Others' thoughts murmured through my head, nothing clear enough to follow, everyone thinking at once. I expected the hum of conversation to fade, anticipating a speech or some other indication that whatever we were waiting for was about to begin. But the rumbling of unfocused chatter continued.

Tomas reached the forest line. A few heads turned to watch him. He raised his nose, sniffing the changing wind. And then he ran.

Just like that. No words were needed. Instinct drove the pack of massive wolves into the forest after him, like a wave rolling back out to sea. Lean bodies stretched in long strides, eating up ground. The hunt was on, and I was in.

All in.

Luke raced at my side. I'd caught the scent of my rabbit, claimed it as mine by following its trail. Luke didn't seem to bother finding one of his own. He stayed with me. We'd work as a team. I liked that. Plus I could use the help. Rabbits were fast and clever, a real challenge.

Twenty minutes into the hunt, the wooded floor of the forest rolled and twitched with movement. Wolves, heads low to the ground, darting like fireflies this way and that, zeroed in for the kill.

The kill. I couldn't think about it. My wolf brain had narrowed to a single mission, a single thought.

Catch. The. Rabbit.

I was getting close, the rabbit's scent filled my nose, every breath drew it into my lungs, and it was seeping into my bloodstream, my mouth. I could taste him, feel him. The rabbit was mine.

A blur of light fur streaked across my rabbit's trail in front of me. And then again. I flicked my gaze ahead and saw her. Madison. She'd picked up the scent of a rabbit. My rabbit.

"Oh no she didn't."

"She's challenging you," Luke whispered to my mind. *"You can bow out. Give her the rabbit and find another. I'll help."*

"Like hell. That's my rabbit." I raced ahead of Madison, taking the risk that I understood my prey better than her, knew its mind, its escape plan, knew which way it would go without confirming my guess with my nose.

The world fell away, my path through the forest narrowed, cleared as though the trees and brush parted for me. My body was air and muscle, light and powerful. I felt my prey running for its life, its heart pounding with mine, its senses flaring out, turning this way then jackknifing back the other way.

I didn't know where Madison was. I didn't care. My eyes judged the distance between me and the four-foot-high fallen tree ahead of me and, beyond that, the rabbit where it sat frozen beneath one of the thick dead branches. I leapt, sailing over the tree, took three strides and scooped the rabbit up with my mouth before its tiny brain thought to run.

I turned around in time to see Madison jump onto the tree. She hadn't judged the distance as well as I had. Luke cleared the tree a second later to land in front of me.

"She didn't kill it," Madison said.

"Uh . . . yeah I did." The rabbit was playing dead. I thought maybe I could fake it. Never mind I could feel its little heart beating like a windup toy.

"She doesn't have to kill it," Luke said. *"She made the catch. It's as good as dead."*

"What is she, a vegetarian?" By the tone of Madison's voice, you'd think a vegetarian was someone who ate poo.

"She wouldn't be the only one in the pack," Luke said. *"She met your challenge. She proved herself the better hunter."*

"Auntie Ella's an alpha?" Zoey asked, trotting around the root end of the fallen tree. Chloe followed right behind her sister.

"Alpha?" The rabbit started wiggling in my mouth. I guess it decided playing dead wasn't getting it anywhere. *"But I'm new. Shouldn't I start at omega and work my way up?"*

"Nu-uh. Madison's an alpha, and you won her challenge. That makes you an alpha, too," Chloe said. *"That means you can be Uncle Luke's mate."*

"Mate?" The rabbit fell out of my mouth and ran.

seven

✳

Later that night it took me forever to fall asleep. My muscles were still charged from the hunt, and my skin kept tingling and crawling on my bones like it'd take off without me. The next morning I opened my eyes to the familiar sensation of Luke's arm draped around my waist, his body warm and soft spooned against mine.

I sighed, nestled my head deeper into the feather pillow. A strand of my hair caught at the corner of my mouth, and I reached my hand up and tucked the slobbery hair behind my ear.

Hair? Hand?

My body shot straight up without the aid of my brain. Luke snorted. I looked over my shoulder to see him lick his lips and roll over. The excitement of last night's pack festivities had worn him out, too.

Thank you, God.

I turned my back to him, my legs dangling off the edge of the bed, and examined my body. Yep, I was me again, two arms, complete with hands and fingers, two boobs—six was just . . . I can't talk about it—two legs with feet, not paws, and all of it absolutely furless.

Luke made another sleepy grumble, and I looked over my shoulder at him again. The urge to snuggle in next to him, inhale his scent, feel the warmth of his body on mine like I'd done every morning for the past several weeks was almost undeniable. But I was a different species then, a different person. It was over. I had to get out of there.

NONE of my clothes fit. I'd swiped shorts and a shirt from Luke but I had to get to work. I'd dropped two sizes but my boobs were only half a cup size smaller. What difference did it make, though, if I couldn't be with Luke? My leaner body wasn't the cure-all I'd always thought it'd be. I was still the same insecure person I'd always been, scared the man I'd come to love would change his mind when he saw the human me again.

The morning flew by, my mind everywhere except on work. I should've been trying to figure out why my seventh grade English class was scheduled to watch *Romeo and Juliet* instead of reading it. Instead I sat at my desk staring at the empty seats between classes, my mind wandering back to thoughts of Luke.

We'd grown so close, but what if things were different when we were face to face instead of face to muzzle. The thought of seeing him again tightened my stomach, made my hands sweat. What if everything was different between us now? What if it wasn't?

I didn't want to face him. I didn't want to lose reason to hope. Stupid. I know.

"Wow, Ms. Blackwood!" One of my students said as a crowd of them shuffled into the room. "You look great. Did you cut your hair or something?"

"No, she's just wearing makeup," another said.

"She wore makeup before. It's something else," said another.

I smiled. The Wolf Watcher's Diet, such as it was, worked. I was healthier, leaner, but I still looked like me. "Thanks."

Problem was, I wasn't sure that was a good thing.

It's a very good thing. Like I said, I'm a big fan of those curves. And I happen to love you just the way you are. I heard his voice flow through my mind like warm chocolate.

I looked toward the door of my classroom. He was still striding down the hall. I could hear him, smell him, and my heart skipped. I stood. He hadn't seen me yet. Not the new me. *You sure you want to say that before you walk in here and see me?*

You're my mate, Ella. I've known it for years. Do you know how hard it's been waiting for you to realize it, too? Waiting for you to want me back?

Your mate? Something clicked inside me—instinct. I knew it was true. I understood in that moment the undeniable need for him. There was nothing I wouldn't do to be with him.

He turned the corner through the door just as my students settled into their seats. In long powerful strides he crossed the room to me. His hands went to my face, cupping my cheeks in his palms. I gasped, my heart in my throat.

"Marry me."

"Yes."

He kissed me, his lips warm, firm, seductive, and oh, so right.

The room erupted with hoots and hollers, and slowly, reluctantly we broke the kiss. In my mate's arms I turned to stare down the pack of teenage beasts that were my seventh grade class . . . and growled. Not loud, but enough they could feel it in their chests without knowing for sure what it'd been. The room fell silent.

Yeah. Being a werewolf wasn't all bad. Being healthy was even better.

a fairy precious love

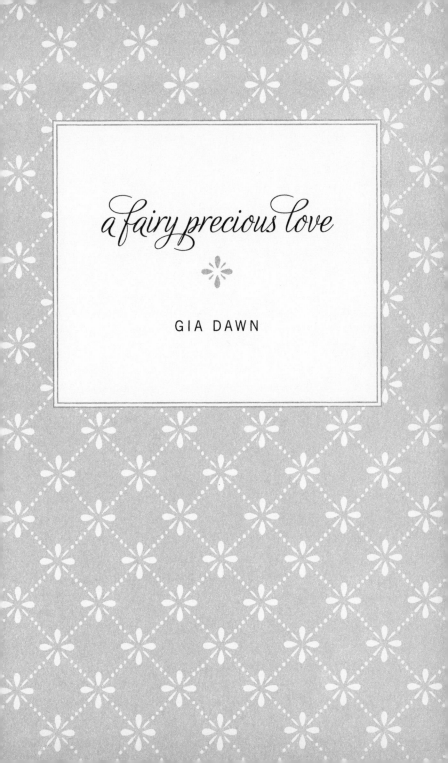

GIA DAWN

This is dedicated to my sister, Summer Eve Williams.

With a most gracious thank-you to our mother,
Marilyn Hutton Chamberlain, for loving us both.

one

❋

Summer watched the fairies fly by at dizzying speed, streaks of iridescent-colored wings cutting across the clear night sky like jewels thrown from the stars above.

A tiny hand tugged at hers, and she knelt beside Princess Honeysuckle, who looked at her through mournful eyes. "Will I still be a fairy once they take away my wings?"

Sorrow nearly made her mute as Summer struggled against a rush of tears. "Of course you will still be a fairy," she explained, pulling the child close to her heart. "But a fairy of a different kind, one that walks instead of flies."

"Foxglove said they will throw me out of the trees and make me live in the dirt."

Summer sighed. "Foxglove doesn't know a single thing about it."

She reached out and smoothed her hand across the little princess's malformed wing, its edge curling and turning black as the blight took hold and spread across the membrane. If left untreated, the disease would eventually work its way into Honeysuckle's bloodstream, condemning the child to a slow and painful death.

Not that the other option was all that appealing.

"I live on the ground," Summer continued, forcing herself to smile. "And after your wings are gone, you can come and live with me, and I will teach you how to walk and run and play games few other fairies know of. Have you ever seen a toadstool from underneath?"

Honeysuckle shook her head, tears spilling over despite her attempt at bravery. "Will my parents come to see me when I am on the ground?"

"Of course we will," came a masculine voice from behind.

Summer bowed as the royal couple floated across the balcony to sweep their daughter into a crushing embrace.

"And the king has promised to have our entire tree wrapped in railing, so you can come home by harvest time and we don't have to worry about you falling off." Crown Prince Stag-fern motioned for Summer to stand. "We cannot thank you enough for agreeing to let our daughter stay with you."

Princess Tiger-lily, Honeysuckle's mother, dabbed at her eyes with one corner of her lovely pink-tipped wings. "You don't know how much this means to us. When we first heard—" She broke off and clung to her husband and child, unable to finish the sentence.

Summer understood how they must feel. It was a terrible blow to find out one's daughter had contracted blight, knowing the only way to save her was to amputate her wings, forcing her into a way of life totally alien to most of her race.

Summer had had her own wings removed when she was seventeen, far older than most who contracted the disease. Old enough to remember how glorious it felt to fly. Old enough to have lost much more than her wings.

"I promise you I will guard her with my life," she said, meaning every word. Although she'd had many wingless children in her care throughout the years, this was the first time the royal house had been affected.

Honeysuckle sniffed and blinked, trying her best to keep her eyes open despite the fact she was up way past her bedtime. "Can we dance, Father? Fly so high we can touch the moon?"

Stag-fern nodded, his face tight with emotion. "Of course we can. Why, your mother was just telling me today she hadn't spoken to the moon for quite some time, isn't that right, my dear?"

Tiger-lily smiled and took her husband's hand. "Talk to the moon? Silly. He never once talks back."

Honeysuckle's giggles lingered as her parents soared high, keeping her safely wrapped in their arms.

Summer knew she should leave. It was a hard climb down to her cozy chambers dug into the ground by the tree's strong roots. But the lure of the ball kept her hostage, the music, laughter, and dancing stirring up memories she'd thought long forgotten.

Their people were separated into two distinct classes. Those who had wings lived high atop the forest, their days spent frolicking in the sunshine or playing games of hide-and-seek in the moonlight.

Those without wings, either lost from blight or other serious accidents such as getting caught in a spider's web or snatched by a bat searching for its dinner, were cast out to toil on the earth below with brownies and gnomes who worked the fields or made the silks and jewelry the flying fairies constantly craved.

Only recently had there been any social interaction between the classes, owing to the heroic efforts of the new fairy king, Wolf-moss, who was slowly making the upper kingdom safe and accessible to Summer and her wingless kinsmen.

She held on tight to the newly installed railing and peeked over at the view, the fairies soaring over the treetops, dipping and diving in an aerial display that left her breathless . . . spellbound by their beauty and grace.

A beauty and grace she would never know again.

With a sigh, she turned to leave, freezing when she caught sight of the man who studied her from where he hovered just out of the light. "Your Majesty," she said, dropping to one knee, her heart beating too fast and her pulse jumping madly.

Wolf was every bit as beautiful as she remembered, his indigo wings a perfect match for his eyes, and his midnight-colored hair hanging long across his shoulders. He moved closer, stunning her again as he folded his wings behind his back and walked the distance between them.

"I've been practicing," he said, taking her hand and pulling her to her feet. "Especially now that my niece has been affected."

Grief darkened the depths of his eyes, quickly hidden behind a thick sweep of lashes.

"She will be thrilled you took the time to learn." The touch of his skin more than she could handle, Summer pulled her hand away. It had been so long since she had seen him, she thought her emotions were well under her control, but where Wolf-moss was concerned, her heart had never done anything she told it.

"I still miss you," he said, his voice a purr in the night.

"You had to make a choice." Summer shrugged and lowered her head, feeling ugly and clumsy in his presence. She tried to sweep by him and make her escape, but he grabbed her arm as she passed and yanked her hard against him, the heat from his body curling around her like sunshine on a cloudless day.

"I made a mistake when I let you go."

"No. You didn't." Summoning up her courage, Summer dared him to see her in all her deformity. "You are king! Our people would never have accepted me as your mate."

"They would have if I'd demanded it." Wolf's mouth thinned, the expression not dimming his beauty in the least.

Summer fought back the urge to press her mouth to his, wishing she had some magic to turn back the hands of time, make them young, happy, before the blight had stolen any chance she had to be his.

"You have done so much to aid our cause," she said instead, stilling in his arms, her voice kept carefully neutral. "Carving stairwells into the trunk of the trees was an absolute stroke of genius, Your Majesty. And the balconies have made it possible for many to return to their families and lead a fairly normal life."

"But you don't." His head dropped, his mouth moved closer, his tone laced with sensual promise. "I could give you anything you wanted, if you would come and live with me. And even if you couldn't be my wife—"

He broke off as a pair of brightly sparkling ladies of the court fluttered over, flaunting their perfect and glorious wings in an effort to capture the king's attention.

Summer broke from his grip and tried to hide in the shadows, but one of them had already seen her.

"She's *blighted*," the fairy whispered, her eyes growing wide in horror. "Don't touch her, she's contagious!"

"And she looks so awful," added the second.

"Enough!" Wolf-moss ordered.

But Summer couldn't bear to hear any more. She fled down the stairs, nearly tripping over her feet in her haste to get away. For years she had advocated education and acceptance, but the old fears died hard. Although their healers had determined the blight wasn't contagious, many of her kind still believed the crippling condition could be spread through contact.

And she didn't have either the will or the energy to fight the superstitions tonight. Not with Wolf-moss watching her every move.

Slowing to catch her breath, Summer realized she was already too far down to stop by her parents' chambers. Not that she visited on any regular basis. Her mother and father were always uncomfortable in her presence, so she made it easier on everyone by staying remote and distant. Although they did make certain she had everything she needed to make her life comfortable on the ground, sending down luxuries such as spun honey and sugared rose petals.

When she finally arrived at her door, the world was nearly silent, most of the ground-folk already tucked in safely for the night. The fairy ball still whirled brightly overhead, but the music and laughter were caught by the wind and didn't carry this far below.

Summer watched for a few moments more, the ache in her chest refusing to subside. Once upon a time, she had loved Wolf, the beautiful fairy king, when she was healthy and whole and had wings the color of starlight. But things had changed, and no amount of wanting in the world could ever change them back.

Although she dreamed of him when the moon was full, hearing his voice call her name and feeling the mist of his breath against her cheek, she kept her tears tucked far away where no one would ever see them.

Not that she would sleep a wink tonight. She would go over every second of their meeting, replay it, savor it, and make up endings where happily ever after was more than a pixie's tale, and crippled fairies still found love with the one they'd always wanted.

She sighed, remembering the feel of his arms around her and the scent of him where it drifted across her senses. Then she went inside and closed the door behind her, shutting out the sparkling light and the world atop the trees.

two

✳

Several days later a terrified Honeysuckle stood in Summer's doorway, one thumb tucked into her mouth and a thread-bare gossamer blanket tucked under her other arm.

Her wings were gone, a thick layer of bandages covering the last of her rapidly healing wounds.

"Hello," Summer greeted her, opening the door and poking her head outside. "Are your parents still here?"

When Honeysuckle shook her head, tears streaming down her cheeks, Summer felt her anger rise. The least Stag-fern and his wife could do was see their daughter safely to the ground, she thought, grinding her teeth in frustration. How dare they leave the child to face the transition on her own.

"U-uncle Wolfy wantsss to s-see you." The little princess popped her thumb out of her mouth and reached for Summer's hand. "B-But his w-w-wings won't—" Her tears came in earnest now as Honeysuckle realized this was a completely different world than the one she was used to.

"I know. My door is so small his wings won't fit. I planned it like that. Really. This is a special place where wings aren't allowed."

Gathering up her courage, she took Honeysuckle's hand and walked outside, a smile plastered into place as she faced the waiting fairy king . . . whose wings had been bound with spider-silk, tucked close to his body and completely useless.

"What on a swallow's tail are you doing?" Summer gaped at him, wondering if she should be furious or grateful.

"Her parents would have come, but I'm the only one who could carry her down the stairs." His eyes glittered with a mixture of pride and pain, the swirl of emotion enough to make Summer's chest clench tight.

"You carried her all the way down?"

"Uh-huh." Honeysuckle nodded vigorously. "I never knew he was so good at walking."

"Neither did I." Now what? Did he expect her to invite him in for tea and cakes?

Summer eyed his trussed-up wings. If he could duck low enough, he would probably fit through the door, and her chambers were much larger on the inside. Plus, it would be wonderful for Honeysuckle to explore her new surroundings with a family member by her side.

His next words, however, nearly did her in. "I promised Honey I would stay for a few days. See her settled. Practice my legwork." He shook one foot in the air, grimacing as he made a huge pretense of trying to get it stilled and back on the ground once more.

Honeysuckle giggled, her cheeks flushing with healthy color. "Silly. Your shoes are torn already."

He frowned at the flimsy scraps of material before glancing pointedly at Summer's sturdy leather boots. "Where can my Honey girl and I get some of those?"

Finding her tongue proved difficult because Summer's mind was still trying to grasp the fact that Wolf was planning to stay ground-side for a few days. Did he mean to stay with her? And could she manage to be in his company for so long without her heart shattering in desperation for his love?

"You don't seem happy." His shoulders drooped, his wings trembling against their bonds. Summer knew his muscles must be cramping, his shoulders unused to being pulled down by the full weight of his wings. That he was willing to go through so much for his niece spoke volumes about the man he had become—and king, she realized when he spoke again.

"I should have come down years ago," he admitted. "These are my people, too, and I have been neglectful in my duty."

"No, you haven't. Everyone knows how hard you have worked fixing things above."

"Then could you invite me in? I really need to sit down, my legs are about to give out." A smile teased one corner of his mouth, turning to a grimace as his wings trembled once more. Summer could see he was tired, but when Honeysuckle's knees buckled, Wolf swept her into his arms without a second thought.

"Give her to me." Summer held out her arms. "You will have to bend very low to make it through the door," she added when he opened his mouth to refuse, moving aside so he could see the tiny opening.

"Done." He handed Honeysuckle carefully into Summer's arms. "I was hoping you might not have an extra room," he whispered wickedly against her ear, "and that I would have to sleep with you."

WOLF didn't know what he was thinking, tying up his wings and trying to see what it would feel like to live on the ground.

He told himself it was to ease his niece's transition, but his brother could have just as easily brought Honeysuckle to her new home and got her settled in.

The plain truth was he missed Summer. He'd jumped at the chance to be with her for a while, however slim the excuse he made up and however foolish he might look to anyone smart enough to see through his ruse.

Although it had taken him too blighted long to get around to it. Carving the stairs into their tree and fitting balconies on all of the public chambers in the upper kingdom had been more difficult tasks than he'd anticipated.

The fickle fairies of the world above vacillated in their support of the project with every passing moon. First they staged protests that lasted for days. Then they changed heart and tried to help, getting in the way of the craftsmen and woodworkers, which slowed the process even more than the protests.

But they were seeing the end of their labors at last, and Wolf fervently hoped that when the improvements were completed, their people could form a more integrated society where worth wasn't based on how high you could fly.

He'd always been intrigued by the ground-side of the world, fascinated by the way the fae had dug themselves in around the tree's massive roots, shops and houses peeking out from every nook and cranny, with gardens planted on every extra expanse of earth.

It was a calm and pleasant place, far removed from the constant flit and whirl of wings that never ceased above.

He ducked to follow Summer through her doorway, nearly having to crawl to get his wings below the jamb. Although he feared he'd feel cramped and suffocated by the smallness of the space inside, the room opened up to a large and comfortable area, with a row of windows high on one wall that let in a glimmer of sunshine and a breath of the fresh late-summer air.

It was cool and dry, with a hardwood floor covered in furs, the walls lined with pitch to keep water out and hung with bright silk tapestries.

Summer sat Honeysuckle on a couch made of pussy willow, and the little girl smiled when she ran her hands across the tufts.

"Blister," Summer called, "our guest has arrived."

The little brownie ran in from the kitchen and prostrated himself on the floor when he saw Wolf looking around the chamber. "M-my k-king," Blister stammered, his nose still pressed to the floor. "You didn't tell me the *king* was coming," he added to Summer in a peeved whisper, turning his head to glare up at her, dust bunnies clinging to his cheeks. "The house is a mess."

"The house is fine, good friend," Wolf assured. "I am certain my niece will be most happy here."

"His *niece*? The king's niece is our new lodger?" Blister's voice soared, and he grew even more agitated, crawling on his knees to stare at the wingless child. "I don't think the bed is soft enough, and I shall have to gather more milk thistle to stuff into her pillows. Such a pretty princess should have all the comforts of home," he added, standing to give the girl a surprisingly graceful bow. "But I made her my special lavender cakes, sprinkled with spun honey."

Honeysuckle's eyes grew round. "I love lavender cakes. However did you know?"

The brownie winked. "I also know you love hot milk and cinnamon. I have had some simmering on the stove all day." He started to bustle out the door before whirling around wildly when he realized he'd missed something. "Your Majesty, what can I bring for your pleasure?"

What Wolf wanted wasn't on Blister's menu, but he wasn't about to say so. "Lavender cakes and milk with cinnamon will be just fine—if you have enough?" He glanced questioningly at

Summer. He hadn't considered his presence might place a burden on her stores.

"Prince Stag-fern and Princess Tiger-lily have been most generous. We have plenty to go around." Her smile said she appreciated the sentiment, despite the lateness of his offer.

"Would you have any mead to flavor the milk?" He gave her
a chagrined look. "My feet hurt, and my wings are killing me."

Now Summer frowned. "Blister, why don't you let me serve
our guests while you call the cobbler. You can gather some extra
milk thistle as you go, and I will save you at least a cake or two."

"Excellent." The brownie counted out the list on his fingers.
"Cobbler, milk thistle. Anything else?"

"Some extra furs would be most welcome. The king will be
staying with us a few days."

Blister's nut-brown face paled. "H-His majesty will be staying
here? Oh, dear, oh, dear. I haven't nearly enough butter or acorn
flour . . . or rose water or—" He continued to mutter a list of
foodstuffs as he bowed before hurrying out to complete his tasks.

"What should I do?" Wolf asked in the ensuing silence. He
glowered at the small door that led into the kitchen. "I seriously
doubt I'll make it through there."

He turned to look for another way in, his wings knocking a
row of plates off a cabinet. He knocked off a vase of fresh-cut
flowers when he turned the other way to see what he'd done before. Honeysuckle giggled as his face turned red, his embarrassment giving way to grateful affection.

"I will replace everything I break," he promised, noting Summer's sly wink.

"Wings can be such a bother," she said, shaking her finger for
emphasis. "See, Honeysuckle, how easy it is without them?"

She spun around in circles, her arms spread wide and her hair
whirling around her like a cloud, every bit as graceful in her
dance as any woman he'd ever seen.

And the way his niece looked at her with such hope and admiration threatened to rip his heart from his chest.

Summer was special. A rare and priceless jewel, and he'd let her slip away, obeying like a good little king when his family and advisers had told him to let her go.

Was it too late to try to win her back? She was clearly successful and contented in the life she'd made for herself. What right did he have to coax her into returning top-side? There she would be fodder for every envious tongue that waggled and hurled insults under the guise of politely proper conversation.

Besides, she'd given no sign that she cared for him in any way at all. Was he dreaming, wishing for things he could never have, a simple life without the obligations and expectations of a king?

Or could he claim some small private victory, finding a way to blend duty with desire?

Summer brushed her hand down his niece's cheek, the gesture gentle and reassuring. "I'll be right back."

She would make a great mother. Strong, determined, but wise enough to teach their children there was more to life than the color of one's wings.

Honeysuckle stood and took his hand, leading him away from any more breakables to sit beside her at the table. After a bit of arranging, Wolf managed to fit comfortably in the chair.

"I like Summer," the princess stated.

"So do I. How are you feeling?"

"Okay, but my shoulders still hurt a little bit."

"Some willow-bark tea will take care of that." Summer said as she returned, setting a silver tray before them, filled with cakes and other goodies.

Honeysuckle grimaced. "I hate willow-bark tea."

"Everybody hates willow-bark tea." Wolf grabbed a lavender cake and put it on Honeysuckle's plate. "Do what your father and I used to do—hold your nose and drink it down fast."

"Really fast," Summer agreed, adding a dollop of butter to the girl's cake.

"Really, really fast," Wolf continued with a grin.

"Really, really, really fast," Honeysuckle piped in, picking up her pastry. "And then I can wash it down with another bite of cake."

"Done." Summer went back to the kitchen and returned with a cup of the loathsome brew. "Ready?"

Honeysuckle nodded. Wolf held his nose right along with her as she quickly swallowed. "Finished," she announced proudly after the required bite of cake.

three

❊

They spent the next few minutes feasting on sugary cakes and cinnamon milk until the cobbler arrived, busting into the room with a whistle.

"Good day, Your Majesty," he said without blinking an eye, "and good day to you, too, young princess." He knelt by Honeysuckle's chair, his expression kindly. "I am told you need a pair of the finest boots in the land, ones that will make you as graceful as a deer when you walk through the forest, and fast enough to outrun the swiftest of rabbits."

"You can do that?" The fairy child gaped at him in fascination. "Make magical shoes?"

"Of the most practical sort." The cobbler opened his pouch and pulled out a thick sheet of aspen bark. "Just place your foot here and let me draw your size."

Honeysuckle held out her silk-clad foot, giggling when he pulled off the flimsy shoe and set her foot on the bark, tracing around it with a charcoal stick. "That tickles."

The cobbler grinned and stuck her shoe back on. "Now give me the other one."

After he had repeated the process, he took out another piece of bark and knelt before Wolf. "Your turn, my king."

Wolf obliged, watching the cobbler with interest. "Do I know you?"

"Yes, sir. Name's Buckthorn. Fought with your father that spring the toads threatened to eat us all. Lost my wings in combat." He traced both of Wolf's feet and put his tools away. "The stairs carved around the trees have really helped my business, Your Majesty. I go up twice a week to take orders and make deliveries. I've even found me a wife with the loveliest set of—" He coughed and turned an embarrassed shade of red. "At any rate, we plan to marry in the fall, when her chambers are fully balconied. I thank you for that."

Buckthorn stood and brushed the dust from his breeches. "I'll have these done by morning. They might not be as sturdy as some, but they'll get you through a few days until I can make the princess a proper pair."

"Excellent." Wolf's eyes beamed. "I cannot wait to go exploring. And Honeysuckle has challenged me to a race."

"Has she now?" He gave the princess another broad smile. "Then I shall have to make your boots too small to make certain she always wins . . . uh, my king," he added with a bow.

Summer thought they'd made a great beginning as she led the cobbler to the door. "Thank you. I didn't know the king was coming or I would have warned you sooner."

"I've got a new apprentice who needs to learn how to work all night." Buckthorn narrowed his eyes at the fading evening light, frowning at the dark shapes that swooped jerkily in the sky above. "Bats tonight. Pray our kin stay safe up top."

Summer also frowned as she caught sight of the erratic flight of the animals. Bats mistook fairies for a food source with alarming regularity, and while they didn't actually eat her people, they could break off wings and send the fae spiraling down to their deaths. There had been more than one occasion when the body of a fairy had been found broken on the ground, a terrible and grisly reminder that danger was an ever-present shadow.

Blister's return broke the somber trail of her thoughts. "Milk thistle and furs, milk thistle and furs," he chanted, his voice muffled beneath the burden of the extra bedding.

Summer grabbed a handful of furs and the brownie gave her a grateful look. "Did the princess like her cakes and milk?"

"She ate three, and she practically had to snatch them off the plate before the king beat her to them."

Blister glowed at the praise. "I plan scones with blueberry jam for breakfast. Oh, dear." Without warning he prostrated himself on the floor, milk thistle flying everywhere. "Your Majesty."

"Rise, Blister." Wolf's grin was both apologetic and amused at the brownie's insistence on protocol. "Ah, I see we have to make some changes in policy."

"You think?" Summer threw the furs in a corner and chased a few rogue strands of the silky plant.

"Blister, I hereby give you royal permission to treat me like any other fairy whenever I am here on the ground." Wolf intoned the words in a commanding voice. "Stand up."

The brownie blinked and turned wide eyes to Summer before slowly clambering to his feet. "I am not worthy."

"Oh, please." Summer patted Blister on the shoulder. "You are the best housekeeper ever, and I couldn't manage a day without you, my friend."

The brownie ducked his head at the praise, only to snap it to attention a second later. "Got to make the princess's bed." He grabbed a fistful of pussy-willow down. "Softer than spider-silk, I promise." He ran to finish his chore.

Honeysuckle rushed after him, the last cake held in her hand. "Don't forget your lavender cake. Saved it special."

"Oh, dear, oh, dear," they heard Blister complain, "crumbs everywhere. Thank you, mistress. If you'll let me finish my work—"

By the time Blister had Honeysuckle's bed as perfect as he could make it, the little fairy had already fallen asleep on the couch. Summer studied the dark circles beneath the child's eyes, and the lingering pallor of her cheeks.

The surgery was never easy; however, the princess had braved her way through it. Summer unwound the swath of bandages and looked at the rapidly fading wounds, assuring herself there was no sign of infection or any evidence at all that the blight had spread beyond the child's wings.

"Is she all right?" Wolf moved and knelt beside them both, his nearness causing Summer's pulse to jump. He traced his fingers down Honeysuckle's arm, gentle and full of true affection.

He would make a wonderful father, Summer realized, the thought cutting hard into her chest. A wonderful father of beautiful winged children who he would teach to fly while his equally beautiful wife soared gracefully by his side.

She banished the picture with a sigh and gathered Honeysuckle into her arms. "I'll put her to bed. Your wings won't fit," she added with a nod to the low doorway that led into the back of the house.

Wolf rolled his shoulders, his jaw clenching as pain radiated through his muscles. "I don't think I planned this as well as I should have," he said, his mouth thinning to a grimace.

"Probably not, but you made a frightened little girl very happy today."

She quickly tucked Honeysuckle into the mass of pillows Blister provided, checking to be certain a thick pile of rugs was on the floor beside the bed in case the princess woke up in the middle of the night and fell, forgetting in her sleep that she could no longer fly.

Taking a deep breath, she returned to the main room to face Wolf . . . alone. Blister was already snoring from his bed by the kitchen stove. Wolf was standing in the middle of the floor, circling his arms as he lowered his head from shoulder to shoulder, trying to work the pain away.

"Let me release your wings." Summer motioned him to sit. "They need to be stretched out at least once a day," she added, dropping to the thick pile of furs Blister had gathered for his bed. "There should be enough room."

He grimaced and turned around, plopping down in front of her. "I really had planned to go without them the whole time."

"I don't intend for you to fly around the chamber." She smiled when he glanced at her over his shoulder, his eyes dark and enigmatic.

"Will it make you uncomfortable?"

"No."

In truth, she wanted to see his wings, smooth her hands across the beautiful membranes, run her fingers over his skin to feel the tightly bunched muscles beneath.

She wanted to touch him, however she could.

He sighed as she unlaced the silk thread and one wing unfurled. He moaned when she released the other, stretching them out cautiously. His wings were perfect. The indigo blue design swirled across the center, fading to the color of a noon-day sky, shot through with streaks of gold and banded by inky-black.

They expanded to fill the space, fluttering softly, shifting the air in rhythmic beats. The sight of them gave her an unexpected sense of pride as their glow mottled the walls with shimmering light.

Summer reached to unsnap his shirt at the shoulders, tugging the material down until it pooled around his hips, her fingers itching to smooth across his body.

In the light his skin gleamed a rich and burnished gold. He'd grown broader these past few years, his body filling out in all the right places, no longer the thin boy she'd adored. Despite the difference, her flesh remembered the feel of his, her hands moving of their own accord to rub the knots from the aching muscles.

But Wolf remained stiff and hesitant beneath her palms as if afraid he'd taken too many liberties already.

"Relax, my king," she chided, kneading her hands down his spine. "I promise not to hurt you."

"Too bad for me."

His voice was rough, thick, and Summer shivered at the emotion that laced his words. He'd always been unabashedly seductive, wooing her with a steadfastness that took her breath away.

But now she knew better. Whatever he said, however he said it, nothing would happen between them. He was king, and she was crippled.

Simple as that, no more to the tale.

Comforted by the turn of her thoughts, she grew bolder, digging deeper into the muscle, finding the knotted tissue and massaging it free. Wolf melted in her hands as she worked, and Summer scooted close enough she could use her elbows on a particularly stubborn spot. His head fell back to rest against her shoulder, his hair soft where it brushed her cheek.

She'd always loved his too long hair. While the other boys had poked fun and ranted on about his girlish appearance, Wolf had smiled and refused to take the bait.

"Women like it," he'd replied, proving his point when a row of fairy lasses flittered past, giggling and blushing and throwing him coquettish glances beneath their lashes.

Summer had been one of those girls fluttering by. It was the spring before the first trace of blight had appeared on her wings, and Wolf had asked her to dance with him at the next Full Moon Ball.

She agreed and spent the next few days digging frantically through her wardrobe for the perfect dress. She needed to look her best . . . especially since his mother was rumored to be looking for a suitable future daughter-in-law.

In those days she had never dreamed her life would turn out the way it had. That she would lose everything in a few short weeks.

Pain lanced into her stomach. What was she doing reliving the past? A past she could never hope to regain?

If she had any sense, she would send him packing on the morrow, back to the upper kingdom where he belonged. Already her heart was splintering back into pieces, the scars ripping open to release a longing so strong it took her breath away.

Her hands trembled against his skin. She pulled them away, startled when he shook his head and turned his face into her throat.

Need and loss and forbidden desire saturated the air between them. He reached back and circled his arms around her waist, dragging her tight against him. Her breasts tingled where they scraped against his back, another ache of want settling hard between her legs, a hunger long buried flying from its sleep.

She'd never taken another man to her bed. What other man could have compared?

"Please," he whispered. "Stay with me."

"I can't." Her voice was coarse, broken, ugly like her malformed body. Only her pride remained strong and perfect—for what good it did when every other emotion she possessed urged her to surrender.

"I would have given it all up for you," he continued in the same strangled tone, "if you'd asked me."

"Then you are a bigger fool than I give you credit for."

She pushed him away and stood at last, brushing imaginary creases from her breeches to hide how much it hurt to let him go. He didn't turn to look at her, keeping his gaze firmly rooted to the wall before him.

"I will have Blister redo the laces in the morning before Honeysuckle wakes up," she said, refusing to acknowledge how bad her voice was shaking. "You will sleep much better this way," she added lamely before ducking into her own bedchamber without a formal good-night.

A broken heart trumped protocol every time, she thought bitterly, tossing and turning as the night wore slowly on. Even a king knew that much.

Dawn found her exhausted, dry-eyed, and determined. She had work to do, and Honeysuckle needed her, whether Wolf was here or not. Still, she braved a glance at herself in the mirror, trying not to notice the empty space behind her shoulders as she brushed her hair and got ready to face them both.

four

They spent the next few days exploring the world around them. With the resiliency only a child possessed, Honeysuckle hiked and climbed and crawled with abandon.

She was fascinated by this new land beneath the trees, and after the very first day never once complained about her feet or legs hurting. If she occasionally forgot and fell while trying to jump for things too high for her to reach, she hid her awkwardness and moved on to some new sport.

Wolf, to Summer's continued surprise, managed to keep up with them fairly well, despite the bulk and dead weight of his tightly bound wings. He greeted the ground-siders with joviality and warmth, gaining their friendship along with their respect.

The time flew by so quickly, Summer was stunned when Tiger-lily and Stag-fern flew down to announce their chambers would be finished in two days and they would be taking Honeysuckle home.

They even presented their daughter with a pair of finely crafted wings exactly like her real ones. She could wear them in public and not feel outcast or ashamed. The child was delighted with the gift, and Summer had to admit there was some merit to the idea.

But she froze when Wolf whispered lightly in her ear. "I could have a pair made for you. I remember exactly what your wings looked like, down to the last flecks of silver that shimmered along their edges."

Her throat tightened at his words, grief and fury threatening to cut off all her breath. She had thought he'd come to care for her exactly as she was, but his offer cut deep, insecurities she'd thought conquered now screaming at the edges of her mind.

"I am not a child. I have learned not to care how I look or to worry that others might think me less than whole."

She lowered her eyes so he couldn't see her tears. She'd known better than to fall in love with him again, that letting him back into her heart was a mistake that would cost her dearly. All her self-respect and discipline went flying in the breeze, swept away on the wings she'd lost and the knowledge her world would never be his.

"Honeysuckle, you look beautiful," she said, bending down to give the little fairy a hug. "If I didn't know better, I would swear they were real. But you must remember the difference," she added in a cautionary tone. "Especially when you are way . . . up . . . there."

They both craned their necks back to look, falling giggling into a heap when they lost their balance and toppled over.

"Will you come visit me sometime? She can come, right?" Honeysuckle gave her parents a pleading look.

Tiger-lily nodded and held her arms out for her child. "Summer is welcome to stay with us whenever she likes."

Trying to keep her smile in place, Summer said, "Next time I get very brave and climb all those stairs, I promise to see you. But in the meantime, I have a brand-new fairy who needs to learn to walk like you."

It was a sad truth. Blight couldn't be prevented or cured, and several fairy children a year were forced to lose their wings. They came to Summer from every household, but while most had been forced to remain grounded before, she had high hopes that more and more would return to their families and friends.

Wolf questioned his brother. "How much work is left to be done?"

"Very little. The public balconies are all in place, and the last set of stairs will be completed next week. After that, every fairy in the kingdom will have full access high and low."

Wolf clapped him on the shoulder. "Excellent. I knew I could count on you."

"Will you be returning with Honeysuckle?" The prince's gaze bounced from Wolf to Summer, although his tone remained neutral enough. "People are talking, wondering if you have had some accident, or caught blight and lost your wings. They need to see for themselves you are whole and healthy. What should I tell them?"

"Tell them to mind their own damned business." Wolf frowned, his mouth thinning in irritation.

Stag-fern matched his brother look for surly look. "You have been away too long, Your Majesty. You have obligations—"

"Duties. Commitments. I am aware of my responsibilities."

"Then I suggest you get back to them."

The prince bowed before turning to give Honeysuckle another hug. "Your mother and I will see you soon, little one. We have missed you terribly. Thank you, Summer." His voice lowered as he faced her, his expression stern when he stepped in front of her to block his brother's view. "I trust your loyalty to your people and your king remains intact."

Meaning she knew her place and would do the right thing, staying below when Wolf returned to his world in the sky. "My loyalty has never faltered," she answered, making a light curtsy.

Stag-fern's look was genuinely respectful when he replied. "So it hasn't."

Taking Tiger-lily's hand, the two soared high, soon lost amid the leaves that talked in the afternoon breeze.

LATER that night, after her charge was safely tucked into bed, Summer came face-to-face with Wolf for the first time all day. Trying her best to remain indifferent, she sat on the couch and plucked at the pussy willow, shredding the tufts between her fingers until she'd torn an entire chunk off one side.

"If you keep that up, you'll be sitting on the floor by winter." Wolf watched her from the shadows. Blister had freed his wings, and they spread around him like indigo fire, all his power and grace on display for her to see.

She felt naked in comparison, a ghost of the woman she should have been, the beautiful fairy who could fly to the heavens. Unnerved by his appraisal, she stood and moved to the door, needing to put some space between them.

"I am sorry," he said, his voice like silk along her skin, "for the stupid suggestion about the wings. I think you are as beautiful now as you ever were."

She shook her head, unwilling to listen. If she was angry, it would be easier when he left. She clutched the emotion close, using it as a shield between them.

"I don't need your pity or your empty flattery."

Rushing through the door and out into the night, Summer willed him not to follow. But Wolf had always been a determined man. Bellowing for Blister, he had the brownie help shove him through the door, both of them cursing as they fought his unruly wings.

"This is much better," he said when he finally made it outside, pinning her against the tree. With his fully spread wings standing guard behind him, Summer found herself well and truly captured.

"Come fly with me." Before she could say no, he hauled her into his arms. "Put your feet on mine, and hold very tight," he ordered, snugging his arms completely around her waist.

"Honeysuckle—"

"Is safe and sound in Blister's care." Wolf pressed his lips against her cheek and pulled her hips tight to his.

Flames of desire licked between her legs, the insistent ache drowning out all rational thought. He nudged her chin up with his until he claimed her mouth with a groan of triumph, his tongue demanding she open and surrender to his kiss.

Despite her best intentions, Summer couldn't resist the feel of his mouth on hers. With a shudder and a sigh, she gave in, granting him access, sanity and reason vanishing like mist beneath the heat of Wolf's glorious presence.

"I actually think I have a better idea," he said at last, spinning her deftly around until her back was pressed against his chest. "I could never do this before," he added in a seriously gloating tone. "This is better than I imagined."

His hands curled around her breasts, strumming their tips into stiff and needy peaks. She trembled, trying desperately to hide her hunger, but Wolf's chuckle of satisfaction proved he wasn't fooled. He pinched harder, drawing the first whimper from her lips, continuing to seduce her as he slowly lifted off the ground.

Sudden fear made her stiffen as the world she was used to slipped away, but his arms were sturdy as oak branches, keeping her locked in his embrace with no chance he would let her fall.

The moon was a chunk along the horizon, its silvered light an ethereal glow. Stars blinked madly as if welcoming her home while the wind sang ancient songs of freedom that resonated in her soul.

But all of it paled beside the way Wolf made her feel, his teeth scraping a path along her neck while one hand dropped to burrow beneath the waistband of her pants.

When he spread his legs, he spread hers with them, giving him better access to stroke and tease the heart of desire nestled at the juncture of her thighs. He slid a finger into her, thrusting deep, biting harder on her neck when she lifted her arms to tangle in his hair.

The sky spun around them in a whirl of sparks as Summer gave in to the power of Wolf's touch. She was home, brought to a place she thought she'd never see again, lifted by the splendor of being held in his arms as her body hummed with growing hunger.

He surged his fingers high into her flesh, forcing a whimper from her throat as her body stretched to take him farther. "Come for me, my love," he demanded, rasping his thumb along the bud of sensitive flesh that ached and begged for more.

As she arched and cried his name, he flew them into a secluded bower, cupping her body against the tree as she trembled in his arms.

This was what she dreamt of when she was alone in the dark. This was the man whose face filled her every waking hour. This was the man she loved, now and forever, no matter that she might not ever have the chance to be with him again.

Tugging her pants farther open, he splayed his other hand on her stomach, sliding beneath her shirt to find her nipple and roll it between his fingers. And all the while he stroked between her legs, burrowing deep and releasing the pressure, only to thrust in hard once more.

Her legs shook as the sensation grew unbearable. "Harder," she urged him, her breath catching on the word. "I . . . uh . . . *please, Wolf.*" If she begged for his touch, she was beyond caring as the slick of his hand gave her all she wanted.

She came in a rush of heat and abandon, her flesh clamping tight around his hand as she scraped her fingers through his hair and buried her face in the thick black strands.

But he hadn't finished with her yet.

In the time it took for her to snatch a breath, he spun her around to face him, letting her pants fall to her feet.

"Take them off and wrap your legs around me."

There was no denying his order. Without a second thought, Summer stepped out of her clothes before smoothing her hands up his thighs to trace the line of his swollen flesh.

A rip of material set him free, and he grabbed her hips when she snugged her legs around his waist.

He was hard and thick, more than ready to take her as he bore her back against the branch. She tensed when he entered, whispering her discomfort as he thrust into her body. It had been so long, so long since he'd loved her.

Wolf swore, stopping his advance, but Summer refused to let him pull away, keeping her heels locked behind his back. A growl of need rumbled against her chest as he bent his head and kissed her, his tongue sliding between her lips, causing another arc of desire to burn between her legs. She relaxed and he plunged deeper, his tongue mimicking the action, over and over until he had settled himself completely inside her, rocking them both against the tree.

"I have always loved you," he moaned against her mouth, breaking the kiss to rest his head on hers. "Always."

A wave of bliss rolled up Summer's spine. "Show me."

Wolf didn't need any more encouragement. She clung to him as he took her, love and desire melding into an emotion so strong, she couldn't speak, couldn't think, could only grip him with wild abandon as she fell over the edge one more time, taking him with her as her body clenched hard around his length, dragging a rumble of pleasure from his throat as they came together in a final burst of ecstasy.

He held her for a long time when it was over, the night air cooling the sweat from their bodies as they cuddled in contented satisfaction.

A stray trill of fae laughter brought Summer back to the present, the reality of their situation digging a sliver of ice into her heart.

They were from different worlds.

Always and forever.

five

Summer let her legs uncurl from Wolf's waist and pushed against his chest.

"Don't do this," he pleaded as she reached for her breeches, tugging them back on.

"What?" She pretended an ignorance they both knew was a lie. "I need to get home. Honeysuckle will be—"

It happened so fast, Summer didn't have time to scream as her foot caught on a sliver of bark and she lost her balance. Wolf's expression turned bleak as she tried to grab his hand, but her fingers missed his and she fell backward, tumbling toward the ground in a nightmare of scratching twigs and sharply cutting leaves.

Wolf dove after her, but his wings were encumbered by the foliage. Summer shrieked, this time for Wolf's safety as one of his beautiful wings was shredded, sending him into a spin that made her head swim and her stomach roll.

And still she fell, the occasional branch slowing her momentum, but she knew she was in trouble. She lost sight of Wolf as she slammed onto a larger branch, unable to catch her breath.

Before she could think to grab on to anything, she was falling again, faster and faster as the ground swelled up to meet her.

And suddenly Wolf was there, his arms strong around her body as he gripped her close to his chest. They still spun madly, and Summer closed her eyes, unwilling to watch as they splattered in the dirt. Then, somehow, someway, Wolf gained control of his one good wing, slowing their fall enough to steer them toward a thick tuft of grass.

And they would have made it, landed safely, until the bat darted from above, biting down on Wolf's last good wing. He dropped her with a curse of agony as the creature careened skyward, realizing in the nick of time the fairy king was not a tasty midnight snack and letting Wolf go at last.

But the damage had been done. Landing beside her with a thud, Wolf's body was broken beyond repair, his face a bloodless mask of pain.

"What have we done?" Summer couldn't take her eyes from his face as she tried to see how badly he was injured. "Wolf. I'll get help. I promise. Don't you dare do anything stupid like die on me before—"

Her words faltered as despair took over. She didn't care if she never saw him again. As long as she knew he was safe in the world above her, she would be satisfied in her world on the ground.

Let him live, she prayed to whatever gods were listening. Just let him live and I will be content.

His eyes fluttered open and he tried his best to smile, but the expression failed as anguish shuddered through his body. "S-Say it," he mouthed, his hand clutching desperately at hers. "Tell me you love me, too."

"I love you. Always," she answered on a sob, squeezing his fingers tight.

Without another sound, he passed out cold, lying so still and lifeless, Summer felt the panic rise once more.

But she had to get help. Covering him with whatever scraps of leaves and brush she could find, she began her run to the village.

Her legs were strong and sturdy beneath her as she flew across the ground, fleet and sure-footed, familiar with the action. In a very short time she made it to the village, her cries of alarm bringing everyone out of their houses.

"The king is hurt," she yelled. "On the ground, just beyond the hedge of roses."

And then she was bounding up the stairs to the upper kingdom, taking them two at a time, not stopping even when her lungs burned as if scorched by fire and her heart thudded so hard in her chest she thought it must surely burst.

At the top of the tree she called for Stag-fern and anyone strong enough to fly Wolf to their healers, all the while continuing her silent pleas that he would live to see the morning sun.

"he will survive."

Summer breathed a sigh of utter relief when Prince Stag-fern sat down beside her. She'd been waiting for hours to hear news of Wolf, hope warring with doubt as the night rolled on and she had no word of his condition.

"His wings?"

"Gone."

Her heart plummeted. "What will you do?"

"Whatever my king commands me." Stag-fern rubbed his hands down his face, his expression grim. "My brother has already decided to abdicate the throne."

"He can't do that." Summer jumped to her feet, intending to speak with Wolf and ask him to wait before he made such a hasty decision, but the prince grabbed her arm.

"If you care for him, leave us. This is a family matter."

His words effectively shut her out, putting her firmly in her place. He was right. She had no business meddling in royal affairs, no matter how much she loved the king.

Wolf was out of her league, over her station, the same as he'd always been.

She nodded, grief curling like iron around her spirit. To have found him only to lose him again— "I understand."

"Honeysuckle has already been brought to our chambers. We thank you for all your help. Our daughter is our life." Stag-fern's voice held a note of compassion, despite the stilted formality of his speech. He gave her shoulder a quick squeeze before he turned to leave. "You saved Wolf-moss's life. That will not go unrewarded."

There was nothing left to say. Summer watched him fly back the way he'd come, disappearing through a doorway.

But Wolf was alive.

It was all she'd asked for, she reminded herself in the days to come when she threw back her head to gaze up at the sky. He was alive.

IN the aftermath of Wolf's injury, the family of Summer's new student decided not to send the child down right away. Because her house seemed so empty with no one to talk to except the faithful Blister, Summer found herself spending more and more time adrift in the forest, roaming farther than she'd ever gone before, sometimes sleeping through the night tucked into a crevice beneath the thick root of a tree, other times arriving back at the village long after the stars and moon had risen.

It was late on one such night that Summer dragged herself through the village, still unwilling to go inside and face the dark alone. She stood outside her door, trying to keep from staring up through the leaves or wondering what Wolf was doing in his world so high above.

"You keep late hours, mistress love," came a familiar voice from the shadows. "I have been waiting here since dusk, and my feet are killing me."

"Wolf!" She whirled, wanting to run and throw her arms around him, but holding back, afraid he wasn't completely healed.

He stepped into the light, hands crossed over his chest, a tentative grin tilting up one corner of his mouth. "Do you recognize me without my wings?"

Of course she did. "You are still the most beautiful man I've ever known," she assured him honestly, understanding at last what he'd been trying to tell her all along.

Love looked beyond appearance. Love could care less whether you had wings or not. Love saw beyond such superficial things. That was the gift love gave to the willing.

When he stepped closer and took her in his arms, she could feel that he was trembling.

"You are still not healed," she chided, curling his arm around her shoulder to help bear his weight. "You should be in bed."

"I'll be in your bed soon," he said with a naughty wink. "That is, if you'll have me."

Summer was already shaking her head. "You can't stay here; you're king."

He managed a tinny chuckle. "How could I be king of earth and sky, when sky is forever out of my reach? Shhh, my love," he continued, placing a finger to her lips when she tried to argue. "My brother will make an amazing king."

"Are you certain this is what you want?" Summer brushed her fingers down his cheek. "To stay here with me?"

"Oh, I don't intend for us to stay ground-side." His face took on an excited glow. "I was talking with Buckthorn, the cobbler, and we've come up with a plan to create a flying machine that will soar higher than the clouds."

Summer frowned. "A flying machine—that sounds entirely too dangerous."

"But exhilarating." An excited glint shone in his eyes and Summer vowed she would do whatever it took to keep that light shining forever. "We should have the first one ready by the spring thaw."

He pulled her away from her door so they could both watch the fairy lights twinkling overhead. "Won't it be grand to see the looks on their faces when we sail to the Midsummer's Ball in our amazing winged chariot?"

"And how will you get this marvelous machine off the ground?"

Wolf had the decency to blush. "Uh . . . we haven't exactly figured that part out yet."

They sat together on the chilly ground, their arms entwined so tight the cold had no way to seep through to their skin.

"How is Honeysuckle?" Summer giggled when Wolf nuzzled his chin into her neck, goose bumps rising along her flesh as desire stirred deep in her stomach.

Wolf nipped at her earlobe and fire licked between her thighs. "Honeysuckle is beyond delightful. She is weaving us several pairs of booties to keep our feet warm this winter." He trailed his hand up her leg and torso until it rested against her breast. Her breath caught and her pulse leapt when his thumb rubbed her nipple into full and aching arousal.

"Will you stay with me forever, have my children and be my wife?" Wolf's voice was so raw with emotion, it caused her throat to constrict and she could only nod in joyous agreement.

"B-But our c-children will have wings," she managed to stammer as he pushed her back against the earth, throwing a muscled leg over hers.

"Beautiful, perfect, amazing wings," he purred against her mouth. "And since we taught his daughter how to walk, my brother has given his solemn vow that when the time comes, he will teach our children how to spread their wings and fly."

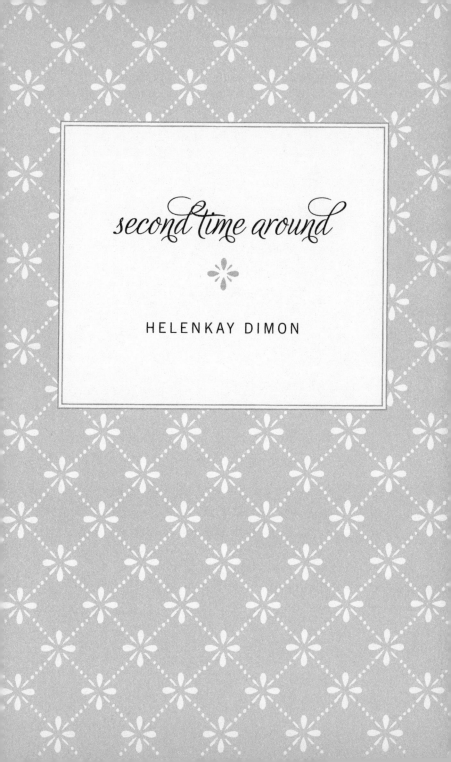

second time around

HELENKAY DIMON

one

Heath Sanders walked into her quiet classroom at four o'clock with the same cocky assurance he'd possessed as the state champion football team's star wide receiver in high school fifteen years earlier. Six foot something of lean muscle and sandy blond hair. A few lines now stretched at the corners of his pale blue eyes, but the handsome gene refused to take a break. Even the dirty flannel shirt and fatigue tugging at his mouth couldn't hide his high cheekbones and firm chin.

Serena Davis had a master's degree and ten years of teaching to her credit, but seeing him still turned her brain to a big puddle of drippy goo. To keep from babbling like one of the lovesick seventh grade girls she taught, Serena kept her butt in her chair. Watched him move—make that stalk—down the row of empty desks and stop right in front of hers.

With his hands at his sides, he nodded his welcome. "Serena."

Insisting he call her Ms. Davis seemed kind of stupid in light of their history, so she let the informality slide. "Thanks for coming in so fast."

"You said Nate was in trouble."

The man had his faults but being a caring dad sure wasn't one of them. Anyone who looked at Heath for more than two seconds could see how much he loved Nate. Heath burned with it even as he worked his body to exhaustion every week.

"Not exactly."

"You said there was a problem, so I dropped everything and got my a—" Heath swallowed. "Butt over here."

Nice job, Serena. She cringed and made a mental note to tone down the drama when leaving phone messages for him. Her concern morphed into something that likely had the poor man in a panic over the safety and well-being of his twelve-year-old.

"I said I wanted to talk with you about Nate." She motioned to the chair next to her. "You can sit down."

Heath's forehead wrinkled in a look hovering somewhere between concern and anger. Hard to tell. "I'm fine here."

"Your choice."

Those long fingers slipped up to rest on his hips. "Since I have four hours of work left to do today and only about three hours of decent light left to do them in, why don't you tell me what's going on."

And he stayed on his feet. Looming. Maintaining the power position. She guessed that was the goal. He commanded everything on the job site and everything in the world around him. Seemed he planned to rule this conversation as well.

"There's an issue with a girl," Serena said with decidedly less flare than her last attempt to communicate with him.

"Meaning?"

Dancing around the subject wouldn't make the discussion go any faster. The embarrassed part of her that wanted him in and out lost to the professional part of her that needed him to understand her concerns. "Has Nate told you about Lexy Young?"

Heath's arms fell to his sides as he blew out a long breath, as if preparing his mind for the bad news to come. "No."

Oh, yeah. She had mucked this one up. She wanted to raise an issue and have a rational talk about kids and peer pressure. Things Heath, who had played the role of most popular kid in school with the super athlete credibility and everyone wanting to be his friend, might not understand. Not everyone sailed through the tough adolescent times the way Heath had. He never lived through the pimply awkward stage. He didn't know about being left, picked last, or ignored. She needed him to tap into those foreign emotions now.

"Serena?"

She picked up her pencil and flipped it through her fingers. It was either that or let all the energy bouncing around inside her come out as fidgeting, and she did enough squirming in Heath's presence without adding some new facial tic . . . or worse.

"She has a crush on your son."

This time those hazy blue eyes narrowed. "Who?"

"Lexy."

"Oh." Heath bit his bottom lip in what looked like an attempt to hide a smile. "Okay, well, I guess girls start young these days. Makes me kind of glad I have a son."

"They can get into just as much trouble. Trust me." She pushed the list of potential horribles out of her mind to stay focused on the Nate and Lexy issue.

"That's the sort of thing that keeps me up at night, but still I don't see the problem here."

"Lexy has been texting Nate."

"So?"

"All the time." Serena whipped the pencil hard enough to send it flying across the desk.

Reflexes still solid, Heath caught it before it thumped against his chest. "Cut through this for me, Serena. Did Nate say or do something to upset Lilly?"

"Lexy."

Heath set the pencil down on the far edge, just out of Serena's reaching range. "Her name isn't the point, is it?"

Serena searched her mind for the best way to explain about young girls and their universal self-esteem issues, how one wrongly spoken word could send their self-image into a death spiral. "Nate is ignoring her texts, and she's having a hard time with his treatment."

Heath's jaw dropped open. It took a couple tries for him to close it again and say something. "And?"

"She's crying, pouting. She spends most of her time staring at the back of Nate's head and ignoring classroom instruction."

"Then shouldn't you be talking with Lexy's parents?"

"I will, but I wanted to ask you for a favor first." Serena thought about making a lunge for the pencil but threaded her fingers together instead. "Could you talk to Nate about this?"

"About what?"

"Girls and their feelings. Help him understand how some people, especially teen-girl people, are sensitive." She knew she had turned the corner and entered the land of babbling, but she kept on talking anyway. "That if he could—"

Heath held up a hand. "Wait a second."

"I know this is difficult for you to understand."

"Not really. You want me to tell my son he has to text back to some girl he's not interested in because she might otherwise get sad, is that about it?"

A steady pounding started over Serena's eyes. The headache came screeching in right about the time Heath's attitude kicked up. "Well, sort of."

"And Nate is supposed to do this thing he doesn't want to do because his English teacher said so? Like it's part of his grade or something."

Her request sounded ridiculous when Heath said it like that. "This has to do with the man you want Nate to be."

"He's twelve."

Serena rubbed her hands together hard enough to draw blood. "And he has the power to hurt a little girl."

Heath leaned down with his fists on the edge of her desk and a knowing smile tugging on the corner of his mouth. "Are we talking about Nate or are we talking about something else?"

Serena refused to dignify that with anything other than a denial. "I don't know what you're referring to."

Oh, but she did. She'd moved away for a few years, got married only to get divorced when her idiot husband cheated, and then eleven months ago had come back to Glen Ridge, the cozy bedroom community just outside of Washington, D.C., to rebuild her life near her sister. But she never forgot Heath. The same handsome senior who had lived across the street and whom she dreamed about marrying in that way only a sophomore girl lost in the confusing space between infatuation and true love could do. All these years later she still blushed when she thought about the awkward fifteen-year-old version of herself and the way she'd thrown herself at Heath. Despite the shyness, she had made a pass and offered him something precious and special . . . and he'd laughed at her.

"You sure we're not dealing with something else here?" he asked, his mouth twitching as if he wanted to laugh at her again.

The adult in her had survived all sorts of heartbreak. With her accomplishments, she should have been immune to the insecurities. If the tumbling in her stomach were any indication, she wasn't.

"We were talking about Nate," she said.

"You sure this isn't about you?" Heath leaned in closer. "Us?"

At this brief distance she could smell the crisp coolness of the outdoors on him. That was enough for her to push back in her chair. If she wanted the scent of sunshine and changing seasons, she could walk outside and take in a big whiff of October. Inhaling the air around this man could only lead to trouble.

"There is no us," she said, ignoring the old sadness that descended over her heart when dealing with that reality.

"Serena, come on."

"I'm a grown woman."

His gaze never left her face. "Obviously, but according to you, these things wreck girls and cause all sorts of problems for years to come."

"Well, they can. Yes."

He slid his thigh on the edge of her desk and let his hand wander closer to her locked palms. "So, is this about Nate or is this about me?"

"My job is to watch over your son. To help guide him."

Heath started shaking his head before she even stopped talking. "Your job is to teach him English. As his father, I can handle the rest."

"We've gotten off track." She tried to push her chair back but the rollers got stuck on something. Stupid chair. "I'm worried about Lexy's feelings."

Heath's eyes narrowed for a second before he pulled his shoulders back again. "If you say so."

"I do."

He dropped his feet back to the ground and stood up, stretching a little and showing off a flat stomach in the process. "I'll consider your concerns."

Just when she thought she could exhale in relief, he threw something else at her. Something vague enough to suggest trouble. "What does that mean?" she asked.

"Exactly what I said."

That explanation did not make his intentions one ounce clearer. "Are you—"

He stopped her words with a simple nod of his head. "I'll handle Nate."

"I still don't know what you plan to do here."

"Maybe you should concentrate on my question instead."

As if she'd be able to think about anything but him for the next two days. She'd turn over every comment he said, every look, and then close her eyes and relive the rumble of excitement that filled her belly whenever he stepped close.

"And when you're ready to discuss that subject—us—let me know." Then Heath winked at her and turned around. He lumbered out the door with the same precision as when he walked in. Only this time he whistled.

two

❖

Despite time ticking away, Heath skipped the rest of the work-day and headed for the house he shared with his uncle and son. Pulling into the driveway of the two-story craftsman-style home Heath had updated through hours of sweat, he made a plan. He refused to lecture Nate on his girl and texting choices, but the gnawing in his gut made him want to spend some extra time together.

The hours had been brutal lately what with the new town-house complex going up on the edge of town. Responsibility for bringing it in on time and on budget fell to Heath. That meant putting in long days to beat the bad weather that could come as early as mid-November.

But if Nate needed attention, Heath vowed to give it to him, even if that meant time away from the one thing that kept him sane. Construction did more than pay his mortgage. It fed his need to stand in the fresh air and see the physical progress from his labor. Used to be the adrenaline rush came with the cheers of the crowd. That all crashed to a halt with a career-ending injury to his wrist right after he made the decision to forgo college and turn pro. Even now his hand swelled and ached at the end of every day. But hammering, throwing wood on piles, seeing a hole in the ground turn from nothing into a house, filled him with a quiet satisfaction he'd once taken for granted.

Twenty and devastated by the loss of the only dream he ever had, with a surprise baby on the way and a girlfriend who yearned for bigger things than the hard work of finding a new life outside of the money and fame his football career once promised, Heath hadn't known where to turn. Then his uncle offered him a job and a home. Having Lucy split right after Nate's birth, complaining about her lost opportunities and ruined figure, turned out to be a relief. Almost thirteen years in, Heath didn't regret the choices he'd made. His uncle handled the bids and office work. Heath hired the workers, acted as the job supervisor, and performed the hard labor.

Yeah, his life finally ran on track.

Except for Serena.

She had moved back to town less than a year before and ignored him every second since. Well, she had until Nate ended up on her class list. Now Heath ran into her as often as he could make it happen without being obvious. Hard to apologize for being a simple teen boy who hurt her all those years ago when she never allowed a moment of privacy between them.

"You're home early," Stan said as he rested his arms in the open window of Heath's truck. "Something wrong?"

Heath fiddled with his keys before finally grabbing them out of the ignition and climbing out. "I need a reason to be here in time for dinner now?"

Stan laughed as he clapped a firm hand on his nephew's shoulder. "Was more worried about the fact you're sitting here with that stupid look on your face."

Heath blamed that one on Serena. Just thinking about her

made his IQ dip. "I had to go to the school." Stan stopped but Heath took a few extra steps until he realized his uncle's reassuring presence had disappeared and Heath turned around to find him. "What?"

Stan's stunned expression said it all. Worry, fear, it all lingered right there on the surface. "Is Nate in some kind of trouble?"

Heath didn't make his uncle wait. "No."

Relief flooded Stan's face. Heath recognized the dizzying feeling since he'd experienced it as soon as Serena started talking about texting instead of fighting or something much worse. Nate was a good kid, smart and dedicated to sports over drinking or drugs. But even the levelheaded ones could stray. Heath knew that from experience. To prevent as much trouble as possible, he and Stan traded off work hours and responsibilities to ensure Nate stayed busy, active, and subtly supervised.

Heath opened the door and stepped into the large foyer, spying Nate sitting on the family room couch in his usual position. Phone in hands, head lowered, and eyes unblinking as his fingers moved over the keys. "Hey, kid."

"Dad?" The cell fell forgotten to the couch. "What are you doing home?"

A little less surprise would have been nice. Heath wondered if he was flunking this dad thing by being away too much and working too hard. "I heard it was pot roast night. Only an idiot would be late for that feast."

Stan passed them both and headed for the kitchen. "Speaking of which, let me get it on the table."

"I'm starving." A huge grin spread across Nate's face as he jumped to his feet and slid to a stop in front of Heath.

"Now there's a surprise." Heath fought the urge to ruffle Nate's hair. Settled for the brief touch of a loving hand across his back instead.

The opportunity came and went that fast as Nate lifted his

phone to eye level and headed for the kitchen at a near run. Heath tried to show a bit more restraint even though the aroma of cooked beef and vegetables lured him in.

By the time he hit the doorway, Nate had the plates on the table and was eyeing the foil-covered platter on the counter. "Can I—"

When Nate tried to sneak a piece, Stan tapped his fingers with the back of a spoon. "Wait until I get it out on the table."

"You know the rules." Heath tried to sound stern but knew he'd failed when Nate tried a second time and met with the same smacked-fingers fate.

Contentment flooded through Heath as he watched the by-play. His parents had divorced and moved on to new families in faraway states right about the time the potential professional-football money train stopped. Stan stuck around. He was rock solid and the best role model Nate could ever have. Stan took them in and loved Nate as his grandson from the day he changed the first diaper. The same kid who now leaned against the counter with worn blue jeans falling off his hips despite the belt cinched at his waist.

The latest growth spurt had taken a good fifteen pounds off Nate's frame and added two inches in height. The sudden shot left him lanky and a bit clumsy, tripping over his feet as if his legs suddenly got in his way with every step. Heath smiled at how in one year his kid went from chubby to a mess of long arms and legs.

The brown hair hanging down in Nate's eyes probably didn't help either. His mother's hair. He never asked and Heath didn't offer, but Nate got the dimple in his check and his wide smile from her.

Just then Nate's phone buzzed, and he broke speed records whipping it up to stare at the screen. Heath wondered how Nate didn't wrench his shoulder with that action.

"Who is it?" Heath asked after a few seconds of silence.

Nate just shrugged.

A tickle of unease moved across the base of Heath's neck. "Does that mean you don't know or you don't care?"

"It's no one."

Uh-huh. That supposed no one had Nate nodding and smiling. Then he dropped the phone on the table and sat down ready to be fed. "Is it dinner yet?"

"Aren't you going to respond to the caller?" Heath asked.

Nate executed shrug number two.

"Let's trying using words. What does the shoulder roll mean?" Heath asked.

"Nah."

Stan stopped cutting the meat to glance at them. With the blade moving in the air, pointing and accenting, he joined in. "I don't see why he even needs that thing. I got through life just fine for all these years without everyone being able to track me down every second."

And then came Nate's third shrug of the early evening. "It's for emergencies."

Stan spun the phone around on the wooden table and stared down at it. "This Lexy person is an emergency?"

Heath stifled a groan.

Nate skipped the shrugging and went straight to denial. "She's no one."

The stupid grin. The rush to the phone the second it rang followed by the nonchalance. Yeah, Heath knew the signs. Nate liked Lexy and was making her work for it. Twelve and already a player.

Conflicting emotions battered Heath. He wanted Nate to be good to women, not use them or take them for granted. He also wanted his kid to maneuver the dangerous road of girl-boy relations without being told what to do.

Rather than rush in, Heath settled for a wait-and-see approach. "No texting at the table. Take the phone into the family room. You can get back to the girl after dinner."

"It can wait until tomorrow." Nate took his time getting up and reaching for the phone. He glanced at the screen about six times as he shuffled his way out of the room.

Heath assumed Nate expected the poor girl to text again before giving up for the evening. "You know, if you don't answer, she might decide you're not interested and stop texting."

Nate shot back a confident smile. "I doubt it."

SERENA reached across her sister's kitchen table and dipped a chip in the homemade salsa. "I met with Heath today," she said between crunches.

Lindsay spun around from the stove so fast she almost dropped the glass casserole dish of enchiladas on the floor. "What?"

"Set that down first and I'll give you the details."

All wide-eyed and staring, poor Linds looked too stunned to do anything constructive. Serena finally took pity on her younger sister and used a napkin to help guide the food to the dinner table without burning either one of them.

Kicking the stove closed behind her, Lindsay slid into the chair across from Serena. "I thought you were avoiding him."

"Hard to do that when his son is in my class." Serena scooped a heaping portion of juicy Mexican food onto her plate then, hoping the tempting smell of the food would put a stop to the inevitable string of questions from Linds.

One of the benefits of moving back home was her sister's cooking. Being the sibling of a caterer had its privileges. Acting as the willing and eager guinea pig was the biggie. And "big" was the right word. Serena knew if she didn't get to a gym soon, the size of her butt could double.

"Is something wrong with the kid?" Lindsay snapped out of her shock long enough to fill her plate.

"There's a girl in the class who has a crush on Nate."

Lindsay snorted. "Sounds familiar."

"Excuse me?"

"Seems to me you know a little something about having a crush on a male in the Sanders clan."

That would teach her to share haunting secrets with Linds. "And to think I once begged for a little sister."

Lindsay wiggled her eyebrows. "I'm a dream come true."

More like a nightmare if Serena didn't get control of the conversation. She knew Linds wouldn't let the subject drop without being dragged in a different direction. "The thing with Heath happened a long time ago."

"Sure it did." Lindsay let out a sound somewhere between a snort and a chuckle.

"I've been married. He has a child. There is a lifetime of experiences separating my moment of stupidity from the people we are today." There. Serena felt a flutter of satisfaction at her reasoned argument. No way could her sister...

Silverware clanged against Lindsay's plate. "Are you kidding me?"

So much for changing the subject. Serena refused to look up. She shoveled the food in her mouth fast enough to make conversation impossible. She even cut off her breath and fought back some wheezing to get it all in there.

Well, she did until Lindsay grabbed the edge of the plate and pulled it away. "Stop eating, Serena."

"Hey!"

Lindsay tapped her fork against the side of her plate. "Are you trying to tell me that you don't relive that day fifteen years ago every single time you look at that dreamy hottie?"

"You think Heath is cute?" The thought of that sent Serena's stomach into freefall. Lindsay qualified as the perfect catch. Twenty-six, semimature, a successful business owner, and stunning with her floaty blond hair and grass green eyes. She'd look perfect standing next to Heath or hanging on his arm.

Serena shook her head to wipe the horrifying mental image out of her head.

"I'm not dead, Serena." Lindsay surrendered the fork back to Serena. "Every woman in Glen Ridge thinks he's hot. It's a combination of his looks, which are smoking, and his dedication to Nate."

Serena didn't need a play-by-play on that issue. She knew exactly how silly women got around Heath because she was one of them. Crushing down the flirting and wanting took all of her strength whenever he came around, which seemed to be more and more often lately.

"I get it," she muttered.

But Lindsay was on a roll and didn't show signs of slowing down. "I've catered parties and heard married women buzz like teenagers about how Heath takes off to see Nate's games and then goes back to work. About how he raised the kid on his own. About how good he looks in his jeans."

Serena ignored the last part, but the way Heath acted with Nate never ceased to send her heart spinning. She had tried to build up an immunity to Heath, but then he walked into parents' night at the beginning of the school year and smiled down at his son with such pride and affection that Serena's will broke. That impenetrable wall around her heart started cracking.

Maybe he didn't understand young girls, but he sure understood his son's needs and filled them. She tried to imagine if there was anything sexier than a man who adored his kid that much.

"The man is swoon-worthy." Lindsay toasted Serena with her glass. "There, I said it. You think it, but I'm the only one in the room brave enough to spit it out."

"Are you done saying it?"

"And you love him."

Lindsay's singsongy voice seeped right into Serena's brain, making her defenses snap into place. "I do not."

"Did you ask him to be your first again?"

Heat rushed to Serena's cheeks at the personal question. It was too late to deny that scene all those years ago since she let the information slip in a sisterly moment of negative common sense. "That day has long passed, and now it's time to change the subject."

"Did you ask him out?" Lindsay kept shifting in her seat as if the energy bouncing around inside her screamed to get out.

"Of course not."

Lindsay's smile fell. "So, you actually kept the discussion to business only?" Her disappointment filled up every corner of the room.

"It was business." Or that was the excuse Serena kept repeating in her mind.

Part of her wanted to see Heath's actions and husky-voiced questions in her office about their past as something more than an attempt to stroke his ego. He sounded almost . . . interested. But that couldn't be the case. He barely noticed her and had certainly made his opinion of her known.

"Why are you blushing?" Lindsay asked.

"The food is warm."

"You're not even eating right now."

Serena knew the only way to move on from this topic was to capitulate, let her sister say whatever she needed to say, and then ignore her. "Why don't you get to the point so I can get back to my enchiladas?"

Lindsay sat up straighter and morphed right into a fake therapist role. "You need to stop mourning a bad marriage. Ned was a loser, all buttoned up and pompous."

Shock stammered through Serena, stealing her words for a second. "But . . . but I thought you liked him."

Lindsay shook her head. "No. No one did."

"That's not true." Wait, was it? Before her parents retired to Arizona, things were strained, but that was because Serena missed so many holidays. Ned preferred staying in town and dining with colleagues to family outings. He wanted . . . that was the point. Back then her life centered on what Ned wanted to the exclusion of everything else.

"If you think back, you'll realize I went out of my way to be in a separate room from the guy. You moving out of the state helped, but it ticked me off that you did. Philadelphia." Lindsay rolled her eyes. "Typical Ned insisted you follow him no matter what. The guy was a self-important loser. And you were out of your mind for agreeing."

Memories crashed in on Serena. Her mother's clipped tone on the telephone. Lindsay's repeated refusals to visit. The swiftness with which her family descended on her Philadelphia condo and moved her back to Glen Ridge when she said her marriage was over. It was as if her life played out with everyone else seeing the truth and her being lost in denial.

"I had no idea."

Lindsay waved in dismissal. "But we're not talking about Ned. He's over and not worth our time. We're talking about Heath."

"I'm thinking we absolutely need to talk about this," Serena said, enunciating each word as the reality of her wrecked marriage settled in on her. Being with Ned touched and destroyed more than she realized.

"He's gone and you're better off. Heath is a different story." Lindsay leaned in closer. "Want to know what I think?"

"I'm afraid to say yes."

"You should let yourself fall for him again, even if it's a short-term thing."

An affair? Her baby sister had been pushing the Heath agenda forever but always as a long-term option. This no-commitment thing had to be a new tactic.

"Why are you so pro-Heath all of a sudden?" Serena asked, knowing she was going to hate the answer.

"It's not sudden. While you were off playing in Philadelphia, I was here. Scoping him out for you." Lindsay pretended to bow. Almost bounced her forehead off the table in the process. "You're welcome."

The visions of Lindsay stalking Heath flowed through Serena's head like a horror film and scared her witless. "Please be kidding."

"He's the perfect fling."

Uh-huh. Not kidding. "Who says I want one? Or that he does?"

Lindsay shot her a you-poor-thing look. "I think your cluelessness is cute."

Serena suddenly felt every minute of her thirty years on the planet and then some. "What does that mean?"

"Next time you have one of your professional talks about Nate and his schoolwork, or whatever boring thing you do to waste time instead of making the move on Heath—"

"It's my job."

"Yeah, well, take a minute and grab a good long look at the man."

Oh, she did that just fine without any coaching. That was part of the problem. "Because?"

Lindsay smiled over a mouthful of food. "You're going to figure out that you're the only one in the room with business on your mind."

three

Heath heard Serena's angry voice before he saw her. He sat crouched on the roof of a townhouse checking the new tile job. She stood on the ground shouting at one of his workers over the mind-numbing sound of the saw.

"I need him now." The construction noise stopped just in time for her words to blare out over the construction site and echo through the trees.

He peeked down over the just-installed gutter and saw his men freeze in place. Burly men who threw out profanity every other word, whether or not the resulting sentence made any sense, stared with mouths hanging open.

It wasn't hard to spot her. The red stain on her cheeks lit up the cloudy afternoon. Looked like perfect and professional Serena Davis stood on the verge of losing her cool.

"Uh, Serena?"

She glanced around, as if trying to detect the placement of his voice.

He sighed, admitting defeat. "Up here."

"What are you doing on the roof?" With her fists slammed on her hips and her head tilted to the side, she sounded furious to find him above her.

"Working."

Something about the word deflated her. She glanced around, more sheepish and less commanding this time around. Could be she noticed the fifteen men surrounding her, waiting to see what she would do or say next. "I need you to come down here for a second."

"So I heard. Everyone within ten miles did." He immediately regretted the comment when he heard his men chuckle. Embarrassing her was not his plan. He'd done enough of that to last a lifetime. "Okay, that's enough. Everyone back to work."

By the time he slid down the ladder and landed at her side, his workers had cleared out and she had launched into full pacing mode. Her wide eyes searched the grounds and stared down the men hovering at the outskirts of the work area and not doing anything to hide their eavesdropping.

"I shouldn't have come here." She mumbled the comment, but he heard it anyway.

He caught her by the shoulders before she could storm off. "Whoa."

"You're working." She motioned around her. "There are all these people."

"It's okay."

In a town the size of Glen Ridge, news traveled with the fury and speed of a raging wildfire. He knew she'd lived through a tough divorce and returned from Philadelphia shaken and a good deal poorer thanks to her high-powered divorce attorney. Ned something was her husband. The guy's name didn't matter. Heath hated him on Serena's behalf for having taken something from her. Something important in the form of self-esteem that she was only now struggling to regain.

What he felt for Serena was the real question. They were so different. Where she thrived on education and intelligence, he'd dropped out of college having gone to only a handful of classes in the two and a half years he'd spent there. She knew every book, every author. He struggled to read. Hell, keeping up with his seventh-grade son's work proved difficult most days.

Despite all that, he wanted to kiss her, hold her . . . make love to her. Something in her sad green eyes tore at his insides. Her scent, her smile, they stayed with him long after she passed him by. Spending almost a year working on a way to break through to her had been a challenge. The idea of apologizing and starting over kept him going.

Every other part of her worked on him, too. Her dark brown hair fell in waves past her shoulders. And her curvy frame, nothing like the stick-straight blondes with plastic boobs that had followed him through college. No, Serena had always been different. Pretty and smart, her body and mind maturing well before her head could catch up. But her days of being jailbait and off-limits were long over.

"This is not what I had planned for today," she said.

That sounded ominous. "Let's go inside."

She looked around. "Where exactly?"

He slipped his hand under her elbow, careful not to scare her since her hands shook. She acted jumpy and uncharacteristically out of control, and he didn't want to add to her distress. "The rooms are only roughed in, but we can have some privacy."

She stared at the front door of the townhouse ten feet away from her as if noticing the building for the first time. "Oh."

He guided her through the would-be family room and to the very interior of the house. From that position, none of his men could sneak a peak. But his biggest concern was her. "Are you okay?"

"Sure."

"I'm not convinced."

"I want to move Nate to honors English class." The words rushed out of her so fast, running together as she went, that Heath barely understood her.

"What?"

She inhaled deep enough for him to see her chest rise and fall.

He forced his gaze back up to her face. Leering at her struck him as the wrong call at the moment.

When she started talking again, her voice returned to a normal decibel level and the racing rhythm slowed. Worse for his nerves, that sexy, husky tone of hers returned full force. "He's smart enough. He's way ahead, and reading well above his grade level."

Well, damn. Of all the things Heath thought she might say when she stepped onto his work site, something about an English class wasn't even in the top hundred. "Honors English?"

"Of course."

She actually made that sound reasonable. "You're saying you're really here about Nate?"

"Why else would I be here?"

Yeah, why. The woman was determined to drive him crazy. No question.

"Do you come to the workplace of all of the parents?" he asked, knowing the answer was no.

"Yes."

Oh, come on. "Really? If I asked around, I'd find out this is a habit for you?"

"Please pass the invitation on to Nate." She turned and bolted for the door.

He waited until she got five steps away from her final escape to stop her. "No."

She shifted around nice and slow. When she finally faced him, her mouth drew down in a severe frown. "Excuse me?"

"You're the teacher. You should ask him."

"You're the parent."

No matter how many hints he dropped, she continued to run from him both emotionally and physically. "Believe it or not, I'm aware of how Nate got here."

The spark returned to her eyes. "Why are you making this difficult?"

"Why are you pretending you came here to talk about Nate and not us?"

Silence filled the wall-less room.

Careful not to spook her, he took a step toward her. She glanced down, watching his feet, but didn't run screaming out into the yard. He took that as a sign of progress. A small success, maybe, but still movement in the right direction.

When he stood in front of her, close enough to keep anything from squeezing in between them, he stopped. "I was hoping you came here today to take me up on my offer."

"What offer?"

Doubt tugged at him until her intense stare gave her away. She knew exactly what he was talking about. The knowledge and understanding played across her face and in direct contrast to her words.

After a quick wipe against his pants to get rid of the dust and slime, he slid his hands up her arms and felt her tremble in response. "The one about us."

"I told you—"

"Let's try not talking for a second."

He leaned in, giving her plenty of time to pull back, slap him, scream for reinforcements, or show him a red light. When she stood there, her body stiff but her eyes dark with need, he went for it. Lips against lips, he kissed her. Not a gentle test. No, this was firm and searching. He wanted to learn her secrets and show her that the man in him appreciated the woman she had become.

With a soft groan, she slowly lifted her arms and wrapped them around his neck. "Heath."

When she whispered his name against his lips, let him taste the words as the smell and feel of her hit his senses, he lost his control. No longer holding back and giving her time to adjust, he fell into her. His mouth slanted over hers, showing her how far past friendship and professionalism he had raced. The guilt he felt over his youthful idiocy gave way to a very adult desire to know her as she was now.

Just as the kiss built and his hands started touring down her back, she broke contact. She moved away, putting a few inches of unwanted air between their heated bodies. "We have to stop."

His mouth trailed to her neck. "Because?"

"Heath, you know."

Her stern teacher voice broke through the sensual haze winding around him. His head shot up. "What is it?"

"This can't happen."

If he reached out, he could pull her back in his arms, cuddle her close, and tell her all those things he kept locked inside, but she had moved away from him in her head. Thrown up the "no sale" sign and relegated him to the stupid jock part of her brain. None of this happened out loud or in the open, but he saw it. Felt it race through every muscle and vein.

The space she stuck between them made his blood simmer. "What's the problem?"

"I am your son's teacher."

A thought popped into Heath's head. A sneaking suspicion that refused to go away. "Do you teach honors English?"

She bit her lower lip. "Well, no."

Just as he thought. The honors program was a ruse. Should he call her on it or not? He waffled. Finally, he went for the home-turf advantage. "We'll expect you around six."

"Why? For what?"

"Dinner and to talk to Nate about the class."

Her eyes widened with a look that could only be described as terror. "That's not necessary."

Since she was such a big fan of logic, he turned it back on her. "You said you're in the habit of dropping in to deliver this type of news."

"That's not what I meant."

"Well, that's what I heard." He took his gloves out of his back pocket and tugged them on. "We'll see you at six."

❊

HEATH made it home by four. He knew his workers would talk about his rush off the lot for weeks. The ribbing had started before he even got to the car. Two of his most loyal, toughest men had asked if he planned to paint his toenails before dinner. The boisterous laughter still rang in his ears.

Yeah, falling for a woman in full view of a construction crew did not count as Heath's idea of a good time. And that was exactly what was happening.

Maybe following her for months had started the process. Watching, learning, studying. The painfully shy and strikingly beautiful girl who offered him her virginity before she was old enough to know he didn't deserve it had become a stunning woman full of life and sunshine she tried hard to tamp down and hide. But in those quiet moments during a school assembly or standing at the front of her class talking with a child, her face would light up with a smile and his world tilted.

With all her outer strength, he saw her fractured core. He possessed one, too, and could recognize the beast. Losing everything—

his dreams, his family, his security—taught him rough lessons that even now left him raw. There were very few people he could count on. Very few he'd risk loving. For so long Nate and Stan had pretty much filled the list. Then Serena came along all haughty and determined to ignore him, and he found her irresistible.

The fact that after all these years she let a long-abandoned teen crush humiliate her in his presence clearly made her feel silly, but to him it showed a soft, vulnerable side. Beneath all the bluster and claims of professional conflict, she felt something for him. He saw it in her sweet eyes and felt it in the kick of her pulse. When he kissed her, every doubt faded away. They had something they could build on and nurture.

But he had to break through her protective shell first and wrestle a few of his own demons in the process. Demanding trust from her was one thing. Giving it back was another. The latter had proved impossible for years, but he wanted to let her in. To trust her with his shame and share the burden.

"Why are you home?" Nate asked the second Heath walked in the front door.

His son put him in his place without even knowing it. Amazing how kids could reach right inside you, find that one insecurity, and twist. "I'm thinking I've been working too many nights lately. The plan is to get home earlier from now on."

"Okay."

Heath took that for the desperate teen plea it was and mentally rearranged his schedule. He could take a little less pay, cut some expenses at home, and give the hours to guys who needed some cash. Nate needed time, not more video games.

Heath plopped down on the couch next to Nate. "What's that?"

"A book I have to read for Ms. Davis's class."

Heath reached over and turned the spine toward him. Never heard of the title before. Not a surprise since Heath couldn't remember the last time he read anything except a sports page. School had come hard for him. Processing the words and information had proven impossible, so he hid his inadequacies under a heap of sports trophies. The stumbling attempts to comprehend something other than a playbook stuck with him. Even now Nate would mention a book or some random fact every adult should know and Heath had to fake it.

He feared his son would discover the problem and find him lacking. Those worries had him thinking about Serena and wondering if she could help without judging him. Seeing disapproval in her eyes would kill him.

"Is it any good?" Heath asked.

Nate's eyes bugged out. "You haven't read it?"

"No."

Nate flipped the book around in his hands, rolling his eyes and sputtering as he went. "Come on, Dad. Everyone's read this."

Nothing like feeling like an idiot in front of the one person you always wanted to impress. "I'm not a big reader."

Nate snorted. "Whatever."

Heath tried to remember a time when he felt so small, so insignificant, that his chest ached with it. The minute when the university told him he'd lost his scholarship and dropped too many credits to remain as a full-time student, the fight with Lucy when she called him worthless—it all paled in comparison to the pain that shot through him with his son's dismissive look.

Heath vowed that would be the last time. If that meant telling Serena about his failings and having her tag him as a loser, so be it. When his son talked about school and his work, Heath wanted to understand. Needed to understand.

four

✣

Serena stood outside the Sanders home for a full ten minutes before knocking. Heath's kiss still lingered on her lips. His sexy smile played in her head until his face swam before her all the time.

She had gone to his job site that afternoon to set the record straight. To let him know her crush had disappeared long ago, thank you. Because of Heath's behavior all those years ago, she knew how Lexy felt. Serena had experienced rejection and cried into her mattress, sure her heart would never mend. The adult in her knew the extreme reaction came from a mix of teen hormones and exaggerated grief, and that the ache faded as other boys came sniffing around. But back in that moment, being ignored had meant everything. So, Heath needed to get his act together and not pass his macho crap on to another generation.

It was a good plan. Tough and clear. Then he'd kissed her and her good intentions had fled.

Over him. *Yeah, right.*

The younger her had adored an image, a piece of him that

played football and walked down the crowded school hallways to turning heads and giggling girls. The woman appreciated the man he'd become. She'd listened for months to hear rumors about Heath treating women poorly, but they never came. He stuck close to home and focused on Nate. Somewhere along the line her boy crush had turned into a worthy man.

And a bossy one.

He'd ordered her appearance, and she'd shown up. If she hadn't messed up so thoroughly this afternoon, she'd have kicked him in the shins and spent the night eating one of Lindsay's take-out trays.

Launching into the honor's English thing instead of her planned personal chat had caused this mess. Not that the class change was a fake. Nate should have been switched long ago. Serena chalked the oversight up to a poor previous teacher who skated through her responsibilities and assumed kids who excelled in sports couldn't also achieve in the classroom. Serena refused to tie up kids in that manner.

The door flew open. There stood Heath. Ruffled hair and shy smile, faded jeans and slim sweater pulled across a most impressive chest.

Even a smart woman didn't stand a chance with this one.

"For the record, it's six-oh-five." Heath glanced at his watch. "Almost oh-six."

"I can leave if I'm too late."

He slipped an arm over her shoulders and tugged her inside. "Nice try."

Warm. The word described her body temperature and the room. Dark floors and light overstuffed furniture defined the open area. From her position in the foyer, she could see the large family room and into the kitchen beyond. Pots rattled and a television played in another room.

"Where is everybody?" she asked.

"Stan is making dinner."

The man in question picked that moment to peek around the corner. "Serena Davis. It's been years." He walked out with an apron tied around his waist and wringing his hands in a towel.

She'd always liked Stan. He had a big teddy bear look to him. Tall with a gruff voice and the biggest smile she'd ever seen. She knew from town gossip he'd amassed a fortune and worked almost nonstop until Heath and Nate dropped back into his life. From then on, Stan had devoted his life to home and hearth.

She lifted her hand but Stan wasn't having it. He wrapped her in a suffocating hug.

"Much more of that and she'll pass out," Heath said, his voice dry and laced with amusement.

"Very happy to see you." When they stepped apart, Stan caught the towel before it hit the ground. "You're staying for dinner, yes?"

"Oh, no—"

"Of course she is." Heath's arm slipped around her back as he talked.

Stan's knowing gaze took it all in. He nodded. "About time."

Serena tried to shrug off Heath's hold. When that didn't work, she aimed her heel at his foot and hissed under her breath. "What are you doing?"

Stan chuckled. "I'll get back into the kitchen. Nate's playing a video game and studiously ignoring that girl's texts. He won't bother you."

She waited until they were alone to turn her wrath on Heath. "What is with the caveman routine?"

"I tried to have a conversation about this. You forced my hand."

"What are you talking about?"

Heath glanced around before taking her hand. "Let's find

somewhere private to talk. Preferably outside of the range of twelve-year-old ears."

The smooth sensation of skin against skin soothed her jumping nerves. Or that was the excuse she gave herself for not throwing off his touch and demanding an explanation. Even showered, with his hair damp and curling at the ends, he smelled like the outdoors. Like fresh grass and clean air. The scent raced through her senses, claiming and hypnotizing her.

Before she knew it, they stood in the center of a room she assumed operated as his home office. Papers piled on the huge desk. Filing cabinets. And a small couch with kids' books strewn all over it.

She nodded at the massive black leather chair, trying to keep the conversation light and her nerves in check. "You work in here?"

"I do paperwork. Nate lounges and pretends to do homework." Heath smiled at the mention of his son's name and glanced quickly at the evidence of his presence.

She fell right there. Stupidly and without a thought to the consequences or her bedrock belief he would hurt her again, her heart shattered.

Maybe she'd always loved Heath. Maybe seeing him walk through his life so changed from the boy he was before played a role. Whatever the reason, she gazed at him and saw hope. And conflict and fear and pain. So many hurdles stood in the way. Some centered on work. Others not.

She inhaled nice and deep, and then dove in. "I've ignored you since I got back into town because you reminded me of a time I wanted to forget. I was young and stupid. It was humiliating, if you must know."

He took her hands in his. "You were a kid with a crush. It's a normal thing."

"You cured me. Believe me."

Regret flashed in his pale eyes. "I'm sorry."

She tried to play it cool with a shrug. "It doesn't matter."

"Of course it does." His fingers gave hers a gentle squeeze. "If I could go back and be more tactful, I would."

"But you'd still turn me down?" Her heart clenched at the thought.

"You were so young. Touching you would have been a bad, bad thing."

He sounded so serious that she couldn't help but laugh. "That sounds almost honorable."

"Don't be fooled. I was a typical self-centered boy and the offer tempted me. All breasts tempted me. But everyone kept telling me how great I was, how much money I could make. Listening to that garbage changed me. My focus centered on getting out and grabbing fame. I looked down on everyone in town and pushed away. I thought I was too good for the people who grew up with me."

She wondered how he only remembered the bad parts. He forgot the good parts of himself. The times when he didn't act like a jerk, like the one where he offered her rides to school so she wouldn't have to wait around for the bus. The one where he stopped bullies from picking on small kids in the school hallways.

Yeah, the immature version of him had faults, but the goodness lingered there, too. Made her think for the first time that his turning her down might have been more of a gift than a humiliation.

"Then you got injured," she said as she crowded in closer to his chest.

"Next to Nate, best thing that ever happened to me." His breath tickled her nose as his hands journeyed to her waist.

"You lost everything."

His gaze centered on her mouth. "I gained more."

Those were the words of a decent man, not a spoiled boy. "That's very adult of you."

"Don't kid yourself. It took years for me to wise up. I was pissed off and nasty when it first happened. Got drunk, did stupid things. Cursed the world and everyone in it. Ran through what little money I had, all illegally given to me by recruiters, by the way."

She gave in and touched a hand to his cheek. When he leaned in, kissing her palm, her stomach performed a little tumble. "I can't even imagine you that way. That far out on the edge."

"My ego outran my common sense. The only thing I ever did well was football, but it was more than that. I had built up this life based on things—fast women, big houses, and interviews on television. None of it was real."

She traced her thumb over his lips. "Not a life I fit into."

"Exactly. Not then."

"What changed?"

"My supposed friends left. My girlfriend bugged out. I ended up alone without hope." The hand pressing against her back pulled her in closer until his mouth hovered over hers and they shared the same breaths. "And then Nate came along, and I stared into his big brown eyes and everything clicked."

Heath's love for Nate flowed out of him like a living, breathing thing. "I figured he was a turning point."

The bleak look on his face broke. "More than that. I did physical therapy for him. Lived for him. Got back to work and away from alcohol for him."

This time she kissed him. Just a quick touch of lips. A gift to let him know his words meant something to her. "You're a good man."

He shook his head. "Just a man, sometimes good and sometimes not."

Her hands were on his shoulders now, her body draped over his. "What if you could play football tomorrow?"

Air hissed through his teeth. "I honestly don't know."

The unexpected response had her pulling back to get a good look at him. "Really?"

"I want to tell you the dream is dead, but life isn't that clean. It lives in me. Now and then I feel cheated and angry for losing out on what could have been. I want to yell and slam into things, but looking at Nate takes the edge off."

He didn't give himself enough credit. She knew the truth. Devoted and strong, he would forgo the dream and stay solid for Nate. Wouldn't subject him to a nonavailable and traveling dad. No way.

She slipped back in his arms. "He's a great kid, Heath. Whenever you think you messed up, remember that."

One of his eyebrows arched up. "Is the honors English thing real?"

"Yes. Nate deserves it. He's smart and driven. His reading comprehension is off the charts."

"Must take after his mom."

The mention of the one woman who'd managed to snag Heath's attention if only for a short time sobered Serena. "She's gone, I take it."

"Forever."

"Good." The word slipped out before she could stop it.

From his wide smile, it was clear Heath appreciated the support on that score. "I think so. She wanted out, and I didn't stop her."

"That's horrible."

"It's good in the end." His thumb slipped over Serena's lips. "The question is whether you're going to let something dumb I did as a kid color what we do today."

Her fears about her feelings for him being nothing more than residual pieces of a long-ago crush faded. This wasn't about idol worship or proving him wrong. This went deeper. The problem of being Nate's teacher and all the propriety concerns that came with that still lingered, but at that moment she didn't care. She'd spent her entire life doing the right thing. She married the "right" guy and then stayed in a bad marriage because she didn't want to admit failure. She followed every rule and played her life as safely as possible. Now she wanted something for her.

For the second time in her life, she reached out to Heath. This time she knew he'd catch her. "I prefer to live in the now."

"Good answer."

"I prefer strong, reliable men to skirt-chasing boys."

"You're my kind of woman."

Before she could agree, his arms closed around her. Enveloped by his warmth and his smell, by strong hands and the need thumping off him and crashing into her, she opened up for his kiss. When his mouth crossed over hers, electricity sparked. Heat and desire washed through her, overtaking everything else.

His lips on hers. His fingers in her hair. This wasn't about the tender infatuation of a girl. What she felt was all woman. Hope, light, and the stirrings of love.

"Ms. Davis?" Nate's startled voice cut through the sensual storm blowing around inside her.

Shaken, her heart thundering, she pulled back. There, standing in the doorway with his hands at his side and his phone hanging loose from his fingertips, she saw Nate.

His eyes grew huge. His gaze took it all in, going from his dad's hands to her body and back to their faces. "What are you doing here?"

She stepped away from Heath, making sure miles of space rushed between them before she spoke. "Nate, I came to talk with you."

His face scrunched up in confusion. "Dad?"

Heath nodded. "She has something to tell you."

"Then why is she kissing you?" Nate almost screamed the question.

Guilt pounded her from all directions. She was a teacher. His teacher. "Nate, I know this is confusing. I'm sorry. So sorry."

Heath joined in his son's frown. "For what?"

She blocked Heath out, had to, and focused on Nate. He was the male who needed soothing. The kid who'd walked in on something strange. Rarely did kids see their teachers as normal people with regular lives. Thanks to her, Nate got a healthy dose of reality shoved right down his throat. And in his own house.

She'd played this all wrong. Messed up every way there was to mess up. "I really did come to talk with you."

Nate snorted. "Sure didn't look like it."

"Nate." Heath's warning tone got through because Nate's gawking eased up.

The timing couldn't be more wrong. "I should go," Serena said.

Heath touched her elbow. She saw his hand move, but couldn't feel his hand against her. Couldn't process anything except humiliation and regret.

"Serena, this is fine." Heath's husky voice fell over her.

She refused to be lured in. "No, it's not."

She grabbed up her forgotten purse, which had dropped at her feet, and slid a quick glance in Heath's direction. "We'll talk later."

"We will?"

"Good night."

HEATH watched Serena run out of his study. Any faster and she would have mowed Nate down.

"What's going on?" Nate asked, his tone more confused than judgmental.

"Sit."

"Am I in trouble?" Nate slumped down on the cushions.

"No," Heath said as he slid in next to his son.

Where to start? Heath searched his mind for the right words but nothing came. In the end, Nate took care of the task in his usual straight-to-the-point kid way of sorting out information.

"Are you dating Ms. Davis?"

"I want to."

Nate's mouth flatlined. "Huh."

"Is that a positive or negative response?"

Nate shrugged. "I can see it. She's pretty hot."

That was just about the last thing Heath wanted to hear from his son. "That's enough of that talk."

"Nah, I get it. She's cool and pretty smart." Nate stared at his phone but didn't turn it on.

"She wants to switch you to honors English."

"So you guys can, you know, do it?" The sparkle in his eye said the kid was testing. Seeing how far he could go.

Heath cuffed the back of Nate's head. "Where do you get this stuff from?"

"Books."

When Nate laughed, the tightness around Heath's heart eased. "I've known Ms. Davis for a long time."

"You were neighbors."

The conversation was killing Heath. "Is this okay with you? Me and Ms. Davis?"

"Sure."

Nate didn't move. Didn't even smile, but Heath could feel it. An excitement radiated off Nate. He clenched the phone hard enough to crack the plastic casing. In this case Heath sensed the "sure" amounted to a wholehearted acceptance of Serena as a potential fixture around the house. Just showed that a guy needed a mother figure sometimes.

Since the first day in her class, Nate talked about Serena in a different way. They had a connection of some sort. A comfort level that nurtured Nate's love for school.

Heath touched his fingers against his son's hair. Memories of the toddler gave way to a burning love for the young man he had become. "I'm proud of you about the honors English thing."

"It's no big deal." Nate's cocky smile said something different.

"School is important. Studying, getting good grades, you handle it all, and I want you to know I'm impressed."

"It's just school stuff."

"I'm very proud of you." Heath hesitated. "I was never good in school. Never really liked reading. It was hard for me to concentrate and understand what I was seeing."

"They can fix that, you know."

Not exactly the response Heath expected. "Who?"

"A lot of kids suck at reading, and teachers help them and stuff." Nate treated his dad to one of those patented teen shrugs. "There's a word for it. It's no big deal."

The deficiency had weighed down every moment of Heath's adult life, worrying he'd never be good enough to be the kind of dad Nate needed, and his kid viewed it as normal. It was humbling. He decided right then that age didn't always bring all that much wisdom.

Heath nodded. "Good to know."

"Besides, you were good at sports."

"That's not everything. You're smart enough to realize that. I wasn't. I regret some of that now."

Nate pushed the buttons on his phone but the screen stayed off. "What stuff do you regret?"

"I haven't read those books you insist everyone has read."

"Ms. Davis might help you with that, but you'll have to take your tongue out of her mouth first." Nate shifted away as he said the words through a bout of laughter.

Heath pressed his hand down on top of Nate's head until he squirmed and begged for mercy. By the time the wrestling match ended, they were both smiling.

"No talking to your friends about Ms. Davis and what you saw. Understood?"

Nate sighed. "Yeah."

"I'm serious." Heath kept staring until Nate finally nodded in agreement. "Don't expect special treatment."

"I got it."

They sat in silence, Nate tapping wildly on his phone keys despite the screen being dark and Heath enjoying the stolen moment. Between his friends and activities, Nate spent more and more time away from the house. Soon he'd hit his teen years in full stride and the quiet times together would all but disappear.

Heath knew how it worked. His son was popular and busy. Girls would soon fill most of his extra time and steal every brain cell in his head. Dad would get left behind. Until then, Heath would savor the minutes Nate gave him.

Nate dropped the phone on his lap. "You're good at other stuff, you know."

The abrupt turn in conversation, including the more serious tone, surprised Heath. Made him wonder what was coming next. "Really? Like what?"

"Yelling." Nate burst out laughing at his joke.

Heath couldn't help but join in this time. "You're hysterical."

"You do."

Heath knew his son was trying to tell him something. What that was, was the question. "Come again?"

Nate started to shrug but stared up instead. "You do okay. You know, with the important stuff."

Heath swallowed to keep from losing it. In simple words, without any fanfare or celebration, his son told him he didn't suck as a dad. Nothing would ever matter more.

"Would you do me a favor?" Heath asked after a few seconds of rapid blinking.

"What?"

"Next time Lexy texts, think about answering her."

Nate looked appalled at the idea. "Why?"

"Do you like her?"

Nate shook his head heard enough to knock something loose. "No."

The answer came too fast and furious to be real. Heath might not know much about women, but he did know about his son. "I'm just saying that if you like her, you should text back. Ignoring her is kind of jerky."

Nate's mouth fell open. "It is?"

"And one of these days she might start thinking you don't like her back and move on."

Nate snorted loud enough to be heard in the next county. "Right."

"You're so smooth with women?"

"They don't run away when *I* kiss them."

Heath knew that smile on his son's face meant trouble. "Excuse me?"

"Aren't you going to go after Ms. Davis?"

The mention of Serena filled Heath with an unexpected lightness. She needed time to calm down, and he'd give it to her, but then he was done waiting around for his shot. "Tomorrow."

"Huh." Nate's turned on his phone and stared down at what looked to be Lexy's last message.

"What's with the grunt?"

"Isn't waiting until tomorrow kind of jerky?"

Heath's good mood shattered. Looked like the kid knew more about women than he did. "Yeah, I guess so."

"Listen to Nate." Stan stood in the doorway. "Get out of here and go find Serena. We could use a woman's touch around here."

Nate grinned up at him. "But don't forget your curfew."

five

Lindsay sat at the bar in Serena's kitchen an hour later and traced her finger around the top of her coffee mug. "Tell me again why you left Heath's house instead of staying for dinner and whatever fabulous dessert the man had in mind."

Serena blocked out the sexy thoughts moving through her. "Nate walked in."

"I'm sure the kid's seen his dad kiss a woman before."

"Thanks for that mental image."

"He's a hottie." Lindsay tapped her forehead. "Remember?"

"How could I forget your description?"

Lindsay smiled over the top of her cup. "Tell me about the kiss."

"No."

Lindsay gave her cell another quick look. Serena didn't know what was on that little screen, but it sure had her sister bouncing around with unspent energy.

"Well, I'm just happy it finally happened. It's been ridiculous trying to throw you two together."

Serena froze in the act of spit-shining the counter. "What did you do?"

"Dropped a hint here and there."

She threw the cleaning cloth down. "What? When?"

"While you were gone, I kept the dream alive in Heath by mentioning you." A dreamy look came over Lindsay. "Not that it was hard work. He always asked about you, so I answered."

Serena felt her simmering anger turn to interest. "He did?"

"Yeah, I'd be catering some event and he'd be there. After only a few seconds in and he'd ask how you were."

She refused to let that matter. "He was just being friendly."

"Well, he never bothered to ask how I was. Never stared at me like he wanted to eat me either. That's just you." This time Lindsay picked up her phone and her grin grew even wider.

"Have you always been this dramatic?"

"You want drama? Answer the door."

"What?"

Lindsay nodded in the general direction of the front of the house. "Answer. Your. Door."

"But the bell didn't ring."

Lindsay rolled her eyes. "Would you, for once, stop being all stuffy and let the moment carry you?"

"I have no idea what you're talking about."

The bell rang. Not once but twice. Whoever stood out there wanted in.

"Now are you happy?" Lindsay asked.

More like terrified. Linds had something cooking and this time it wasn't a spectacular meal. With her feet dragging and her anxiety bouncing around inside her, Serena went to the door. One peek in the skinny window by the entrance, and she knew what had her sister jumping around like a silly teenager on prom night.

Serena shot her sister a will-kill-you-later look. "You invited him?"

"Nope."

"Serena?" Heath's voice boomed through the door. "Open up."

More orders. That was one thing about him she planned to work on.

But she did obey . . . this time. "You bellowed?"

With the door out of his way, Heath stepped right inside. "About time."

"I was thinking the same thing." Lindsay toasted them with her mug before dropping it on the counter. She scurried to find her purse. "I'll be leaving but expect a full report."

The days of oversharing about her love life were over as far as Serena was concerned. "I don't think so."

"I hate to ask what 'full' means," Heath said at the same time.

Lindsay didn't bother to respond. She just kissed them both on the cheek and then breezed out, closing the door behind her.

Serena rushed to fill the silence. "I'm sorry I ran out on you like that."

"Why did you?"

"I saw Nate's face and panicked. He look horrified at seeing me in your arms."

The worry lines around his eyes eased. "He was just surprised. If you had stayed a few minutes longer, you would have heard him give his blessing."

The air whooshed out of her lungs. "He did?"

Heath closed in on her. Hands fell on her shoulders and tugged her close. "Well, as much of one as a teen boy can give. Mostly, he shrugged. He does that a lot."

"They all do."

His fingers clenched against her arms. "Let's talk about us."

"Okay."

"I know we're different."

The switch took her off guard, but she followed him just fine. "Heath—"

"No, let me get this out."

She rested her palms against his stomach in a silent show of support. "Go ahead."

"I'm not super smart. My grades would terrify you. I had to leave college because I was so bad at it. But it's more basic than that." He glanced around the room, looked everywhere but at her. "Reading makes me nervous. I see the words, but I can't get them to make sense."

She hadn't expected that honest revelation. It obviously hurt him to force the words out. "Really?"

"Nate assures me a lot of kids have this problem."

Her heart broke for Heath. Everyone spent so much time encouraging his football skills and so little reassuring the other parts of him that sorely needed attention. She wouldn't make that mistake.

With her fingers under his chin, she lifted his face to see his eyes. "It's a learning issue. There are skills you can learn to make it easier."

"It never mattered before, but it does now. For you. For Nate." He swallowed hard enough for her to see his throat move. "Will you teach me? I want to get it when Nate talks to me about a book."

A sob lodged in her chest. This strong, proud man stood there admitting his imperfections. She knew it stole a piece of him to be so honest and open. She also knew it meant she owned a place in his life.

Her fingers trailed down his cheek. "Of course."

He kissed her open palm and peeked up at her, all the vulnerability and worry mirrored in his face. "Still want to try dating?"

"You think telling me about a learning disability will scare me away?"

Heath borrowed from Nate and shrugged. "Intelligence is important to you."

"Decency and honor, good parenting and love. Those are the things that matter. Someone who sticks it out during the tough times and values what he has enough to guard it and hold it precious." He wasn't the only one who had learned something. She had, too. "The number of classics you've read doesn't amount to much at all. I had that guy. Married and divorced him."

"I'll never cheat on you."

It was an unbreakable vow delivered in a clear, ringing voice. She felt the sureness of it down to her toes. "I know I can count on that. On you."

He leaned down and placed a soft kiss on her lips. When he raised his head, the worry had disappeared. "All I want is a chance to show you I'm not that stupid kid who pushed you away."

"What are you?" She knew but she wanted to make sure he did.

"A grown man who wants you very much. A guy who wants to build something with you. Learn from you. Grow with you."

She closed her eyes on a wave of happiness. It winged through her hard enough to knock her over, but Heath's strong hands kept her on her feet. "Those are the words of a smart man, Heath."

"I've been falling for you for months now." He balanced his forehead on hers. "Loving you is not hard."

Tears pressed against the back of her eyes. "I feel the same way about you. It was easy to love the man and forget the boy."

His lips met hers in a kiss that went on, pressing and caressing, stealing their words and sapping their strength until they leaned against each other for support.

When it ended, she buried her head against his neck and inhaled the musky smell of his skin. "Now what?"

His shoulders tensed. "Depends on how slow you want to take this."

The way his tone dropped low and his body shifted had her wondering. She lifted her head to get a good look at him. Wasn't hard to see where his mind had traveled. She could feel his muscles tremble. See the question in his eyes.

"Are you making a proposition, Mr. Sanders?"

"Nate told me to be home by curfew." Heath pretended to look at his watch, but his arm was bare. "That gives us a few hours."

She glanced over his head at the bedroom. "So the answer to that question I asked all those years ago is finally yes?"

"Definitely. See, I'm a lot smarter these days."

So was she. "I plan on letting you prove that to me for a long time."

"Like, maybe forty years or so?"

She slid her hand in his and led him toward the bedroom. "Sounds like a good start."

Copyright Notices

"For the Love of Wendy" by Lori Foster copyright © 2010 by Lori Foster.

"Ava's Haven" by Jules Bennett copyright © 2010 by Jules Bennett.

"Skin Deep" by Heidi Betts copyright © 2010 by Heidi Betts.

"Atticus Gets a Mommy" by Ann Christopher copyright © 2010 by Sally Moore.

"The Redemption of Brodie Grant" by Lisa Cooke copyright © 2010 by Lisa Cooke.

"The Wolf Watcher's Diet" by Paige Cuccaro copyright © 2010 by Paige Cuccaro.

"A Fairy Precious Love" by Gia Dawn copyright © 2010 by Gia Raterman.

"Second Time Around" by HelenKay Dimon copyright © 2010 by HelenKay Dimon.